Jilly Cooper

Lisa & Co.

Originally published as

LOVE AND OTHER HEARTACHES

CORGI BOOKS

LISA & CO
A CORGI BOOK : 0 552 14839 3

Originally published in Great Britain by
Arlington Books Ltd

PRINTING HISTORY
Arlington Books edition published 1981 (published as LOVE AND
OTHER HEARTACHES)
Corgi edition published 1982

19 20 18

Set in 10/11pt English Times.

Corgi Books are published by Transworld Publishers,
61–63 Uxbridge Road, London W5 5SA,
a division of The Random House Group Ltd,
in Australia by Random House Australia (Pty) Ltd,
20 Alfred Street, Milsons Point, Sydney, NSW 2061, Australia,
and in New Zealand by Random House New Zealand Ltd,
18 Poland Road, Glenfield, Auckland 10, New Zealand
and in South Africa by Random House (Pty) Ltd,
Endulini, 5a Jubilee Road, Parktown 2193, South Africa.

Printed and bound in Great Britain by
Cox & Wyman Ltd, Reading, Berkshire.

For Rosemary Nolan with love and gratitude
because she encouraged me to write these stories in the
first place

Contents

Introduction

All my life I wanted to be a writer and scribbled away at short stories, plays, and the first chapters of frightful novels, but never tried very hard to get anything published. When I was twenty-nine, while employed in the publicity department of William Collins the publishers, a friend, Cherry Lewis, told me she was working on a new Odhams magazine for teenagers called *Intro*. She introduced me to the editor, Marjorie Fergusson, who asked me if I'd like to edit the fiction. She was looking for stories, she said, which were funny and realistic, and would appeal to the new, optimistic, flower-power mood of the late sixties.

At first, the only stories I could find were either too heavily romantic and humourless, or too pornographic for a teenage magazine, which still didn't allow you to mention any parts of the female anatomy between the neck and the kneecaps. We did publish, however, a lovely story by Virginia Ironside, and another by a then unknown writer called Beryl Bainbridge.

Finally, in despair of ever finding enough stories, I sat down and wrote one myself. For a week I bit my nails, then Marjorie Fergusson sent for me. "You're a rotten editor," she said, "and this story is no good for us, but it's well written. If I were you I'd give up any ideas of editing, and concentrate on writing."

I walked back to Collins on air. For the next year, I did very little work for either of my two jobs, but instead spent my time in office hours writing stories. The first one, *Temporary Set-Back*, was published in *Intro* in 1967. Others followed: *The Red Angora Dress, Christmas Stocking* and *An Uplifting Evening*. Few experiences have ever equalled the ecstasy of seeing my name in print for the first time. With *Sister To The Bride* and *May The Best Girl Win*, I even achieved the dizzy heights of *Woman's Own*. *The Square Peg*, one of my favourite stories, appeared in *Woman's Weekly*. *Petticoat* published *Lisa* and *Forsaking All Others*. *Johnnie Casanova* appeared in *19*. *Political Asylum*, written in 1968, never found a home in a magazine at all, everyone then considering it to be far too risqué and probably libellous as well.

It was on the strength of these stories, which are all gathered together in this book, that another friend, Ilsa Yardly, introduced me to Godfrey Smith, then editor of the *Sunday Times* colour magazine, who asked me to write a piece on being a young wife. As a result of this article, Harold Evans, then editor of the *Sunday Times*, gave me a column on the *Look* pages, and I was suddenly launched on a brand new journalistic career.

This book also contains three long stories started in the sixties, which I finally finished this year. They are *Kate's Wedding, A Pressing Engagement* and *The Ugly Swan*.

I cannot pretend that these stories are literature. They are written purely to entertain. I have updated where possible but their mood is rooted firmly in the sixties, when we all lived it up and had a great deal more fun, I think, than people do today. It was a time before the women's movement had gained so much ascendency, when the young were still optimistic about marriage, and believed that God was in his Heaven if all was Mr Right with the world.

Jilly Cooper, 1981

A Pressing Engagement

Darrell French did not look like a film director. He wore a pin-striped suit, a regimental tie, and a watch chain looped across his waistcoat. He was washing down Rennies with Perrier water, drunk straight from the bottle, and he had the most chaotic office Hester had ever seen. Books, scripts, papers, copies of *Spotlight* and *The Stage* were piled so high on his desk, it was like talking to someone over a garden wall.

'My last P.A.,' he said wearily, 'spent all day painting her nails, talking to her girlfriends on the telephone, and screwing my most important clients. She couldn't type, or do shorthand, or spell, or even make Nescafé. She once tried to book Nanette Newman for the lead in a war film instead of Paul Newman.'

Hester burst out laughing.

'Believe me,' said Darrell French, 'it was not funny at the time.'

The telephone rang. It was several seconds before he could locate it in the débris on his desk.

'Well put him through . . . Hi, David, how are you . . . Bugger,' he rattled the receiver button hysterically, 'you cut him off, you imbecile . . . well get him back again . . . David, yes Niven, at the South of France number . . . you'd better go through the exchange then.'

He sighed and put down the telephone receiver, staring at Hester beadily. 'As you can see, I am up the proverbial ordure creek. I'm entirely dependent on a

11

decent P.A. and I'm fed up with flash, beautiful, illiterate girls who are not prepared to work, but who find the idea of movies glamorous. In the last two days, I have interviewed more than a hundred girls. You're the only one who's taken the trouble to wear a skirt.'

He looked at Hester again, taking in the round sweet face, the gently curving mouth, the shiny copper hair drawn loosely into a coil at the nape of the neck, and the skin as clear and brownly glowing as Pears' soap.

'You seem a nice girl,' he went on dubiously, 'but I could be wrong. I must also tell you that I am a happily married man with three children, for whom I have to pay nine thousand pounds a year in school fees after tax. This I am capable of doing if things are running smoothly at the office. I have never made a pass at any of my P.A.'s.'

'You seem to have had an awful time,' said Hester sympathetically.

'I need a lot of cherishing,' said Darrell French. 'I'm off to Nairobi on Monday fortnight to make a television series of *The Grass is Singing*.'

'Doris Lessing?' asked Hester.

'Well, that's a step in the right direction,' said Darrell French. 'Can you get away from your present job by then?'

'Oh, yes please,' breathed Hester.

'Well, you'd better go and get some jabs—cholera, yellow fever, T.A.B.—that one's nasty, probably lay you out for twenty-four hours. Is your passport in order?'

Hester nodded incredulously. 'Are you actually offering me the job?'

'I am. Is a thousand enough?'

'A year?' asked Hester, her face falling.

Darrell French laughed. 'No, a month. You're not married or heavily involved or anything are you?'

Hester's mind was spinning at the thought of so much money. She hesitated for a moment before answering—you could hardly call her involvement with Julian heavy. 'No,' she finally said, 'definitely not.'

'Good—this job is likely to take you abroad for weeks, even months on end, and husbands don't like that very much.'

Hester tried to ring Julian from a telephone box the moment she was a safe distance from Darrell French's office. She absolutely hated being the one to call him, particularly as he hadn't telephoned her for over a week. But a dazzling new job was surely a legitimate excuse. It was Julian after all who had always nagged her to get out of her present job, and she could sound happy and on top of the world, instead of stiff and stammering as she would have done normally. Her hands grew damp on the receiver, as the number rang on and on. Julian must be out or not answering. He often switched off his telephone when he was immersed in work.

Coming out of the telephone box, Hester went straight into an off-licence and bought a bottle of Dom Perignon. Then she hailed a taxi. If she was going to be earning twelve thousand pounds a year, she could afford a few luxuries.

'I got the job,' she shouted, as she rushed into the outer office which she shared with Beverly, the Sales Director's secretary.

'Fantastic,' said Beverly, who had finished her frugal lunch of cottage cheese, flavoured with prawns, and was now stirring Sweetex with a ballpoint pen into a paper cup of black coffee.

'I can't believe it,' said Hester, unpinning her hair, so it fell bronze and shining to her shoulders. 'Oodles of money, and such a sweet man, and David Niven rang up in the middle. I've bought this to celebrate.' She waved the bottle of champagne.

'I'm on a diet,' said Beverly, 'and you've got the Fisher-Holmes report to type this afternoon.'

'I don't care,' said Hester, ripping the gold paper off the top of the bottle with her finger nails, 'two weeks on Monday, I'm off to Kenya on location.'

'Blimey,' said Beverly, getting a couple of plastic mugs out of the cupboard. 'What on earth will Mr. Petrie say?'

Yes indeed, wondered Hester, what would Mr. Petrie say? She had worked for him for six years, ever since she'd left her secretarial college. Although the work had been hard and often boring, she had been so fond of everyone in the office, and Mr. Petrie had always looked so mortified every time she suggested she might move on, that she'd been unable to tear herself away.

Recently, however, she'd reached the end of her tether. She had been working late every night, Julian seemed to be showing less and less interest in her, and she never met any new men. Well, she'd got herself out of the rut by landing a new job. Now she had to face the awful task of telling Mr. Petrie.

The cork flew out of the window, endangering the lives of two pigeons mating on the roof, and the champagne, shaken in Hester's excitement, gushed all over the faded green carpet, as she filled up the two mugs.

'To your brilliant career,' said Beverly. 'How many calories are there in champagne?'

'Hardly any,' said Hester. 'I know—I'll tell Mr. Petrie I've got engaged.'

'You haven't,' said Beverly.

'I can pretend I have. Not to Julian—I'm much too superstitious to risk that, but I'll say I've had a whirlwind courtship and am suddenly going to marry someone else.'

'Dodgy,' said Beverly, 'he's bound to want to know who he is.'

Hester had another brainwave. 'I'll say I'm going to marry Nico.'

'Who's he?'

'Nicholas Calvert—we were brought up together, he's the only platonic friend I've got.'

'Won't he mind?' asked Beverly.

'He won't know,' said Hester.

14

*

Mr. Petrie had had a good lunch. His white hair was slightly ruffled, his face more magenta than ever. As a gesture to the heat of the day, he had discarded his waistcoat. When Hester brought in her shorthand book, he smiled fondly at her, as well he might. Mr. Petrie's continuing existence at Bateman and Mathers, when he was well beyond retiring age, was entirely due to Hester's efficiency. All day long she was a captive audience, forced to listen to his jokes and his troubles, smiling at his dictated quips, correcting his grammar, and steering him with skilled anonymity through the day's routine. Mr. Petrie only appreciated that Hester was sympathetic on the ear, and almost more delightful on the eye. He thought how particularly fetching she looked today, lushly spilling out of her new willow-green suit.

He gave her some letters. Hester reminded him he would need the draft of the Fisher-Holmes report by that evening, double-spaced so that he could tinker about with it at home. Then buoyed up by half a bottle of champagne, and doodling frantically around the spirals of her notebook, she gave in her notice.

Mr. Petrie's magenta face lost a few degrees of colour. 'Oh Hester, you can't leave me.'

'I must,' she said, going scarlet at the thumping lie, 'I'm getting married you see.'

This was a different matter altogether. Mr. Petrie was a deeply sentimental man. Immediately he waddled round the desk and kissed her on the cheek. 'My dear! Congratulations! It couldn't have happened to a nicer person. And who is the very lucky young man—is it Julian?' he asked a shade doubtfully.

Hester crossed her fingers behind her back. 'Well, actually no, it's an old friend from my childhood called Nicholas Calvert. We've known each other for ages, but suddenly the whole thing gelled.'

'Splendid, splendid,' said Mr. Petrie, 'I wouldn't have liked it if you'd abandoned me for another boss. And I'm so relieved this young man can support you,

15

without your having to go on working. I always feel so sorry for poor young Mrs. Davies in accounts, staggering home with all those carrier bags every evening, and then having to clean the flat and cook her husband's dinner. Now when do you want to leave us?'

Hester stepped up the doodling. 'Well, in a fortnight's time, I'm afraid, we're getting married in—er—six weeks, and I really need a month at home first to organise the wedding.'

'That's all right,' said Mr. Petrie, suddenly looking doleful. 'I suppose you'd better put an advertisement in the paper—perhaps you could interview the applicants. But oh Hester, I shall miss you.'

Fortunately for Hester, at that moment the internal telephone started ringing. It was the Managing Director wanting Mr. Petrie, who promptly started to flap. 'Where's the background to the Marsh and Follifoot deal?'

'I put the memo on your desk this morning,' said Hester soothingly. 'Here it is.' She extracted it from under the *Sporting Times* and a copy of *Playboy*.

'Thank you,' said Mr. Petrie, scuttling out of the office, 'I hope you're going to ask Nancy and me to the wedding.'

There were tears in Hester's eyes, as she went out of his office. 'I've done it,' she said to Beverly, 'I haven't felt such a heel since I let my brother's gerbil out of its cage when I was seven, and the cat ate it.'

'Can I be bridesmaid?' said Beverly. 'I wish you hadn't made me drink all that champagne, this letter is straight Tippex.'

Mr. Petrie sent for Hester later in the afternoon and said he had just telephoned his wife, Nancy.

'I can't tell you how delighted she is, sad for me, of course, but thrilled for you. She was always saying she couldn't understand why a lovely girl like you wasn't snapped up years ago. She wants to know what your fiancé does.'

16

'He's a stockbroker—in the City,' said Hester, sensing trouble, but not sure from what direction.

'Splendid,' said Mr. Petrie. 'Well, Nancy's got to come up to London some time for the Constable exhibition at the Royal Academy, and she wants us to give a little engagement party for you both at the office that day, so she can say goodbye to you.'

Hester turned as green as her suit. 'Nico's going abroad next week.'

'Well, make it the week after,' said Mr. Petrie, 'it'll be your last week, so we can give you a royal send-off.'

Nico was with a client, when Hester telephoned his office. He rang back when she was in Mr. Petrie's office giving him the Fisher-Holmes report and the remaining letters to sign.

'Your "fiancé's" on the 'phone,' said Beverly, popping her head round the door, with a malicious gleam in her eyes.

'Put it through here, I won't listen,' said Mr. Petrie untruthfully.

'Hullo, Nico,' said Hester picking up the telephone, and once again blushing scarlet.

'Hes, how nice to hear you.'

'Darling!' Hester dropped her voice an octave, 'Are we meeting up later this evening?'

Nico sounded surprised. 'Were we meant to be? I've got to drive Annabel to the airport.'

'Well, after that then, it doesn't matter how late it is.'

'Can't we make it tomorrow?' said Nico.

Hester looked at Mr. Petrie's fountain pen—static over the blue writing paper. 'I do *so* want to see you, darling,' she said even more huskily.

'Okay, I'll drop round about eleven,' said Nico, a little taken aback by Hester's insistence.

'That'll be lovely.' She took a deep breath, 'And, Nico darling, I do love you.'

Nico sounded startled. 'Hes, have you been drinking?'

'Me too, darling, I can't wait to see you. Bye, my

angel,' murmered Hester, and slamming down the receiver she fled out of the room.

Ah young love, thought Mr. Petrie.

'How the hell did Machiavelli do it?' said Hester, collapsing behind her desk and putting her burning face in her hands.

'Oh, what a tangled web we weave,' said Beverly. 'I must say your "fiancé" sounds delicious on the telephone.'

'He's infinitely too nice to get caught up in a mess like this,' agreed Hester.

Hester bought a bottle of whisky, and sat in her empty flat, wishing Julian would ring her. She looked at his photograph on the mantelpiece: surly, hopelessly good-looking, dark eyes brooding with an intensity that he certainly didn't feel towards her. On the table, with the top page coated in ginger cat fur, were the three copies she had typed of his latest book. It was called: *Stratification, Gender-Role Stereotyping and Sexual Behaviour Patterns Among Middle Class Siblings, with Special Reference to Canvey Island.*

Hester hadn't understood much of it, but believed Julian, who was senior sociology professor at London University, when he told her it was a deeply significant, seminal work. The typescript had been ready for him a week now, but she liked to keep an excuse to ring him up her sleeve, just in case she got too desperate. Now she had her new job to tell him about as well, but although she'd tried his flat several times that evening there was no answer. She had been in love with Julian for two years. On good days, she fantasised about their future together. On bad days she felt cut off from all human warmth.

Above the forest of shiny green plants on the window ledge, she watched the colour drain out of the Cambridge-blue sky, and the great plane trees round the common fill up with black shadows. It was one of those stiflingly humid nights that descend on London like a blanket. Every window was open in the flat in the hope of inducing some breeze to enter.

Instead, Hockney, Hester's ginger tomcat, pushed his way through the plants mewing disapprovingly, and landed with a heavy thud at her feet. He started to weave furrily round her bare legs, then thinking better of it, gave her a right and left on the calf with fat, unsheathed paws.

'Nasty, ungrateful creature,' chided Hester. 'I bought you a tin of salmon to celebrate. We're in the money, Hockney.'

In the kitchen, she opened the tin. Hockney, however, took a few mouthfuls, and then disdainfully scratched up all the newspaper under the plate, and wandered off into the drawing-room to wash himself on Julian's typescript. Hester shooed him away, and shook the ginger fur off the top copy.

If Julian had had this typed professionally, she thought, it would have cost him at least two hundred and fifty pounds—his writing had been absolute murder to decipher. Then she felt guilty. Of course she had done it for love, but one needed a little love in return. She knew it was nearing the end of the university term and he must be desperately busy. Perhaps in the long summer vac, he'd have more time for her.

She looked at her watch—a quarter to eleven—Nico probably wouldn't have eaten. At least she could make him an omelette. She picked some thyme and marjoram from the window box, and went into the kitchen to chop them up.

Nico Calvert had been the school friend of her elder brother, Michael, that she had liked the best. He used to stay with them often in the holidays, and she'd had a mild crush on him, because he was clever, and quiet, and laughed easily, and never expected her to be anything she wasn't. She was also impressed by the way he didn't mind if he lost at the endless games of tennis, croquet, poker and vingt-et-un, they'd played through those long, hot summers. In a way she felt he was more of a brother to her than Michael.

Michael, who'd been back to stay with Nico's family in Somerset, had often implied that Nico was rather smart. His mother was a peer's daughter, the family seemed to own a lot of land, and after Nico left school, he'd been considered something of a Deb's Delight, and often appeared in the gossip columns photographed with a succession of pretty girls. But he never dropped names, or boasted about the invitations, thick as a pack of cards, on his mantelpiece.

Nor did he ever grumble that (because of the crippling estate duties when his father died) he was the first member of the family who'd seriously had to earn his own living. He was obviously miserable working as a stockbroker—it was rather like keeping a gun dog cooped up in a stuffy London bed-sitter.

For the last eighteen months, since Nico had fallen in love with Annabel, Hester had seen much less of him. Annabel was a model, with infinitely more beauty than talent, who wanted to break into acting. She was enormously fancied in the market place, and, rather like Hockney, was all soft curves and melting eyes one moment, then scratching and clawing the next. She gave Nico a hard time because he wasn't rich enough to take her to night clubs every evening, or fly her—when she felt so inclined—to exotic parties in distant corners of the world. Yet she raised hell if he looked at other women. Hester had met her twice and disliked her exceedingly. She was the sort of person who only watered plants when they were about to expire.

Nico arrived about eleven. He was wearing a yellow and white striped shirt, and had taken off his tie, and the jacket of his dark grey suit. He looked tired and very pale. Annabel must have been playing him up, thought Hester savagely. He was tall and rangy, with straight sandy hair, and nothing exceptional about his bony face, except freckles, a flat nose and sleepy amber eyes. Hester poured him a very stiff drink.

'I bet you haven't had anything to eat,' she said.

'I had lunch, I think,' said Nico collapsing onto the sofa. 'I'm not very hungry, too bloody hot.'

'It must be hell in the City.'

'My office is like a sauna.'

'How's your mother?' asked Hester.

'Still missing my father, but getting over it—slowly. Her real problems are financial. The farm manager's ripping her off right, left and centre. I really ought to pack in the Stock Exchange, and go home and run things.'

'Why don't you?' said Hester. 'You always wanted to.'

'Wouldn't earn enough money,' said Nico. 'My father let things go so badly at the end, it'll be five years before we start breaking even, and that's dependent on good summers. I can't see Annabel as a farmer's wife either.'

'She might get used to it,' said Hester unconvincingly. 'She'd have you.'

'And hay fever,' said Nico. 'She hates the country.'

'How is she?' asked Hester, noticing that the little bunched lines at the corners of his eyes had deepened since they'd last met.

'Never at her best before a flight.'

'Where's she gone?'

'Rome, modelling for *Vogue*, and auditioning for some film part.' He looked miserably down at his glass, 'We had a hell of a row before she left, she threw a telephone directory at me.'

'Which one?' said Hester.

Nico smiled slightly. 'The E-K, at least it wasn't Debrett's. Fortunately she missed and smashed that Meissen bowl Mickie Middlesex gave her for Christmas, which put her in an even worse mood. We didn't speak on the way to the airport. Then I'm sure I saw Jamie Cavendish going into the departure lounge just ahead of us.'

'Doesn't he have rather a nice wife?' said Hester.

'He's had several,' said Nico gloomily. 'It doesn't stop him running after Annabel.'

'Might have been a coincidence,' said Hester soothingly. 'He was probably flying somewhere quite different.'

Nico shook his head. 'Probably explained why she was in such a foul mood, expect she was terrified of being rumbled. Christ, I'm sorry, I must stop belly-aching.'

'Annabelly-aching,' said Hester, going into the kitchen. 'Help yourself to another drink, I'm going to make you some supper.'

She broke three eggs into a bowl with cream, salt and pepper, and was just adding the herbs when Nico wandered in.

'What was the reason for that extraordinary conversation we had on the telephone this afternoon?' he said, stooping to rub Hockney behind the ears.

'I was just coming to that,' said Hester cautiously.

As she waited for the butter to smoke in the frying pan, she told him about the new job. Nico was delighted.

'I've been moaning on about my boring miseries, and you've been bursting with this amazing piece of news. I'm so sorry, Hes. Tell me more about it.'

'Well, it's going to take me abroad a lot.'

'That's a good thing for a start—get you away from the History Man.'

'I wish you wouldn't call him that,' snapped Hester, tipping the eggs into the frying pan. 'Julian isn't always having affairs with his students, nor any of the dons' wives either. He just works terribly, terribly hard.'

'Producing rubbish like that typescript next door —Julian knows as much about sexual behaviour patterns as Hockney knows about hang-gliding.'

Hester giggled. 'Hockney's very good at hang-gliding, you should have seen him half way up Julian's trouser legs when he was a kitten.'

'How's Julian's marriage?'

'He's not living with his wife anymore, and he keeps talking about getting a divorce,' said Hester, pulling forward the cooked edges of the omelette so that the liquid in the centre ran out into the hot fat.

22

Nico admired the opulent curves of her bosom and hips, and the ankles, still slender despite the punishing heat of the evening.

'You're a very attractive girl,' he said, 'totally wasted on Julian. Why don't you find some nice, uncomplicated chap for a change?'

'Why don't you pack in Annabel, and find *yourself* some nice, uncomplicated girl?'

'Annabel is not in the same league as Julian,' said Nico coldly, 'who is a man of deep and frequent idiocy.'

'Annabel is a four-star bitch,' snapped Hester.

For a second they glared at each other, then Nico laughed. 'You are speaking of the woman I lust after. All right, pax, let's keep off the subject of both of them.'

'All right,' muttered Hester, turning a perfect omelette onto an emerald green plate. She buttered two pieces of French bread, and put them on either side. 'There. Now eat it while it's hot.'

'Not likely to get cold in this weather,' said Nico. 'You are an angel, what it is to feel cherished.'

He took the plate into the drawing-room. Hester followed with some Brie which was beginning to slide off the plate, and a bowl of greengages.

'Tell me more about the job,' said Nico, settling himself on the sofa. 'You'd better watch it, film crews get frightfully lecherous when they're abroad.' He took an unenthusiastic bite of the omelette.

'My new boss is heavily married,' explained Hester.

'Just like Julian,' said Nico. Then seeing the expression on Hester's face, 'All right, pax, pax. This really is a most delicious omelette, perhaps I am hungry after all.'

After he'd wolfed it down, and eaten the two slices of bread, and a large piece of Brie and five greengages, he got out his cigarette case, and offered one to Hester who shook her head.

'I've given up. I'm a slave to propaganda.'

'Now tell me why,' Nico said, 'you were so amorous

23

on the telephone this afternoon and why it was so vital that I came round this evening.'

Hester scuffed the carpet with her foot. 'I've got myself into a bit of a spot, and you're the only person who can get me out of it.'

Nico gazed at her through a haze of cigarette smoke. 'That sounds horribly ominous.'

Blushing, she told him about pretending to be engaged in order not to hurt Mr. Petrie's feelings.

Nico grinned. 'Bloody idiot, but typical, I've never forgotten you crying your eyes out when Michael ran over that weasel in the road.'

'But that's not all,' she went on miserably. 'Mr. Petrie's insisting on giving a farewell party at the office for me and my fictitious fiancé.'

Nico whistled. 'Wow—that *is* tricky. Won't Julian oblige?'

'I said it was you,' said Hester in a small voice.

'You what!' It was like a clap of thunder. Even Hockney jumped off Julian's typescript.

'I couldn't think of anyone else, and now he wants to give the party any day in the next fortnight.'

Nico shook his head. 'Uh-uh, you just tell him I've been posted to the Paris office.'

'He caught me off guard, he already knows you're here.'

'But it's bound to leak out.'

'It won't—no-one in the office knows anyone who knows you.'

'Everywhere,' said Nico, with a total lack of conceit, 'someone knows someone who knows me.'

'Just one evening for a couple of hours,' pleaded Hester, 'for the sake of our long and trouble-free friendship.'

'No,' said Nico. 'I'd have to miss *The Archers*—take Hockney instead.'

But Hester sensed weakness. 'Oh *please*.'

'Well, I was rather good as Orsino in the school play,' reflected Nico, 'and the boy playing Olivia—it was Charlie Paignton-Taylor actually—wasn't nearly as attractive as you, Hes, so I suppose I shouldn't find it too hard to play an infatuated lover. All right, I'll do it —just for one night, then.'

He stubbed out his cigarette, and reached for his diary. 'Now I know why it's called an engagement book. What about Wednesday week. We'd better have lunch that day too so you can brief me.'

Hester went over, and crouched down beside him. 'I can't thank you enough. You are the dearest, dearest person in the world.'

'May I get myself another drink then?' said Nico. 'And then can we watch *Soap*.'

'Oh yes please,' said Hester, turning on the television. 'Julian never lets me watch it, he thinks it's too silly for words.'

'Never send to know for whom the Bells toll,' said Nico, pouring two fingers of whisky into his glass, 'Annabel says I drink too much.'

'Probably drives you to it,' said Hester. Then seeing the mutinous, bulldog expression on his face, 'Oh, sorry, pax pax.'

The temperature rocketed, London wilted. Hester spent the next twelve days working late at the office to make sure everything was in order for when she left. She trailed round the shops in her lunch hour looking for clothes for Kenya, and wondering if she really wanted to spend the next few months in a country that was probably full of snakes, and twice as hot as this. The necessary jabs made her feel awful, and almost too weak to drag herself out in the evening to catch up on old Darrell French films, which were so romantically bitter-sweet, they made her long and long for Julian. He still hadn't rung. She wished she could have a jab against him. The rest of the time was spent worrying frantically whether Hockney would survive being looked after by a girlfriend while she was away, and even worse, whether poor Nico would survive the engagement party.

The whole thing seemed to be snowballing alarm-

25

ingly. Not only did everyone in the office know about her engagement, and keep bombarding her with questions, but also all the reps who called on the firm, and all Mr. Petrie's numerous business cronies who rang up, seemed to have heard the good news, and were anxious to congratulate her. She couldn't sleep at night. She felt very pulled down.

Hester spent the morning on the day of the party avoiding the office junior, who was hawking a manilla envelope round the building in a cloak and dagger fashion, obviously collecting for Hester's leaving present. Nico met her in a nearby pub for an early lunch. He'd been playing cricket at the weekend, which had stepped up his freckles and bleached his hair.

'Are you hungry?' he asked.

She shook her head. 'Not at all.'

He bought a bottle of Muscadet and some smoked salmon sandwiches, and they took them into the park, picking up a bag of nectarines on the way. The heat was putting paid to the blossom. Every path was strewn with purple lilac and yellow laburnum petals. Reddening secretaries in bikinis stretched out on the whitening grass, office boys removed their shirts and raised spotty backs to the merciless sun. Hester, who had washed her hair that morning for the party, was wearing a pistachio-green shirt, and a rust red skirt over bare brown legs. Nico noticed how every man's head turned as she passed. They sat down under the shade of a plane tree. Beneath them the dry earth was separating and cracking from lack of rain.

'I feel so awful landing you with this evening,' sighed Hester, as she watched Nico fill up two paper cups.

'Your apologies are getting marginally more boring than the actual event,' said Nico. 'I'm looking forward to being engaged—rather like a public lavatory.' He handed her a cup. 'Now will you please brief me. Where are we supposed to be getting married?'

'At home,' said Hester, 'but it's only a very quiet, tiny family wedding,' she blushed furiously, 'because your father's just died.'

26

Nico's eyebrows shot up. 'But he died eighteen months ago.'

'I know, but it's the only excuse I could think of for not asking the entire office. Then we're going on honeymoon to Kenya—I thought I'd better stick to half truths.'

'Whereabouts in Kenya?'

'Oh, the game reserves,' said Hester airily.

'Doesn't sound very peaceful.'

Hester giggled. 'I'm game if you are. And Bev is the only person in the office who knows we're not engaged at all. You can't miss her, she's going to wear cherry red matador pants, if she's taken off enough weight by six o'clock this evening to get into them.'

'Why are we getting married in such a hurry, you're not having a baby, are you?'

'Oh no,' said Hester, biting into a nectarine. 'That would horrify Mr. Petrie. We're just terribly in "lerve", and as we've known each other for ages, there was no need for a long engagement.'

'Why aren't you writing for *Woman's Own*,' said Nico lying back on the grass. 'I must say it's all rather erotic, like an arranged marriage,' he reached up and removed a lilac flower from her hair. 'I'm beginning to look at you with new eyes.'

'Don't be silly,' said Hester blushing.

'What happens when you come back from Kenya, and everyone discovers we're not married?'

'Oh, we just say we broke it off, because we weren't suited.'

'Why not? Did you discover I was a closet queen or a secret drinker?'

'There's nothing secret about your drinking,' said Hester, filling up his paper cup. She suddenly noticed how tired and drawn he looked beneath the freckles. 'Have you heard from Annabel?'

'Only one postcard, asking me to pick up her pearls from the jewellers and not displaying any overwhelming wish that I was with her.'

It was when they were walking back to Hester's office, that the truth came out. Nigel Dempster had rung Nico the previous night to say that Annabel and Jamie Cavendish had been inseparable since they arrived in Rome, and had Nico any comment to make.

'Dempster's a mate,' said Nico, 'so he perfectly understood when I told him to go and stuff himself. I don't think he'll use the story, but if he doesn't someone else'll get onto it soon.'

'I can't bear it,' said Hester in horror. 'Oh poor Nico, Annabel's probably just bored talking Italian all the time, and hankers after some English conversation.'

'No-one's ever been interested in Jamie Cavendish for his conversation,' said Nico bitterly. 'I've been trying to get her on the telephone all morning—in between discussing investments with ancient widows —but either she's out or not answering. I'd like to jump on an aeroplane and fly to Rome, and take them both apart, but I can't leave my unutterably bloody job at the moment.'

Hester was overwhelmed with contrition. 'And I'm dragging you along to this awful party this evening. I'm so desperately sorry,' and putting her arm through his, she reached up and kissed him on the cheek.

They were so engrossed that neither noticed a photographer, hovering inside the green curtain of a nearby weeping willow, who quickly took their picture as they passed.

Nico dropped her back at the office at half-past one, but instead of going inside, she waited five minutes then took a taxi to Piccadilly, where she bought a pale pink dress, a blue silk shirt from Turnbull and Asser, and the entire collection of Mozart's piano concertos —none of which she could afford. She must ring her bank manager and tell him about the new job— particularly as she'd just drawn out three hundred pounds in travellers cheques.

She slunk back into the office, feeling frightfully guilty about skiving, to find the place deserted. Everyone had gone to the hairdressers, except Beverly, who was reading Cosmopolitan, and putting fake tan on her legs.

'Mr. Petrie's got enough booze to float a battleship,' she said. 'And at last I'm going to get a chance to have a crack at young Mr. Bateman.'

'*He's* not coming?' said Hester in horror. Young Mr. Bateman was the Chairman's handsome son, so terrified of being ensnared by the typists that he never patronised office parties.

'He is, *and* Mrs. Bateman,' said Beverly gleefully. 'They're looking in before some dinner party. Even Miss Fishlock's gone to the Hydro Beauty Clinic to have her legs and arms waxed. Everyone wants to wish you well, Hes.'

'Oh shut up,' said Hester.

Mr. Petrie trotted back about three-thirty, as excited as a small boy on Christmas Eve.

'My dear,' he stopped at her desk, breathing brandy all over her, 'your mother rang before lunch.'

'But she's abroad,' said Hester aghast.

'Well, evidently she and your father have been having terrible storms in the Mediterranean,' said Mr. Petrie happily, 'and their boat ran aground. She thought you might have read about the storms in the papers, and be worried, but both your parents are fine. They're in Cannes now, and are flying back on Sunday. I told her how absolutely delighted we all were about you and Nico.'

'Oh no,' said Hester, sitting down very suddenly.

'My dear, I'm so sorry, I assumed she must know. But don't worry, she couldn't be more thrilled. Like me, she was a little worried it might be Julian, but she was simply amazed it was Nico. She told me he's an absolute charmer. She's going to ring back later.'

Hester was trapped in the office, admiring the newly waxed legs of Miss Fishlock, the head of the typing pool, when her mother rang back—obviously after a long and celebratory lunch.

'Darling, darling—crackle, crackle,' went the telephone—'we couldn't be more thrilled, it's absolutely wonderful news—we always hoped you and Nico might finally hit it off, you were such friends when you were younger. I can't imagine anyone nicer as a son-in-law. I can't wait to ring up Elizabeth Calvert. It will cheer her up, she's been so depressed since Georgie died.'

'Oh please don't,' said Hester in panic, 'Nico hasn't told her yet, it's supposed to be a secret.'

'Mr. Petrie said you were getting married in six weeks' time, darling—crackle crackle—you're not?'

'No I am not,' said Hester firmly.

'Well, that's a relief, not that it would have mattered these days, but people always count from the wedding and say "Hum", don't they? Darling, Daddy and I are also so pleased it isn't Julian, we never said anything in case you did marry him, but I didn't think he was right for you. And Daddy would have had a heart attack if you'd married a socialist.'

'He's *not*, he's a sociologist.'

'Well, it's all the same thing, dirty finger-nails and disapproving of one for living in a nice house. I must ring Michael, he'll be so fascinated you're marrying Nico. Do you think he'll be best man?'

'Oh please don't,' Hester almost screamed, acutely aware of the flapping ears of Miss Fishlock, and of Beverly helpless with suppressed mirth in the corner.

'We're staying with the Montgomerys, they're all thrilled,' went on her mother. 'And they send love, and Daddy wants a word with you too.'

Fortunately, Hester's father, more aware of the cost of long distance telephone calls, kept it brief, but there was no doubt about how pleased he was.

Hester put down the telephone receiver, gave a whimper of terror, and rushed off and hid in the loo, which looked like a wholesale dress house with all the secretaries' party clothes hanging up. If only she could go out to a telephone box and ring her mother back, but she didn't know the number of the Montgomerys' villa. She had grisly visions of them all celebrating over a bottle of Armagnac and ringing up half England.

At half-past five, feeling as if she was in a rowing boat, bucketing towards Niagara Falls, Hester changed into her new pink dress. It clung everywhere, and gave a rosy glow to her brown skin, which completely belied the churning sickness and nerves inside her.

'Do I look fat?' she asked Beverly, who inch by inch was easing herself into the cherry-red matador pants.

'No, absolutely gorgeous, you've lost weight in the past fortnight,' said Beverly grinning evilly. 'Getting engaged must be such a strain.'

'Your fiancé won't know where to put himself when he sees you in that dress,' said Marie from the typing pool.

The party was being held in the Boardroom. To begin with everyone stood around under the chandeliers, eyeing each other's dresses and wondering what to say next—funny when they had no difficulty in working hours.

Mr. Petrie, who had a friend who was a wine merchant, had ordered five cases of sparkling wine, and a bottle of whisky for the Board. Like an army waiting to come to the rescue, the serried ranks of bottles gleamed on the white tablecloth. Mr. Petrie was soon circulating them freely, and the roar of conversation started to spread through the whole building.

Everyone in the office seemed to have contributed to the food. Miss Fishlock had cooked a whole tin of cheese straws with baker's droop, the typing pool had filled bridge rolls with chopped-up boiled eggs and bloater paste. The Sales Department had provided two large quiches from the local delicatessen. The Managing Director had sent his secretary out to buy a tenner's worth of smoked salmon which she had spread on slices of brown bread that were already curling up at the edges, and the packer's wife had made a large, iced rainbow cake, across the top of which was written: "*Nico and Hester: All the best*", in loopy turquoise writing.

31

Hester felt a great lump in her throat. 'Oh, you are all angels,' she said in a shaking voice, 'I really don't deserve it. Thank you so much.'

'Don't cry,' said Beverly, 'it'll ruin your make-up. Bloody hell, Debby Austin from Accounts is wearing the same red matador pants as me—the cow! She must have seen me trying them on in the loo, yesterday.'

'Your fiancé's downstairs, Hester,' said Marie from the typing pool. 'Hasn't he got a lovely smile.'

Perhaps Annabel's rung him after all, thought Hester.

Nico was smoothing his hair in the hall mirror as she came down the stairs. 'Goodness, you look desirable,' he said. 'Like a fondant. I shan't have to act at all. How are you, my dearest darling. It seems a million hours since I saw you at lunch-time, darling, I've missed you so much, darling.'

'Don't overdo it,' hissed Hester.

'In six weeks we shall be married, darling, and you will be mine for all eternity, darling,' said Nico.

'You've been drinking,' said Hester.

'Co-rrect, but cross my heart, no-one will know but you, darling.'

And they wouldn't. Nico behaved impeccably: talking to Miss Fishlock about the fallibility of the photo-copying machines, discussing the third test with Mr. Bateman, telling Mr. Petrie what a wonderful employer he'd been to Hester, admiring photographs of Mrs. Petrie's bull terriers, and even managing to eat a piece of rainbow cake, and drink several glasses of sparkling hock, which Hester knew he detested.

He spent some minutes talking to Debby Austin from Accounts, and admiring her cherry-red matador pants.

'I thought she wasn't supposed to show that she knows we're not engaged, but she kept winking at me,' he muttered to Hester afterwards.

'Shush, it's just a nervous twitch,' said Hester, suddenly overcome with a fearful desire to giggle.

'Have some pilchard dip,' said Miss Fishlock, brandishing a mangled looking blood-red mess under Nico's nose.

'I won't, thanks awfully,' he said. 'It looks terrific, but I must make feeble attempts to stick to my pre-wedding crash diet.'

'*You* don't need to lose weight,' said Miss Fishlock skittishly.

'I might not get into my morning coat,' said Nico.

He's as adaptable as a thermostat, thought Hester in passionate gratitude. Julian would never have behaved so well, even if he and Hester really had been engaged.

As everyone was trying to congratulate Hester, she found it difficult to keep as close to Nico as she would have liked. She was talking to Mrs. Petrie about wedding cakes, when Nico (trapped by two of the Directors' wives), suddenly turned round and hissed out of the corner of his mouth, 'I've forgotten where I'm going for my honeymoon.'

'The game reserves,' hissed back Hester, 'for six weeks.'

'But isn't it the rainy season?' she heard one of the Directors' wives saying in a perplexed voice.

'How's your mother, Hester?' asked Mrs. Petrie.

'She's sailing in France,' said Hester, then froze as she heard Fiona, the Managing Director's secretary saying to Nico, 'I hear you got Hester's engagement ring at lunch-time today, what's it like?'

Leaving Mrs. Petrie in full flood, Hester swung round once again, brandishing her left hand, with its cracker ring of fake rubies and diamonds glittering gaudily on the third finger. 'Isn't it heaven,' she gasped.

'Lovely,' said Fiona looking at Nico in awe, thinking he must be rich if he could afford diamonds that size.

'But no more than you deserve, darling,' said Nico, putting an arm round Hester's waist.

'Where are you going to live?' asked Fiona.

There was a pause.

'Well,' said Nico. 'Probably,' said Hester, both at the

33

same time. Then together they said: 'No, you go on, darling.'

'We're tossing up between her flat and mine,' said Nico eventually. 'Mine is more central, but hers is more rural. We'll probably live in mine during the week, and go to Hester's for weekends.'

Two of the Directors had just joined the group, and were being introduced to Nico, when Marie from the typing pool came rushing in.

'Look, you're in the paper,' she said brandishing the *Evening Post.*

'Let's see,' said everyone crowding round.

Hester felt as though icicles were being slowly dripped down her spine. She shot an agonised look at Nico.

'Let's have a look,' he said calmly.

Underneath a photograph of Nico and Hester, arm in arm, obviously returning from lunch in the park, was written: *'While his girlfriend for the last two years, model Annabel Blair-Hopkinson, has been whooping it up in Rome, stockbroker Nico Calvert has secretly got engaged to his childhood sweetheart, Hester Milne. Neither of them was available for comment this afternoon, but Hester's office confirmed that her boss is holding a celebration party for her and Nico this evening. What will the volatile Annabel—not renowned for the evenness of her temper—do next? Watch this space.'*

'Oh my God,' said Hester under her breath.

Nico's face didn't flicker. 'Well, that's nice,' he said easily, 'and a very good picture of you, Hes darling.'

'Nico, it *is* you, I thought it must be. Congratulations,' said a voice. It was young Mr. Bateman, closely flanked by a large, chinless girl in a shirtwaister dress.

'Nico, darling,' she screamed, 'it really *is* you. How sudden and dramatic. Have you told Annabel?'

'Hullo Charlie, Hullo Selena,' said Nico kissing the large, chinless girl on the cheek. 'I thought you were in the Seychelles. Have you met Hester?'

Hester nodded, utterly speechless.

'We're all devastated to lose you, Hester,' said Charlie Bateman, looking at her with interest for the first time in six years. 'I didn't know you even knew Nico. Are you coming up to Melchester for the twelfth, Nico?'

Mercifully they were saved by a rap on the table.

Mr. Petrie, wiping away rivulets of sweat and the odd tear, then launched into an emotional farewell to Hester, thanking her for six years' devoted service.

After five minutes, old Mr. Bateman, who wanted his dinner in Cadogan Square said, 'That's enough, Cyril.'

But Mr. Petrie, not to be deflected, soldiered on for another five minutes. Hester didn't take in a word he was saying. All she could think about was what the hell was Annabel going to say to poor Nico when she read the piece in the paper.

At last when Mr. Petrie asked everyone to raise their glasses to Hester and Nico, she was still so stunned with horror, that she raised her glass and drunk a toast to herself.

Worse was to come. A large pile of presents was unearthed from under the white tablecloth. It included a set of saucepans from Accounts, coffee cups from the warehouse, a picnic basket from the sales force, a painted cock from the General Trading Company from Mr. and Mrs. Petrie, and four beautiful, fluffy towels from the typing pool.

'I thought mushroom went with everything,' explained Miss Fishlock.

'You see we all love you, Hester,' said Mr. Petrie.

Hester burst into tears. 'I can't bear it,' she sobbed. 'You've all been so kind, you don't realise . . .'

'Shut up,' interrupted Nico icily, so only she could hear, 'you can't back down now.'

He handed her his red silk handkerchief, and realising she was quite incapable of saying anything, made a short speech. He thanked Mr. Petrie for the party, and everyone else for their presents and their cooking and finally he thanked them all for the present of Hester, who he knew would make him very happy.

35

Everyone was surging forward to kiss Hester now, and clap Nico on the back.

'I think we'll push off,' Hester heard Nico say in an undertone to Mr. and Mrs. Petrie, 'it's all been marvellous, but rather a strain for Hes.'

'Quite understood, it's been pretty tear-jerking for all of us,' said Mr. Petrie, his face shining like a Dutch cheese.

'See you all tomorrow, thank you so much,' stammered Hester.

While two of the sales reps helped Nico down to his car with the presents, she had time to nip into her office and collect the wrapped-up Turnbull and Asser shirt and the Mozart piano concertos.

Outside the heat hit her like a furnace.

'Don't say anything,' said Nico, as she got into the car beside him. 'They're watching from the window.'

He drove for half a mile, then pulled up. For a minute he stared at her, his amber eyes suddenly narrowed to slits; then he proceeded to laugh until he cried. 'What a glorious, glorious cockup,' he gasped finally.

'But it's awful,' said Hester, appalled, 'Young Mr. Bateman and the piece in the *Evening Post*.'

Nico wiped his eyes.

'It really doesn't matter,' he said. 'They were all so sweet, let's go out and get absolutely smashed.'

A pink evening sun glittered behind the plane trees, as he drove her across London to Chelsea. Every so often he started to laugh again. Hester was faintly relieved by his reaction, but wondered how much was due to the drink he had consumed. He took her to a very pretty restaurant, where they dined outside under a dense canopy of dark green vine leaves. Vases of pink snapdragons stood on the pale green tablecloths. Was it Hester's imagination or did a lot of the diners look up and nudge each other as she and Nico came in?

'Congratulations, Mr. Calvert,' said the head waiter, 'congratulations. Miss Milne. I saw the article in the evening paper. This must be a very special evening for you both. I hope you will accept a bottle of champagne on the house.'

Hester shot an anguished look at Nico.

'That'd be great,' said Nico, smiling broadly. 'Thanks, Eduardo. All this free loading's wonderful,' he added to Hester, as they sat down at their table. 'With any luck we can live in the lap of luxury for the rest of our lives.'

Within the next few minutes, four people came up and congratulated him.

'Do you come here a lot with Annabel?' said Hester miserably, as the last one drifted off.

'I used to come here a lot before I met her,' said Nico. 'But she doesn't like it much, not noisy enough, nor full enough of smart people to shriek at.'

As Hester seemed quite incapable of making a decision, he ordered asparagus and poached salmon for both of them, and a bottle of Sancerre to follow the champagne.

'Nico,' she said desperately when the waiter had gone, 'you must let me pay tonight.'

'Don't be ridiculous, I'm having a wonderful time.'

'In five days time,' she persisted, 'I'll be on a plane to Kenya, and you've got to stay here and face the music.'

Nico shrugged his shoulders. 'You know what London's like, they'll have forgotten it in a few days.'

'Your optimism is truly record breaking,' said Hester gloomily.

After they'd drunk the bottle of champagne, however, she began to cheer up. She still felt close to tears, and bitterly, bitterly ashamed of herself but Nico was so nice to dine out with. He listened to what she said, and put himself out to amuse her, instead of yawning and staring at other women, and becoming irritated like Julian did if she didn't immediately get the gist of some abstruse sociological argument.

Even so she jumped out of her skin every time a dark girl came into the room. 'I keep thinking it might be Annabel.'

37

Nico laughed. 'You're more frightened of her than I am. It's amazing,' he went on, managing to talk and eat asparagus at great speed at the same time, 'how every single person at that party said how pleased they were you weren't marrying Julian.'

'I don't want to talk about Julian,' said Hester. She was horrified that she hadn't even wondered yet what his reaction would be to the piece in the *Evening Post*.

'I do though,' said Nico. 'It's high time someone talked some sense into your head.'

'He's just working terribly hard at the moment,' muttered Hester. 'He gets so stuck into things, he can't think of anything else.'

'Are you sure it's work he's stuck into?' said Nico drily.

'Of course, at least when he does turn up, it's so wonderful,' she stammered. 'I feel as though I'd been given the kiss of life, or a Leonardo of my very own.'

'Go on,' said Nico gently, 'you ought to talk about him to someone.'

Hester knew she had drunk too much, but under Nico's kind, exceptionally friendly gaze, she felt her resolve weakening. 'I want to touch him all the time when I'm with him,' she said. 'But he doesn't like it, he even thinks holding hands in the street is risqué.'

'That's probably because he's married,' said Nico. 'More married than you think. Married people are completely ruthless about maintaining the status quo. As long as their own marriage isn't endangered, they don't mind who they hurt.'

'And Julian m-makes me feel so . . .' began Hester.

'What,' said Nico.

'Hopeless in bed.' She *must* be drunk. She'd never discussed this with anyone, even with Beverly. 'He says I'm boring and unimaginative. I've read millions of sex books, but I don't really get enough practice to apply them. When we do go to bed, I'm so nervous I can't relax.'

Her voice was trembling. With one hand she was nervously opening and shutting the mouth of a snapdragon.

'Have you ever been to bed with anyone else?' asked Nico.

'Once or twice—but they were only odd scuffles after parties. They left me feeling awful afterwards. I think you have to be in love for it to work.'

Nico picked up her other hand, examining the engagement ring, and the pink, very clean, shell-like nails. Then he turned it over and kissed the palm slowly. 'You're such a nice girl, Hes. Life would be so much simpler if I loved you and not Annabel.'

'And I you, and not Julian,' said Hester sadly.

They found that neither of them had much in the way of appetite. They left their salmon virtually untouched, but got a doggy bag and took the rest home for Hockney. They did, however, finish the bottle of Sancerre, and two large brandies each. They left abruptly, with Nico overtipping.

Outside the sun had set, and the street lamps were lighting up the new, pale buff leaves on the plane trees. As they got into the car, Hester unearthed her carrier bag.

'These are for you, for being so good to me, Nico.'

She gave him the blue silk Turnbull and Asser shirt, and the Mozart piano concertos.

Nico was appalled. '*Darling*! I don't need presents like this.'

'Yes, you do, you've risked the most precious thing in your life for me.'

'Give them to Julian.'

She shook her head. 'Julian prefers Wagner, and he looks hell in blue.'

Hester lay back in the car, seeing London through a haze of alcohol. The pink and white chestnut trees were covered in candles, the laburnum and the wisteria had candles hanging down—the whole world's lit up, she thought dreamily.

It was ten minutes before she realised Nico was driving to his flat in Kensington, rather than taking her home. 'I ought to go back to Putney, it must be terribly late.'

39

'I want to play my records first,' said Nico.

He parked the car under a huge chestnut tree in the square.

Hester loved Nico's flat. It was shabby, and the curtains and chair covers, in soft faded colours, were practically falling to pieces, but it was terribly comfortable, and overflowing with records, books and pictures. Over the fireplace, there was a painting of the house in Somerset, square and Queen Anne with its russet walls, and sweeping green lawns. On the desk was a picture of Bentley, Nico's beloved black labrador, whom he saw most weekends, but refused to keep in London.

'It looks quite tidy,' said Nico, 'Mrs. Harris must have been. I'm going to have a pee, get a bottle of wine out of the fridge.'

Despite the suffocating heat of the night, Hester was assailed by a fit of shivering. She went to the window, breathing in the heady smell of lilac and wall flowers from the garden outside. Turning, she saw Nico's large double bed through a door on the right. It somehow seemed to have assumed a tangible presence, like a great grisly bear waiting to pounce on her. Don't be ridiculous, she told herself furiously, Nico loves Annabel.

In the kitchen, Mrs. Harris had left a note on the draining board, *Your lady rang, can you ring her, very urgent,*' followed by a Rome telephone number which seemed to go on for ever. Hester suppressed a terrible urge to tear it up into little bits and swallow it like a spy. Instead, she got the wine out of the fridge.

'There's a message to ring Annabel,' she said, as Nico came out of the bathroom.

'Thanks,' he said, and taking the bit of paper picked up the telephone and started to dial.

Hester retired to the loo. She was amazed that after all the drinking and emotion she still looked so pretty. I hate Annabel, she thought savagely. She lingered, washing her hands and combing her hair, as long as possible. She put on some scent, then washed it off again, thinking it too much of a deliberate come-on. Get a grip on yourself, she thought for the umpteenth time that evening.

Back in the sitting room, she found Nico lounging against the wall, his face in shadow, still letting the number ring. Hester sat down on the corner of the sofa at the other end of the room, to keep a distance between herself and the conversation.

Nico dropped the telephone back on the hook. 'Why are you hiding over there?' he said. 'To pay me back for ringing Annabel? You can ring Julian if you like.'

'Don't be so utterly bloody.'

Hester got to her feet and went over to the window once more. She wished the trembling would stop. She watched a shooting star careering across the indigo sky, then realised it was an aeroplane. Perhaps it was Annabel on her way home.

Suddenly the room was flooded with Mozart. Hester didn't move, she only knew the music seemed to be expressing all the loneliness and longing inside her.

'Hes,' said Nico softly, 'stop sulking,' and he crossed the room and took her in his arms. He looked at her for a second, as if he was trying to memorise every curve and line of her face. She could smell the faint lemon tang of his aftershave. Then he kissed her very gently.

'You've cleaned your teeth,' she muttered. 'That's not fair.'

Then he kissed her much harder—and almost before she knew it they were in bed. And she never dreamt in a million years that anyone could be so tender and skilled, and unshymaking, and utterly dedicated to giving her pleasure. It was like hearing the "Merry Peasant" strummed out for years on an out-of-tune, upright piano, then suddenly having it played by Arthur Rubenstein on a Bechstein.

Afterwards, she mumbled, 'But you're absolutely brilliant.'

'Plenty of practice,' he said, kissing her on the shoulder. 'Annabel is extremely demanding, but I

41

don't want to talk about Annabel. God, you're so warm and sweet, and you've got such a lovely cushiony body.'

'Julian says I'm too fat.'

'Julian ought to be horsewhipped,' he said roughly, 'and you should have him for slander—you're utterly adorable in bed.'

'I don't want to talk about Julian,' whispered Hester.

Nico lay back and reached for a cigarette. A match flickered in the dark like a firefly. He settled her into the crook of his arm. Hester thought she had never been so comfortable in her life. She was just drifting off to sleep, when a terrible thought struck her. 'Nico, I must go home.'

'Don't be stupid, the night'—he looked at his watch—'or rather the day, is still young. If you want to change, I'll drive you over to your flat before work tomorrow morning.'

With his left hand he began to stroke her left breast, and she felt her resolution weaken. Then she said, 'I must go back, I haven't fed Hockney.'

There was a long, long pause.

'Bugger Hockney,' said Nico.

'You needn't get up, I'll get a taxi,' said Hester, as she'd always done with Julian.

'No, you won't, I'll drive you home.'

Outside, the roof of the car was covered in white chestnut blossom—like confetti, thought Hester. The sky was already lightening to a cool, clear turquoise, as they drove through the deserted streets. Nico's hand rested on her bare thigh, in a comforting gesture of companionship. He didn't kiss her when they got back to the flat. She was relieved: her mouth tasted like a parrot's cage. But he broke a branch off the white lilac tree in the next door garden and gave it to her.

'Little Hester,' he said, running his finger lingeringly down her cheek, 'whoever would have thought it? Go and get some sleep. I'll ring you in the morning.'

Hockney, torn between rage and relief that she had finally come back, attacked her ankles viciously.

'I've got some real salmon for you tonight,' she said,

42

reproachfully unwrapping the tin foil, 'and all you can do is abuse me.'

Hockney went on mewing piteously until she put the fish down on the floor. Then after one sniff, he shot her a dirty look, and wandered off on stiff, furry, orange plus fours into the bedroom.

'And I came all the way back for you,' Hester called after him indignantly. 'Nico's right, you're a pig, Hockney.'

She bashed the stem of the white lilac, and put it in a vase by her bed, breathing in the soft, heady smell. Then she lay down and gazed at the ceiling. 'I am not at all drunk,' she said out loud, 'just totally intoxicated.' When Hockney climbed onto her stomach, and started kneading it with open claws, she didn't even notice.

She woke with an absolutely bone-crushing hangover. It took her a long time to get up and bath, and reach the office. She travelled two stops beyond her station on the tube, bought four bunches of pink snapdragons at the barrow for Mr. Petrie, and when she passed a man in the street playing "Greensleeves" on the flute, she put two pounds into his cloth cap.

'You've got your shirt on the wrong way round,' said Beverly as she wandered into the office. 'It's supposed to be lucky. You're going to need it, people have been ringing up to congratulate you all morning.'

For the next half an hour, various members of the staff trooped into the office to tell her how much they liked Nico. He rang during the coffee break.

'How are you?' she asked, suddenly overwhelmed with shyness.

'Well, if you pour two bottles of Sancerre on top of a bottle of Dom Perignon, on top of four glasses of Asti Spumante, on top of at least half a bottle of whisky, on top of half a bottle of Muscadet drunk yesterday lunch-time, you can't expect to feel like a mountain stream in the morning. Added to that, my telephone has been ringing since seven o'clock this morning. Apart from four of our national newspapers, the calls included my mother, my grandmother, and three aunts, all of whom seem delighted, and a couple of friends eking out a living as photographers, who want to take your picture. Everyone has been telling me what a lovely girl you are, Hester, and how relieved they are I've finally ditched Annabel. How are you?'

'All right,' said Hester truthfully, but next moment she knew she wasn't, as Nico went on:

'And as the *coup de grace*, Annabel has just telephoned breathing fire, having been informed by a dozen of her best friends, as well as her mother and her two step-mothers, that you and I are shortly to be married. She's flying home this morning. And guess who's got to meet her at London Airport at half-past twelve? It is no longer a question of my giving up the City, the City will give up me, if I don't spend a bit more time there.'

'Oh Nico,' said Hester, horrified, 'I'm so, so sorry.'

'So you should be, I'll ring you later.'

Hester sat down at her desk, feeling ludicrously depressed. Stop it, she told herself in a rage, don't be so wet, you've got your lovely new job to look forward to on Monday. You'll feel better once you're out of England. But all she could think about was poor Nico having to face up to Annabel's fury, and even worse, of them both making up afterwards.

At eleven-thirty, the telephone stopped ringing for a second, and Marie from the typing pool came in with an envelope delivered by hand and typed rather badly.

Opening it, Hester read, '*Dear Miss Milne, I saw the report of your engagement in the paper last night. While I must congratulate you, and wish you every happiness, I did stipulate at the interview that I was not interested in anyone with emotional ties, so I am afraid I have filled your job, and am no longer in need of your services. Yours sincerely, Darrell French.*'

I can't bear it, whimpered Hester. She ran out to a telephone box, and tried to ring Darrell French to explain, but the number was permanently engaged —probably David Niven ringing from the South of France, she thought miserably. Then she remembered the fortune she had spent in the last fortnight on the expectation of her fat new salary. She felt as though the Hoover bag containing her life was suddenly exploding. She went back to the office, put her head on the desk, and fell into a short, miserable sleep. She was woken by the telephone. It was Julian. He had seen the engagement in the paper, or rather his secretary had drawn his attention to it. Surely there was some mistake.

'Yes,' said Hester wearily, there was a colossal mistake.

Could they have lunch, asked Julian.

'He's taking me to the Etoile,' said Hester in awe, as she put down the telephone.

'He's never taken you anywhere that grand before,' said Beverly. 'The bait must have been taken.'

' "Bate" is the operative word,' said Hester. 'Annabel's flying home in a rage to have it out with poor Nico.'

For the first time since she'd known him, Julian was waiting for her at the restaurant. As always, determined to repudiate any suggestion of academic stuffiness, he was wearing a black shirt, tight white trousers, a gold necklace, and several pints of Aramis. He was immersed in a weighty tome entitled: *Gender Role Stereotypes: A Reappraisal*, and drinking a glass of Chambery. His spectacular good looks were further enhanced by a mahogany suntan. Hester thought she'd never seen him look more devastating.

'You've been away,' she said, sliding into the seat beside him.

He nodded. 'I went to a conference on World Poverty in Florida, and then on to a seminar in San Francisco, where I delivered two papers.'

'Like a paper boy,' said Hester, giggling nervously. Julian frowned.

'Did people like them?' asked Hester hastily.

'They were not unwell received,' said Julian, 'I felt I had to get away from London. It's very invigorating to

45

spend a few days mixing with the top minds in one's own field.'

Nico has hayfields, Hester was alarmed to find herself thinking. She must concentrate. Just as Julian was about to launch into a detailed description of his trip, she said, 'Can I have a very large gin and tonic, please.'

Julian looked alarmed. 'But you don't believe in drinking at lunch-time.'

'Co-rrection, Buster,' she replied quite amiably, 'it's *you* who don't believe in my drinking at lunch-time.'

I really must stop being lippy, she thought, and as Julian summoned the waiter and ordered the gin and tonic, she concentrated on his beauty. He had washed his hair for her, it was still wet at the back. Aware of her scrutiny, Julian explained that he'd been swimming before they met. Nuts, thought Hester, he'd never achieve those uniformly windswept waves without the aid of a hair dryer.

'How's my typescript getting on?' he asked.

'I finished it nearly a fortnight ago, I tried to ring you. I was a bit nervous of sending it by post.'

'Quite right,' said Julian. 'Much too precious. I'm sorry I didn't have time to tell you I was going away. I was rushed off my feet before I left. I sent you a postcard from Florida.'

'I haven't got it yet,' said Hester sweetly, then drained half her gin and tonic in one gulp.

Julian was beginning to look at her with some alarm. 'What are you going to eat?' he asked. 'It's so hot, I don't feel like much.'

Hester was not going to fall for that old trick. So often in the past, Julian had told her he wasn't hungry, and she'd frugally asked for grapefruit and a plain omelette, to find that he'd suddenly recovered his appetite, and ordered smoked salmon and a huge steak.

'I'd like a large Dover sole and a tomato salad,' she said.

By the time Julian had finished describing even the

most minor triumphs of his trip to America, their food had arrived. First Julian sent back the wine because it wasn't chilled enough, and then he summoned the waiter. 'These quenelles are very disappointing,' he said, 'I don't think you've added enough seasoning. I'll have cold salmon instead.'

Hester blushed scarlet and helped herself liberally to tartar sauce. It's sacrilege to complain here, she thought furiously, when they do everything so perfectly. He's just pig-ignorant and showing off.

'Not too much tartar sauce,' chided Julian. 'You've managed to shed some weight since I last saw you. We don't want you gaining it too soon. Perhaps I should go away more often,' he added playfully, 'and make you lose your appetite.'

'Absolutely heavenly sole,' said Hester defiantly to the waiter, when he returned with Julian's cold salmon, 'and wonderful tomato salad, and spiffing tartar sauce.'

The waiter gave her an almost imperceptible wink. 'Thank you, Madam,' he said solemnly.

'Now,' said Julian, 'what's all this nonsense in the paper last night?'

Hester told him. Julian was horrified. 'That doddering old ruin, who's been exploiting you for the last six years! And you didn't have the guts to tell him why you were leaving.'

'It wasn't anything to do with guts,' protested Hester, 'I just love Mr. Petrie, and I didn't want to hurt him.'

'And Nico Calvert went along with this charade. I suppose it's the sort of silly idiot, ragging-in-the-dormitory, practical joke he would appreciate—talk about delayed adolescence.'

'Nico has been wonderful,' snapped Hester, 'and behaved like a perfect gentleman throughout.'

'Meaning I wouldn't,' said Julian nettled.

'No, no,' said Hester hastily, 'I'm sorry, Julian.'

'What happens if your new boss gets to hear of this?'

'He has,' said Hester sadly. 'He sent me round a letter this morning, saying the job has gone to someone else.'

47

'How old are you, Hester?'

'Twenty-six.' He ought to know, she thought irritated.

'You're very infantile for twenty-six.'

She didn't need *him* to tell her.

'I realise you're a caring and concerned person, but to fabricate such lies. You obviously consider Nico has been very supportive, but he's merely encouraged you in your duplicity. You deserved to lose that job. What did your mother say when Mr. Petrie told her?'

'She was absolutely delighted,' said Hester. 'She adores Nico.'

'Naturally,' sneered Julian, 'one would expect her to be heavily into endogamy.'

Hester bit her lip. She was not going to give Julian the opportunity to put her down by asking him what "endogamy" meant. He was lecturing her on and on now. She found it very hard to concentrate. She suddenly thought what a common voice he had, a sort of ironed-out Birmingham with American overtones, then felt appallingly ashamed of herself for being such a raging snob.

The richness of the fish, the oil from the salad, and the tartar sauce, were beginning to make her feel sick. She took a slug of white wine, and felt the sweat rising under her hair. She still had three-quarters of the sole to get through. Julian, who'd nearly finished his salmon, disapproved strongly of waste, but even more of doggy bags.

At the next table, a blond man had taken the hand of a beautiful girl sitting beside him. They both looked so besottedly in love. Hester found her thoughts straying to Nico, and how he was getting on. Had Annabel drawn first blood yet? Perhaps they were already making it up in Nico's double bed? She was filled with a pain so intense it astonished her.

'I think it was just as well your job didn't come off,' Julian was saying, 'I'm not sure you have the moral fibre to withstand entire film crews abroad and, although I admire Darrell French's work, as a director he lacks seriousness. One can't make films just to entertain these days.'

He took her hand. 'If you had the right person to guide you, Hester, I think you could grow into a beautiful human being.'

'I could harly grow into a beautiful carthorse.'

Julian frowned, but was not to be deflected. 'You would find the field of sociology very rewarding. I have more paper work than I can handle at the moment, I need to be released from all the trivial pressures of everyday life, in order to get on with my next book.'

'What's it going to be called this time?' asked Hester, her heart sinking.

'A short but telling title: *Whence Sisterhood?* The male can no longer bury his head in the sand where the women's movement is concerned. This should be my most meaningful work to date. I didn't tell you before, because I needed the space to think, but my divorce has come through. I realise that'll be a great relief to you.'

Hester put her knife and fork together. 'What are you trying to say, Julian?'

'That you should move in with me, then we could extend the parameters of our relationship. You can sub-let your flat—that should give us two hundred and forty pounds a month, and you can help me with all my research, and, if need be, do extra typing for some of the other professors.'

Hester was absolutely speechless. Julian, she thought, wants a housekeeper and a free secretary.

'I appreciate this is a shock for you,' said Julian smugly. 'When you've wanted something as much as I know you've wanted this, you can't assimilate it straight away.'

'I'd like some fresh air,' said Hester. 'I'm terribly sorry,' she added to the waiter who was ruefully shaking his head over her hardly touched plate, 'it was lovely, but the weather's too hot,' and she fled out of the restaurant.

Outside a white hot sun blazed relentlessly out of a white hot sky. Julian walked her back to the office, wheeling his bicycle, and talking and talking, little of which Hester took in. The pavement scorched her feet through her soles.

Outside her office, she turned to him, looking at his face as carefully as Nico had studied hers last night. 'Julian, will you kiss me?' she said, adding *'Please,'* as he hesitated.

Rather reluctantly, he put his arms round her. She could feel the bar of the bicycle against her stomach, the oily chain against her leg. His kiss was as perfunctory as the "Thank You" stamped at the bottom of a supermarket tag. She drew away from him.

'I'm sorry, Julian,' she said sadly. 'But I can't move in with you, because I don't love you anymore.'

Julian looked thunderstruck. 'Oh c'mon, I know exactly how much you feel about me. You're just erecting defensive barriers, because I didn't get in touch with you for a few days. Believe me, I had some thinking to do myself, some very real conflicts had to be resolved. I didn't know if I was ready for a caring and committed relationship again.'

'Also,' said Hester, 'I don't think you'd make a very good step-father for Hockney.'

Julian was furious. 'You've been seeing far too much of Nico Calvert recently,' he said, 'I can detect the flip, ridiculously trivialising influence. You are down and out, Hester, with no job, no fiancé, and when Annabel gets back from Rome, and makes absolute mince meat of you, you'll be a laughing stock. I don't want you to see any more of Nico, and I expect you round at my flat at eight o'clock tonight with the typescript.'

'Taxi,' screamed Hester, seeing an orange *For Hire* sign approaching like an angel of mercy. She tore across the road, narrowly avoiding a car coming in the opposite direction, and leapt frantically into the waiting cab.

She only had enough money to take her to Putney Hospital, and had to walk home across the common. A heat haze shivered above the bleached grass. Every tree was a boiling, midgy, ebony cauldron of shadow. Dried-out pink blossom rained down from the chestnut trees. Hester just made it home in time, and threw up all the wine and the Dover sole.

Hockney was totally unsympathetic as she cleaned her teeth, mewing round her legs and leading her huffily into the kitchen, where last night's salmon was buzzing with flies.

'You wouldn't have enjoyed moving in with Julian,' said Hester, throwing the salmon into the dustbin. 'He'd never have let you shed hairs on *Whence Sisterhood*?'

She gave him some Kit-e-Cat, the smell of which made her feel sick again. She went next door and rung the office.

'I'm sorry, Mr. Petrie, I've got a blinding headache. I'll come in at crack of dawn tomorrow and clear all my work up.'

Immediately she put the telephone down, it rang again. She snatched it up praying it was Nico, but it was the *Daily Mail*.

'Wrong number,' she screamed slamming down the receiver, then she took it off the hook. In her bedroom, she found the lilac branch Nico had broken off for her last night already dropping white petals all over her bedside table.

'This place is a tip,' she said, and settled down to clean the flat from top to toe, crying great tearing sobs as she worked, until her hair was dark with sweat, and her face streaked with dust. When at last she was finished she collapsed onto her bed.

'I'm a stupid idiot,' she said to herself, 'falling in love with someone I know as well as my old teddy bear,' and the tears spilled over and she started to cry again.

She was interrupted by the doorbell. She didn't answer it, probably some rotten journalist. But whoever it was, was leaning on the bell. She put on a huge pair of dark glasses, and went to answer the door.

To her amazement it was Nico, also wearing dark

51

glasses, which he took off at once. 'Where the hell have you been, I've been ringing you all afternoon? The office said you'd gone home.'

'How was Annabel?' she asked quickly.

'Fine. Everything's sorted out there.'

Hester felt the tears welling up again. 'I'm so pleased,' she said in a frozen voice. 'We'd better have a drink to celebrate.'

He followed her into the drawing-room. 'Why are you wearing those ridiculous dark glasses?'

'I'm hungover,' she muttered.

Despite her frantic protests, he whipped them off. 'Darling,' he said in horror, 'what's the matter?'

'I had lunch with Julian.'

The amber eyes hardened. 'If that bastard's been bullying you.'

'No, no, he asked me to move in with him.'

His hand tightened on her arm so sharply that she winced. 'He what!'

'He wants me to sub-let this flat and move in with him.'

'And what did you say?'

'Nico, please, you're hurting me,' she cried out. 'I suddenly found I didn't want to move in with him at all.'

'The Past-History Man,' said Nico with a grin.

Rubbing her arm, she went over to the window, and started frantically removing dead leaves from one of the geraniums. Some of the pale red petals fell onto the window sill. She noticed they were heart-shaped. 'I'm terribly pleased everything's all right between you and Annabel,' she mumbled. 'Did she give you hell?'

'Appalling at first. It seems my stock, like yours, has rocketed during our twenty-four hour engagement. She's decided she wants to marry me, but first I've got to ring up the *Evening Post*, and get them to print a retraction of last night's piece, and then put an announcement of our engagement in the *Times*.'

So that's that, thought Hester dully. Out loud she said, 'I'll get us a drink.'

'So I drafted the announcement,' went on Nico, 'I thought you might like to look at it.'

'I'm sure you'll be terribly happy,' said Hester in a choked voice.

'I know I will,' said Nico, 'I've never been so happy.'

He got a piece of paper out of his pocket, and handed it to Hester. 'Go on, read it.'

I can't bear to, she thought in agony. Then she remembered how angelic Nico had been to her, not only over the engagement party, but also during the time when there had been a very real prospect of his losing Annabel. It was so churlish not to share in his happiness.

She forced herself to look at the piece of paper. The first words were a mist of tears, then she read, *The engagement is announced between Nicholas Gerald Christopher, elder son of the Hon. Mrs. Gerald Calvert, and the late Mr. Gerald Calvert of Penhaldren Hall, Somerset, and Hester Jane,*' she read on incredulously, '*only daughter of Mr. and Mrs. Anthony Milne, of Lime Tree House, Chichester, Sussex.*'

Her lip began to tremble. 'I don't understand,' she whispered.

'I absolutely adored being engaged to you,' said Nico softly. 'But I'd much rather we were married.'

'We can't,' she said in a stifled voice. 'I've compromised you.'

'I know you have, and I couldn't be more delighted.' He took her by the shoulders, gently turning her round to face him, and her heart failed.

'Annabel went on and on and on, yakking and yakking. I suddenly thought, "you're in the wrong pen, mate, you'd better hop out at once, and go back to where you belong." '

He looked into her red, swollen eyes, 'I adore you, Hes, you look like one of the piglets on the farm, and you're the most lovely and familiar thing I've ever held in my arms.'

'It was the same with me,' she muttered damply into his shirt. 'Julian was rabbiting on and on, and he was so pompous and conceited, and he could never have been as fantastic as you were last night.'

'Which part of last night?'

'That was this morning,' said Hester. 'I mean at the party, and then when Marie rolled up with that thing in the paper—'

'I behaved well,' said Nico stroking her hair, 'because I didn't give a bugger. I think I've been in love with you since you were a little schoolgirl with pigtails. Annabel was just a hiatus.'

'Oh, that's such a very kind thing to say,' said Hester going very pink in the face.

'Darling, I'm not railroading you, am I?' he said suddenly. 'You do feel the same about me, don't you?'

'Oh yes,' sighed Hester, 'I so liked being engaged to you last night, I've been having the most awful withdrawal symptoms ever since,' and she flung her arms round his neck and kissed him until both their hearts were hammering.

'Just one more thing before we get down to more serious matters,' said Nico, 'do you mind terribly if I chuck in stockbroking and take you back to Somerset to run the farm? It'll be a hell of a struggle at first, but if I've got you with me, I know I can do it.'

'As long as Hockney can come too,' said Hester.

'Won't he chase sheep,' said Nico, going towards the bedroom.

'No,' said Hester following him. 'And he'll be awfully supportive, and caring and concerned and meaningful about keeping the rats down too.'

Forsaking All Others

One of the greatest shocks of Julia Nicholson's life was the discovery that being happily married doesn't stop one falling in love with other people. Before she was married, she was always in love—plunging into each new involvement with the alacrity of the high diver, who doesn't realise the water has been drained out of the swimming pool. After each affair, she emerged bruised and shattered, but perfectly willing, after a few weeks, to take the plunge again with somebody else.

Then, when she was nineteen, she met David Nicholson, a successful underwriter, who fell in love with her about five minutes before she saw and fell in love with him. They were married in three months.

Julia blossomed. David bought her a ginger kitten called Kitchen, and after she had played with her wedding presents and spent six months painting their mews cottage, she took an unexacting job working for a property company.

Then came the Hornbys' summer party. The Hornbys were both successful architects and twice a year they filled their starkly furnished penthouse flat with other successful people. That afternoon the telephone rang.

It was David. 'Darling!' she cried delighted, 'I've missed you. I thought your meeting went on till six.'

'I've missed you, too.' He sounded nervous. 'I'm afraid we're running behind schedule. I haven't a hope of making the Hornbys' party.'

55

'Oh, darling!' she wailed.

'Never mind. It'll do us good to have an early night.'

'An early night,' Julia's voice was sharp. 'But I can go.'

'You can't,' said David flatly, 'not without me. I know what happens to married women who go to parties without their husbands. Sitting duck for every wolf in sight.'

Julia was outraged that he could trust her so little after eighteen months of marriage, and told him so.

'It isn't you I don't trust, darling—it's other men.'

'But I've spent a fortune getting my dress out of the cleaners!'

Someone was shouting in the background. 'Look, I've got to go,' said David. 'All right, go to your precious party. I'll pick you up about nine.'

'Thank you, darling—darling?' But he had rung off. Bland, handsome, he smiled at her out of the photograph frame on her desk. Having got her own way, Julia decided she didn't want to go to the party at all.

She took a long time getting ready. She wanted to overwhelm David with her beauty when he arrived, and she very much enjoyed making an entrance. As a result, the Hornbys' flat was crowded by the time she got there. Sarah Hornby met her at the door. Tall and slim, her long hair wound about with ribbon like a maypole, her eyes glittered when she saw that Julia had come on her own.

'Darling—you're on the loose at last. I'm frightfully short of girls, come and meet some lovely men.'

After a quick check round the room, Julia was relieved to see that apart from a flat-chested girl in red chiffon, she was easily the prettiest girl in the room. Sarah introduced her to a sleek man in a primrose shirt, who said he worked in advertising.

'Which is your husband?' he asked her.

'He's not here.' She saw the gleam in his eye. David was right. 'But he's coming later,' she added hastily. The gleam subsided.

The party ebbed and flowed. Without David to ask

them the right questions, Julia found the people less interesting than before. Trapped between two male ballet dancers drinking tomato juice, their feet in first position, her eyes started to wander. With amusement she noticed three women, hopping about like sparrows, competing for the attention of a very tall, broad-shouldered man with long, dark red hair. He had his back to her, and Julia edged round so she could see his profile. He had a bony, sunburnt face and a big nose. What an ugly man! she thought. He looks like a fox!

Suddenly he turned round and caught her staring at him. Julia blushed and looked quickly away, but when she looked back a few seconds later, he was still staring at her.

For the next quarter of an hour, try as she would to concentrate on the ballet dancers, her eyes kept tangling with his. He had disconcerting eyes, very light grey, with heavy lids and thick dark lashes. She was relieved when he shrugged off the three women and elbowed his way across the room to Sarah Hornby. Julia tried not to notice them both looking in her direction. When she looked again the tall man had disappeared and Sarah was beckoning imperiously.

'Sorry you got stuck with those two,' she said, when Julia had battled through the throng. 'Come and meet the most devastating man in London!'

Sarah always exaggerates, Julia thought, as she followed Sarah into the next room. It was empty except for the man who looked like a fox. He was gazing out of the window at the sunset. He turned round and smiled at them.

'It's a sin to introduce two such ravishing people to each other! But I can't resist it. Julia Nicholson—Richard de Lisle! Now, you're on your own, darlings, I've got a party to run!' Sarah whisked back into the throng, ribbons flying.

Julia longed to follow her. Richard de Lisle! What a fool she'd been, making eyes at him—he must think her an out of work actress angling for a part in his next film! She looked down at her glass, unable to say anything.

'It's all right,' he said gently. 'Sarah makes the most paralysing introductions. It takes people at least five minutes to recover.'

'I'm not an actress,' Julia said.

He laughed. 'I didn't think you were. Actresses don't blush. I'm sorry I stared at you—you threw me off my stride. Come and see the sunset.'

The Hornbys' flat boasted one of the most magnificent views in London. Across the feathery green of the trees, the sky was deep gold slashed with purple and scarlet.

'I always think,' said Julia, 'that when great artists die, they take it in turns in heaven to paint the sunset —to give them something to do.' What a precious remark, she thought as soon as she'd said it.

But Richard de Lisle merely smiled and said, 'I wonder what happens to indifferent directors when they die—straight to hell I suppose.'

Julia noticed he had a slight stammer which made him much less alarming.

A man was mowing the lawn in the next garden and suddenly Julia shivered. 'Cold?' he asked, leaning over to shut the window.

She shook her head. 'It's the smell of newly cut grass. It takes me straight back to school when the pitches were being cut. I was so fat I couldn't run then, and everyone laughed at me.'

Richard de Lisle got out a packet of cigarettes and offered her one. 'When I was at school, I was miles taller than anybody else. They ragged me! Then I started to broaden out, and I found there were compensations. I can always see at race meetings, and look down women's dresses.'

Julia laughed and raised her glass to him. 'Well, here's to all misfits then.'

'God, you're pretty,' he said. 'Where the hell's your husband?'

'He got held up at the office—we had a row about my coming alone.' Instantly she felt disloyal.

'He's quite right. If I were married to you, I'd keep you locked up.'

The crowd was beginning to overflow from the next room. People—particularly women—kept trying to break them up. But it was as though Richard de Lisle had drawn a magic circle round the two of them which excluded everyone else.

She had never found anyone so easy to talk to. She found he had two children at boarding school, which meant that he must be quite old, and that he was shooting a film in a studio near her office. In her turn, she told him about David and Kitchen, the cat.

'We've got four cats,' he said, filling up both their glasses. 'They rule our lives.'

They were comparing cat food brands, when the beautiful, skinny girl in red chiffon came rushing up to them.

'Ricky!' she shrieked, 'I never saw you come in! We must have a private talk.' Julia moved tactfully away, but Richard de Lisle grabbed her elbow like a vice. She was quite happy to lean against the wall, almost—but not quite—touching him.

'You never called me back,' reproached the skinny girl. 'I wanted to tell you about the ball I had in the States.'

And tell them she did, only deflected by Sarah Hornby, shouting that Richard was wanted on the telephone.

'I'll be right back,' he said to Julia. In a daze, she watched him crossing the room. She wondered how on earth she could have thought him ugly—he made every other man in the room look insignificant. The skinny girl rattled on . . .

'I've got to go,' he said regretfully when he came back. 'My wife was coming to pick me up, but she's gone home instead and she's complaining that she's tired and hungry. Thank you so much for talking to me. I hope we meet again soon.'

Julia felt deflated as she watched him saying good-bye to the Hornbys. He hadn't even asked for her telephone number. Then she shook herself. For goodness sake, she was married now! But she was comforted when he turned at the door and looked at her for a long time . . .

A few minutes later, when David Nicholson arrived, tired and badly in need of a drink, he thought he had never seen his wife look more radiant.

Later, their love-making was more passionate than it had been in weeks. What a perfect marriage, thought Julia as she fell asleep.

The next day in the office, however, she did not thumb through recipe books or read the gossip page. She gazed out of the window. The cigarette ends mounted in her ashtray. At four o'clock, she rang Sarah Hornby to thank her for the party.

'I thought it went well,' said Sarah. 'We still had people there until well after midnight. You certainly made a hit.'

'I did?'

'With Richard de Lisle. Ten minutes after you arrived, he comes pounding up to find out who you are and stays glued to your side for the rest of the evening.'

'I thought he was rather attractive,' said Julia calmly.

'Attractive? He's lethal. He's the most run-after man I know. But I've never seen him go ape like that before. Has he rung you?'

'No, why should he?'

'He will. He rang me this morning—you know how he stammers. It took him five minutes to ask for your telephone number.'

'But why me?' Julia said.

'Search me,' said Sarah tactlessly. 'There's no accounting for tastes.'

'What's his wife like?'

'Attractive, quite tough. They go their separate ways. At least, she does. I've never heard any gossip about him. He buries himself in his work. But you want to

60

watch those reserved types. Before you know where you are, you've got a tiger by the tail.' Or a fox, Julia thought.

Every time the telephone rang she jumped like a terrified horse. But he didn't ring that day, nor any of the following days.

One afternoon she slipped out to buy some coffee for the office. Coming back, clutching a large tin, she saw a taxi draw up in front of her. A man jumped out. There was no mistaking the dark red hair. Richard de Lisle had seen her and was waving his arms like a windmill. They were twenty yards apart, Julia didn't know where to look as she walked towards him.

'Hello,' he said, 'playing truant?'

Julia brandished the tin of coffee. 'We ran out.'

'Come and have a drink.'

'At this hour?'

'I know a little place round the corner where you can drink all round the clock.'

After a half-hearted show of reluctance, Julia agreed to go—but only for five minutes. The little place round the corner was all red plush and soft pink lights. Several expensive-looking men with red, veined faces eyed Julia with interest. Apart from a close-cropped blonde in a maroon smoking jacket, who was playing "Night and Day" on the piano, she was the only woman in the place.

'What would you like?' said Richard de Lisle.

"What's best in the middle of the afternoon?'

'Brandy—go and grab a seat and I'll bring them over.'

Julia sat down and watched him joking with the barman. She noticed once again the broad shoulders and the powerful thighs, and was horrified to find herself wondering what it would be like to be in bed with him.

When he sat down, she noticed how tired he looked. 'You've been overworking,' she said.

'No—well—yes, I suppose I have. Nothing seems to be working out—all the cast are throwing tantrums.

61

They were so frightful this morning, I walked out on them! How are you, though? That's much more important.'

'I'm fine.'

His heavy-lidded eyes ran over her. 'You look marvellous—those knickerbockers absolutely slay me.'

Because she had no eye make-up on, Julia was reluctant to look him straight in the eyes.

'Do you know what I'd like to do now?' he said.

'What?' said Julia, fiddling with the plastic roses on the table.

'I'd take the biggest suite at the Ritz, draw the curtains, curl up with you in a huge bed and sleep for a month.'

Julia laughed. 'If you were going to sleep for a month, you'd hardly need me.'

'Oh, I would, I would. I couldn't sleep unless I knew you'd be there when I woke up. I had the most disturbing dreams about you last night.'

'About me?' Julia was flattered. 'What did I do?'

'Marvellous and quite unmentionable things.'

He picked up one of her bunches of hair. 'These are pretty fetching.'

Suddenly Julia felt the current of electricity flowing between them so strongly that she was frightened.

"I ought to go in a minute,' she said, taking a huge gulp of brandy and choking. As he patted her on the back, he said, 'Let's have a drink after work—one day this week.'

Julia was flustered. Drinks in the middle of the day were all right. After work, that smacked of adultery!

'It's difficult, I have to rush home and cook David's dinner.'

'Doesn't he ever go away?'

His strange, light eyes bored into her. In the pink light his red hair seemed to be on fire. Suddenly, he looked like the devil. Terrified, Julia leapt to her feet, clutching her tin of coffee.

'I must go back,' she said.

Out in the brilliant sunshine, her fears evaporated.

How foolish she must seem. He didn't look like the devil at all—just a big man with weary eyes.

They walked back to her office.

'I'm sorry, I didn't mean to rush you. It's that Lolita kit you're wearing and too much booze at lunch-time.' She noticed he was stammering more than usual.

On impulse she said, 'Will you come to my birthday party? It's next Wednesday. You and your wife, I mean.'

'I think we'd love to,' he said. 'How old will you be? Sixteen?'

Julia made a face at him. 'Six-thirty then—just drinks . . .'

'Can I have a small party on my birthday?' she asked David, as they were going to bed that night.

'We ought to pay the gas bill first and the rates.'

'They can wait—I'll get a fat cheque from Granny for my birthday. Just a small party, darling . . .'

In her blue cotton nightgown, fresh from the bath, David Nicholson could deny his wife nothing.

'Of course, my sweetheart, as long as you do the asking—and not more than thirty people!'

The day before the party, Sarah Hornby telephoned. 'Darling, Mark's gone to the States.' Julia suppressed her dismay. They were already short of men. 'Can I bring someone else?'

'Of course, who is he?'

'Rather glamorous actually—he's Brazilian.'

'How exciting—what's he like?'

It was like opening the sluices of a dam. Half an hour later, when Sarah ran out of breath, Julia reflected it was the first time that Sarah had admitted to her that she had lovers.

That evening she showed David the guest list. He whistled. 'But I don't know any of these people. Who the hell are Duck and Piggy?'

'Dick and Peggy Fanshawe—you know, that nice couple we met at Henley.'

'For about five minutes—and who's Geranium?'

'Genevieve, darling, Richard de Lisle's wife—the film director I met at the Hornbys.'

'It's like a page out of *Who's Who*. Thank God I asked the Mittons and Suzy to add a little roughage.'

Julia stiffened. 'Oh no, not the Mittons—they always row when they're drunk. And why on earth ask Suzy? It fouls up the numbers.'

Suzy was David's secretary—a natural scene-stealer, who wore her clothes too tight and too short. Julia hated the idea of her taking dictation from David for hours a day.

'Well, I'll ask old Roley Farebrother to drop in.'

'No,' snapped Julia. 'There I draw the line. If that man ever crosses my threshold again—I walk out.' Roley Farebrother was like the worst kind of street dog, with an unengaging habit of laughing at his own off-colour jokes and singing ghastly Rugger songs when he was tight.

Julia was holding hands with Richard de Lisle on the Hornbys' black leather sofa when the ceiling fell in. She was struggling desperately to crawl out of the debris, when she woke up to find the cat treading water on her stomach and David holding a breakfast tray.

'Kitchen and I have come to wish you a happy birthday,' he said, kissing her.

Julia was so relieved it was only a dream that she flung her arms around David and hugged him. 'Oh, darling, I do love you,' she said.

David gave her a cashmere twinset and a new handbag. Kitchen gave her a box of Turkish Delight. She was slightly dismayed that her grandmother gave her a rather ugly diamond brooch instead of the usual large cheque, but she cheered up when she found a small parcel waiting for her in the office.

It was a volume of modern and incomprehensible poems. Inside Richard de Lisle had written, *'Happy birthday—love from Richard.'*

I'll have to keep them in the office, she thought, but she sang all the way to the hairdresser at lunch-time.

Everything was going like clock-work, she decided several hours later, as she dried herself after a bath. She had three-quarters of an hour to get ready. To Julia, making up one's face was something of a religious ceremony, which should be carried out in complete silence without interruption. She had just gathered all the necessary bottles and brushes round her when the doorbell rang.

It was David, complete with Suzy, his secretary. 'Sorry darling,' he said, 'I forgot my key. I thought it would be nice for Suzy to have a bath and change.'

'What a good idea. Come along upstairs,' said Julia, smiling rather tightly. She had just cleaned the bathroom.

She gave Suzy a towel and left her to it. But her ritual was ruined. Every few minutes, Suzy popped in to borrow something or to ask who was coming.

At last Julia gave up in despair, as ready as she could ever be with that creature around.

'What on earth have you got on?' asked David, suddenly noticing her pink culotte dress.

'Do you like it?' said Julia.

'It's interesting,' he said cautiously. 'Rather low at the back. Still, the colour suits you.'

The doorbell rang. No-one was due for ten minutes. Julia went to answer it. The welcoming smile on her face froze when she saw it was Roley Farebrother. She was about to shut the door in his face when he thrust a big bunch of tulips at her and gave her a smacking kiss.

'Many happys, old fruit. You don't look a day over fifty. That's a fine pair of pyjaws you're wearing —ready for bed?' He was wearing a tartan tie and a maroon velvet waistcoat.

'David said there was plenty of crumpet coming. I thought I'd get here early to stake a claim.'

'David's in the kitchen, Roley,' said Julia. 'You'd better go through.'

She couldn't trust herself to speak to David just now. How dare he sneak Roley in under her nose?

In the drawing-room, Roley Farebrother was laying

seige to Suzy. She was wearing a slit black skirt and no bra under a transparent white frilly shirt. Unbelievably tarty! thought Julia.

Julia's boss and his wife were the first to arrive. 'We came early, as we've got to go out to dinner,' he said, handing her a large bunch of roses. 'How pretty you look!'

Determined not to introduce Roley and Suzy, Julia kept them talking in the dining-room as long as possible.

Then a rush of people started to arrive. Soon Suzy was in her element holding court to five men. And in horror, Julia saw Roley Farebrother regaling her boss's wife with his bluest story. Everyone suddenly seemed to have empty glasses, and Julia and David were kept busy filling them up.

The telephone rang. It was Sarah Hornby. The Brazilian, she said happily, didn't feel like getting out of bed. 'We just rang up to wish you a very happy Richard de Lisle, darling,' she said as she rang off.

Julia turned round nervously. David was behind her, talking to a woman who had just arrived. She smiled at Julia and held out her hand.

'Happy birthday,' she said, 'I'm Genevieve de Lisle. Richard's finding a place to park. I am sorry we're so late. I got waylaid in the country.'

She was well into her thirties and she wore a crumpled red dress and no make-up except sunburn. But she had a sleepy, well fed air about her.

David, obviously impressed, took her off to meet people. Julia went into the hall—her heart was going like a pneumatic drill. Looming in the doorway, looking like a thundercloud, was Richard de Lisle. His face softened when he saw her. Julia wanted to throw herself into his arms and beg him to take her away from all these people. Instead she put on her brightest smile.

'Richard, how lovely!'

'Happy birthday,' he said looking at her intently.

'Everything all right?' One would never be able to keep any secrets from this man, she thought. .

She nodded. 'Thank you for the book,' she whispered. 'Come and get a drink.'

David met them in the doorway and Julia introduced them. She had always thought of David as tall, but he was dwarfed by Richard de Lisle.

'I've just been pole-axed by your wife,' said David, handing him a large drink. 'Come and meet my secretary. She's a tremendous fan of yours and she's dying to meet you.'

Julia gritted her teeth.

Soon Suzy was nose to nose with Richard de Lisle and every time he looked like extracting himself, David rolled up another beautiful girl.

She went into the kitchen to get some more tonic out of the fridge and found Kitchen the cat sitting like Ferdinand among her boss's flowers. When she picked him up, he rumbled with purring like a tumble dryer.

'Oh Catkin,' she said, 'I'm so miserable.'

She heard a footstep and turning round saw Richard de Lisle at the door. 'This is Kitchen,' she said.

'He's beautiful,' he said, coming over and ruffling the cat's fur. Then he ran his hand over her hair. 'But not nearly as beautiful as you.'

Taking Kitchen from her, he dropped him gently on the floor, and held out his arms. Julia went into them like a dog out of a thunderstorm. For a moment they clung to each other without speaking, then he said, 'I know I oughtn't to be doing this to you. I'm so terribly sorry it's happened. But I'm haunted by you, completely obsessed, I can't work, I can't think—I don't know what's hit me. I know I shouldn't ask you, but we must see each other again.'

His voice was like a sedative, his hands were warm on her bare back. Julia felt the strength drain out of her.

'I've got to go to Rome for three days, but I'll be back on Sunday.'

In a voice she hardly recognised as her own, Julia

said, 'David's got a cricket dinner on Monday. He never gets back until long after midnight.'

'I'll ring you on Monday, and arrange where to meet.'

He took her face in his hands. 'Promise not to get cold feet between now and Monday,' he whispered. 'Just remember I love you.'

Not a moment too soon, he let her go. David came through the door. Julia wondered how long he'd been outside, but he was smiling quite amiably.

'There you are!' he said to Richard. 'Your wife says you ought to be off.' In a daze, Julia said goodbye to the de Lisles.

'I think it went well,' she said, when finally the last guests, who were naturally Suzy and Roley Farebrother, had gone.

'The best party we've ever given,' said David.

Julia could bear it no longer—the desire to talk about him was too strong. 'The de Lisles *are* nice, aren't they?' she said.

'She was fabulous. I didn't much care for him.'

'Why not?' said Julia carelessly. 'Too intense?'

'I don't mind that. But he really fancies himself. Poor Suzy had a terrible time with him.'

'Suzy?'

'He spent all evening pestering her to go to Rome with him, and in the end she had to fob him off with lunch tomorrow. She's commandeered me to ring him up in the morning to say she's ill.'

'Are you sure you've got the right person?' said Julia.

'Yes, the man with red hair, who looks like a fox. He's got the most frightful reputation anyway. That's why I followed you into the kitchen. I didn't want him bothering you.'

For a minute, Julia didn't speak. Then she noticed someone had stubbed out a cigarette on their white silk sofa. She burst into floods of tears. 'Oh, the pigs,' she sobbed. 'Look at our beautiful sofa!'

David put his arms round her. 'Darling! Don't cry,' he said soothingly, 'not on your birthday.'

Gradually, the first wild intensity died down and subsided into a succession of wrenching and destructive sobs. David congratulated himself on handling the situation with aplomb. He felt a little guilty about all those lies he had just told Julia about Richard de Lisle and Suzy. But he hadn't liked what he had overheard in the kitchen. De Lisle was obviously besotted with Julia, and she was so impressionable. These fancies should be nipped in the bud, early.

Besides, he thought as he stroked her hair, it would be an excuse to take Suzy out for a long lunch tomorrow. It was vital that they both told Julia the same story.

Temporary Set-Back

My first job was with a small publishers, Mildew and Rambridge. And how I hated it—nothing but washing up and running errands and cutting off people on the switchboard. I stayed there only because my typing school had gone on about holding down a first job for at least a year and, far more important, because I was nuts about Mr. Rambridge. We all were: Miss Winn, his secretary, fairly drooled over him, and even fat Miss Truslove, who worked for Mr. Mildew, was very free with the Devon Violets if she had to go to see him.

I don't know what made him so lovely. He was at least thirty—and he always looked tired out: like a weary lion, with his beautiful ravaged face, hair and great powerful body, that always seemed too big for his clothes as he sat reading manuscripts all day with his long legs up on his desk. I saw him only occasionally but he gave me a marvellous smile every time I took him his coffee, and I made sure that he and nobody else got the top of the milk. Recently his marriage had cracked up and, hope surging, Miss Winn had a home perm and Miss Truslove took to plucking out her beard with tweezers every morning.

The only other man in the firm besides Mr. Rambridge and old Mr. Mildew was Mr. Curtis in Sales. Both Miss Winn and Miss Truslove disapproved of him and were pleased he was leaving at the end of the month. I was rather sad. He was lecherous but I liked him. He had a nice gipsy face and was a snappy dresser. But let's face it, he wasn't really in the same class as Mr. Rambridge; I never gave Mr. Curtis the top of the milk in his coffee.

It was a hot July and Miss Winn suddenly took a week's holiday. Mr. Rambridge never gave her many letters, and I hoped she might let me do his work while she was away.

But she was quite determined to get a temporary in.

'Don't let her touch the filing,' she told me. 'Just see she does his letters and keeps his desk tidy. I told the agency to send us a really sensible older woman.'

At eleven o'clock on Monday the 'sensible older woman' rolled up. She was about nineteen, and she wore a tight sweater and short skirt. She had long hair, small eyes and a pug dog in her arms.

'I'm Stephanie Bathurst,' she said. 'Have I come to the right place?'

'You're late,' snapped Miss Truslove.

'Sorry, I overslept.'

'Is that your dog?' asked Miss Truslove. 'We can't have dogs here.'

At that moment Mr. Rambridge wandered out of his office looking distraught.

'Could you ask Miss Winn to come in?' he said.

'She's on holiday,' said Miss Truslove.

'Oh God, I forgot.'

'This is your temporary,' added Miss Truslove with a

sniff. 'She's brought her dog, but I told her we can't have dogs here.'

'He's very good,' said Stephanie, smiling dazzlingly at Mr. Rambridge. 'He pines if he's left at home.'

'I don't see why he shouldn't stay,' said Mr. Rambridge. 'Will you come in when you're ready?'

It took Stephanie at least half an hour to get ready. She looked ravishing. Her small eyes had become huge and thickly lashed, and she had put marvellous hollows in her cheeks. Mr. Curtis in Sales, who'd just arrived, gave a long whistle.

'I say, I say, I say,' he said. 'Things *are* looking up.'

'Mr. Rambridge is waiting,' snapped Miss Truslove. 'Will you go in at once.'

I was left to look after the pug, who was called Pomeroy. He was nice, but a perfect nuisance, whining and yapping and casting covetous eyes at Miss Truslove's knitting.

Stephanie was in with Mr. Rambridge for hours. She came out yawning and I asked her if I could get her some sandwiches for lunch.

'No, thank you,' she said. 'I'm meeting someone, but I'll walk down the road with you if you like.'

She was just back from six weeks in the South of France, she told me.

'I'm so broke it isn't true, that's why I'm doing this awful temporary work. I can't type or do shorthand so I just smile all the time and show a lot of leg—it seems to work. Tell me—what gives with Rupert?'

'Rupert?'

'Rupert Rambridge—he's quite a dish! Married, I suppose?'

'Yes, very happily,' I lied.

'Pity! I really fancy him, and the other one—with the dark hair—he's not bad either.'

She got back from lunch at about half-past three and went into Mr. Rambridge for more dictation. She then disappeared to do her face.

'Goodness, it's five o'clock,' she said, looking at her watch as she came out of the loo. 'Long past my

71

going-home time. I can charge up to the agency for an extra half hour. Goodnight everyone,' and scooping up Pomeroy, she whisked out of the office before a spluttering Miss Truslove could say anything.

On Tuesday she arrived late, took two hours for lunch, spent ages in Mr. Rambridge's office taking dictation, and didn't type a word of it back. She was amazed he made no advances.

'He's still in love with his wife,' I told her crossly.

'They all say that,' sighed Stephanie, 'but it never makes any difference.'

On Wednesday afternoon Miss Truslove could bear it no longer and, as soon as Stephanie left the office, she waddled into Mr. Rambridge.

'Three hours for lunch,' I heard, 'and not a single letter typed.'

'Never mind,' said Mr. Rambridge mildly, 'I shall be away in Brighton most of tomorrow, so she can catch up then.'

But on the morning of the fourth day, Stephanie came in wearing a string vest over a body stocking and immediately disappeared to do her face.

'This is it,' Miss Truslove said and, marching into Mr. Mildew's office, she slammed the door behind her.

'She spends all day in the toilet,' I heard Miss Truslove shouting, 'and today she's wearing a dress that makes her look quite nude.'

'I beg your pardon?' said Mr. Mildew.

'Quite nude,' repeated Miss Truslove, warming to her subject. 'She's a bad influence on our little Jenny, it's only her first job, and they can pick up bad habits so easily at that age.'

'Can Jenny cope with Rupert's letters for the rest of the week?'

'I don't see why not, there are only two more days now.'

I couldn't believe my luck: I skipped round the office, hugging myself. At last—a chance to have a crack at Mr. Rambridge. Perhaps I could nip up to Oxford Street in the lunch hour and buy a new dress.

Stephanie's face was quite expressionless when she came out of Mr. Mildew's office.

'Goodbye,' she said to me. 'Thanks for looking after Pomeroy. Give my love to Rupert.'

Over my dead body, I thought. I was never so glad to see the back of anyone. Not that I disliked her, but it disturbed me to have her sitting hour after hour looking sexy in Mr. Rambridge's office. I forgave her all, however, when I found she had written *Dorothy Truslove has had more men than I've had hot dinners* in lipstick on the wall of the loo.

The weather grew hotter. Miss Truslove's ankles swelled and swelled, and I wilted as I typed Mr. Rambridge's letters over and over again until they were perfect. Mr. Curtis badgered me to have a drink with him, and his gipsy face darkened when, as always, I turned down his offer.

By the time Mr. Rambridge got back to the office after his day in Brighton everyone else had gone. Having driven an open car to the coast and back, his gleaming beauty was almost overwhelming, and I stammered as I explained the ousting of Stephanie.

'You shouldn't have waited,' he said, putting his beautiful black-ink signature at the bottom of each letter. 'These are splendid, you must have worked like a slave. How about a drink?'

He opened a cupboard and from it took a bottle of whisky and two glasses. Then he changed his mind. 'On second thoughts, let's go to a pub, it's too hot in here.'

I was too shy to ask if I could do my face so I only had time to comb my hair and empty a half bottle of scent over myself.

We sat in a lovely pub garden, surrounded by great wafts of Charlie. I was quite speechless with happiness, but Mr. Rambridge seemed perfectly happy to do most of the talking anyway. I just listened.

'I hope you're enjoying the job,' he said.

'Oh yes, it gets better and better as I get more experienced.'

I was not used to drinking, and under the sun of his interest and a second drink I expanded like a flower. I told him all about myself and exactly why Stephanie had been thrown out and what she had written on the wall about Miss Truslove. Mr. Rambridge loved that.

'She certainly was an odd girl,' he said. 'I used to be at school with some Pankhursts. I wonder if they were any relation?'

'Hardly,' I said. The drink was making me giggly. 'Her name was Bathurst.'

'Oh, Bathurst! I suppose she lives in extreme sordidity with hordes of girls, all draping their underwear over the bath.'

'No,' I said, 'she's staying in Kensington with her brother and his wife.'

Mr. Rambridge looked at his watch. 'Heavens, I must go. Look, I'll drop you off at the nearest tube.'

I reeled home in a haze of drunken euphoria. I was so glad Mum and Dad had gone out to the pictures.

All night I was kept awake by delicious fantasies of becoming the second Mrs. Rambridge: young, tender and understanding as I soothed away the hurt of his first marriage.

It was a beautiful morning next day, and I arrived at the office very early. I pinched twelve of Dad's prize roses, all velvety and dew-drenched, to put in Mr. Rambridge's office. Then I decided that was going it a bit, so I picked out three with greenfly on them for Mr. Mildew's desk. I spent hours in the loo doing my face, and when I came out Miss Truslove was answering the telephone.

'These summer colds are so treacherous,' she was saying, really laying it on. 'Now keep warm. I'll tell Mr. Mildew you won't be in till Monday.' To me she said crossly, 'You should never leave the switchboard unattended. That was Mr. Rambridge, he's caught a terrible chill and won't be in.'

I kicked myself for not being there to answer the telephone. Mr. Rambridge knew I was always on the switchboard at that time and must have rung up especially to talk to me. Perhaps he even wanted me to go round and look after him. Now I'd have to exist for three long days until I saw him again. I imagined him lying in his great empty bed as sick with disappointment as I was.

That morning, Mr. Mildew had one of his sporadic bursts of efficiency and discovered two manuscripts were missing. Eventually I tracked down *British West Hampstead, A Geographical Survey* among the telephone books, but we couldn't find *Stubby, The Story of A Royal Corgi* anywhere.

'Perhaps Mr. Rambridge has got it,' I said hopefully.

'Good idea,' said Mr. Mildew. 'Ring him up and ask him.'

I was so excited, I could hardly pick up the telephone. If Mr. Rambridge had the manuscript I could collect it. I could take him grapes and cook him a light lunch—me, who can't even boil an egg.

'Chinese laundry,' said a voice at the end of the telephone.

'Sorry, wrong number,' I said, and dialled again. I was completely thrown by a woman answering. 'Can I speak to Mr. Rambridge?' I said. 'Wrong number,' said the voice and slammed down the phone.

I dialled carefully this time. The telephone rang for ages.

'Hello,' snapped the female voice; a dog was yapping hysterically in the background. 'Shut up, Pomeroy,' said the voice. 'It's all right, darling, go back to bed. Who did you say? Mr. Rambridge? Sorry, you've got the wrong number,' and once again the phone was slammed down.

It took a few seconds to sink in—lovely, lovely Mr. Rambridge and horrible Stephanie, or lovely, lovely Stephanie and horrible Mr. Rambridge. But how had they got together? Then I remembered how last night at the pub I'd told him her surname, and that she was staying with her brother. Despite his lazy manner, he must have moved like lightning. I couldn't cry out loud, but I felt the tears pouring down my cheeks.

At that moment, Mr. Curtis came in and said, 'Hello gorgeous,' then with real concern, 'Hey, what's the matter?'

I cried all over my desk, but bit by bit I managed to tell him the whole story.

He shrugged his shoulders. 'I could see it coming a mile off,' he said. 'There's a bird not famed for the strength of her knicker elastic I said to myself. She was sitting on his desk on Tuesday when I went in—skirt hitched up showing half a mile of thigh.'

'But Mr. Rambridge isn't like that,' I sobbed.

'You've got him wrong, duckie. He's a really smooth operator.'

'I don't believe it, he was miserable when his wife left him.'

'And do you know why she left him? Because he was chasing every available skirt in London. She never knew where he was. Why do you think he always looks so clapped out in the mornings?'

'He never made a pass at anyone in the office.'

'He doesn't believe in shitting on his own doorstep. Anyway, can you imagine him having a go at Truslove or Winn?'

'Stephanie is terribly pretty,' I said.

'Sure, she's well packaged. You're much prettier —you just need to take your skirts up a few inches, get your hair cut properly, and stop letting old Mother Truslove dictate what you wear.'

I digested that for a minute. 'D'you think Mr. Rambridge would fancy me then?'

'Course he would, if you're silly enough to want him.'

I stood up when Mr. Curtis said that and looked at him. He was staring out of the window. I took my hand mirror out of my desk and had a quick look at my face: bloodshot piggy eyes and all my mascara running.

'You're a right mess,' said Mr. Curtis, and took me in his arms and kissed me. That's the funny thing about men. You really don't know whether you fancy them until they touch you.

As suddenly as he had grabbed me, he let go. 'Sorry, I got carried away,' he said, taking a pair of dark glasses out of his pocket. 'Put these on and I'll buy you lunch.'

'I've got to get Miss Truslove some sandwiches.'

'To hell with Miss Truslove, she can live on her hump.'

'Thank you for being so kind,' I said.

'Purely ulterior motives,' he said.

That weekend I pottered down to the shops to get my hair cut and buy a new dress. I avoided thinking about the office or Mr. Rambridge.

When I arrived on Monday, Miss Winn was having hysterics over the state of her in-tray. The friend she had expected to join her on holiday had not turned up and she was pouring out her heart to Miss Truslove, who had lost her tweezers and was surreptitiously trying to pluck her beard out with a bulldog clip.

'You've cut your hair,' Miss Truslove said to me. 'It's much neater. New dress, too, a bit short for the office. Taking a leaf out of that temporary's book,' and she started to tell Miss Winn about Stephanie.

Mr. Rambridge came in at about ten. He looked exhausted. I was sitting by the switchboard.

'How's your cold?' I asked.

'Much better, thanks awfully. I stayed in bed all weekend, and managed to sweat it out.'

I bet you did, I thought sourly. He was looking at me with interest.

'I like your hair,' he said, 'and the dress. I did enjoy our drink, we must do it again soon.'

As I smiled at him very sweetly, I noticed that his hair was thinning, and where once I thought his great hairy body had seemed too big for his clothes I realised now that he just wore his clothes too tight.

While I was making coffee, I heard Mr. Curtis come

in. I poured the top of the milk into a cup and, picking it up, started for the door.

'I'll take Mr. Rambridge's,' Miss Winn said, jumping up.

'This is for Mr. Curtis,' I said shortly.

'But it's got cream in. You know Mr. Rambridge always likes the cream.'

'Funny, so does Mr. Curtis,' I said.

Sister To The Bride

Sally, as usual, was late for supper. The pork chops shrivelled in the oven. My father, who has given up his pre-dinner drink since the Budget, rattled the evening paper in irritation.

'Sally is the limit,' said my mother. 'Shall we start?'

I looked out of the window and saw a long blue car draw up at the gate. 'She's here,' I said, 'with Charles.'

I watched my sister jump out of the car and run up the path, leaving Charles to shut the car door and the gate behind her. Sally never shuts doors; she knows someone will do it for her. Always, always laughing, she is as beautiful as the spring and everywhere as welcome.

'Hello everyone,' she shouted.

'You're late,' said my father mildly.

'Is Charles staying for supper?' asked my mother, wondering how to divide four chops between five people.

'Darlings,' cried Sally, hugging first one and then the

other, 'I've got heavenly news for you. Charles and I are engaged.'

There was a stunned silence—then everyone seemed to be laughing and kissing each other. Charles Tankard is charming-looking, and has the added advantage that he is absolutely loaded. Sally is only eighteen, and I know my parents wouldn't have approved of her getting married so young if they hadn't been sure Charles would support her in a style to which she was quite unaccustomed. From now on, it would be yachts and oil-fired central heating all the way.

Charles came into the room looking sheepish but very pleased with himself. 'I meant to ask your permission first, sir,' he said, shaking hands with my father, 'but Sal seems to have jumped the gun.'

'And Helen will be a bridesmaid, won't you, darling?' said Sally, beaming at me. They all turned and smiled at me, as though it were ample compensation for not being the one to get married.

'Of course I can't,' I said roughly. 'It's ridiculous. I'd be a laughing stock being a bridesmaid at my age.'

I am twenty-seven, nearly eight years older than Sally. One of my recurrent nightmares was that she would get married before me. Now, in one horrifying stride, I seemed to have turned into an old maid—Sally's spinster sister.

Sally's face had fallen when I refused, and later in the evening my mother took me aside. 'Daddy and I know what a terrible knock you took over Simon so we haven't fussed you. But you can't mope around for ever, or you'll miss the boat. It's nearly a year now.'

Was it only a year? It seemed like an eternity. For six years Simon and I had gone out together and, tortured with misgivings, I had battled to make him love me. Everyone said be patient, he would marry me in the end. Instead, he came back from a skiing holiday and said he had met someone else. I behaved very well at the time—no hysterics, no fuss, just a loss of brightness, and a feeling of total emptiness. Hour after hour,

I sat in my bedroom, gazing out of the window at passing cars—thousands of men and women driving along, all paired off, except me.

Of course, in the end, I gave in and agreed to be a bridesmaid. Sally was enchanted. 'I'm so pleased,' she said, 'and there'll be lots of talent for you at the wedding.'

Talent? I knew the Tankard set—arrogant, handsome, self-assured, with their fast cars and their helicopters. They were not likely to be interested in me.

The three months before the wedding were a nightmare. I must have been hell to live with. I realise now I was consumed with jealousy. My mother never stopped worrying about everything being good enough for the Tankards; the fuss that went into choosing the right flowers, and cake, even the right guests. And every night when I got home tired from the office, the hall was littered with packing straw; and I would be called in to rave over all the latest presents. Charles' father, obviously completely besotted with Sally, gave them a fantastically mod-con house as a wedding present. Charles gave Sally an emerald and diamond necklace.

There was another row about the bridesmaids' dresses. I am not pretty like Sally. I'm tall—five feet nine inches—and big with it. When I'm happy, I light up and give the illusion of being beautiful. But when I'm miserable, I look like a pudding.

The other bridesmaid was Charles' sister Bridget, who is tiny, with bold black eyes and olive skin: she looks sensational in brilliant colours. Her only fault is her awful legs, which she was determined to cover up. As a result, she got into cahoots with Sally—very much under the Tankard sway at the time—and together they chose a full-length dress in cyclamen with masses of frills. Nobody took any notice when I stormed that I was far too large for full-length frills and my face clashed with cyclamen.

The wedding day dawned—trust Sally to bring the sun out—and at three o'clock, we stood in the church porch waiting for her to arrive, Bridget looking devastating, I like a badly wrapped Christmas cracker. A few guests who were late scuttled in clutching their hats.

Suddenly here was Sally. A ripple of pleasure ran through the onlookers. The white blossom floated down from the cherry trees in the church yard, but none floated more gracefully or merrily than she. She was radiant, and not at all scared. My father, clutching her arm, looked terrified.

Then came "The Wedding March"—and off we went: Sally drifting in front like a goddess, Bridget and I following like Dignity and Impudence. I felt exposed to every staring eye, acutely conscious of my wide shoulders in the cyclamen frills. Everyone must be looking at me and recognising me as Sally's spinster sister.

'Dearly Beloved . . .' intoned the vicar.

Not until the waves of misery had subsided a little did I notice the man in the pew just beside us. Perhaps he was in his early thirties, perhaps more—a tall, rangy thoroughbred of a man, with powerful shoulders, right out of my class.

But it was not his outstanding looks that held my attention, it was his stillness; there was a strange, guarded look about him, as though he didn't belong to the people around him. His hands clenched the pew so hard his knuckles showed white, and a muscle was going like a sledge-hammer in his cheek.

He must have felt me watching him, because he suddenly turned my way. Beneath the suntan, there was a terrible greyness about his face. Involuntarily I smiled at him, as one would reassure a frightened child. Instantly his face became a mask, and he looked straight through me.

'Oh dear,' I thought, 'how awful! He's so good-looking, he must think I'm trying to get off with him.' And as I jerked my eyes away, I felt a great blush seeping over my face, neck and shoulders.

Half an hour later, we all lined up to welcome the guests. It was like working in a factory—as each guest came by, I smiled, shook hands and made some fatuous welcoming comment; then on to the next one, smile, shake, comment. I stood between Bridget and Mrs. Tankard, who gushed like an oil well and always kept people talking too long.

Suddenly I heard Bridget draw in her breath. 'Look,' she whispered to me. 'There's lovely David Carlisle. I used to have a crush on him.'

It was the man I had noticed in church. His face was quite expressionless as he started to make his way down the line.

'David,' cried Mrs. Tankard, 'I'm so glad you made it.'

'Hello, Vera,' he said, still unsmiling, as he leaned forward to kiss her cheek.

'I was so upset to hear about everything,' she said. 'I kept meaning to write. But one doesn't. How are the poor little ones?'

'They're fine.' It really was unfair—even his voice was sexy.

'And how are you—are you managing all right?'

'I'm fine, too.' He'd looked anything but "fine" in church.

'You're back in England for a bit?'

'A month or so, anyway.' The queue was buckling behind him.

'For God's sake stop holding up the traffic, Vera,' snapped Mr. Tankard.

And then he was in front of me, looking me up and down—and he was certainly a man who knew how to look. Furious, I found myself blushing again. 'We saw each other in church,' he said, holding out his hand.

'Did you see me too?' chipped in Bridget, seizing his hand and holding up her face to be kissed. 'Have I changed since you used to buy me all that ice-cream?'

'You're obviously eating less ice-cream,' he said.

'Where are you staying?'

'At the Grand.'

'Will you come and see us tomorrow? We shall be feeling so flat.'

The queue buckled again. 'We seem to be holding up the traffic,' he said. 'See you later.'

'Isn't he glorious!' said Bridget, gazing after him. 'Who is he?'

'David Carlisle—he's an architect. He married a stunning model about six years ago—it was all over the papers. Hello, Uncle Dennis, how are you? Then he landed this plum job in Africa—the next thing we heard, she'd run off with his partner out there, taking the children with her.'

'How dreadful. Will she come back?'

'Not a hope, thank goodness!'

At last people stopped arriving, and we were free to circulate. I spent an agonising half-hour chatting up relations. Sally is a rotten letter writer and most of them wanted to know if their toasters and table-mats had arrived. Several people who hadn't seen me for ages asked where Simon was—it was very harrowing.

I was on my way to talk to my favourite great-aunt when a voice said, 'You haven't got a drink.' David Carlisle towered over me. He summoned a passing waiter and exchanged our empty glasses for full ones. Overwhelmed by shyness, I watched the bubbles rising in my glass.

'If anyone else tells me they haven't seen me since I was so high, I'll kick their teeth in,' he said.

'Are you related to Charles?' I asked.

'Vera's my godmother, so the place is stiff with my parents' friends. And you're Sally's sister?'

'Yes,' I said, shrinking from the inevitable comparison.

'It seems only yesterday,' he said, 'that we were taking Charles out from Radley. I was shattered when I got his wedding invitation. They both look so young.'

'Too young?' I asked.

He shrugged his shoulders. 'Who can tell? I was much older when I got married.'

'And yours came unstuck,' I said without thinking.

'How do you know?' he asked brusquely. 'Who the

83

hell told you?' That muscle in his cheek was going again.

'Bridget did,' I stammered. 'But I asked her. I'm sorry.'

He was still glaring at me when a waitress came up with a plate of smoked salmon sandwiches. He looked down at it, blinked, and then shook his head. He reached for his cigarette case.

'I'm terribly sorry . . .' I began.

'It's I who should be sorry,' he said. 'I'm afraid my nerves are a bit raw at the moment. Let's get some more champagne.'

'It must be terrible,' I said slowly, thinking what it would be like if Simon had actually married me and then swanned off. 'So terrible . . . I mean, it's rare enough to find someone you really click with, enough to get married to. And then all the ghastly palaver of getting married—we've been living with it for months now—and then it all goes wrong. Coming home every evening to an empty house . . . You must despair of ever finding the right person again—it must be like trying to climb Everest in ballet shoes. I'm so sorry about it.' My voice trailed off in a thin line of drivel. I stared at my hands in embarrassment.

'You're not a bit like Sally, are you?' he said gently.

Across the room stood Sally, surrounded by admiring guests. 'She's devastating, isn't she?' I said.

He looked at her thoughtfully. 'A bit chromium perhaps. People always crowd round the picture with the red "sold" sticker on. You're far prettier. You're just badly framed.'

'What do you mean?' I said furiously, acutely conscious of my hot face clashing with the cyclamen frills.

'I'm sorry.' He smiled for the first time. 'We really must stop apologising to each other. But that dress is atrocious—I'm sure Bridget chose it, and I bet you got that appalling, matching hairstyle at Aunt Vera's hairdresser.'

'How do you know?' I asked, curious in spite of myself.

'I know the Tankard family extremely well—they're all bullies.'

He must be dying to go off and talk to all the pretty girls, I thought, and I was half-relieved when I saw my great-aunt descending on us—at least it would give him a chance to escape.

Clothes are not my great-aunt's strong point and, although she had made heroic attempts to come into line for the wedding, her wispy hair was already escaping from beneath her smart hat, and her stockings were concertina-ing round her ankles. I purposely didn't introduce David Carlisle but he showed no sign of escaping.

After we had swapped family gossip for about five minutes, she said, 'Sally looks exquisite, but I thought as she went up the aisle, this is wrong: it should be Helen and Simon. Whatever went wrong, my dear? I was so distressed when your mother wrote that it was all off.'

'He met someone else when he was skiing,' I said, horribly aware of David Carlisle taking it all in.

'Well, silly him, that's all I can say. Mind you, I never trust men with close-set eyes, don't you agree?' she said, turning to David.

'Absolutely,' he said gravely.

'You're nice and brown,' she went on to say.

'I'm just back from Kenya.'

'Kenya,' breathed my great-aunt, who keeps eight cats. 'All those wonderful animals!'

He was in full spate about the game reserves, when she suddenly looked down at her feet: 'Good gracious, I've forgotten to put on my party shoes! Will you excuse me?' And she strode off towards the door.

'What a marvellous old girl,' he said, laughing. Then he turned to me. 'You were crazy about this Simon fellow, weren't you?'

'He hung the moon for me for six years,' I said lightly.

'That's why you were so eloquent a few minutes ago

on the subject of being left. Have you found anyone else?'

I shook my head. 'People keep trying to fix me up —but I'm afraid it doesn't work.'

'Don't I know it. As soon as my wife walked out, all her friends were queueing up to console me.'

I didn't say it was different in his case—if you looked as marvellous as he did, you had to fight people off.

'It's very easy,' he went on, 'to drift into the state where there's a different head on the pillow each morning. And talking of that, here comes my Aunt Vera with another candidate.'

Mrs. Tankard was bearing down on us with a beautiful girl with half Chelsea Flower Show on her head. 'David, darling, you must meet Amy.' She turned to me. 'Helen, I think you had better join the others. Charles and Sally are going to cut the cake.'

It could hardly have been more pointed. Depression descended on me like a cloud. Bridget came up and took my arm. 'Come and meet the darling man we've lined up for you this evening. I know he's your type.'

'My type'—God help me—was called Tubby Langley, had no chin, crinkly ginger hair, and the beginning of a paunch. He was so wet he ought to have had a damp course installed. Was this all I was fit for? Fortunately we only had time to exchange pleasantries.

When the toasting and the clapping were over, there was a silence; then the room became a vast, twittering aviary again. Children—beginning to get over-excited —were charging through people's legs, playing tag. The grannies had returned to the edge of the room to drink coffee and rest their swelling ankles. Out of the corner of my eye, I was amazed to see David Carlisle shake off the flower-hatted beauty and come prowling like a great panther across the room. Heavens, he was coming in my direction.

'Let's get out of the crush,' he said. 'I've cornered a bottle of champagne.' In a daze I followed him to the other end of the room.

'God, what rubbish people talk at weddings,' he said.

'Well, why did you come if you don't like parties?' I said. I felt that as it was my parents' wedding and he had already drunk vast quantities of their champagne, I ought to be vaguely annoyed.

'The only parties I like are for two people.' He looked straight into my eyes. 'Will you have dinner with me tonight?'

'I can't,' I said. 'There's the bridesmaids' party.'

'Of course. I should have thought.' His face was quite expressionless again. I was about to tell him that I would a million times rather have dinner with him, when Mrs. Tankard came up.

'Helen,' she said rather tartly, 'Sally's gone to change. Oughtn't you to go and help her?'

Sally, of course, was in chaos. She'd just stepped out of her wedding dress, and a mass of petticoats lay all over the floor. I tidied up a bit, and then escaped to the bathroom to repair my face. David Carlisle was right. I looked awful and my hair was terrible.

There was a knock on the door. It was Charles in a smart new suit, come to collect Sally's smart new suitcases—and in a few minutes they were gone, waving through a shower of confetti and good wishes.

Suddenly I felt terribly tired. Champagne never does anything else but depress me utterly. Although the bar was closed, David Carlisle seemed to have cornered yet another bottle and was making good progress down it. I have never seen a man so little affected by drink. 'I've only got one glass, you'll have to share it,' he said.

We just looked at each other, not saying much. Then he took a bit of confetti out of my hair. You know how it is—some people maul you about for years and nothing happens and then one man touches your hair and a thousand volts go through you.

'I know I shouldn't press you,' he said, 'but don't you think it would be better for both of us if you chucked that bridesmaids' party?'

His physical presence was quite overwhelming. I was

just about to haggle and say I'd slope off from the party early, when Tubby came dripping up.

'There you are, Helen of Troy,' he said. 'I've been looking for you everywhere. Your carriage awaits you.' I could have knifed him.

'Goodbye,' I said to David Carlisle. I hoped he'd ask me out tomorrow, but he didn't. The terrible greyness had returned to his face.

We went on to someone's flat and drank huge gins and tonics with no ice. They were all Tankards—except me—and I knew they wanted to let their hair down about the wedding and probably bitch about my family, but felt inhibited by my presence. Bridget was getting off with the best man. The other couple had just returned from their honeymoon. Tubby droned on. I sat on the sofa beside him and fretted. It was ten o'clock before we moved on.

You should go to a night-club only with someone who attracts you. The Black Gypsy was very dark inside, but all around I could distinguish couples wrapped around each other like wet towels. To crown it, we had to eat our way through a huge dinner—though in the gloom, one couldn't tell if it were steak or horse meat. Tubby ate all mine.

Later we danced decorously together, making polite conversation. Perhaps I ought to settle for this, I thought sadly, a string of fat children, and Tubby coming home from the City every night. Then I thought of David Carlisle coming home to me every night and my knees turned to water.

If only I could have had the chance to take that haunted look out of his eyes and make him happy and not miserably lonely anymore.

We went back to the table and Tubby asked Bridget to dance.

The best man lounged beside me, arrogant and bored. 'You don't want to dance, do you?' he said, watching Bridget, who winked at him over Tubby's shoulder. It's embarrassing sitting in the dark next to a man who is totally indifferent to you.

'That was an awfully good speech,' I said timidly.

'I was president of the Debating Society at school,' he said, as though that settled it.

Suddenly I could bear it no longer. I had to telephone David and see if he was all right. The man on the door looked at me sourly when I asked him where the telephone was, and got progressively more sour when I made him dig out the local directory and change a pound.

David needs me, I kept telling myself, as I dialled the number with trembling fingers.

'Grand Hotel,' said a voice.

'Can I speak to Mr. Carlisle please?'

There was a long pause.

Oh, hell, I thought, he's probably passed out.

'We're getting no answer from his room, madam.'

Even worse, he'd probably picked someone up, and would be furious at being interrupted at this late hour.

There was another long pause.

'I've just rung reception,' the voice said, 'and I'm afraid Mr. Carlisle's checked out.'

The room reeled—I nearly blacked out. 'Checked out, but he can't have done. He was booked to stay with you till Monday.'

'I'm sorry, madam, he paid his bill and left about three hours ago.'

Slowly, I put down the receiver. And it hit me like a thunderbolt. Who was I fooling with this junk about wanting to restore his confidence because he was in a terrible state? He was the most ravishing man I'd ever met, and I'd fallen hook, line and sinker for him—and was trying to pass it off as pity.

I escaped into the loo and repainted my stiff lips with shaking hands; then I hurried back to the noise and the dim lights. When Tubby and I danced, I closed my eyes in agony and allowed him to press his fat cheek against mine. At last the band played the National Anthem.

'Drinks at my flat?' said Tubby.

'Yes, please,' shrieked Bridget.

They were all anxious to prolong the evening. 'I'm sorry,' I said, 'I'm absolutely whacked.'

They looked at me in concern. 'You do look a bit peaky. I'll drive you home,' said Tubby. But in the end I persuaded him to put me in a taxi. 'We must have lunch next week,' he said.

It was only in the safety of the taxi, with a four-mile ride in front of me, that I let myself go. I cried and cried until my hair came down—not in lovely shining tresses, but in an ugly lacquered mass; so I cried even more. At last the town gave way to the country, and I saw the beech trees at the top of the road. I made the taxi stop fifty yards from our house; I was anxious to creep in without a post mortem.

I walked down our road. Suddenly in the dark under the trees, I saw a cigarette glow. My heart gave an insane leap.

'Helen,' said a voice. David Carlisle walked towards me—his face was ghostly pale in the moonlight. With an effort I stopped myself running straight into his arms.

'How did you find your way here?' I gasped.

'Your address was on the wedding invitation.'

'But you must have been here hours.'

'I've waited two years for something like you to happen. I can wait two hours.' He shouldn't make remarks like that unless he were serious.

'There was a cable from Africa when I got back to the hotel,' he went on.

That's that, I thought dully, his wife wants him back.

'The firm's run into a spot of trouble, I've got to fly out tomorrow and sort it out.' He put his hand under my chin and gently turned my face towards him.

'Darling,' he said, 'you've been crying. I shouldn't have let you go to that party. This wedding's obviously been a terrible strain for you. You looked so crucified in church. And you've got such sad, sad eyes,' he went

90

on, 'I want to take all the pain out of them. I want to make you happy and not haunted anymore.'

'But that's what . . .' I began, and then thought better of it. Let him think he was the one doing the rehabilitating.

'I've been doing my nut ever since you went off with Tubby,' he said, 'wondering if you were all right.'

And all the time, I'd been fretting over him. 'Please hold me,' I whispered.

He took me in his arms, and one thing I couldn't have invented was the way he trembled as he kissed me.

'How long will you be gone?' I asked.

'Four weeks, perhaps a couple of months, no more. And when I come back I'll woo you properly with theatres and roses and things. Will you write to me?'

'Yes, of course, if you like.'

'I do like, and while I'm out there I thought I'd start divorce proceedings.'

I didn't say anything. I took his hand and held it against my cheek. I was too busy fighting back the tears that he should have found me when it had seemed impossible.

Christmas Stocking

Christmas got off to the worst possible start this year, with Audrey the telephonist getting tight at our office party and telling me a few home truths.

'It's no good you making eyes at Mr. Blantyre any

more,' she said, 'he's just told me he likes you, but he doesn't fancy you. He's a legs man, you see.'

I did see—only too well. With legs like mine, how could I expect Mr. Blantyre or anyone else to fall in love with me? My face is all right and my figure's not bad, but my legs are terrible. As my brother Matthew said, 'Old Caroline doesn't have ankles—just calves all the way down.'

Christmas, too, with all its togetherness and compulsory good-will is the worst possible time to be unhappy in love. I'd hate to be on my own, but even in the bosom of one's family, it's a pretty lethal brand of loneliness if there's no special man to love you.

The bosom of my family this year consisted of my mother and father, my sister who's still at school, and my brother, who had written at the last moment to say he'd be arriving the night before Christmas Eve and would be bringing two friends (sex unspecified). Finally, to round off the party there was my Aunt Gertrude, a big bossy schoolmistress, whose mind is as narrow as her beam is broad. She treats us like the Upper Fourth.

We live in a Victorian house on the edge of the Yorkshire moors, and I got home from the office party to find it completely transformed. Great banks of holly and spruce softened the tall, angular rooms, and in the drawing-room glittered a huge Christmas tree. Mistletoe hung in a cluster from the hall light, but alas I couldn't imagine anyone wanting to kiss me under it.

My father and sister had already left to meet my brother's train from London, and I was just combing my hair and pulling a pair of long black boots over my fat legs, when I heard Conrad, our border terrier, barking and a car drive up. My mother rushed out to meet it.

'Matthew, darling—you've grown a moustache,' she cried, hugging my brother and leaving flour marks all over his smart, dark blue coat. My brother was rather sheepishly helping a girl out of the car. With her tight curls, heavily blacked eyes, red shiny mouth, and sideboards of pink rouge, she looked like a blonde golliwog. She was wearing a squashy, blonde fur coat.

'This is Anthea,' he said.

I was so busy gaping at this apparition and her vast quantities of luggage, that at first I didn't notice the other man with them. His black hair was tousled, and there was a glazed expression on his pale green face. He swayed slightly.

'Jamie's not very well,' said my brother. 'He's just getting over a vicious bout of red 'flu, and I'm afraid he got up too soon.'

'Poor lamb,' said my mother, all sympathy. 'He must go straight to bed. There's a nice fire in his bedroom.' And putting her arm around the young man she steered him gently upstairs.

'Actually,' said my brother as soon as my mother was out of earshot, 'Jamie got smashed out of his mind at the office party; Anthea and I had great difficulty getting him on to the train. I brought him as a Christmas present for you, Caroline. He's nice when he's sober.'

'He looks just like Bob Geldorf,' said my sister ecstatically.

Later that evening when I took his supper up, I found my "Christmas present" snoring slightly and fast asleep with the light on. I stood looking at him for a few minutes before I put some more coal on the fire and turned off the light.

The cold weather really set in the next morning, and the house had pulled the sky down over its ears as an icy wind came hurtling off the moors. Neither Anthea, nor my brother, nor Jamie surfaced for breakfast. I sat in the gloom, watching Aunt Gertrude work her way through a plate of porridge, sausage and bacon, five pieces of toast and the morning paper. Perhaps I'll look like that in thirty years, I thought with a shiver.

My sister was cracking nuts with her teeth. 'I wish someone would give me Adam and the Ants and a big hotel bedroom for Christmas,' she said.

Jamie wandered down about eleven, armed with boxes of goodies for my mother. He looked much better. 'I'm sorry I arrived in such a state last night,' he said. 'I must have caught one of those forty-eight hour bugs. How marvellous your house looks.'

A real soft-soaper, I thought, and by lunch-time he had the entire household, except me, eating out of his hand. He'd read all the same books as my father, he discussed religion with Aunt Gertrude and regaled my sister with scurrilous stories about pop stars. My mother was enchanted because he offered to peel the potatoes for lunch.

And at me, he just looked. He wasn't nearly as handsome as Mr. Blantyre. He wasn't anything near six feet, and his broad shoulders made him look even shorter, and his mouth was too wide and rubbery, and his black hair too unruly. (Mr. Blantyre had sculptured blond waves.)

But it was the way he looked at me with those sleepy, dangerous eyes. I kept dropping things, and I iced far more of the table than the cake.

My brother and Anthea, looking somewhat battered, put in an appearance just before lunch and said they were off to Leeds for the day. 'She's got love bites all over her neck,' hissed my sister.

Before they left, my brother sidled up to me. 'I say, Caroline, I'm awfully broke. I've obviously got to get a present for Anthea, but can I share your presents to the rest of the family?'

After lunch, I announced I was going into Skipton to do some late shopping.

'I'll come with you,' said Jamie.

'Take the car,' my father told him. He never lends his precious car to me.

I changed out of my old jeans into a new pair of cords. I had little doubt that once he saw my legs, Jamie would stop leching after me, but I wanted to foster the illusion a little longer.

The afternoon was fading as we drove off. Patches

of rusty bracken were the only colour in the grey wintery landscape.

His hands, I noticed, still bore traces of last summer's suntan. 'It's nice to be here,' he said. 'My parents live abroad, and this is the first proper Christmas I've had in years.'

'You should have come in an Uncle Tony year,' I said.

'Uncle Tony?'

'Our black sheep uncle. Aunt Gertrude won't stay in the same house as him, so they have to come on alternate years. He drinks a bit, and we usually have to put him to bed, and give him his fare back to London, but it's always a riot the years he's here.'

'Sorry,' said Jamie. 'I haven't got used to these winding roads yet.' It was the third time he'd swung fast round a corner throwing me against him—I wondered if he were doing it on purpose.

Skipton was packed. Armed with Christmas trees and holly, last-minute shoppers were fighting their way ten-deep along the pavement. Loud-speakers belched out carols and Christmas cheer. Bad-will was rampant.

Jamie said he hadn't bought any cards yet and, as the only ones we could find were covered in loopy writing and spangles, he bought birthday cards instead. Then he insisted on looking in every bookshop to find the right book for my father, and spraying every scent in every chemist shop on to my wrist and sniffing it before he found the right one for my mother. I had great difficulty stopping him buying a pair of false eye-lashes for Aunt Gertrude.

Reeking like a tart, I braved the market with him for chestnuts and cooking apples. It was almost impossible to battle through the crowd. Jamie put his arms round me to protect me, and every time I tried to move away the crowd jostled us together again. His nearness disturbed me.

We de-birthdayed his cards in a café.

'Make your writing like mine, and write "Happy Christmas, love from Jamie" on them; I'll do the

95

addresses,' he said. I didn't really see the point of sending them since they wouldn't arrive until well after the festivities, but Jamie was insistent. I tried terribly hard not to look to see how many he was sending to girls.

'I'll join you in a minute,' he said as we left, giving me the keys of the car.

I was sitting wondering why I hadn't thought of Mr. Blantyre for at least an hour, when Jamie dropped a parcel on to my lap.

'Not for Christmas, just a present,' he said.

They were sheepskin gloves. 'Oh how lovely!'

'I couldn't bear to see you with purple paws,' he said.

Christmas Eve panic was at its height when we got home. Everyone wanted to wrap up presents, and we'd run out of paper. My sister was pulling it out of the bottoms of drawers. 'Caroline,' she said, sidling up to me.

'I know, you're terribly broke and you want to share all my Christmas presents.'

It was absurd to get so excited over a pair of furry gloves. Twenty-four hours ago, I had been devastated by Mr. Blantyre—now I could hardly remember what he looked like. Jamie has a kind heart and he hasn't even seen my legs yet, I kept telling myself as I soaked in the bath before dinner. But I still couldn't face shattering his illusion, so I cheated once more, putting on a black jersey and hiding my legs under a black and red skirt and boots.

The wine flowed at dinner, and even Aunt Gertrude seemed to be mellowing.

Afterwards we all sat down to watch the circus, but in the middle of the performing dogs, the television suddenly flickered, gave a groan, and went dead. No amount of tinkering and fiddling could bring it to life again. We were faced with the appalling prospect of entertaining ourselves.

'Let's play charades,' said Jamie. Normally we would have groaned, but he seemed to have infected us all with his high spirits. Even my father joined in, prancing around in my mother's hats. The *pièce de résistance* was Jamie in a long dress and mufflers doing an hilarious impersonation of Aunt Gertrude coaching the netball team, with my sister and Anthea leaping about in gym tunics.

I thought Aunt Gertrude was going to be furious at the roars of laughter which greeted it, but she was actually smiling—talk about the taming of the shrew.

'I wouldn't let him loose among my girls,' I heard her telling my mother, 'but I must confess I like that young man.'

Oh dear, I thought, I must confess I'm beginning to like him too.

My father looked at his watch. 'I doubt if any of you are in a state of grace,' he said, 'but if we're going to Midnight Mass we'd better get going.'

My mother, father, sister and Aunt Gertrude went up to get ready, and eventually my brother and Anthea decided to go too.

'Get it over with now, you won't feel a bit like church in the morning,' said my brother, patting her on the bottom.

'Let's stay behind,' said Jamie to me.

We sat on the sofa after they'd all gone, watching the glowing embers until the silence became unbearable. I got up to put a log on the fire.

'Would you like some coffee?'

He shook his head, looking me up and down with those sleepy, dangerous eyes until my stomach disappeared. 'No,' he said, getting up and taking me in his arms, 'only you.'

Oh God, the terrible beauty of that kiss.

'Caro, Caro, Caro,' he said dreamily.

Never before had I heard my name spoken like that, and never before had the ceiling reeled and the furniture gone round and round. He pulled me down on to the sofa.

'I'm so happy here,' he said, into my hair. 'I like all

97

your family so much. And even old Anthea seems less awful now.'

'Don't you find her attractive?' I said.

'You must be joking—all that make-up and those terrible legs.'

His words took a good second to register. Her legs were super—long and thin. If he thinks *her* legs are awful, I thought in horror, he must be even more of a legs man than Mr. Blantyre.

I pulled away from him and, muttering a few broken sentences about how impossible the whole thing was, I fled upstairs to my bedroom and locked the door. There was nothing else to do but to throw myself down on the bed and cry my eyes out.

A few minutes later, Jamie rattled the door and spoke to me, but I refused to answer, and in the end he went away. When the family came back from church, I pretended to be asleep. All night I watched the snow growing like white icing on the window ledge, and heard the grandfather clock tolling hours downstairs in the hall. When I got up next morning with gritty eyes and a heavy heart, the stark Yorkshire countryside had been transformed into a fairyland, with every tree carrying armfuls of thick white blossom, and the little houses in the village gleaming like palaces.

I found it impossible to be jolly at breakfast. Jamie appeared quite cheerful, but his eyes seemed tired. We avoided looking at each other. Everyone rhapsodised over their presents, however awful they were. Aunt Gertrude gave me a set of mauve plastic egg-cups —'for your bottom drawer,' she added.

'Just what I wanted,' she cried, opening Jamie's bottle of scent, but she wasn't so pleased when my brother gave her a breathalyser kit.

At the bottom of my pile of presents I found a small parcel, with a card saying: *'Caroline. All my love, Jamie'* and he'd underlined the 'all'. It was a pair of fishnet tights. Tears stung my eyes, as I thought of the irony of my legs in black fishnet.

Aunt Gertrude, my sister who has a crush on the

vicar, Jamie and I sat in a red-nosed, blue-knuckled row at Morning Service, and sang at the tops of our voices to keep warm. Without any hope of success I prayed to God to get me over Jamie, or to give me legs like Joanna Lumley.

When the collection plate came round Aunt Gertrude, with much rustling ostentation, put in a pound note; then my sister, with equal rustling ostentation, took out a fiver and laid it carefully on top.

Little beast, I thought, no wonder she said she was broke and wanted to share my Christmas presents. Aunt Gertrude looked furious, and I caught Jamie's eye and tried not to giggle. He moved closer to me, and when my sister and Aunt Gertrude were chatting up the vicar after the service, we walked on ahead down the street, with the church bells echoing.

'I'm sorry about last night,' he said, bending down and picking up a handful of snow. 'Are you in love with someone else, Caroline?'

I shook my head.

'But you keep running away. Every time I think I'm making progress, in the market or last night, you're suddenly off like a frightened animal.'

I scuffed at the snow with my long black boots.

'You're even harder to get through to than Aunt Gertrude,' he went on.

'You can't win all the time,' I said.

'I'm sorry,' he said, 'I won't pester you any more,' and he hurled the snowball miles down into the valley. We walked the rest of the way home in silence. Twice I slipped and twice he steadied me, but he removed his hand immediately.

After lunch my brother and father gingerly tried out their new cigars, Aunt Gertrude wrote her thank you letters, and my sister solemnly worked her way through an entire box of liqueur chocolates, draining out the liqueur, and giving the chocolate shells to Conrad the dog. Anthea and Jamie did all the Christmas quizzes from the newspapers, and I was reading the same page of my book over and over again, when suddenly the television came miraculously to life in time for the Queen's speech. Conrad was sick.

I escaped into the kitchen and started on the Christmas dinner. I tried not to cry as I peeled the chestnuts for the stuffing.

'Are you all right, darling?' said my mother, coming in later. 'I've never known you to do so much housework. You look awfully tired.'

'It's only because she's being so nasty to Jamie,' said my sister spitting a date stone into the coal bucket.

'We can manage perfectly well now,' my mother said to me. 'Run along and have a nice bath, darling, and do put on your new dress, it suits you so well.' Miserably I went upstairs. I knew the moment I got out of the room they'd start discussing how uptight I was.

I really had run out of camouflage now. This evening, for the first time, Jamie would see my legs in their true glory. My face took hours, because I kept crying and my eye make-up ran. I wore the dress my mother had given me for Christmas: black velvet with side slits in the skirt. I was just about to put on my stockings when there was a knock at the door.

'Come in,' I said without thinking. To my horror it was Jamie.

'Your mother said, please put the potatoes on, then come and have a drink,' he said formally.

'I'll be down in a minute,' I said, but my voice broke.

'Oh, darling,' he said, 'what's the matter?'

'These are,' I wailed, pointing to my awful legs.

'I should think so. Silly idiot, you'll get frightful chilblains if you wander round with bare feet in this weather. For God's sake, put some slippers on.'

'You don't understand,' I said with a sob, 'you've never seen my legs before.'

'Of course I have,' he said. 'There's a fantastic photograph of you in Matthew's flat—all legs and falling out of the top of a bikini. Ever since I saw it in September, I've been angling to be asked down for the weekend.'

100

'You mean you've seen them and you don't mind?' I said incredulously.

'Of course not. I hate chicken legs like Anthea's.'

I couldn't believe the joy I was feeling, like getting back the circulation in one's fingers when they've been numb.

'I wish you'd wear those tights I gave you,' Jamie went on. 'They'd look great with that dress.'

I shook my head. 'They're lovely, but I'd be a laughing stock in black fishnet.'

'Put them on,' he said firmly.

With trembling hands, I rolled the tights up over my legs. The transformation was incredible. I couldn't believe my eyes.

'Oh,' I said in ecstasy, 'I've got ankles! Real, real ankles!'

'They look ravishing,' he said, putting his arms around me, 'and I meant every word on the card that went with them.'

'If you can stop necking,' shouted my sister, banging on the door, 'Mummy says don't put the potatoes on yet. Uncle Tony's got the year wrong. He's just rung from the station, complaining that no-one's there to pick him up. And Aunt Gertrude was going to leave, but she's decided not to, having smelled the turkey cooking.'

Suddenly I thought, it's going to be the best possible Christmas after all.

The Ugly Swan

Jessica raced down the High Street deep in thought. She was trying to work out an opening paragraph for the big stabbing story she'd heard at the Juvenile Court that morning. A teenage boy had plunged a knife into his stepfather, who'd come home drunk from the pub and started beating up the boy's mother. The whole case had upset Jessica very much. The accused boy had looked so dead-eyed and defeated when the magistrates remanded him in custody for a fortnight. But she knew she had to get over her squeamishness and sensitivity if she were going to be any good as a journalist.

She was so preoccupied as she galloped along that it was a few seconds before she realised her name was being shouted.

'Jessica. *Jessica*!'

She stopped in her tracks, long legs sprawling like a colt, short, spiky dark hair standing on end, looking everywhere but at the blond young man in the dark green Lamborghini who was shouting at her. He backed the car until he was level with her.

'Jessica,' he said patiently, 'I'm here.'

'Oh hello, Oliver,' she gasped, blushing crimson and dropping her paper bag and her notebook, 'How are you? Are you better now?'

Oliver Cotswold was one of the string of golden boys who'd run around with Jessica's sister, Helen, before she married. A racing driver, he'd been badly burned in a multi-crash at Silverstone last year. As he turned to talk to her, she could see the livid scars disfiguring the left side of his face.

'Totally recovered,' he said. 'I'm giving a party on Saturday to celebrate my return to the circuit. I'd love you to come.'

'Gosh, how incredibly kind,' said Jessica, retrieving her paper bag and notebook from the gutter. 'I'd simply adore to if I'm not working.'

'On Saturday night?'

'The W.I. are doing *Dear Octopus*. I'm supposed to be covering it.'

'Well, come on afterwards, it'll go on all night.'

'Shall I bring a bottle?'

'No, just yourself—Danny's coming down for it by the way.'

Jessica's knees seemed to buckle. Her heart stopped beating. Thank goodness Oliver was lighting a cigarette, and therefore didn't see her total confusion. Her voice would hardly come out of her dry throat, as she whispered, 'Did you say Danny?'

'Yes. Danny McCarthy—you remember, he went out with your sister, Helen.' He started up the green car with a dragon's roar which had the passers-by clicking their tongues. 'See you Saturday then.'

Jessica stood in the street clutching her packages. Looking down she realised she'd squeezed her paper bag so hard that the egg and tomato in her sandwiches had burst through the cellophane, and got all mixed up with the leaking coffee. She'd promised Victor Price, the Editor, that she'd have her Juvenile Court reports written by four o'clock, but instead she chucked the coffee and sandwiches into an adjacent litter-bin, and went into a nearby café and sat down by herself in the corner.

'Danny's coming back,' she muttered, and putting her burning face in her hands, tried to rub away the blaze of excitement.

Helen, Jessica's eldest sister, had been so beautiful she had always had hoards of admirers, but the one the

103

family always remembered and talked about was Danny. All Jessica's four sisters, and even her mother, had gone out and had their hair done for the weekends Danny came down. It wasn't that he was particularly handsome. He was thin, very dark and small, and had the saddest, bony, harlequin face when he wasn't laughing, which was most of the time; but he had beautiful hands, a soft Irish voice, and he seemed to have time for everyone. At a party, he would talk to the plainest woman in the room, and within ten minutes she'd be glowing and happy with a crowd gathering round her. People warmed themselves on Danny; he was like a bonfire on a raw winter's day.

Jessica, the youngest of the sisters, was the ugly duckling in a houseful of beauties. When Danny had gone out with Helen, she'd been only fourteen, ignored or nagged about her appearance by the rest of the family. Danny, however, had singled her out, always teasing her and talking to her. He never arrived from London without some crazy present: a three-foot teddy bear from Fortnum's, a stuffed fox in a glass case, a scrap-book full of Victorian Christmas cards, a pink sugar mouse still hardening on her mantelpiece nearly four and a half years later. He had even discovered the secret hollow in the oak tree down by the river, where she used to hide out whenever she was miserable, or just wanted to be alone.

Gradually as the weeks passed, and he seemed to be coming down more and more often, Jessica was horrified to find herself not only thinking about him continually, but also to be wracked by jealousy of the lovely Helen who could attract men so effortlessly. She started to avoid being in the same room as the two of them, in case they guessed her guilty secret.

On New Year's Eve, there was a party at home, and Danny came down for it. While Jessica's four sisters were getting dressed beforehand—all scented, bathed, shining-haired, and applying perfect make-up with practised hands—Helen had suddenly sat down on the bed in her scarlet dressing-gown and announced that she had a feeling Danny was going to ask her to marry him that night.

'Lucky thing,' said Victoria, the second sister, enviously. 'Will you say "yes"?'

'I might, I might,' Helen said, brushing out her blue-black hair.

But her voice was so full of laughter and confidence that Jessica, who'd been hiding in the shadows, crept back to her own bedroom, stabbed to the heart.

How listlessly she'd put on her first long dress —Victoria's violet taffeta taken in—acutely conscious of her bony shoulders. Even when Danny told her with a completely serious face how pretty she looked, she only half cheered up.

Later Jessica had to endure the agony of watching Danny dancing with Helen as the New Year approached. Helen was so tall that their eyes were on a level, and she had looked radiantly happy as his hands moved slowly over her white back beneath the inky curtain of hair. Then it was midnight, and everyone was kissing everyone else, and bursting balloons, and blowing hunting horns. Suddenly Jessica had come face to face with Danny, and he'd pulled her into his arms, and without thinking kissed her.

'Happy New Year, darling,' he said, and then his merry, laughing eyes had looked into hers and seen the confusion and turmoil, and for a second they had just gazed at each other. 'Oh my God,' he said, 'I'm sorry, Duckling.'

At that moment, Helen had come up, and slipped her arm through Danny's, saying with a slight edge to her voice, 'Come *on*, darling, Duckling monopolises you quite enough as it is.'

Jessica had slunk off to bed. The next morning she had risen at dawn, and walked and walked for miles through the frozen countryside, not even aware of the cold, trying to compose herself to face Danny at lunch. But when she got back, he had gone. Helen was locked in her room.

'What happened?' asked Jessica in bewilderment.

'I don't know,' sighed her mother. 'They had some row last night, matters came to a head, and Danny's gone back to London. He sent you his love.'

Later, Helen spoke about it, not to her parents, nor to Jessica, but to Victoria. It was a difficult thing for such a sought-after girl to admit, but Danny had evidently got some glamorous new blonde in London, and wasn't ready for marriage. Soon afterwards, Helen got engaged and married to the most eligible and handsome of her suitors, and was now living, beautiful and happily cow-like, in the depths of the countryside, expecting her second baby any minute. Every year, Danny had sent the family a Christmas card. The last three had been post-marked New York, but had no address inside.

After four and a half years, Jessica's longing had subsided to a dull ache. At eighteen she'd left school and joined the local paper, because she'd always wanted to write, and because Danny had been a journalist. She dreamed of making it one day to Fleet Street—like the Three Sisters longing for Moscow —and bumping into Danny once more. Every time she went to the cinema, and afterwards day-dreamed of Robert Redford or Clint Eastwood, their features would blur into Danny's. She had an old photograph of him taken with Helen, but she'd cut Helen off, and each New Year's Eve the photograph was transferred from one diary to the next, in memory of the night he had kissed her.

And now he was coming back. In three days she'd see him again. Perhaps he'd changed—he'd be nearly thirty now—and she'd been cherishing a dream all this time. She glanced at herself in the mirror on the opposite wall. She was still an ugly duckling, still skinny, flat-chested and as gawky as ever, with a pointed face in which you noticed only the huge grey eyes. Oh *why* hadn't she persevered with growing her hair, instead of always having it hacked off when it started dividing on her collar. Her eyes strayed to the café clock. Heavens, it was nearly two-thirty! She left her cup of coffee undrunk, and bolted back to the office.

Somehow she got her Juvenile Court reports finished by four o'clock. The Editor made her re-write the intro to the stabbing story three times, but at least he gave her a bi-line and an inside page lead. She sat down to type-up a couple of wedding reports, which inevitably started her off fantasising about Danny. She was just drifting up the aisle on her father's arms in a white, wild silk dress with a high neck to hide her collar bones, when the banging of the outside door brought her back to reality with a start. Guiltily turning back her typewriter, she read the last sentence:

'The bride, given away by her uncle, wore a weeding dress of white chiffon and French lace.'

Shades of Vita Sackville-West and Sissinghurst, thought Jessica. She was giggling and changing "weeding" to "wedding" when Rosie, the office temptress, wandered in. She'd been out of the office since eleven o'clock, interviewing the manager of the local football team.

'He is superb,' said Rosie, chucking a completely unused notebook onto the desk, and collapsing into a chair. 'We didn't get much interviewing done, except of a nature far too intimate for a family newspaper, but he's asked me to have dinner with him tonight, and then no doubt we'll get down to the nitty-gritty of his defence policy.' She pushed her amber fringe out of her eyes, and gave Jessica the full benefit of her most bewitching smile. 'You wouldn't cover the vicar's retirement party for me, tonight?'

'Okay,' said Jessica, 'if you'll do *Dear Octopus* for me on Saturday.'

'Have you got a date?' asked Rosie in surprise.

'Oliver Cotswold's giving a party.'

Rosie whistled enviously. Football managers were foothills, compared with the dizzy heights of Oliver Cotswold and his rich racing driver friends. 'Lucky thing—bound to be loads of talent there,' she said, looking at Jessica critically. 'You must get something fantastic to wear.'

'Will you come and help me?' asked Jessica. 'I thought I might go blonde, but I'm a bit scared of dyeing my hair.'

'Paint it on,' said Rosie. 'You can wash it out next day if you don't like it.'

Over the next three days—in between amorous skirmishing with the football manager—Rosie took charge of Jessica's appearance. At eight-thirty on the Saturday night, Rosie had still not allowed Jessica to look at herself in the mirror in case she got cold feet. They were in Rosie's flat, in case Jessica's mother had a heart attack over her daughter's appearance. Rosie had cajoled her into high-heeled, silver sandals, and a glittering, silver body stocking, high at the front, then plunging to positive indecency at the back. Her bare feet and long swoop of back were thickly covered with a frosting of glitter. Silver polish gleamed on her finger and toe-nails. Her hair had been brushed forward in a thick, side-ways fringe over her eyes, and back into two smooth wings on either side of her head, then sprayed with layers of silver, gold, pink and blue, so she looked like a rainbow blonde. Jessica was only too glad to let Rosie put on her make-up, her hands were trembling far too much to do it herself.

'You must have really dramatic make-up to stand out in the dim light at a party,' said Rosie authoritatively, brushing a final coat of silver glitter along Jessica's cheek-bones. 'Christ, you look stunning,' she said, standing back to admire her handiwork. 'Quite amazing that no-one's realised before what a beautiful girl you are. Now you can look.' She swung Jessica round.

'It can't be me,' gasped Jessica, going up to the long mirror and touching her reflection in wonder.

Her grey eyes, even larger now with the silver shadowing and three layers of black mascara, were set off by a smiling, wanton scarlet mouth. Her shimmering body didn't look skinny and gawky anymore, just seductively supple and slender. The multi-coloured

Greek youth hair gave her a strangely exotic, sexually ambiguous look. Danny couldn't possibly ignore her looking like this.

'I'm like an anorexic seal,' she stammered, joking to cover up how incredibly delighted she was.

'Charming,' said Rosie, 'after all my hard work.'

'Oh, I don't mean to be ungrateful,' said Jessica. 'It's so lovely to look sophisticated, wicked and predatory all at the same time. You're so clever, I don't know how you do it,' she added humbly, about to fling her arms round Rosie who went sharply into reverse.

'Don't be so free with your favours, that glitter comes off. And don't go clutching any men in white suits, they won't thank you,' said Rosie. Then her hard little face softened, 'All the same, Jess, you do look absolutely stunning, it was about bloody time the duckling turned into a swan.'

'God, I feel nervous,' said Jessica, turning round and examining her expanse of frosted back, 'Do you think I ought to wear my velvet blazer for the first half of the evening?'

'Like hell you will!' said Rosie, 'And beauties' teeth don't chatter either. It's no good looking sophisticated, you've got to act it too. You'd better have a couple of stiff drinks before I drop you off.'

In the lime-scented twilight, the huge trees lining the Cotswolds' drive seemed to tremble in the stifling heat like dark bells. All the square windows of the big Georgian house had been thrown open, and music pounded over the green velvet lawns. Two sleek, grass-plump horses, excited by the unaccustomed din, were careering through the buttercups of a nearby paddock.

'Wow,' sighed Rosie, looking enviously at the sports cars fanning out like sleeping beasts on the gravel in front of the house, 'there are Ferraris at the bottom of the garden.'

'I want to go home. I had a terrible horoscope this morning,' moaned Jessica. Despite two large drinks, her teeth were chattering worse than ever. She could feel the sweat seeping down her ribs.

'You're not going to the scaffold,' said Rosie, stopping the battered Mini with a jerk. 'Oh do look, they've floodlit the swimming pool, I'll bet you'll all be doing nude breast stroke before the night is out.'

She dropped Jessica off very slowly, in the hope that Oliver might come out and invite her in too.

'Life is hard,' was her parting shot. 'You to your jet set ball, I like Cinderella to the Woman's Institute and the last act of *Dear Octopus*,' and she drove, off, loudly singing "Jerusalem".

Oliver Cotswold didn't recognise Jessica when he answered the door. 'Hello, come in,' he said, instinctively turning the unscarred side of his face towards her. 'You must be a chum of Smokey's, she does have the most knee-trembling friends.'

'No, I'm not . . . I mean, it's me, Jessica,' she stammered.

Oliver whistled. 'Jessica!' he said incredulously. 'Little Jessica Eliot. My God!' He turned her round, 'You *have* come out of the chrysalis. You'll need a bodyguard. D'you want to take anything off?' Then he laughed, 'No, I don't think you could.'

Jessica glanced nervously at the hall mirror and, not recognising the spectacular blonde for a few seconds, was reassured that she looked all right.

'All the girls seem to be dressed as pirates tonight,' said Oliver. 'Rather like Peter Pan, it'll be a nice change to have a Tinkerbell. Although with all that glitter you look more like Jack Frost,' and he shook his head. 'It's really most disturbing.'

The doorbell rang.

'Smokey!' Oliver yelled into a door on the right.

A girl emerged from the melée, wearing a white frilled shirt slashed to the waist, and red, blue and gold striped knickerbockers. She had long, bare brown legs, and her ash-blonde hair fell casually to her shoulders. She was very beautiful.

'Smokey, darling, this is Jessica Eliot, Helen's baby sister,' said Oliver. 'Get her a drink, and look after her while I answer the door, she doesn't know anyone.'

Smokey looked Jessica up and down with hostility. 'She soon will,' she said, leading Jessica into a study on the right, where a huge table, big enough to take a nap on, was covered with glasses and every kind of drink.

'What d'you want? I'll pour the first one, after that everyone helps themselves, there's another bar in the drawing-room opposite.'

'Oh white wine, please,' said Jessica. 'Smokey's a lovely name,' she added, in an attempt to placate, 'is it a nickname?'

'No,' snarled Smokey.

'How did you get a name like that?'

'Because my mother's a pratt,' said Smokey, filling up a half-pint mug to the top with white wine.

Jessica giggled, warming to her. 'And those flowers are wonderful,' she said, admiring the orange golden tiger lilies, yellow irises, and salmon pink carnations, which were fanning out against the silk apricot wall.

'Oliver's mother did them,' growled Smokey. 'She's a pratt too, going away for the weekend and giving Oliver and his Dionysiac friends the run of this house. Look, someone's already ground a cigarette into the carpet.' She picked up the butt and flung it out of the window.

She handed Jessica the half-pint mug, and then led her across the hall into a double drawing-room, embowered in William Morris olive leaves, and furnished with good-looking people yelling their heads off. Everywhere there were candles throwing soft light on sun-tanned faces. Jessica entered with extreme trepidation, like a swimmer testing the Brighton sea on Christmas Day.

'Which of these swollen-headed creeps do you want to meet?' demanded Smokey.

'I used to know Danny McCarthy, years ago,' stammered Jessica, totally failing to sound casual.

Smokey shot her a sidelong, feline smile. 'The irresistible Danny—eh? He isn't here yet—probably sleeping off jet lag. He only stepped off a plane this morning.'

The doorbell rang again.

'Smokey!' yelled Oliver from the hall.

'Why the hell didn't he hire some flunkey to answer the door?' snapped Smokey and disappeared.

For a second, Jessica stood alone shaking with terror. Then a smooth, expensive, whisky-soaked voice said, 'That's what I want this evening,' and a leisurely finger ran down her spine.

Jessica jumped, and turned round, to find herself looking into the familiar, swashbuckling, playboy face of Mikey Carpenter. He was heavily sunburnt, and wearing a pink-and-white-striped seersucker jacket, with a pink rose in his buttonhole.

'How do you do,' said Jessica, blushing because he was so famous.

'I do ladies very expertly so they all tell me,' said Mikey, showing strong, very white teeth, 'And you are some lady.' His dissipated blue eyes travelled over her body. 'Where did you spring from—out of the sea? You look like a water nymph.'

'Who's talking about nymphos?' said a good-looking dark boy in a navy-blue sweat shirt, who was drinking out of a Coke can.

'Bugger off, Butler, I saw her first,' said Mikey Carpenter.

'All's fair in love and whoring,' said Bobbie Butler. 'What a steaming girl.'

And Jessica blushed some more, because Bobbie Butler was probably the second most famous racing driver in England. The next moment Rupert Bentley, the third of the illustrious trio, came over. In one hand he was holding a whisky bottle, with which he darkened Mikey Carpenter's glass, and in the other a bottle of champagne.

'Oliver tells me you're Helen's sister,' he said to Jessica. 'Jesus, they breed good-looking girls in your family.' Seeing her glass was still full, he turned to

112

Bobbie Butler, and started to pour champagne through the hole in the top of the Coke can.

'For Christ's sake, Rupe, this is brandy,' howled Bobbie Butler, jerking the can away so that the champagne cascaded onto the carpet.

'Never mind,' said Rupert, pushing his white-blond hair back from his forehead, and grinning at Jessica. 'You're now having a champagne cocktail.'

Yet another driver, a hot-eyed, swarthy Italian in a red shirt, joined the group. Immediately Mikey Carpenter dispatched both him and Rupert Bentley to another part of the room.

'You insisted on bringing him, Rupe, so you can bloody well talk to him. I didn't come to this party to be bored by a load of Wops. I want to talk to Jessica.'

For Jessica, it was a completely new and at first exhilarating experience. Before, she'd always felt invisible at parties, now every man in the room seemed to be vying for her attention. Even the ones who weren't grouped round her, seemed to be hanging around on the outskirts of the room, waiting like auctioneers for a sign. Soon she was mixing her drinks, as all the men who wanted an introduction came over with a bottle on the pretext of topping up her glass.

She also realised that, despite behaviour very much to the contrary, Mikey, Rupert and Bobbie had girl-friends at the party—interchangeable Formula One girls, as highly tuned as any racing car. They were the kind who washed their streaked Schumi hair three times a day, and had such blank, expressionless faces that you felt they were still wearing sunglasses even when they took them off. Despite their exaggerated coolness, however, all three were looking at Jessica as though she were a typhoid carrier.

'Mikey, we ought to circulate,' said his girlfriend pointedly.

'Have another drink,' said Mikey, 'and the room'll circulate by itself.'

'It was the starter's bloody fault,' said Bobbie Butler. 'When the green light went on, half the drivers in the middle of the grid were still coming down into neutral.'

'It was like pouring a bag of Dinkey cars down a funnel,' said Mikey.

'The bloke behind got off to a flier,' said Bobbie, 'and whacked me up onto the bank on the left, and it was all over before I'd gone two hundred yards. I ended up with a bump on my head like a unicorn. Feel,' and he put Jessica's hand up to his head to touch the lump.

'My neck muscles took a hell of a hammering too,' said Mikey, firmly removing the hand from Bobbie's head, and putting it round his own neck, which was as strong and brown as an ox. Jessica rubbed it tentatively.

'That's nice,' said Mikey, blue eyes raking her face. 'God, you're pretty.'

She could feel his hip bone rammed against hers. Jessica dropped her eyes. 'How did you get on today?' she asked shyly.

Everyone laughed a great deal at this.

'He won,' said Bobbie Butler. 'There you are, Mikey, take you down a peg.'

'D'you like motor racing?' demanded Mikey.

'I've never been,' said Jessica, hot with embarrassment.

'Never been,' he looked thunderstruck. 'I'll take you to Silverstone next weekend.'

'I'll probably be working.'

'You'll have to go sick,' said Mikey with all the arrogance of one shored up by a large private income.

Rupert Bentley returned to the group with an armful of bottles and filled up everyone's glasses.

'I'm utterly exhausted with talking Italian,' he moaned, 'I can't keep it up any more.'

'That's never been your problem before,' said his girlfriend nastily.

'I hear you're Helen's little sister,' said a man in a pin-striped suit.

'Beat it,' said Mikey Carpenter.

The evening wore on. Anecdotes about other drivers

and the cost of motor cars were exchanged; gossip multiplied. Jessica found that as long as she laughed, and looked as though she were passionately interested, she could do no wrong. But every time the doorbell rang, her heart lurched in case it was Danny. Mikey was now concentrating all his considerable charm in her direction. Superficially, she was amazed and flattered, but uppermost in her mind was Danny. Why, she wondered, is it that while I'm listening to talk about drifts and acceleration and inside curves, all I can think about is when will Danny arrive, and why am I standing here talking to Mikey instead of him?

'Are you on the Scarsdale diet?' said Mikey's girlfriend to Jessica, trying to break up the tête-à-tête.

'No,' said Jessica.

'You must be on something?'

'Not really,' stammered Jessica, as they all looked at her narrow, silver body. 'I just forget to eat.'

'It's giving up booze that I can't take,' said Mikey's girlfriend sourly, sipping Perrier water. 'It makes one so boring.'

'You can say that again,' said Mikey, turning to Jessica. 'Come and dance.'

'Yes please,' said Jessica.

She felt horribly guilty about Mikey's girlfriend, but she wanted an opportunity on the way to the dance floor to scour the drawing-room and the hall, and glimpse into the study in a desperate search for Danny. Perhaps he would keep on sleeping and not turn up at all, she thought in despair.

The floor was already packed. Mikey was a superb dancer, completely relaxed, but agile as a great jaguar. Jessica, unsteady from too much drink and her high silver heels, was often forced to cling onto him, and he held her like a man who is very accustomed to handling women. During a rock number, he whizzed her around like a ball-bearing in one of those glass-topped puzzles, but when the music slowed, he drew her into his arms, pressing his hard, muscular body against hers, running his hands up and down her spine, and placing his cheek against her hair. When he removed it, his face was streaked blue and silver.

Crossing back into the drawing-room, Mikey bumped into yet another motor racing crony—an Australian with a black eye, a bandage round his head and his arm in a sling.

'That was a beaut win, Mike.'

'How did you get on?' said Mikey, holding onto Jessica's wrist like a vice.

'Lost a back wheel at Paddock Bend,' said the Australian. 'Next moment I was dumped on the bank, bleeding like a pig. My mechanics were scared shitless.'

'You okay now?'

'Boozing my way through it,' grinned the Australian, raising a bottle to his lips.

Leaning in the doorway to the drawing-room was Smokey. She was eating a slice of turkey between two pieces of bread, and looked bored and misanthropic.

'Has Danny turned up yet?' asked Jessica out of the corner of her mouth.

'He's in the kitchen, talking to Oliver,' said Smokey.

Jessica's legs seemed to give way beneath her. 'Must go to the loo,' she muttered, and stumbled upstairs to one of the bedrooms to find a mirror. How could her reflection gaze back at her so intact and perfect, when her heart was crashing around like a peachstone in the waste disposal?

As she made her way back down the stairs, she realised that she'd never been so drunk in her life. She must get a grip on herself, or she'd start blurting out all sorts of nonsense the minute she came face to face with him. She wiped her sweating hands on her body stocking, and edged into the drawing-room, looking frantically round, but there was no Danny.

'There you are,' said Mikey, drawing her back into the group surrounding him. 'And you haven't got a drink.' He filled up an empty glass with wine and handed it to her. She took a slug in a desperate attempt to stop all the confidence draining out of her.

'You have to take the bend from memory,' Bobbie

Butler was saying, 'a foot out, and it completely buggers up the corner.'

'There was a really bloody traffic jam at Druid's End,' said Mikey.

'I want to dance with Jessica,' said Rupert Bentley.

'Well you can't,' said Mikey.

Bobbie Butler's girlfriend was so stoned, she was helping herself to pot-pourri out of a blue and white bowl.

'Disgusting crisps,' she said.

'That's an attractive man,' said Mikey's girlfriend suddenly, running her fingers down her parting to give her blonde hair more height. 'Over there by the door, talking to Oliver.'

'Bit small,' said Rupert's girlfriend. 'Yes, maybe you're right, he's got terrific eyes.'

Jessica didn't need to look round, she knew it was Danny. I'm going to black out, she thought. Then she remembered that she must appear glamorous and sophisticated. She turned her attention to Mikey and Bobbie.

'You've got to be accelerating all the time,' said Mikey.

'*Really!*' said Jessica.

Although she was expecting it, she nearly went through the roof when Oliver tapped her on the shoulder. 'If you can extract yourself from these cowboys for a second, Jess, come and say hello to Danny.'

She turned round, and there he was just two feet away.

'Hello, Jessica, I used to come and stay with your family a few years ago, d'you remember?'

'Heavens, so you did,' said Jessica, pretending to be terribly surprised, 'How *amazing* to see you again.'

Despite her silver shoes, he was still a couple of inches taller than her. His face seemed thinner, the dark, watchful eyes, heavily shadowed, the sallow skin drained of colour—a muscle was moving in his cheek.

He was wearing a clean, blue-striped, button-down shirt, but his grey suit looked as though he'd slept in it.

'When did you get here?' asked Jessica, thinking how much older and grimmer he looked.

'This morning.'

'I hope you've been to bed.'

'Haven't had time yet.'

'What time is it now in New York?'

Danny looked at his watch. 'About six o'clock in the evening, I guess.'

'Way past opening time,' said Mikey's girlfriend filling up his glass. 'Jet lag,' she added with a vacant smile, 'is the true disease of the twentieth century.'

'What are you doing now?' Danny asked Jessica.

'Working on the local paper.'

'Enjoying it?'

'Oh yes, I love it—there's so much variety.' Oh hell, she thought, I'm sounding like Jennifer's Diary.

'I know it all,' said Danny. 'The Fordingbridge Young Farmers practised sheep shearing, while their wives held a competition to dress a clothes peg, with refreshments in the shape of hot dogs and coffee, prepared on a novel barbecue by Mesdames Hilda and Edna Harrison.'

Jessica giggled..

'I used to be the Mother's Union mystery tour special correspondent,' Danny went on. 'I even wrote a fashion page, and had a huge following by telling readers what the budget-conscious over-thirties would be wearing this autumn.'

Suddenly he smiled, deepening all the laughter lines round his eyes, and showing the extreme kindness and friendliness of his face. He hasn't changed, thought Jessica with a simultaneous thud of relief and panic. She felt absolutely wiped out by love. She wanted to tell him about the "weeding" dress and the stabbing story, but next minute a dark, intense, rather scruffy girl in a red dress came up to them.

'Danny, this is great, how long are you back for?'

'About a month,' he said, kissing her on the cheek.

'I'm over to cover the royal wedding. The Yanks are utterly obsessed with it. D'you know Jessica Eliot? Jessica, this is Bridget O'Hara from *The Observer*.'

'Hi,' said Bridget, nodding perfunctorily in Jessica's direction.

'I hear you've got a big piece on Reagan in the *Times* tomorrow.'

'That's been a complete cock-up,' said Danny. 'The subs lost half the copy, and I'd left the black in the States, so I had to go straight to the paper this morning, re-write two thousand words, and then hang about for hours waiting to correct the galleys.'

'What a frightful drag,' said Bridget in horror. 'What d'you think of Reagan?'

Danny shrugged his shoulders. 'Well, he's not all there—like my piece. I like the stuff you've been doing on India, very good,' he added.

'Thanks,' said Bridget.

Danny's voice was so soft that, particularly at a party, you had to draw close to catch all he was saying. Bridget O'Hara seemed to have no objections. Jessica remembered how, in the old days, she used to close her eyes and listen to him talking, imprinting the beauty of each word in her memory.

'How's Helen?' asked Danny.

Jessica started. 'Oh, terribly well, about to have another baby.'

'What did she have the first time?'

'A girl—Clemency—she's absolutely adorable, Helen's a wonderful mother.' She had to speak with great precision, so as not to slur her words.

'And your mother,' went on Danny, 'did she ever get her dishwasher? I always felt so sorry for her, washing up for all of you.'

'We all clubbed together, and gave her one for her Silver Wedding—ouch!' Jessica jumped out of her skin, as Mikey Carpenter dropped a piece of ice down the back of her body stocking.

'Hello, Mikey,' said Danny. 'You had a good win

119

today. The *Sunday Times* have got a big picture on the inside back page.'

'What am I doing in it?' asked Mikey.

'Oh, drenching the crowds with champagne, in a somewhat ejaculatory fashion,' said Danny.

Mikey laughed. 'Didn't you once go out with Helen?'

Danny nodded. 'And lost out like everyone else.'

'But Helen was never a fraction as sexy as this pretty baby,' said Mikey, putting an arm round Jessica's waist about six inches too high, so his fingers rested caressingly on her right breast. Jessica wriggled away giggling, but not before she saw Danny's eyes change for a second from dark grey to granite.

As the evening progressed she and Danny became like two islands, further and further divided by a rising tide of people: old friends coming up to talk to Danny; different men trying to get off with Jessica. Over and over again her glass was filled as she laughed and flirted. She would show Danny how desirable and fascinating she'd become. Back and forth, back and forth she went to dance with Rupert, with Bobbie, with Oliver, with the Italian, and they all returned with blue and silver faces. But Mikey Carpenter was always waiting to claim her when she came back, drinking steadily, accepting the adulation of the multitude, biding his time, utterly certain of his prey. Occasionally, Jessica caught Danny looking at her, as though she was a message he couldn't decode. Oh why doesn't he ask me to dance, she thought, near to tears.

He was talking to Bridget by the fireplace now, listening to what she was saying, his dark head still, his eyes watchful. He hasn't lost any of his magic, thought Jessica, looking at the wrapt expression on the girl's face. Why don't you come over here, she wanted to scream, and pull me out of this quicksand. But instead she tossed back another drink.

'Good girl,' said Mikey, 'let's go and dance.'

'All right,' said Jessica meekly, like a child accepting a dentist appointment as inevitable.

'Another Lamborghini owner to the slaughter,' she heard Danny saying to Bridget as she went past.

It was very dark on the dance floor now. Most of the candles were burnt down. An occasional shaft of light lanced the room when the door was opened. Jessica had kicked off her silver shoes and was dancing in her bare feet. All around her, powder was melting on beautiful faces, breasts spilled out of plunging necklines, jewellery gleamed in the dim light as the deafening music blared out.

'Oh poor thing,' said Jessica, as Mikey's pink rose fell from his buttonhole to the floor. She dived, desperate to retrieve it. Her head swum, and she wanted to cry as next minute the rose was crushed beneath a stampede of feet.

'Leave it,' said Mikey pulling her up and drawing her close. He seemed to burn with fitness and sheer animal energy. His hand slid down her back, under her body stocking, and began to stroke her bottom. Jessica wriggled away frantically with a writhing that Mikey misconstrued as intentionally erotic.

'That's my angel,' he whispered into her hair. 'This is only the warm-up lap.'

As she turned, the door opened and a couple went out. In the shaft of light, she saw Danny barely three feet away. He was dancing with Bridget, they were swaying close to each other and talking. Jessica couldn't bear it. Suddenly it was New Year's Eve four and a half years ago, and Danny was dancing with Helen. She gave a low moan.

'Yeah—it is nice, isn't it?' said Mikey, pulling down her body stocking and slowly kissing her bare shoulder. Over his head, she saw Danny looking across at her. Despite the stifling warmth of the night, it was as though a wind was coming straight off the North Pole and wrapping itself round her neck. Then she saw him look at his watch, speak to Bridget and, taking her hand, lead her off the floor.

Five minutes later, when Jessica managed to persuade Mikey she needed another drink, he led her out

121

into the hall, where they were accosted by some noisy, late arrivals all wanting to congratulate Mikey on his victory.

'Must go to the loo,' said Jessica, breaking away from him once more. Over the din of the party, there was a terrific clap of thunder. She couldn't find Danny in either the dining-room or the kitchen, or the study or the huge, double drawing-room. He's gone, she thought in horror.

In the hall she found Smokey sitting at the bottom of the stairs, blacking out the teeth of the beautiful girl on the front of *Vogue*.

'Have you seen Danny?'

'You have got him bad, haven't you?' said Smokey lifting glazed eyes to her and smiling beatifically. 'I think he left with Bridget O'Hara about five minutes ago. On the other hand I should check upstairs if I were you, it's like a floating brothel up there.'

Jessica started to cry, and bounded up the stairs two steps at a time, cannoning off the wall and the banisters. Frantically she rushed from room to room turning on lights, surprising horizontal couples enmeshed on beds, tripping over a man who'd passed out cold, searching and searching for Danny. Another huge clap of thunder rocked the house, as she reached the last bedroom on the last passage. She caught her breath because the lights were on, but the room was empty. The window was open, and the rain was falling with a steady hiss, drenching the bottles on the window ledge. Oh God, I can't bear it she sobbed. In the long mirror, she could see that her mascara was running down her cheeks. Like a child she wiped it away.

'So that's where you've got to,' said a triumphant voice, and the overhead light was snapped off. It was Mikey. He looked out at the rain for a minute. 'That should bring the fornicators in from the garden,' he added, closing the window with a laugh.

Jessica edged towards the door.

Mikey turned, his brilliant blue eyes glittering with drink and lust. 'Come here,' he said.

'I must go,' gabbled Jessica, diving for the door.

Mikey, although drunk, was a man used to making the kind of major decisions in one-hundredth of a second that most people don't make in a life time. In a flash, he had crossed the room and barred Jessica's exit. Grabbing her, he kissed her, forcing her mouth open with his tongue. She could taste the whisky and the cigar fumes.

'No!' she said, utterly revolted.

As she backed away, she tripped over the carpet. Instantly, Mikey pushed her back onto the bed, and like a very undear octopus, was ripping the silver body stocking from her shoulders.

'Please, no,' gasped Jessica, 'you'll tear it.'

'Shut up,' said Mikey. His face above hers was as red and brutal as a Regency rake after the third bottle. His mouth ground into hers.

'No!' screamed Jessica, struggling frantically, but he was far too strong for her, pinning her hands above her head.

'You've been asking for this all evening, my precious, and my God I'm going to give it to you.' He kicked the door shut with his foot. 'Let's get you out of this armour plating. Jesus,' he said, his breath quickening, 'you've got a body just like a boy's.'

Suddenly the light went on. There was a long, long pause. Jessica shut her eyes. Next minute they were drenched in a flood of cold water. For a horrified second, she thought the roof had caved in, and the heavens opened on them in retribution. Then as she opened her eyes, gasping and blinking away the water, her horror quadrupled for there, standing in the doorway, swinging a metal bucket, with two spots of colour blazing in his pale cheeks, was Danny.

'What the fuck,' snarled Mikey, who'd received the bulk of the downpour.

'Get off, Mikey,' said Danny icily. 'I've got to take Jessica home.'

Relief, humiliation, remorse, misery swept over her.

'Go and gate-crash someone else's party,' howled

Mikey, getting to his feet, lunging at Danny and missing.

'I wouldn't,' said Danny, holding the top edge of the bucket with both ends, 'or I'll crown you with this, and it'll cut your head open.'

Jessica pulled up her torn body stocking, and got unsteadily to her feet.

'Go and get your coat,' said Danny.

As she passed the mirror, she saw her lipstick had smudged as though her scarlet mouth was bleeding. Mikey, impervious to the bucket, took another slug at Danny, caught his foot on the edge of the bed, and crashed to the floor. As Jessica ran down the passage, she could hear his voice shouting, 'I'll get you for this, Danny.'

It took Jessica hours to find her shoes, and even longer her bag, because she'd forgotten she'd brought Rosie's pearly grey one instead of her own scuffed leather. Outside, the storm had stepped up its pace, rain sluiced out of the sky, each zip of lightning was followed instantly by a drum roll of thunder.

Jessica was not quite drunk enough not to appreciate that Danny's car was unusually clean. In the old days Helen had always complained that he drove around in a tip, with piles of books, old yellowing newspapers, cigarette packets, beer cans and discarded clothes littered all over the back and front seats.

'I've hired it,' explained Danny. 'I hope the bloody thing starts. Where the hell are the windscreen wipers?' he added, pressing buttons, making windows shoot up and down, and lights flash on and off. 'Got it,' he said at last.

Several sets of windscreen wipers seemed to be waving in front of Jessica's eyes. Hastily she shut them. I mustn't be sick, and I mustn't cry, she said to herself.

A torrent of water swept with them down the drive. As they turned onto the main road, Danny lit a cigarette. Jessica glanced at his profile, hair tousled and wet, eyes screwed up against the rain, mouth set in a thin, hard line.

'Thank you for rescuing me,' she said in a small voice.

'Mikey's girlfriend was of the opinion that he was more in need of rescue than you were,' said Danny grimly.

Jessica winced. 'W-where did you find the bucket?' she asked.

'Oliver gave it to me to put under a leak in one of the bedrooms. When I got upstairs I found a better use for it.'

'It's supposed to work on dogs,' said Jessica.

'And on bitches,' said Danny savagely.

Jessica bit her lip, desperately trying not to cry.

Danny had no difficulty in finding the way back to her house. He must have made the journey so often, thought Jessica, with Helen under happier circumstances. As he turned into her road, he suddenly said, 'I never got around to asking you, whatever happened to Duckling?'

'Duckling?' Jessica stammered.

'Helen's youngest sister. I got very fond of that little kid when I used to come down for the weekend.'

Jessica swallowed miserably. Was it possible that Danny had muddled her up with one of her elder sisters?

'How old is she now?' asked Danny.

'Just nineteen.'

'Is she pretty, they always called her the ugly duckling but I thought she was the one with the most potential.'

'She looks all right,' muttered Jessica.

'Did she ever get on a paper? She was always talking about it, bombarding me with questions.'

'She's at University,' said Jessica wildly, 'N-newcastle.'

'Pity—I had hoped she might be at Oliver's party this weekend.'

Jessica gritted her teeth in a frantic attempt not to cry. How insane to be hopelessly jealous of oneself. I can't bear it, she thought.

The car drew up outside their house. In the front garden, the delphiniums and the white iceberg roses were bent double from the rain.

'Do come in,' she said, 'Mummy and Daddy'd love to see you again.'

Danny looked at his watch and stifled a yawn. 'I doubt it at two-thirty in the morning.' He went round and opened the door for her, so she had no option but to get out. He held her elbow as she lurched up the path, and he found her keys for her, after she'd tried fruitlessly to open the front door with a lipstick.

'Are you sure you don't want a drink?' she pleaded.

He shook his head. 'I'm dying on my feet. Run along in, don't get any wetter.' He started to walk down the path.

'Are you going back to London tomorrow?' she called frantically after him.

'Yes,' he said, not even turning his head, 'I've got a lunch date. Good luck with the journalism.' And he was gone, running to his car to get out of the rain. As he drove off, a great crack of lightning seemed to carve open the livid sky with a meat axe.

'All right, darling?' called her mother as she went upstairs. 'Had a lovely time?'

'Fine,' said Jessica, speaking very precisely. 'See you in the morning.' Thankfully, a great clap of thunder obliterated any further need to talk.

Hereward, the springer spaniel, who was terrified of thunder, scuttled out from under her parents' bed and shot through Jessica's legs into her bedroom. Soon his freckled, brown and white head and shoulders were drenched with her tears, as they lay shuddering together until, with the coming of dawn, the storm moved off.

Every pipe and chirrup of the birds seemed to murder Jessica's splitting head. At last she heaved herself out of bed, and managed to get to the bathroom, where she took four Alka Seltzers, and nearly threw the whole lot up. Then she had a bath and scrubbed every

126

bit of glitter and make-up off her face and body, and washed the colours out of her hair. The rainbow had come and gone forever, nothing but desolation lay ahead. Slowly she digested the truth that, however many Mikey Carpenters ran after her, she would always love Danny, and he would never love her. She would never again be as beautiful and desirable as she had been last night, and even that hadn't been enough to attract him. He'd rescued her from the dragon, an indifferent, fastidious St. George, and ridden off into the night forever.

Hearing sounds of her parents getting up, she pulled on jeans and an old shirt and fled out of the house. Her mother had been so excited about her going to Oliver's party and meeting some nice (if only she knew) young men, that she would want a blow-by-blow account of the evening. Jessica couldn't stand it at the moment.

As she took the path down to the river, everything was sparkling. The young bracken held up clenched brown fists in a power salute to the sun, the rose-pink turrets of the willow herb swayed above the dark green moat of the nettles. Hereward, overjoyed that the thunder had gone and that he was having a walk so early on a Sunday, bounded ahead, snorting ecstatically.

Reaching the river, which had become a raging brown torrent after last night's rain, Jessica walked listlessly along the tow path until she arrived at her favourite oak tree. She was so uncoordinated as a result of her hangover that it took several attempts to clamber up the seven feet to settle herself into her special hollow. Hereward, who'd plunged into the water, snapping at the racing ripples, charged back on shore, and circled frantically until he had located her. Then, reassured that she was safe up the tree, he set off on a rabbit hunt.

Jessica pulled her sadness round her like a shawl. Her hangover had subsided to a dull, throbbing pain, leaving her alone with the far more blinding intensity of her grief. Yesterday she'd had her daydreams. Today nothing. How much better if she'd gone to the party as the shy, retiring Duckling Danny had remembered with such affection. He'd never have fancied her, but at least they might have become friends. But then she realised she couldn't have borne that—just friendship with Danny would never be enough. She wanted love as well.

For a long time she watched the water lapping at the shore, sometimes khaki sometimes silver, and the darting insects flashing above it. As the climbing sun began to filter through the canopy of oak leaves, a tear splashed onto the lichened branch beneath her, and then another and another.

Whatever will become of me, she sobbed.

Through her tears, she couldn't at first distinguish the slight figure walking down the tow path. Slowly she realised it was a man in a navy-blue jersey, dark hair lifting in the breeze. She stiffened—it couldn't be, she must be dreaming. She saw Hereward bound forward, and the man bend to pat him. Then Hereward's name tag flashed in the sun as the man examined it. Straightening up, he gave the dog a final pat, and quickened his pace towards her hideout. Yes, it was definitely Danny, and she with a blotchy face, and eyes all red and swollen from crying. She huddled into the hollow of the tree.

'Hello, Duckling,' said Danny.

'Oh gosh, hello—Danny! Whatever are you doing here?' said Jessica, nearly falling out of the tree in an attempt to simulate surprise.

'I came down for Oliver Cotswold's party,' he said.

Jessica opened her mouth and shut it again.

'I didn't expect to find you here,' he said softly, 'I heard you were in Newcastle.'

Was he laughing at her? She didn't dare look at him. She stared fixedly at the oak tree, noticing tiny acorns already sprouting between the leaves.

'Who told you that?' she muttered.

'One of your sisters—the blonde one.'

128

'Was she at Oliver's?'

'And how she was—looking sensational. Every man in the room was going crazy with desire trying to get off with her.'

Jessica felt herself blushing. This is ridiculous, she thought, scraping at the lichen with her fingernails.

'Even you?' she asked.

'No,' said Danny, 'I've never liked blondes.'

'But I thought—' replied Jessica too quickly.

'What did you think?'

She scuffed the branch with her foot.

'Nothing, I don't know—that you did.'

'Who told you?'

She was acutely aware of his scrutiny, but she couldn't bring herself to look at him. She tugged a leaf off the branch and began tearing it to shreds. 'Helen did,' she mumbled. 'She said the reason you never married her was because you'd fallen for some sexy blonde in London.'

Danny lit a cigarette—inhaling deeply. 'Well, I suppose she had to say something. I couldn't tell her the truth either. I was very fond of Helen, I nearly married her, it would have been so easy and streamlined.' He was speaking very softly now so that Jessica had to bend her head to catch the words.

'I couldn't marry Helen because I suddenly discovered that the real reason I enjoyed coming to stay so much was a scrawny little kid. Everyone dismissed her as ugly, but whenever I talked to her she lit up like a star on a dark night. The family were always putting her down, so I started bringing her presents to cheer her up, then I realised I wanted to give her everything in the world—even myself.'

Jessica couldn't speak. She sat stunned, knowing that if she opened her mouth all the love and emotion would pour out with the force of a Japanese tidal wave.

'Aren't you going to come down?' said Danny. 'I'm fed up with shouting up the stairs like a bus conductor.'

Jessica slid down the tree. Landing about two feet

away from him, she leaned against the trunk, frantically examining the beading on her moccasins.

'I had to put her out of my mind,' Danny went on, moving nearer to her, 'or I'd have been up on a rape charge. She was lucky she had my conscience to chaperone her. So I went to America, and worked myself into the ground, and tried to fall in love with lots of other girls, but the memory of her still lingered. So I came home to see if this great passion was a figment of my imagination. Last night I discovered to my horror that the ugly duckling had turned into a swan.'

Jessica gave a strangled sob. 'Then you knew all the time it was me.'

'Yep. My heart sunk the moment I came into the room. There you were, beautiful, besieged, with racing drivers prowling round and round you with as much rivalry as if you'd been the Silverstone circuit. It was only when I heard you pleading with Mikey Carpenter, that I realised it was all a front.'

'I behaved so badly,' whispered Jessica. 'I knew you were coming to the party and I wanted to knock you sideways. I'm simply not used to people running after me like that, they never do normally.'

Danny threw his half-smoked cigarette into the river. 'I was the one who behaved badly,' he said ruefully. 'I expected a little kid with huge eyes hanging on my every word, and I found instead a raving beauty who every man in the room was trying to get into bed with. I was so blinded with rage and disappointment, I behaved like an absolute sod. I could have kicked myself the moment I let you go last night. I gambled on the fact that if you were feeling anywhere near as suicidal as I was this morning, you might hide out down here.'

For the first time, Jessica looked at him properly, and the expression in the dark eyes made her stomach turn a somersault.

'I don't like swans,' he said softly, smoothing her cheek with his hand, and running his fingers over the swollen eyelids. 'They've got mean little eyes, and they bite and hiss. I've always preferred ducklings, awkward, fluffy and utterly adorable.'

He ruffled her hair, then drew her gently into his arms and kissed her.

'Jessica, little Jessica, there's nothing to cry about any more. All the nightmares are over.'

'I was so jealous of myself,' she sobbed. 'Oh Danny, I've loved you ever since you started coming down with Helen, never anyone else—it's nearly five years now, it can't be calf love any more.'

Danny grinned, and getting out his handkerchief wiped her eyes. 'Ducklings don't have calf love anyway.'

She clung onto him. 'You won't go away again, will you?'

'I daren't. If I weren't around to look after you, you might keep getting into the same ghastly mess you got into last night.'

And this time he kissed her very hard for a long time, until Hereward bounded out of the river and shook muddy water all over them.

'He's doing the very best he can without a bucket of water,' giggled Jessica.

Hereward looked from one to the other, onyx eyes shining, freckled head covered in grass seed, stumpy tail making his whole body shudder.

Danny laughed. 'He's on a losing wicket,' he said. He put an arm around Jessica's shoulder. 'Come on, let's go and break the news to your parents.'

An Uplifting Evening

Lunch with Elizabeth always depressed me. 'Don't you think Colin is beginning to take you for granted?' she was saying, ladling French dressing over her salad. 'I mean, he gets his shirts washed, his meals cooked —when he's in,' she added darkly. 'You're always going round to his flat to clean it up. And what do you get out of it? Precisely nothing.'

'I love him,' I said, wondering how I would ever get through my spaghetti.

'You've been going out with him for two years now,' she went on, 'and he doesn't seem to be showing any signs of marrying you.'

'I don't want to get married,' I lied weakly. 'Not for years yet.'

Elizabeth had got marriage on the brain. After eighteen agonising months of marching her boy friend up and down in front of the Gas Board showroom, she'd managed to get engaged—and was horribly smug about it.

'Of course you want to get married,' she said. 'And Colin's quite a catch.'

She was right—Colin was a marvellous catch. Neck-crickingly handsome, much fancied at the tennis club and doing phenomenally well at his job. But Elizabeth was also right about him using me, and although I defended him hotly, he did take me for granted. We'd reached that awful stage in our relationship—hell when we were together because we ratted so much, even more hell when we were apart because I never knew what he was up to.

That day, however, Elizabeth's lunch-hour sermon depressed me less than usual, for in the evening Colin —for the first time in weeks—was taking me out.

I went straight round to his flat from the office, but there was no answer, so I let myself in. In the hall was a pile of washing with a note on top: '*Angel*,' it said —always 'angel' when he wanted something—'*I may be held up at the office after all. Be a duck and pop round to the laundrette with these. Love, Colin.*'

Sometimes I hate Colin. I'd got all tarted up for nothing again. I sat fuming in the laundrette watching his white shirts and pants dancing round. I was thumbing through a pile of last year's colour supplements with all the best bits torn out, when a voice asked me if I'd got fifty pence.

It was a man's voice, attractive and husky, so I promptly looked up. He was not at all the sort of man Elizabeth would have approved of—very tall, with dark glasses, lovely plasticine features, dark blond hair and a quarter of an inch of stubble on his chin. He was deathly pale. He also looked hungover to the teeth.

'Have you got fifty pence?' he repeated, smiling at me. I ferreted around in my purse until I found one.

'Ta,' he said, dropping a shoal of five pences into my hand. He put his washing into the next machine. His shirts, in dark blues and mulberries, looked far more interesting than Colin's.

'Hell,' he said. 'Now I need twenty pence for the soap. You haven't got any change for a quid have you?'

I shook my head and handed him Colin's packet of Daz. 'Be my guest.'

'Thanks awfully,' he said, pouring it into the machine. 'I'll repay you in kind—come and have a drink.'

'No thank you,' I said.

'Why not?'

'I don't want to.'

He took off his dark glasses and looked at me. If

133

they hadn't been bloodshot he would have had very good eyes—slanting and slate grey.

'Really not?'

'No,' I said.

'Pity,' he sighed. He sat down a couple of seats away, pulled a crumpled envelope out of his pocket, smoothed it out and started to draw.

'What are you doing?' I asked crossly.

'Don't move, you've got just the right expression on your face.'

'What for?'

'I've been commissioned to illustrate a feature on career wives.'

'I'm not a wife,' I snapped.

'Good—I couldn't see with your hand shoved into your pocket. Living with someone?'

'No,' I said.

He peered into my washing machine. 'I must say your boy friend has a pretty dreary line in shirts. What does he do? Soap commercials?'

'He's an executive in a textile firm,' I said. I was damned if I was going to tell him that Colin worked for a firm called the Cuti-Curve Corset Company. 'What do you do?' I asked him.

'I'm a graphic designer. Unfortunately, I leave everything to the last moment. I've a major panic on now, so I've been working non-stop since yesterday.'

No wonder he looked clapped out.

He added another pencil stroke to his drawing and examined it. 'There you are,' he said, holding it out to me.

It certainly was me—sulky as an old crow on a telegraph wire, but brilliantly, unmistakably me. 'It's very good,' I said reluctantly.

'Have dinner with me, and I'll do you one of your own.'

'I'm going out already,' I said, stuffing Colin's clothes into a polythene bag.

He yawned and rubbed his eyes. He really was

attractive, but you can't pick up stray artists in the laundrette.

'Well,' he said, holding open the door for me. 'If you get bored, drop in and see me. I only live at No. 9 across the road.'

Colin was marvellous to me when I got to his flat. He gave me a bear hug and even offered me a drink. 'The Managing Director sent for me this afternoon,' he said, satisfaction oozing out of every pore. 'He's asked me to join his party on Friday night.'

'What for?'

'The Foundation Garment Manufacturers Association are holding their Ladies Night at the Belmont Hotel. It's quite a slap-up do and the M.D. always takes a party of Cuti-Curve directors and their wives. This year he's asked me to go too.'

'That's wonderful,' I said.

'It is rather. Worthington says it's quite unprecedented for him to ask anyone so young. It means I should be on the Board in six months' time.' He looked so happy that I rushed over and hugged him.

'You're coming too,' he said. 'You've got to chat up all the important people.'

Elizabeth was thrilled when I told her the good news. 'I hear wedding bells,' she said archly. 'With Colin, "come and meet the boss" means the same as "come and meet mother". You must wear a long dress.'

'I can't afford one,' I said.

'You can borrow my black taffeta. Come and try it on this evening.'

Elizabeth is much slimmer than me, and her dress was so tight I could hardly breathe. It was also strapless and blush-makingly low cut.

'I can't possibly wear it,' I protested. 'It's indecent and anyway, no-one wears strapless dresses any more.'

'That's where you're wrong,' said Elizabeth firmly. 'They're so far out they're back in fashion again. I saw two in the paper this week.'

I peered at myself in her long mirror—there was no

denying that the dress suited me. I made one last protest. 'I haven't got a strapless bra.'

'You don't need one with a dress as tight as that,' said Elizabeth.

On Friday night, I decided, I would be sophisticated, scintillating, slightly mysterious and sweep the entire Association of Foundation Garment Manufacturers off their feet.

I found a magazine feature for brides on *'Preparing for the most important day in your life'* and followed it implicitly. I lived on steak and oranges, whitened my elbows with lemon, washed in milk and smothered my face in egg white. By Friday I looked much the same —just more exhausted.

My boss, realising something was up, let me off early, and Elizabeth insisted that I went to her hairdresser's, Bernard of Knightsbridge.

'You'll just have to jettison the *Alice in Wonderland* kick for once,' she said. 'Have it up, with a few ringlets to soften the effect.'

By the time I'd been high-lighted, cut, washed, rinsed, conditioned, blow-dried and brushed out, and Mr. Bernard had had two screaming matches with Mr. Crispin who kept nicking his hair-dryer, I looked like a cross between Medusa and Little Lord Fauntleroy. It was almost six o'clock when I emerged and I stood fretting at the bus stop. Two buses sailed by full, and as Colin was collecting me at seven, I got more and more panicky. Suddenly, a navy-blue Renault shot past, then shrieked to a halt and backed up almost as fast.

The handsome man who leaned across and opened the door seemed faintly familiar. Perhaps he was a pop singer, or I'd seen him on telly? Then I twigged, it was the artist from the laundrette, so spruced up I hadn't recognised him. I shot into that car.

'I was hoping we'd bump into each other again,' he said.

'Oh please,' I gasped, 'could you possibly drive me home?'

'I'd much rather buy you dinner, but I suppose that glamorous hairstyle means you're already booked. Where do you live?'

'Cranbury Crescent—just round the corner from the launderette. I'm being picked up at seven.'

He looked at his watch as he drove off. 'Relax, it's only five past six now.'

'I'm sorry I didn't recognise you at first,' I said.

He looked completely different—the bloodshot eyes, the stubble were gone. He was wearing a blue and white striped jacket and very tight white trousers.

He laughed. 'I've had some sleep since I saw you and I'm all tarted up for my publishers. Everyone's very pleased with me. On the strength of that sketch I did of you, I've been commissioned to illustrate a whole series of book jackets. I really do owe you a decent dinner now. Where are you off to this evening?'

'It's some frightfully important company dance of Colin's.'

His eyes gleamed. 'You'll love that. You won't see much of Mr. Whiter-Than-White, he'll be too busy feathering his nest. But you'll be so busy fending off senior executives you won't have a dull moment.'

'It won't be at all like that,' I said pompously. 'It's very high level.'

He certainly knew how to shift that car. People must have thought we were on the run as we careered down streets and tore round corners. James Hunt couldn't have done better.

'Well, when are you going to come out with me?'

I looked down at my hands. 'I don't know,' I said.

'You're serious about Mr. Whiter-Than-White?'

'We've been going out for two years.'

'And you love him?'

'Yes, I think I do.'

'Okay, you win, I've never been one to screw up a perfectly good relationship.'

Suddenly, irrationally, I wished he had been more insistent.

As the car drew up outside my flat, he looked at his

watch. 'There you are—in fourteen minutes flat. You've got forty-six minutes to blast off. And tell Mr. Whiter-Than-White I'll come and duff him up if he doesn't look after you properly.'

I raced up those stairs. The *'most important day in your life'* final preparations are supposed to take two and a half hours, and I had to cram them into forty-five minutes. But at last I was ready, except for my dress. Then without Elizabeth to tug I found I couldn't do it up. I screamed downstairs to my landlady, Mrs. Horrobin, to come and help.

'Hi say,' she said with a sniff, 'we are done up like a dog's dinner, aren't we.'

In spite of the steak and oranges, I didn't seem to have lost much weight up top and we had a terrible struggle doing it up.

'I need a shoe'orn,' panted Mrs. Horrobin, 'and you oughta wear somefink underneath.'

In the gloom of Elizabeth's bedsitter, I hadn't realised quite how tight the dress was. Every stitch was straining and I was spilling over the top like an overfilled ice-cream cornet.

'You could carry a tea tray on them,' commented Mrs. Horrobin.

'Do I look all right?' I asked dubiously.

She handed me the black feather boa Elizabeth had lent me too. 'You'll be okay if you keep them fevvers on.'

The doorbell rang.

'Hell,' I said, 'he's here already.'

I had never seen Colin in a dinner jacket before. His staggering beauty was only marred by a very recent haircut, there was too long an expanse of red neck between his collar and his hairline.

'Hello, angel,' he said, hardly looking at me. 'You look smashing. We're giving some people a lift,' he continued, as we walked out to a waiting taxi. The back seat was overflowing with two large people. With their small eyes, puffed out cheeks and vast bulks, they looked like a couple of well-dressed whales. As Colin and I perched uncomfortably on the tip-up seats, he introduced them as Harold and Deirdre Bligh.

'So pleased to meet you,' they said without enthusiasm. 'It was good of you to make up the numbers at the last moment,' said the girl. A remark which struck me as rather odd.

After initial welcoming grunts, the three of them ignored me completely. The girl was worse than the boy, with her ghastly put-on voice. I wasn't mad either about the way she patted Colin's knee every time she wanted to emphasise a point.

Colin was acting in a most uncharacteristic way, leaning eagerly towards them and punctuating their conversation with remarks like, 'You're so right,' and 'I couldn't agree with you more.'

I was relieved to feel a foot pressed against mine. Colin must be just playing up for the office. Although it hurt my chilblains, I pressed back hard. It wasn't until the lights streamed into the taxi from the Belmont Hotel that I realised, to my horror, that the foot belonged to Harold Bligh.

When Deirdre Bligh shed her expensive fur coat, I was able to study her in more detail. Any fear that Colin might be after her evaporated. The full resources of the Cuti-Curve Corset Company had failed to give her even the suggestion of a waist, and the tightly-fitting, pink watered silk made her look almost grotesque.

She was unwrapping a tissue paper parcel. It contained two orchids with a mass of greenery attached. 'One for you, one for me—from Daddy,' she said advancing towards me. 'Shall I pin yours on for you?'

'I don't think it quite goes with black taffeta,' I stammered. It was as though I had spurned the O.B.E. at Buckingham Palace.

'Daddy will be hurt,' she said threateningly, and looking at my bosom with disapproval, she pinned the spray so that the maidenhair-fern concealed as much of my cleavage as possible.

Colin and Harold Bligh were waiting when we came

out of the cloakroom. Colin's eyes flickered disapprovingly over my *décolletage* and then moved more happily on to Deirdre. 'You look lovely,' he said.

'Who's the creep who welcomed us?' I asked Colin, once we were inside.

'Shut up,' he hissed, looking round in agony unless anyone had heard. 'That's Deirdre's father—the Managing Director.'

Oh God, I thought, a cold fear creeping over me. That's his little game—the Managing Director's daughter.

We joined a crowd of people standing in front of a bar at the end of the room. Colin was in his element, exuding a completely spurious bonhomie. I noticed he'd developed a terrible habit when he shook hands with people, of taking their hand in both of his—like a vicar. He seemed to know everyone, and people he couldn't reach through the crowd to double shake with, he made thumbs-up signs to and winked. He also managed to trail Deirdre Bligh like a favourite dog.

I stood on the edge of the throng, sipping sherry and trying to look coolly animated. I wanted someone to talk to me so I could impress them with my executive wife potential. My feet were agony and the dress was so tight, I could hardly breathe.

'Don't you work in Foam Rubber Padding?' said a little man with a huge ginger moustache.

I shook my head and gave him my most gracious smile.

'Well, Pantie Girdles then, I know I've seen you somewhere.'

'You might have seen me one day when I picked up Colin Lang.'

'Colin Lang from All-in-Ones?'

I nodded, and he looked at me rather oddly. He was about to say something when the toast-master banged the table and summoned us, in Sergeant Major tones, to dinner.

The Cuti-Curve contingent was massed along the

top table, and I was put at the end between Harold Bligh and a pillar. Colin sat opposite, a couple of places down the table next to Deirdre. I was beginning to get seriously worried, but I decided I'd better try and involve Harold in conversation to please Colin.

'What department do you work in?' I asked him.

'I've just taken over the Strapless Department,' said Harold, spearing four pats of butter with his knife. 'It's been rather in the doldrums lately. But as the strapless dress seems to be coming back'—he gave a mock bow in my direction and had a good look through the fern —'the future looks fairly rosy.'

I was terrified he was going to ask me if I was wearing a Cuti-Curve bra, so I hastily started talking about the theatre, a subject in which he had no interest, for he promptly turned his back on me and started discussing the price of whalebone with the Amazon on his left.

As we ploughed through five courses, I looked out, in vain, for a conspiratorial wink from Colin. But he was too busy paying compliments to Deirdre.

The faces around me got redder and redder, my dress got tighter and tighter. A balloon burst overhead. Lucky thing, I thought enviously.

The ladies were each presented with a red leather address book, and Colin, with much giggling, wrote his name in Deirdre's book to cries of 'Good work, Colin' from adjacent corseteers.

I was bored to tears and suddenly I wished the gorgeous artist from the laundrette were here for me to giggle with.

When the women retired to the loo, I tried to avoid Deirdre, but she tracked me down. 'Colin tells me you're old friends,' she said.

'Very old,' I said grimly, trying to ease my dress a little.

'He really is a charmer. Daddy thinks the world of him.'

'Have you been out with him a lot?' I asked, trying to keep my voice steady.

'Oh, several times a week over the past three months. Ever since I came back from finishing school' (I wished they had finished her off altogether). 'He's such a responsible person,' she went on. 'He never keeps me out late, as he thinks it might worry Mummy and Daddy.'

And then he turns up at my place, I thought furiously. The two-timing snake.

In a rage I went back to the table. I should have walked out there and then but I hadn't enough money for a cab.

Colin came and sat beside me. 'For goodness sake, cheer up,' he whispered, 'it's not a funeral.'

'It may well soon be yours,' I hissed at him. 'Deirdre's been telling me how wonderful you've been to her recently.'

He didn't bat an eyelid. 'Don't be ridiculous,' he said coldly. 'It's just business.'

'What's just business?' said a gay voice behind us.

Colin nearly jumped out of his skin. 'Deirdre,' he cried, taking her hand. 'Come and dance.'

Wobble, wobble, like a pink blancmange, she went as she danced.

'Aren't they with it?' said a corseteer next to me.

'Such a handsome couple,' said another in a loud voice, hoping that Deirdre's father would hear. He did, and looked round and caught sight of me sitting alone. My maidenhair-fern had slipped and like father, like son, he was over in a trice.

'You look lonely, little girl,' he said, 'come and tread a measure.'

The rest of the table were charmed. Jehovah himself had descended from heaven to dance with an ordinary mortal.

'You're the girl Colin found for my son Harold, aren't you? A lad of infinite resource, our Colin—I don't know what we'd do without him.'

He smiled and waved as Deirdre and Colin bounced past. The band broke into a quickstep. Deirdre's father was a most energetic dancer, fishtailing, reversing, telemarking in vast strides across the floor. Crippled by my chilblains, hampered by my tight dress, and a lousy ballroom dancer at the best of times, I kept tripping up and apologising.

'I expect your talents lie elsewhere,' he said with a meaningful leer.

The band switched to a Gay Gordons. 'My favourite,' cried Deirdre's father, and off we went at the double, round and round, faster and faster. Suddenly the whole room started spinning, and our feet seemed to get caught up together. I managed to right myself, but Mr. Bligh overbalanced, and caught hold of me to save himself. There was a hideous splitting sound and the zip went right down the back of my dress.

For a nightmare second, I stood naked to the waist in the middle of the dance floor. Then snatching my dress together I held it against me and fled through the nearest exit. It led straight into the kitchens, and a hoard of Italian waiters descended on me crying, 'Bella, bella,' and trying to be helpful. At last I was rescued by the manageress, who took me into her office and got out a needle and thread.

'What a thing to happen,' she kept saying, shaking her head.

Suddenly Colin barged in carrying my feather boa and bag. He was furious. 'Little idiot,' he said, 'not to wear anything underneath.'

I swear he was more annoyed because I wasn't wearing a Cuti-Curve bra than that I'd been seen naked by four hundred people. I started to cry. 'I want to go home.'

'Don't be ridiculous, of course you can't. What about Harold?'

'I can't face all those people again,' I said. 'Please take me home.'

The manageress coughed discreetly. 'I'm afraid Madam's dress won't meet,' she said.

'You'll have to go home and change,' said Colin.

'I've nothing else to wear,' I wailed.

Colin's control snapped. 'Stop bawling,' he shouted. 'You're letting me down.'

'Letting you down?' I screamed back. 'What about you, two-timing with that—' Words failed me.

'Go and get your coat,' Colin muttered.

When I came out of the loo, Colin was talking to Harold Bligh. 'She just came to pieces in Dad's hands,' I heard Harold say. 'Mind you, she's a perfect C cup, I would say.' They looked round and saw me. Harold went pink.

'Harold will run you home to change,' said Colin heartily. He was smiling, but his eyes were as cold as the grave.

'I haven't got anything to change into,' I said and, bargaining on Colin's dread of scenes, I burst into tears again. It did the trick. Harold disappeared like a discomfited beetroot, and Colin found me a cab. I made one last attempt. 'Please come back with me,' I pleaded, 'I haven't any money.'

Furiously, he gave me a fiver. 'You don't realise,' he said, 'that I happen to be working this evening.' And he strode back into the hotel.

When I got home, I couldn't believe it was only nine-thirty. Colin's final words kept ringing in my ears. Perhaps I'd misjudged him, and all this chasing after Deirdre and souping over Harold was part of his campaign to get to the top and make enough money to marry me.

But was it worth it? If Colin really got to the top, how many more appalling evenings would I have to sit through? And if he loved me, he would have understood how upset I was when my dress fell off in front of all those people.

All night during crying fits, I vacillated between these two viewpoints. I suppose love, like an insect, goes on kicking long after it's dead.

About six in the morning I finally fell into a deep sleep, only to be disturbed a few hours later by Mrs. Horrobin banging on my door and shouting, 'Telephone.'

144

I staggered downstairs. It was Colin, blithe as a disc jockey. 'Good morning, darling,' he said.

'Go away,' I croaked.

'Angel, I know I behaved badly, but I'll explain everything, I promise. I'll be right over.'

'Oh no you won't,' I said, 'I'm going shopping.'

'Call in on the way. Please darling, I'll make it up to you.'

I was too sleepy to argue. 'Okay,' I said, 'I'll be round in about an hour.'

'Don't be too long, darling,' he said in his special Casanova voice which once had caused such havoc.

He's feeling lecherous, I thought sourly, and the weekend lies ahead and he can't face the thought of Deirdre.

It was nearly twelve by the time I reached his flat. He really laid it on with a trowel. He was playing my favourite record, and was wearing a big ear to ear smile, and the dark green sweater I'd given him for Christmas.

'Darling!' He pulled me into his arms and I was practically drowned in Paco Rabane Pour Homme. I struggled away and went and sat on the sofa. For the first time in two years, I knew I had the whiphand.

'Darling,' he said again, sitting on the floor at my feet and trying to look little-boyish, 'I can explain everything. I should have told you before, but when Deirdre came back from Switzerland in the autumn, old man Bligh took me aside and asked me rather firmly to show her around a bit.'

'Why didn't you tell me?' I said.

'I wanted to tell you, but I didn't want to jeopardise our relationship. I thought you might be upset.'

'And how do you think I felt last night? I suppose you think I didn't mind.'

'I know I behaved like a heel. It's just that I'm so anxious to get on and earn enough money to . . .'

'Keep Deirdre Bligh in petit fours,' I said nastily. I got up to go.

He came towards me. For the first time, he was

almost pleading with me. 'Please let me take you out and buy you lunch. We'll have a bottle of wine, several bottles if you like. I'll pick you up in an hour, and I promise you things won't go on as they have done in the past few months.'

'All right,' I said, weakening as I had so often weakened before. 'I'll just go home and change.'

'Marvellous,' he said, as though he'd never been in any real doubt about the outcome. 'You know you made a fantastic impression on everyone last night,' he added, putting an arm round me and escorting me to the front door. 'Harold can't wait to meet you again. Old man Bligh also sent special regards, and said if you ever want a job as a model, he'll willingly give you one.'

Suddenly, as though from nowhere, he whisked out a blue polythene bag crammed with washing. 'Could you just drop these in on the way home?'

Once more I sat fuming in the laundrette. I'd only just added my soap when the gorgeous artist walked in. He was wearing a navy-blue sweater and he'd already got paint all over his white trousers.

'Hi,' he said, 'I was just having breakfast when I looked out of the window and saw you coming in here. I said to myself, there's Mrs. Whiter-Than-White up bright and early after the festivities.' He looked at me closely; he must have noticed how horribly red and puffy my eyes were.

'I've got a terrible hangover,' I said defensively.

'Well, it's high time you had some hair of the dog. Come and have a drink at my flat.'

'Okay,' I said.

'Here, you've left some of your washing out.' He picked up something from the floor and dropped it into my machine.

His flat was chaotic—canvasses lying everywhere, the bed unmade and a half-eaten piece of bread and butter on the sideboard mingling with a mass of books

146

and magazines. Yet the whole place had the same sort of unkempt elegance that he had himself.

'My breakfast,' he explained, taking a bite out of the piece of bread. 'Would you like some?'

I shook my head.

'Well, sit down.' He scooped up a pile of canvasses to make room for me on the button back sofa. He poured us both a large glass of whisky and then sat down in the rickety armchair opposite.

'Now, tell me all about last night.'

'There's not much to tell,' I said. 'Colin went off with the boss's daughter.'

'That sounds pretty standard practice,' he said, pulling at the sole of one of his black leather boots.

I took a deep breath. 'And my dress fell off.'

He looked up.

'And I wasn't wearing a bra.'

'Wow!' he said with a grin. 'I wish I'd been there.'

And then all the events of the evening poured out in a great rush.

He wasn't grinning when I'd finished the story. 'I'd like to take that bastard apart,' he said. 'Why the hell are you still doing his washing?'

'It's the last time,' I said. 'I must leave things tidy.'

'Then we can spend the weekend together?'

'I've promised to have lunch with Colin and I must give him back his washing.'

'You're still hooked on him?'

'No,' I said, 'not any more. But after two years, one must talk it over.'

'You're crazy,' he said, getting up and pouring himself another drink.

I looked surreptitiously at the long tawny hair, the broad shoulders, the narrow hips and long, long legs. Oh heavens, I thought, I could do a king-sized rebound on to him. He came across and stood over me. Then stretching out a hand, he gently ruffled my hair.

'I'm glad you've brushed out that appalling hairstyle,' he said.

'Didn't you like it?'

'Not a lot,' he said. 'But you weren't in any fit state last night to be told it was awful.'

I restrained an impulse to throw myself into his arms and cry my eyes out.

'Don't go back to him,' he said, his eyes suddenly serious. 'Stay here and we can have a long, leisurely lunch and get mildly tight, and then we might or might not go to the cinema. And then I've got a huge steak in the fridge for supper, and after that I might paint you.'

He had such a lovely face. I wondered how I'd ever found Colin attractive. 'I'll take Colin's washing back,' I said, 'and I'll have lunch with him. Then I'll come back here.'

He shrugged his shoulders and drained his glass. 'Please yourself. I'll walk you back.'

We found the laundrette in pandemonium. One of the machines was belching out clouds of pink foam and everyone was crowding round.

'I think it's your machine,' my artist said. To my horror I realised he was right. I rushed through the foam and opened the lid.

Inside, all Colin's beautiful white shirts were streaked with scarlet, like the dawn. His white vests and pants were dyed a deep rose pink.

'Fantastic,' breathed my artist. 'Unbelievable. Look at those colours. Turner himself couldn't have done better.' And he put his hand into the machine and groped around in the mass of foam until he at last found a wet red rag.

'I can't afford to waste my best handkerchief,' he said.

'*You* did it,' I said in wonder. 'It was your handkerchief. You put it in on purpose.'

A gentle smile spread across his face. 'Yes,' he said, and a stream of red dye fell into the machine as he squeezed the handkerchief out. 'I did it once before by mistake with a purple silk handkerchief, and I had to wear mauve underpants for months. I thought Mr.

Whiter-Than-White was about due for his come-uppance.'

I giggled. 'Colin will be insane with rage,' I said. Suddenly I didn't want to be around when he found out.

'If that offer of lunch is still open,' I said, 'I'll take you up on it.'

Johnnie Casanova

Richard scowled at his reflection in the mirror. Maybe Johnnie could get away with unbuttoned Lacoste t-shirts worn next to the skin—but he couldn't. His neck was too long and thin—he looked like a faggotty giraffe. Sighing, he peeled off the Lacoste, put on a dark blue shirt and tie and a pale blue linen jacket, and doused himself in Johnnie's aftershave.

He went down the passage and banged on the door of the other bedroom. 'It's after nine,' he said. 'I'm off.'

There was a scuffling inside, then a voice shouted, 'Hang on a minute!'

Johnnie came out wrapped in a towel, his black hair tousled, and shut the door behind him. 'Stick around,' he said. 'I'll be through in a quarter of an hour.'

'Like hell you will,' said Richard. He pointed to the bedroom door. 'You're not bringing her, are you?'

Johnnie grinned and shook his head. 'The invitation didn't say bring an enemy. Look, tell Miranda I'm working late. I'll be along before the pubs close.'

Richard picked up his car keys. 'I'll tell her to keep

someone hot for you,' he said, and slammed the front door behind him.

Richard noticed the girl as soon as he arrived at the party. She looked entirely out of place, hovering on the edge of a group who were ignoring her, bewildered as a puppy put out on the motorway.

'Who's the girl in the purple dress?' he asked, taking a drink from Miranda, his hostess.

'My little cousin Gemma, just out of school and completely out of her depth.'

Gemma. Richard kicked the name around and decided he liked it. 'Shall I go and chat her up?' he said.

'Oh, darling, would you? I'd be awfully grateful. It looks so bad at a party, people standing around looking spare. Johnnie is coming, isn't he?' she added, fluttering her long sooty eyelashes.

'Sure,' said Richard. 'He was working. He said he might be late.'

He tasted his drink, which was revolting, and wondered where the whisky was hidden. Girls always kept a bottle tucked away for Johnnie. By the time he'd battled his way across the room to the girl in the purple dress, the group around her had dispersed. She was clutching her drink looking terrified.

'Hello,' he said.

She turned to him gratefully. 'Oh, hello.'

'It's too noisy here, and I'm not very good at lip-reading,' he said. She followed him over to the window.

'That's a nice dress,' he said.

'Isn't it lovely? I borrowed it from Miranda.'

She had big blue eyes and a pink skin, and her innocent, anxious face looked quite out of keeping with her full voluptuous body. Rather as though she'd borrowed that for the party as well.

'And Gemma's a nice name,' he said. 'It suits you.'

'How did you know I was called Gemma?'

'Miranda told me.'

150

She looked disappointed. 'And sent you over to rescue me?'

'Not at all. I asked who you were, and sent myself over.'

She was just seventeen, he learnt, starting her first job, living in a bed-sitter quite near him. This was her first big London party, and she'd been worrying about it for days.

Their conversation was continually interrupted by girls coming over to find out where Johnnie was.

'Who's Johnnie?' asked Gemma, as a blonde drifted away.

'My flatmate.'

'He has a lot of admirers.'

'You could put it that way.'

'What dies he do?'

'Makes havoc.'

She laughed. 'In what way? What's he like?'

Richard shrugged his shoulders. 'Mad, bad, dangerous to know,' he said lightly. 'One calculated smoulder from those heartless blue eyes, and wives leave husbands, girlfriends leave boyfriends, and they all leave their possessions littered over our flat—as an excuse to come back.'

'Have you known him long?'

'Oh, ages. We were at school together, and Cambridge, and we've been sharing the same flat ever since. I'm just employed there as an answering service. I also have the dampest shoulder in London.'

She looked at him steadily. 'I can understand that. If I wanted to cry on someone's shoulder, I think I should choose yours.'

Cheered on, Richard told her a few jokes and pointed out who was who at the party. Music was playing very loudly, and people were dancing, getting drunk, getting amorous and quarrelling. As he talked to her, Richard kept wondering what she would look like first thing in the morning, that lovely luxurious body all warm, her smoky, dark hair streaming out over the pillow.

Their eyes met, combined, turned soft. Suddenly, it was vital to get her away from the party before Johnnie arrived.

'What are you doing after this?'

'Nothing,' she said.

'Shall we shoot off and have dinner somewhere?'

'Oh, I'd love to. I'm starving. I couldn't eat any lunch.'

Johnnie arrived just as they were leaving. He stood grinning in the doorway, barring their escape, wearing a pink suit with a carnation in his button-hole, looking tall, thin and very, very sexy.

He put his arms round both of them. 'Sneaking out on me, huh? With the prettiest girl in the room.'

'We're just off to dine,' said Richard.

'Hang on. Don't rush off. Aren't you going to introduce me?'

'This is Gemma,' said Richard flatly.

'Gemma.' Johnnie let his voice purr caressingly over the name. 'G-e-m-m-a. I've never met a Gemma before.' Lazily he let his eyes wander downwards, not missing an inch of the girl's body.

'Very nice, Richard,' he murmured. 'Really exceptionally nice, and at Miranda's party, of all places. What a turn-up for the books!'

Gemma blushed scarlet. But, at that moment, Miranda rushed up, giving a shriek of delight and flinging her arms round Johnnie's neck.

'Darling, you've arrived at last. I'll get you a whisky.'

She disappeared, and Johnnie peered into the soupy darkness of the party. 'Looks pretty unappetising,' he said. 'Where are you having dinner?'

'We haven't decided yet,' said Richard, who didn't like the way Johnnie's eyes were still travelling over Gemma, with that casual expression which always meant he was interested.

'Look, there's Johnnie!' cried a girl in a see-through dress.

Richard took Gemma's arm. 'Come on, let's go,' he said.

*

To throw Johnnie off the scent, Richard took Gemma to a restaurant he'd never been to before. It was wildly expensive, and he was pleased that she ate like a horse.

He didn't take her back to the flat that night—he wasn't going to risk her meeting Johnnie again so soon —nor did he take her there on the string of dates that followed. He didn't kiss her either, frightened of the torrent of emotions it might unleash.

He found he couldn't stop thinking about her— uneasy, obsessive thoughts, that kept him from sleeping at night, and made him abstracted during the day. He was also alarmed that he kept thinking of her in terms of marriage. It would be insanity to marry a girl who was only seventeen.

Johnnie, frankly curious, plagued him with questions. 'There was something very suductive about that little cousin of Miranda's. I wouldn't mind teaching her a thing or two. Why don't you bring her round one evening?'

'And have you annex her on the spot? No thanks!'

'Richard baby, I only want to look her over to see if she's good enough for you.'

'Or bad enough for you.'

'Look, ask her to dinner tomorrow. I'll get Birgitta round to cook and, Scouts honour, I'll behave myself.'

Richard sighed and agreed.

Surprisingly, the evening was a success. Birgitta cooked a magnificent dinner, a great deal of wine was drunk and, although Johnnie went out of his way to put Gemma at her ease, he made it quite clear that it was Birgitta he was interested in.

When he left the sitting-room, he bent over and kissed Gemma lightly on the cheek. 'Nice to meet you, baby. You're good for old Richard. Stick around.'

As Richard was driving her home, he swerved to avoid a taxi coming out of a side turning, and she was thrown against him. She made no attempt to move away. He could feel her warm as an oven against him. His throat went dry.

He stopped the car outside her house, and took her in his arms and kissed her. He was only aware of the blood thundering in his head and the warmth and honey softness of her flesh.

'Come on,' he said. 'We'd better stop this.'

'Why? Why?' she breathed, snuggling up to him. 'Don't you want me, Richard?'

'That's got nothing to do with it.'

'Look at Johnnie and Birgitta,' she said.

'You're not Birgitta,' he replied.

As he drove home, he wondered what had stopped him. He was not usually backward at coming forward, where girls were concerned—and it had been handed him on a plate. She's too young, probably not even on the pill, he told himself. I don't want that from her —not yet, not until I'm sure I want her for good.

When he rang her the next day, the warmth had gone out of her voice. She sounded bruised, cold, almost resentful. No, she couldn't make that evening, nor the next, and the next time they went out together, she was very cool.

He decided to let her simmer for a week, but within two days found that he was missing her so much he couldn't work. He decided to pick her up from the office.

He stiffened when he saw Johnnie's Lotus Elite parked outside the building. Johnnie was lounging against it smoking a cigarette. Gemma came running out, straight into Johnnie's arms.

He tackled Johnnie next morning at breakfast. 'I saw you and Gemma.'

Johnnie looked at him. 'So?'

'You promised to leave her alone. I don't mind you nicking scrubbers from underneath my nose. But Gemma's only a kid.'

'She's learning fast,' said Johnnie. He lit a cigarette. 'I was never more surprised than when she rang me.'

'Rang you?' said Richard.

'Yes, rang me, the day after she came here to dinner, and said could I meet her. I thought it must be

154

something to do with you so, naturally, I said "yes".
The poor little thing was in a terrible state. She . . . er
. . . said that you didn't seem to want to make a pass at
her, and was she so frightfully unattractive?'

'Unattractive?' echoed Richard. 'Oh, my God!'

Johnnie shrugged his shoulders. 'Well, of course, my
dear, I had to console her, she seemed to want it that
way. But I'll certainly lay off, if you want me to.'

Richard shook his head. That, he thought regretfully, was that. At least, he supposed he hadn't had
time to get really hooked on her. Yet, several times in
the days that followed, wanting her became so unbearable that he had rung up and asked her out—to be
met, every time, with the same cold refusal.

Richard buried himself in his work, played squash,
spent a lot of time out of London, rang up old friends,
but the ache showed no sign of subsiding.

One evening when he went to the flat, he bumped
into Gemma coming out of the bathroom. She was
wearing only a scarlet towel, smoky hair tumbling over
her pale shoulders. Richard caught his breath. He'd
forgotten how lovely she was.

She turned pale when she saw him. 'Hello, Richard,
how are you?'

'All right. You look well.'

'Hurry up, love, I'm getting cold,' shouted Johnnie
from the bedroom.

Blushing crimson now, Gemma fled past him.

Richard went and sat on his bed with his face in his
hands. He felt as though someone was slowly pulling
his toenails out.

A week later, he came home from the office and
found Johnnie dressing to go out. 'The most fantastic
temp turned up at work today.'

'When are you moving her in?'

'As fast as possible, as far as I'm concerned.'

'Taking her out this evening?' asked Richard.

'Yep,' said Johnnie.

'What about Gemma?' How hard it was to sound casual.

'Gemma, my dear, has gone the way of all female flesh, into bed and out again.'

Richard was horrified. 'But you can't just pack her in!'

'Who said anything about packing her in?' Johnnie shrugged himself into a canary yellow jacket. 'I'll just have her on a weekly basis instead of daily.'

Gemma rang next evening. Richard told her Johnnie was out. They chatted amiably, but Richard could sense the tension in her voice.

She rang the next day sounding desperate.

'Anything I can do?' asked Richard.

'No, thank you. Just tell Johnnie I rang.'

The next evening, she rang as Johnny was changing to go out.

'Hi, baby,' he tucked the telephone between his shoulder and chin, and went on fixing his cuff-links. 'How've you been? Great. We must get together soon. I've been up to my ears the past few days. I'll call you, huh?'

Johnnie got a high-powered new job, which involved a number of nightly business calls. He installed a recording machine in the flat to take messages. Richard, who was making a half-hearted attempt to get off with a nurse he had met at a party, spent a lot of time out of the flat.

One evening a few days later, he came in and flicked on the recording machine.

'Johnnie, Johnnie.' It was Gemma's voice, with no melting softness in it now. She sounded frantic. 'Please, Johnnie, I've got to see you, please don't fob me off any more with that awful machine,' and she burst into tears. It sounded terrible, heartbreaking, her sobs echoing round the room.

Richard couldn't bear it, he switched off the machine and scrubbed out Gemma's voice.

'I'm sorry,' he said to the nurse, who'd been waiting for him in the other room. 'I've got to rush out.'

For a second, on opening the door, Gemma's face lit up, when she saw it was him. 'Richard! What are you doing here?'

'I heard your message on the machine. I scrubbed it off. You won't get Johnnie back that way,' he said gently. 'May I come in?'

She nodded dumbly. He was appalled by her appearance. There were marks all over her skirt, her hair was lank, her skin blotchy. She won't get Johnnie back that way either, he thought.

'Would you like some coffee?'

He shook his head. She was twisting her handkerchief round and round.

'What's the matter?' he asked.

'It's Johnnie,' her lips trembling. 'Have you seen him?'

'He's been around.' He went over and looked out of the window. 'You're better off without him,' he said bluntly. 'I know it sounds brutal, but I've seen him go through so many women. He's incapable of keeping up a steady relationship with anyone for very long.'

There was a long pause.

'But he said he loved me, and now—now I think I'm pregnant. Oh God!' she put her hands over her face and broke into great sobs.

Richard crossed the room in an instant and put his arms round her. 'Oh, poor love—are you sure?'

'Well, almost . . .'

'You could just be upset over Johnnie.'

'But I'm so frightened.' She beat her clenched fists against her forehead. 'It's like being in hell. What will my parents say? And people at work. I couldn't help it, Richard. That first time he rang me—the night after I'd been to dinner with you and Birgitta, I didn't want to go out with him.'

'He rang you?' asked Richard sharply. 'But I thought . . . never mind, go on.'

'And I didn't want to go to bed with him, either. But he's so terribly attractive. Every time he puts his hands

157

on me, I turn to marsh-mallow. And he promised it would last for ever and he would marry me.'

'He may have to!'

'No!' She sprang away from him. 'He mustn't know. I don't want him to be forced into it.'

'We'll wait another week,' said Richard, 'and then he'll have to be told.'

Over the next few days, Richard spent every moment of his free time with Gemma, taking her to the cinema, forcing her to eat properly, trying to make her relax.

One evening, he arrived to find her swaying, her eyes glazed, her face dripping with sweat. 'Hello, darling,' she said, her voice slurred. 'Come and join the party.' She waved a three-quarters empty bottle of gin at him. 'I've just drunk this in a boiling hot bath.' She took another slug at the bottle, and grimaced.

Richard snatched the bottle from her. 'Bloody little fool!' he shouted. 'Trying these cockeyed old wives' remedies.'

'I want Johnnie,' she cried, 'oh, I need him! Why should I suffer this nightmare alone?'

She was screaming hysterically now, and Richard, who detested any form of physical violence, steeled himself, then slapped her sharply across the face. She collapsed in a crumpled heap on the sofa.

'I'm sorry, so sorry,' she whispered. 'But I'm so scared, Richard.'

Later, she was violently sick. He put her to bed, and sat holding her, soothing her like a child, until she became calm.

'Tell me about Johnnie,' she said. 'Where did I go wrong?'

'Nowhere. Johnnie just can't stand too much love.'

'Has he ever been serious about a girl?'

'Not that I can remember. Violent pursuit and then petering out. Almost as though he was fleeing from something he dreaded, rather than chasing after something he loved.'

'I suppose that's why he's such a marvellous lover,' she said. 'Because he's so detached.'

Richard stroked her hair. The thought of Johnnie making love to Gemma excited him. He felt the softness of her pressed against him. I want her, he thought. I've never stopped wanting her.

He knew it was crazy but gently, caressingly, he began to make love to her. And when it was over, she cried and cried, and he told her over and over again how much he loved her and that he was going to marry her, until she fell asleep in his arms.

The following afternoon, she rang him at the office. 'Richard, it's all right. I'm not pregnant, so you don't have to marry me after all. And guess what? Johnnie's just rung and asked me out.'

'Are you going?' he asked flatly.

'Of course,' she said happily.

'Be careful,' he said.

He couldn't face going back to the flat and seeing Johnnie get spruced up. He went to the cinema, then on to a midnight movie. When he got back to the flat, all the lights were on.

But when he went into the sitting-room, he found Johnnie stretched out on the sofa alone. His white ruffled shirt was open at the neck, a bottle of whisky stood beside him. His eyes were glinting dangerously.

'I've just been with Gemma.'

'I know,' said Richard.

'And she told me the funniest thing. She said that last night you asked her to marry you.' He got to his feet, swaying slightly. 'You're mad! You don't have to marry her. She's a pushover. Anyone could have her.'

'I don't want to discuss it,' said Richard. He realised Johnnie was extremely drunk.

'Well, I do! I'm not having you throwing yourself away on a little tramp like that.' There was a wheedling note in his voice now. 'Why don't we both pack her in? You don't really want to marry her, Richie. You're much better off living with me.'

Suddenly it struck Richard like a flash of lightning.

'So that's it,' he said slowly. 'You're not really interested in women, are you? You just like them liking you, so you can kick them in the teeth. And you can't bear me liking them either.'

Johnnie was moving towards him, his eyes like slits of thread.

'I always thought it was accidental,' Richard went on, 'the way you muscled in and broke it up every time I was keen on a girl. But now I see it was quite deliberate.'

Johnnie hit him then, knocking him across the room. Through a haze of stars, Richard looked up from the floor and saw Johnnie bending over him, his face disintegrating in horror.

'Richie,' he stammered. 'I'm sorry. I lost my temper. I didn't mean to hurt you.'

Richard fingered his jaw, and got to his feet. 'Yes, you did,' he said not unkindly. 'You've always meant to hurt me. Punishing me for wanting girls, when I should only have wanted you. I suppose that's why I've put up with it because, subconsciously, I've known why you were doing it.'

'Don't go, Richie, don't go. You've got it wrong!' pleaded Johnnie.

But Richard had slammed the door behind him. He set off down the road at a run. On the way, he passed the house where Gemma lived. Her light was burning and, for a moment, he paused, toying with the idea of going up to see her.

What a bloody stupid triangle, he kept telling himself. It was all part of love's strange and vicious geometry, he supposed, that he, Johnnie and Gemma should be caught up like this. Each one loving the wrong person.

The river was thick with mist. The cranes hung like tall drunks over the water. Up in the sky, a solitary aeroplane was moving across the stars, its lights flashing, now emerald, now red. I wish I were on that plane, he thought.

He fingered his jaw again. It was numb now. Soon, like everything else, he supposed it would begin to hurt like hell.

And May The Best Girl Win

We all worked in the same office and thought about nothing but men. Fiona Davis specialised in guards officers; Susan Black—Blackie—liked twitchy little modern boys in television or advertising. Neither regarded the other as serious competition.

They were both knockouts in completely different ways. Fiona was one of those blondes who come gift-wrapped in Scotch mist and cashmere on the end of a long yellow labrador. Blackie had a pale, pointed little face, short black hair, wore crazy clothes, and used up at least one bottle of eye-liner a week.

I myself have a neat face, average figure and longish, thick brown hair. I get by, but I don't have mass media appeal like the other two. My name is Kathleen Burgess.

I had just come back from a fortnight's holiday, and was settled in my corner trying to catch up on some sleep, when Fiona strolled in wearing a very tight grey jersey tucked into a very tight crimson skirt—not her usual style at all—and lashings of scent.

'Hi,' she said. 'How are you?' Obviously not the slightest bit anxious to know, she sat down and immediately started to do her eyes.

Hello, I thought to myself, Fiona never wears eye make-up in the daytime.

Stranger was to come. In walked Blackie, fully made-up, false eyelashes and all. Blackie always hides behind huge tinted glasses until lunch-time. 'Hi,' she said perfunctorily and got out her hairbrush.

'What's come over you two?' I said. 'What's happened to those dear old slagheaps I knew and loved?' They both glared at me, and as no-one obviously wanted to know about my holiday, I trotted off to get the post for our department. It was all for someone called Charles Townsend, who had a string of qualifications after his name. Blackie had disappeared when I got back.

'Who's Charles Townsend when he's at home?' I asked Fiona.

She dropped her eyelash curler with a clatter. 'Give those letters to me,' she cried, snatching them from me.

'Okay, okay. But who is he?'

'The new scientific consultant. He's been brought in just below Board level to take over our department.'

'What's he like?'

'Oh, delightful—and amazingly intelligent.'

'Married?'

'I really wouldn't know.' Fiona gets very pompous at times.

'Who's working for him?' I asked.

'That's the ridiculous thing. He's got so much work that both Blackie and I are, and Blackie's got this stupid crush on him. She won't give him a moment's peace. Oh well, I can't stand here gossiping all day. I'd better take his letters in.'

Blackie returned, wearing several more squirts of Fidgi and a new padded bra.

'You look nice,' I said.

'Do I?' she said gratefully. 'Where's Fiona?'

'Delivering somebody Townsend's mail.'

Blackie looked furious. 'Trust her to get her mitts on it.'

'Why?' I asked.

'She's fallen hook, line and sinker for poor Mr. Townsend; she's never out of his office.'

'What's he like?' I asked.

'Oh bliss, but in a nice way. The ideal husband type. He was a don and this is his first taste of industry, so he gets terribly bemused by things like memos and the intercom. Which reminds me, his desk must have gathered lots of dust over the weekend.' And brandishing a duster, she whisked out of the room.

This I must see, I thought. I waited until the coffee trolley arrived, producing the unedifying sight of Fiona and Blackie squabbling over who was to take Mr. Towsend's cup in, and then I sneaked into his room with the biscuit tin.

He was gazing out of the window, so wrapped up in thought that I was able to study him in detail. I couldn't see what the fuss was about; to me he seemed just a thin, untidy-looking man with long dark hair, a lean, ascetic face, and half moon spectacles. He just waved the biscuit tin away.

'Well, he's no Adonis,' I said, as I went back into our office.

Fiona and Blackie looked at me stonily. 'Mr. Townsend doesn't have biscuits,' they said in unison.

I saw more of what they were getting at that afternoon when I took minutes at a meeting. Mr. Townsend may have been no Adonis, but he could talk—oh boy, could he talk! In the most disarming way, speaking in a slow, deep, gentle voice, he tied all those fusty old directors in knots.

When old Antrobus, the Managing Director, was churning out the usual platitudes, Mr. Townsend looked up, caught me in the middle of a king-sized yawn, and smiled. And he had a devastating smile—it illuminated his thin, rather nondescript features like a search-light. I decided that I did think he was attractive after all. But I wasn't going to chase after him like the other two.

Certainly no boss was ever so well filed, so tidied up,

so looked after as Mr. Townsend. Gone were those jolly little two-hour lunches we had had together; now Fiona and Blackie had cottage cheese and yoghurt in the office, to stop the other being alone with Mr. Townsend. Both were permanently on diets and talked endlessly about calories.

I took to having lunch round the corner at Jimmy's cafe with my boss, Mr. Pringle. Blackie and Fiona despised Mr. Pringle, because he had a red nose, put cotton-wool in his ears in cold weather, and was always broke. I liked him. His wife was expecting a baby, and we used to sit over our egg and chips, discussing whether it would be a boy or girl, and giggling over Fiona's and Blackie's latest absurdity.

'I can't see what they see in Mr. Townsend,' I lied.

'It's a combination of helplessness and brilliance,' said Mr. Pringle. 'Women immediately want to mother him and sew buttons on for him, yet know he's got the upper hand intellectually.'

On the day that Blackie frenziedly turned her skirt up four inches with the office stapler and Fiona wore the tightest pale blue jersey I'd ever seen, Mr. Pringle staggered in, his face grey with exhaustion, shouting: 'It's a boy! Seven pounds.'

'Marvellous,' I said, hugging him.

'Today, you and I are going to celebrate,' he said. 'To hell with egg and chips.'

We went to the French restaurant in the High Street. We had a bottle of champagne to start with and a bottle of white wine with lunch. Mr. Pringle's nose got redder and redder as he toasted me, his wife and baby Crispin in turn. In fact, we were making so much noise that we didn't notice the group of men who sat down at a nearby table. Then the pudding trolley came round and suddenly, through the rum babas and crême caramels, I saw Mr. Townsend staring bleakly at me. Mr. Antrobus was next to him, with his back to us.

'Waiter, two large brandies,' shouted Mr. Pringle.

'Hush,' I whispered. 'Mr. Antrobus and Mr. Town-send are here!'

'You're a lovely girl, Kathleen,' said Mr. Pringle, putting an arm round my shoulders, and raising his glass.

By this time Mr. Townsend had taken off his spectacles and his eyes were like chips of ice. At the end of lunch he watched me support Mr. Pringle round the back of the dining-room so that Mr. Antrobus shouldn't spot us. We took a taxi back, and I deposited him in his office where he promptly fell asleep.

Back in the big office, I found Blackie in floods of tears. What a day! 'What's the matter?' I asked.

'I've been fired!'

'What?'

'That foul old bag from Personnel saw my skirt and sent me a memo about office decorum. Half an hour later, she came barging in here to see if I'd read it, and I'd made a paper dart of it! So she sacked me.'

'Oh, poor Blackie,' I sympathised.

'And now Fiona will get lovely Mr. Townsend after all,' said Blackie, breaking into fresh sobs.

At that moment Mr. Townsend sent for me. He looked as bleak as a grey winter's day as I closed his door.

'I don't know how to begin, Miss Burgess,' he said, playing nervously with a green paperweight on his desk. 'Pringle is a married man, you see, and although I've noticed you going off for lunch with him every day, I haven't said anything. I don't believe in interfering in people's private lives. But when they make them so excessively public as you and Pringle did at lunch-time today, I must put my foot down. I noticed Pringle becoming (a) amorous and (b) paralytically drunk.'

'That's not fair,' I said furiously, 'Mr. Pringle has a weak head on account of poverty. It's the first time he's had champagne since he was married. He never drinks at lunch-time normally. How can he on the rotten salary they pay him!'

Mr. Townsend stared at me, obviously considering my outburst proof of my infatuation.

'Mr. Pringle and I are just friends,' I said sulkily.

A silence fell, which I refused to break. Mr. Townsend got up from his chair and peered through the Venetian blinds. The sight of his tall, rangy body with the slumped shoulders, took all the fight out of me. You can't row with a man wearing odd shoes.

Then he turned round and said slowly, 'I don't think you realise, Miss Burgess, how potent the boss-secretary relationship is.' (Didn't I just.) 'It's an artificial situation, you see. You're so used to Mr. Pringle telling you to write a letter or get a customer on the telephone that it's terribly difficult for you to say "no" if he asks you out to dinner, or to go to bed with him.'

'I haven't been to bed with Mr. Pringle,' I squeaked indignantly.

But Mr. Townsend wasn't listening and went on, 'When I told the Master of my College that I was going into industry, he said, "Well, make it a rule, Townsend, never to get involved with the women in the office. If you fall for them, you won't get any work done; and it's damned awkward when you get bored with them."'

Then he smiled that devastating smile. 'It's good advice, Miss Burgess,' he said gently. 'If you're really keen on Pringle, get another job and see things in perspective.'

Suddenly I wanted to cry on his shoulder so badly I couldn't say anything. So I just fled from the room.

I found Blackie still sniffing, but sufficiently recovered to eat a bar of chocolate, with Fiona suppressing a Cheshire cat smile and trying to look sympathetic. 'You're quite right to get sacked,' I told her. 'Mr. Townsend's just told me he'd never dream of having an affair with a girl working in the same office.'

'My God!' shrieked Fiona, seizing the evening paper and thumbing through it to the Situations Vacant page. 'What are we waiting for?'

Fiona and Blackie spent the next week going to interviews. Both were convinced that the day they started their new jobs they would get a telephone call from Mr. Townsend asking them out. Both of them, however, were determined to stay for the office party next week.

'I must buy something spectacular,' said Blackie.

'I'm really going to knock darling Charles for six,' said Fiona.

The party began at seven-thirty. I arrived a few minutes early and was just combing my newly-curled ringlets in the ladies' loo when Fiona sauntered in. For a minute I didn't recognise her. Her lovely straight blonde hair had been frizzed into tight little curls, which didn't suit her at all, and she was wearing a slinky, high-necked cyclamen pink dress. 'You've changed your hair,' I said stupidly.

'Well, I thought I'd change my image,' she said.

When she went to the mirror to comb her hair, I saw her dress was so low at the back you could almost see the cleavage of her bottom. She certainly got noticed —as we went into the ballroom everyone was gawping at her. Even Mr. Townsend looked up and smiled.

'Did you notice Charles noticing me?' whispered Fiona. Suddenly she stiffened beside me. 'Look,' she hissed.

Another identical blonde with frizzy curls in a brilliant yellow cat suit came wiggling through the door towards us. It was a few seconds before I realised it was Blackie. 'Have you dyed your hair?' I said in awe.

'Course not, it's a wig. I thought I'd out-blonde Fiona for a change—gentlemen preferring and all that.'

Her cat suit was almost as low cut at the front as Fiona's was at the back. I felt such a frump in my black velvet.

The evening passed like a bad dream. We worked our way through a five-course dinner and then there was dancing. Mr. Pringle came over and asked me to dance. He couldn't stop laughing at Blackie and Fiona's matching hairstyles.

Mr. Townsend danced with darling Mrs. Pringle, who hadn't lost an ounce of weight since the baby was born. They were talking earnestly and kept looking in our direction; and when the dance ended, they came over to talk to us. I carefully avoided looking at Mr. Townsend. I hoped he hadn't been spreading vile rumours about me and Mr. Pringle.

'Would you like to dance, Miss Burgess?' he said.

It was one of those waltzes they only play at office parties, swoop, two, three, swoop, two, three. 'I'm afraid I dance very badly,' he said shyly.

Round and round we went, completely out of time, and oh, the exquisite agony as his feet crushed my chilblains.

'I like your hair, ' he said. 'It reminds me of an oil painting of my great, great grandmother. She was considered very beautiful,' he added hastily.

Bliss was shortlived. The band moved into a Paul Jones, and Mr. Townsend and I were separated. I felt a great sadness as I saw Blackie corner him, and then watched Fiona join the fray. For the rest of the evening they never allowed anyone near him.

'We're off,' said Mr. Pringle beside me.

'Must get back to the baby,' Mrs. Pringle added happily.

'Do you want a lift?' Mr. Pringle asked, giving me a quizzical look.

I nodded dumbly. I couldn't take any more.

Next morning before work, I was trying to reduce my hangover with pints of orange juice in Jimmy's cafe, when Mr. Townsend walked in and headed towards me like a homing pigeon. He was white and shaking.

'Miss Burgess,' he said, sitting on the stool beside me, 'I wonder if you could spare me ten minutes.' He was wearing odd socks I noticed. 'I did something terribly foolish last night . . . I hardly dare go into the office.'

Which one got him? I thought, and a sharp stab of pain ran through me.

He lit a cigarette with a trembling hand. 'As you know, I had my hands somewhat full with Miss Black and Miss Davis last night . . .'

'I had noticed,' I said bleakly.

'I hadn't got my car, so I decided the best thing was to get them on their last trains. I took a taxi first to Victoria and put Miss Black on the Brighton train.'

I began to say encouragingly that that was clever, when he added, 'And then I took the taxi to Paddington and put Miss Davis on the Oxford train. But just as the train was moving, she leaned out and waved so frantically that her wig fell off, and I realised she wasn't Miss Davis after all.'

'It was Blackie!' I said.

'I put them on the wrong trains. It was so hard to differentiate between them . . . and they were both rather, er, tight.'

I looked at him for a minute and then I laughed and laughed until the tears ran down my cheeks, and I nearly fell off my stool.

'Do you think they'll be all right, all night on alien stations?' he said in a worried voice.

'I should think they'll survive,' I said. 'Although it might have cooled their ardour somewhat.'

Mr. Townsend blushed. 'Well, it's not that I have anything against them. They're very nice girls, but they never give me a moment to myself. Besides,' he added firmly, but not quite meeting my eyes, 'I'm keen on someone else.'

All the laughter drained out of me after that and I muttered some excuse about not being late for the office. But when I got back there, I was far too miserable to do any work. The two Babes in the Wood, having had to get home from the middle of nowhere the previous night, didn't get in until midday. They didn't feel much like talking either, until I passed on Mr. Townsend's remark about being keen on someone else. Strange to say, that cheered them up; so long as

Fiona knew that Blackie wasn't getting him, and Blackie knew Fiona was out of luck, they seemed faintly relieved that the whole tussle was over.

'Let's go and have lunch,' said Blackie.

'Good idea,' said Fiona. 'We might see Henry . . . Coming, Kathleen?'

'No, I'm lunching with my godmother,' I lied.

'Oh well, see you later.' And they sauntered out together.

I was sitting at my desk feeling suicidal when my buzzer rang. 'Will you come in a minute, Miss Burgess?' said Mr. Townsend.

I found him kneeling on the floor surrounded by papers, his hair ruffled, his spectacles on the end of his nose.

I turned to the door when he suddenly stammered: 'Miss B—Burgess, I've just had a word with a friend of mine who's in shipping. It seems they desperately need a secretary in the Oil Tanker Department to start next Monday. Very easy hours . . . ten till five . . . good pay, long lunch hours . . .'

'It sounds wonderful,' I said listlessly.

'Would you be interested in it?' he asked, scrambling up and coming towards me. Then I saw the expression on his face and the earth reeled under me.

'Dear, darling, Miss Burgess,' he pleaded. 'Please, please take this job, then I can ask you out, as I've wanted to from the first moment I saw you.'

'Me?' I squeaked.

'Please, say you'll take the job,' he said in that slow, persuasive voice he used to hypnotise the directors at meetings. 'I couldn't bear you to be exposed to all that awful office gossip and nudging—but I don't think I can hold out much longer.'

He ran his hand slowly, wonderingly down my cheek as though it were the most precious thing in the world. 'I'm afraid I'm going to have to break my golden rule,' he said, bending his head to kiss me.

'There's no need,' I whispered. 'I've just resigned.'

Political Asylum

Tetbury Court has always been one of the smartest blocks of flats in London—the names board in the hall reads like a page out of *Debrett*, and as it is only a stones-throw from the House of Commons, some members of the Cabinet find it convenient to live there during the week.

Jenny and I, in our first London flat in the sixties, rather lowered the tone. We only got in there because we knew a friend of a friend who was the secretary of an M.P. who had once lived there. Before we moved into No. 4 we had to sign a lengthy agreement about noise and not playing budgerigars after ten o'clock. We soon discovered to our intense excitement, that across the passage in No. 3 lived the Right Hon. Anthony Hudson, Minister for Public Relations, the handsomest man in the Cabinet.

We couldn't wait to meet him. But so far we had only smelt his expensive cigar smoke in the passage, and heard him splashing about like a great leviathan in the bath. His wife had fat legs and lived in the country, but Jenny had frequently seen another very glamorous woman letting herself into his flat.

Jenny, who loathed her job and longed to be a kept woman, was much more preoccupied with getting to know him than I was—but in the end it was I who met him first.

I had had a particularly awful day at the office, William my steady boyfriend hadn't rung as promised,

171

it started to pour on the way home, and I hadn't got a coat. When I got home, absolutely drenched, I discovered Jenny had already gone out, and I hadn't got my latch key. It was the last straw, I didn't know a great number of four-letter words in those days, but I was in full spate when the push button light went out.

'It's too much,' I wailed into the darkness, 'too bloody much.'

'What's too bloody much?' said an expensive voice behind me, and the light went on, and there was the Minister towering out of the gloom, a few raindrops glistening on the velvet collar of his overcoat. 'Good evening,' he said, 'what a foul night.'

Heavens, how large he was, much bigger than he looked on telly.

'What's the matter, my dear?' he went on, beaming at me expansively.

'I'm locked out,' I stammered. 'But my flatmate should be back any minute.'

He looked me up and down. My dress seemed to have shrunk and was clinging like a wet rag. 'You're soaking,' he said. 'You'd better come and have a drink with me and dry off.'

'Please don't bother,' I said, overwhelmed by his size, his bonhomie and those heavy-lidded grey eyes. 'I'm quite happy waiting.'

Jenny, I thought, would strangle me for lack of initiative.

'Come on,' he said firmly, unlocking the door. 'It's absurd to stay outside.'

He had not been a *tour de force* as chief whip for nothing. Feeling like the fly walking into the spider's parlour, I followed him inside.

His flat was stunning, full of books and the biggest drinks tray I've ever seen. Amid all this splendour, I stood dripping, my teeth going like castanets.

'You'd better get out of those wet things,' said the Minister.

'I'm quite okay,' I said, 'and anyway I've nothing else to wear.'

172

'I have a large dressing-gown which you may borrow,' he said, leading me into a bedroom. 'Don't look so alarmed, I won't eat you.'

That may be, I thought. But I leant against the door as I peeled off my dress, and kept on my bra and pants for protection. His dressing-gown went twice round me and trailed along the floor.

'That's better,' said the Minister as I braved the drawing-room again. 'You've gone all fluffy.'

He handed me a drink. 'Brandy to warm you up, it looks large but it's mostly ginger ale. I suppose I ought to introduce myself. I'm Anthony Hudson, the boy next door.'

I giggled. It seemed silly put like that, he must be nearly forty.

'And you must be Virginia or Jenny?'

'Virginia, how did you know?' I asked.

'I've looked at your post on the table, and I sometimes hear you shouting to each other in the evening.'

'Goodness, I'm sorry,' I said, remembering the rules about noise.

'I like it, I've wanted to ask you over for ages, but the nearest I got was singing in my bath.'

'We heard you,' I said. 'It was much appreciated.'

'I know your flat quite well,' he went on, 'a great chum of mine, Buffie Angland, used to have it before he was sacked from the Ministry of Agriculture. Did you ever meet him?'

'No,' I said, 'but he gets the most peculiar telephone calls in the middle of the night from strange women offering him French lessons.'

After being initially tongue-tied, I found the Minister very easy to talk to. The cartoonists usually portrayed him as a sleek black cat, but to me he looked more like a handsome, friendly dog—or could it be wolf?

'Where's your friend, Jenny?' he asked.

'I don't know,' I said. Jenny had a nasty habit of making a night of it.

'And you, were you going out?'

173

I was suddenly overwhelmed by the memory of William, who hadn't rung for three days, and who, because I was locked out, couldn't get in touch with me at all. William the Conqueror, who was playing me up like mad.

'No, I wasn't,' I said, looking glumly into my empty glass.

'What a waste,' he sighed. 'We could have had a jolly little supper together somewhere, but I'm already dining in Cadogan Square.' He looked at his watch. 'In fact, I'd better go and get ready. Do have another drink.'

'Will it be fun?' I called after him.

'No, absolute hell,' he shouted from the bedroom. 'Sulky faces over the Nationalisation Bill, and Piggy Bridlington's bound to pass out before the main course. Doody Harbottle's supposed to be flying down from Edinburgh.'

Funny that he expected me to know all these people with their outlandish names.

When he came back to do up his tie in the drawing-room mirror, I made another attempt to go, but he wouldn't hear of it.

'Make yourself at home. There's television, wireless, scrabble, an exercise bicycle, masses of food and drink. I must go, but I won't be late. I'll be very disappointed if you're not still here when I get back. If Jenny arrives, ask her over too.'

He selected a red carnation from the vase on the table for his button hole, and frowned at his reflection in the mirror. He looked devastating, like a Moss Bros ad., only more so.

The moment he slammed the front door, I hared over to the mirror to have a look at myself. Not bad really, my hair had dried all blonde and curly, and the rain had made my skin glow.

I wonder if he fancies me, I remember thinking, as I dialled William's number. William was out of course. Then I rang the pub he called in at after work, but he wasn't there, and then I buried my pride and rang his

174

best friend who sounded embarrassed and said he hadn't seen William for days. There was much guffawing in the background, and I had a horrible feeling that William was there.

To cheer myself up, I poured another huge drink and started to explore the flat. In the Minister's bedroom there was a vast double bed and lots of photographs of horses and dogs. Pushed to the back was a photo of his wife. She was wearing pearls and a strapless evening dress. The toucher-up had made valiant attempts to give her a cleavage but you could see there was nothing there. I thought she looked pretty wet.

I was feeling hungry and decided to raid the larder. I found some gorgeous garlic pâté, and was just making my second lot of toast when I heard a key turn in the door. Perhaps the Minister had got the wrong day for his dinner party.

'Coo-ee,' said a husky voice. 'Tiger darling, you are naughty, you said you were going out. It's Eunice.'

Footsteps came racing down the passage, and framed in the doorway was a beautiful woman. *Soignée*, sleek-haired, she looked as though she spent her life on a candlelit terrace discreetly swallowing After-Eights like communion wafers. She gave a shriek of horror when she saw me. 'Where's Tony?' she cried. She had a very slight foreign accent.

'He's gone out to dinner,' I said, 'he'll be back later.'

'Who are you?' she asked, 'and what on earth are you doing here?'

I thought she was jolly rude and jolly old too when you looked closely. Her body must be like crêpe under all those smart clothes.

'It's okay,' I told her soothingly, 'I'm from next door. I got locked out, so Mr. Hudson said I could wait here.'

'So you're one of the girls who's moved in next door. Locked out! I don't believe it. It's all a put-up tale to get yourself in here.'

She looked furious. Suddenly there was a terrible smell of burning. I thought for a moment that she was going up in flames. Then I remembered the toast—I made a great show of scraping it into the sink.

Meanwhile she'd noticed the ravages I'd already made on the pâté. Her face looked like milk coming to the boil, and she launched into a flood of French and English on how she had especially made that pâté for the Minister (I bet she bought it at Fortnum's) and how I'd no right to make a cochon of myself. In the end, she snatched up the bowl and bore it off like some sacrificial urn.

'You can tell Anthony, Eunice called, and I'll speak to him later,' she shouted, flouncing out and slamming the kitchen door and then the front door behind her.

She'd quite spoilt my appetite, so I decided to have a bath to pass the time. The bathroom was really kinky—all mirrors, even on the ceiling. I was having a nice soak, admiring my multiple reflection from all angles when the doorbell rang. At first I ignored it, but as it went on ringing, I grabbed a towel and went to open the door, praying it wasn't Eunice again. It turned out, however, to be a middle-aged man with a red face, magnificent handlebar moustache and a nebulous chin receding into his stiff white collar.

'Hello, is Tony in?' he said, leering at the parts of me that weren't covered by the towel. I said the Minister would be back later, and was about to shut the door on his eager, furry face when he pushed his way in.

'Good, I'll wait for him, haven't seen Tony for ages.' He tossed his bowler onto a hook in the hall, and headed straight for the drinks tray.

'I'll get dressed,' I said, but my clothes were still soaking, so I put on the Minister's dressing-gown again, and went back into the drawing-room.

'What would you like to drink?' said Handlebars.

'Brandy and ginger,' I said blandly. I was taking to High Life like a duck to water.

'I must introduce myself, my name's Monty Angland.'

'Not Buffie,' I cried, swinging into the lingo splendidly, 'from next door.'

'How extraordinary,' he said, 'I don't think we've had the pleasure.'

'We haven't,' I said, 'but we took your flat.'

Comprehension dawned in a great grin over his face. 'Tony's neighbours,—well, well. Wily old devil, there's gross foxage for you. Love your neighbour, what?' and he roared with laughter showing long, discoloured teeth. 'He's kept you pretty dark, hasn't he?'

'We only met this evening.'

His monocle fell out, and his mouth opened and shut several times.

'I got soaked and then found I'd left my key behind, so he lent me his flat and dressing-gown, you see.'

But he obviously didn't see at all. I reflected how odd it was that neither Buffie nor Eunice believed my story.

'I say,' he said, 'd'you mind if we turn on the News? I had a terrible pasting from the Race Relations Board this morning, and I want to see how I made out.'

He seemed very disappointed that the television hadn't witnessed his humiliation, but the news did show a film of the Minister opening the *Communications Sixties* Exhibition at Earl's Court that morning. He spoke indifferently, but he looked terrific, and there were brief shots of him touring the stands with all the pretty girls craning forward to have a gawp at him.

'There's no doubt about it,' said Buffie rather sourly, 'Tony does get the girls. The only reason he's still in the Cabinet is because the P.M.'s wife has a soft spot for him, and the P.M.'s more frightened of her than the electorate. I used to think Tony was after Eunice at one time.'

'Eunice?' I said faintly.

'My wife, damned attractive woman, bit high-spirited, but that's because she's half French, you know?'

I certainly did.

'I don't think Tony's really her type, she likes her men a little less obvious,' Buffie stroked his moustache smugly. 'But the vanity of the man is astounding. If you'll forgive me saying, my dear, I should watch it. He likes young girls, but he's inclined to love them and leave them.'

'Does he have lots and lots?'

'Millions,' said Buffie. 'It's the pressure. When you're working as hard as he is now, you haven't the time to be tied to a proper relationship, so you have casual affairs. It's so easy—women fall over backwards for a 17,000 majority and a Ministry with it. I found the same myself when I was in charge of Agriculture.'

Minister of Agriculture! The thought of this imbecile having been in charge of all the poor cows and pigs and chickens and horses and turkeys and ducks in the country was appalling.

Eric Robinson and his band followed the News, with the Luton Girls Choir singing "Nymphs and Shepherds". Buffie beat time with a swizzle stick. They really are a pair, I thought. Buffie with his spooky telephone calls, and the Minister knocking off Buffie's wife.

Was I dreaming, or was Buffie's leg brushing against mine? We both had our eyes glued to the telly, but as I edged my legs away, Buffie's skinny black ones kept following, until we were both riding side-saddle on the sofa.

'Have another drink,' I said leaping up.

'Allow me,' said Buffie, filling both our glasses.

'Where's your wife this evening?' I asked, hoping to divert him.

'She's dining with a girlfriend. She's a great one for girlfriends, my Eunice. So I decided to pop over here, and see if there was anything up.'

He advanced towards me. I was vastly relieved to hear a key in the front door, but I looked around for a hiding-place in case it was Eunice again.

'Hello,' shouted Buffie.

If the Minister was put out at seeing Buffie, he didn't show it. They greeted each other affectionately.

'Eunice sent her love,' said Buffie.

'How very kind,' said the Minister smoothly. 'Do send mine back.'

'And how are you, my little one?' he said to me. 'How nice that you're still here. Isn't she charming,' he said to Buffie. 'I found her shivering outside your old flat, so I had to bring her in. Have you both had a nice time swapping notes about No. 4?' He helped himself to a drink and sat down. 'It was as I predicted, an appalling evening.'

'Who was there?' asked Buffie. And off they went into an orgy of name swopping about Doody and Piggie, and wasn't it awful about poor Sybil, and how Rupert and Charlie were going to cope with the Re-shuffle, etc.

I listened to them in a happy, drunken daze. I couldn't take my eyes off the Minister. I liked the way his black-grey hair was brushed back smooth, and winged up over his ears. He looked up suddenly and caught me staring at him and smiled. Golly, I thought, if he looks at his women constituents like that I know exactly why he's got a 17,000 majority.

'Virginia's been telling me you've been taking midnight French lessons,' he said to Buffie, with a gleam in his eye. Buffie went puce but, before he had time to answer, the telephone rang. The Minister held the receiver very close to his ear, but I could hear the screeching from where I was. Buffie grinned, and came and sat on the arm of my chair.

'One of Tony's birds sounds a bit ruffled,' he whispered to me.

The Minister let the screeching run down. 'How nice to hear you, Eunice,' he said politely, 'you guessed right, the old rascal is here, you'd better have a word with him.'

Buffie had leapt from the chair, as though it were white hot, when he heard her name. 'What does she want?' he whispered.

'I don't know,' said the Minister, 'but she's pretty upset about something.'

'Hello, darling,' said Buffie picking up the receiver.

He listened dutifully for a minute. 'All right, my dearest, I'd no idea it was so late. I'll be back as soon as I can. She wants to go to bed,' he added to us. He was out of the flat like greased lightning. His face had gone ashen. He didn't even bother to say goodbye to me. I felt so sorry for him being saddled with that virago.

'Poor old Buffie,' said the Minister grinning from ear to ear. 'I hope nobody clobbers him for dangerous driving. I gather from Eunice that the two of you met earlier?'

'I didn't mean to upset her,' I said, 'but she didn't seem to believe I was locked out—nor did Buffie for that matter. I hope I haven't ruined anything.'

'You haven't,' said the Minister. 'Eunice is getting far too demanding, she also has a talent for barging in when she isn't wanted.' He poured himself a large glass of whisky, 'Poor Buffie won't know what's hit him.'

'I really ought to go,' I said. 'Jenny doesn't seem to be coming back, and I can't keep you up any longer.'

'Have you anything planned?' asked the Minister unhelpfully.

'I could find a hotel,' I said.

'Not a hope at this hour of night. You'll just have to put up with my spare room. Would you like another drink?'

I shook my head. If I drunk anymore, I'd have seen two of him, and it was bad enough fending off one.

'Well, be a good girl and come and sit down.' He patted the sofa beside him. 'I'm sorry you had to put up with Eunice. I'm afraid you'll have to watch Buffie too. He seems determined to grow old disgracefully, and now he knows where you live he'll be descending on you at all hours.'

'I've never seen anyone as jealous as Eunice,' I said half to myself. 'I wish I could make William erupt like she did.'

'William? Your boyfriend? Is he giving you a hard time?'

It was like asking for beer, when the Minister was offering me a magnum of champagne. Jenny was

180

always lecturing me about not talking about one man in front of another. But suddenly I found myself telling the Minister all about William, and how he was going off me, and how awful it was.

'He picks me up after dinner now instead of before and he keeps saying he's got to work even on Sunday,' I went on, hardly noticing that the Minister had taken my hand.

'It sounds awfully facile,' he said, 'but you're going to love a lot of other people before you're through. One day, you'll look back and wonder what you ever saw in him.'

I nodded dolefully.

'Meanwhile,' said the Minister, 'I think it's high time we made him jealous,' and he drew me gently towards him and kissed me. Now, whatever his defects as Minister of Public Relations, at private relations he was a genius. I wanted to go on kissing him for ever. Practice makes perfect I suppose.

At first we didn't hear the doorbell, but whoever it was, was obviously leaning on it. Then the knocker started as well.

'Hell and damnation,' said the Minister, smoothing his hair, 'I suppose I'd better answer it.'

It was Buffie. The Minister obviously wasn't going to let him in without a struggle.

'Sorry to bother you, old boy,' I heard Buffie saying, 'but Eunice has thrown me out.'

'Whatever for?' asked the Minister.

'Well, I got back to the flat, and she seemed in such a foul temper that I told her all about that little fancy piece you've got here—ha, ha, to amuse her, don't you know?'

'I don't,' I heard the Minister say icily, 'but go on.'

'Well, she went mad and started throwing all those bottles and jars on her dressing-table at me. She's a damned good shot for a woman who never played cricket, and then she told me to clear out. So I did —pretty damned quick. She'll get over it, but can I shack up on your spare bed for the night?'

'Virginia is going to sleep in the spare room.'

'Ho, ho, ho, ho,' chortled Buffie. 'That's a good one.' I didn't hear the Minister's reply. He had closed the drawing-room door firmly.

In the end Buffie was allotted the sofa, and the Minister hustled me into the spare room.

'I'll just bed Buffie down,' he whispered, 'and then I'll come and say goodnight.'

I lay in bed wrestling with my conscience. In a few minutes my fidelity to William was going to be put to the test. Anyway you couldn't leap into bed with men the first night you meet them. Jenny always said you should wait at least a fortnight to let them work up an appetite. But it was going to be terribly difficult to say "no" to the Minister, he was *so* persuasive and *so* attractive—as I've said before, he hadn't been a success as chief whip for nothing. Besides, after eating his food, drinking his drink and antagonising his mistress, it seemed very ungrateful to say "no". It's all Jenny's fault, I thought crossly as the light went out under the door.

I stiffened as I heard a step in the passage. Slowly the door opened and I was engulfed in a waft of after-shave. I was touched that he should tart himself up for me.

'Where are you, my darling girl?' he whispered.

'Over here,' I whispered back, hoping he wouldn't disturb Buffie as he tripped over a chair. He sat down on the bed and as he reached for me, I felt something soft and furry brushing my face. It took a moment to dawn. 'Oh my God, no! *No!*' I shrieked for help at the top of my voice.

It seemed ages but it can only have been a matter of seconds before the light went on. Leaping around in long grey underpants in the middle of the room was Buffie. In the doorway, breathing fire, stood the Minister wrapped in a towel.

'What the bloody hell are you doing?' he roared at Buffie. 'Can't you ever learn to behave yourself.'

I looked at them. What an entry into High Life—in

bed in my bra and pants, with one Minister in a towel, and an ex-Minister in grey underpants with a matching hairy chest. Suddenly it struck me as ridiculous—drink and slight hysteria I suppose—and I went off into peals of laughter. Buffie and the Minister looked at each other and then they joined in, and we all sat on the bed with tears pouring down our cheeks.

'What about a night cap?' said Buffie hopefully.

'No,' said the Minister firmly, 'we're all going to bed, and if I hear another squeak out of you, I'll have you up on a rape charge.'

Across the way, a light went on.

'Oh dear,' I said wistfully, 'Jenny's home, I can go back to my own flat now.'

For a minute, the Minister looked at me with infinite regret. Then he gave a deep sigh. 'Under the circumstances, perhaps you'd better,' he said. 'I'll see you home.'

In the drawing-room, he picked the red carnations from their vase, wrapped them dripping in a page of the *Evening Standard*, gave them to me and led me out of his flat.

He was standing behind me in the shadows and Jenny didn't see him when she opened the door. 'Ginny!' she whispered. 'Thank God you're back. William's here. He's been trying to ring you all evening and didn't know where you were. I said you'd gone out with a devastating man, so he's doing his nut. You've got him over a barrel, duckie. For God's sake though, don't be too nice too soon.'

'Thoroughly sound advice,' said the Minister, unhurriedly kissing me. 'I insist that you follow it.'

The funny thing was that neither of us saw William standing behind Jenny—also in the shadows. I've never had a moment of trouble with William since.

Kate's Wedding

As soon as they reached the motorway, Hugh gave the dark blue B.M.W. its head. 'Good thing we waited until after the rush hour,' he said. 'Who are you writing to?'

'Some people called Lacey,' said Kate.

'The Talbot-Laceys? They've sent us a present even though they can't make the wedding? That's interesting. What did they give us?'

'Wine glasses—twelve of them, not awfully pretty.'

'Vera Talbot-Lacey has exquisite taste,' said Hugh rather coldly. 'You should see their house in the country.'

'Who are they anyway?' asked Kate.

'He's the senior partner at Burns and Marlowe,' said Hugh, lighting his pipe. 'I've defended one or two of his clients—not unsuccessfully, I may say. It wouldn't be a bad idea to add something at the end of the letter about asking them to dinner as soon as we've settled in.'

Kate sighed. All Hugh's friends appeared to be extremely successful, and also had to be asked to dine after they were married to further Hugh's legal career. At this rate she might as well open a restaurant. Half the guests at the wedding would be influential solicitors, barristers and even judges. The reception was going to be like something out of Gilbert and Sullivan. Hugh was destined for great things in life. Her parents were delighted she was going to marry him.

She glanced at his regular-featured, handsome

profile: dark hair, just beginning to go grey at the temples, brushed into smooth wings over very clean ears; dark-brown eyes, shrewd behind heavy horn-rimmed spectacles. At thirty-seven, he had been considered a confirmed bachelor by his friends. Oh definitely not queer, my dear, he'd had loads of suitable, even glamorous girlfriends, but just cautious about making a mistake. He had handled too many seamy divorce cases, seen the appalling underside of so much domestic life, to enter into marriage lightly.

Kate went back to her letter. The next moment, Hugh swerved to avoid a car that had pulled out in front, and Kate's pen shot across the page. She clenched her fists so hard that even her nails, bitten down to the quick, dug deeply into her palms. She counted very slowly to ten—then tore off the page and crumpled it up. She mustn't snap at Hugh, not after yesterday's appalling demonstration.

She had gone straight from work to the house they had bought in Canonbury in order to be near the Law Courts. When Hugh arrived, she was up a ladder painting the kitchen ceiling. He had poured himself a drink, and was just telling her about the case he'd won against all odds that morning, when suddenly her hand had slipped, and the tin she was holding crashed to the floor splashing white gloss all over the newly laid cork tiles.

Hugh had then pointed out that it would have been advisable to have covered the floor with newspaper first, and Kate had thrown a complete fit of hysterics. Hugh had done nothing, just sat watching her helplessly until the screams and shouts subsided into choking sobs. Then he'd poured her a large slug of whisky into a white mug.

'I'm desperately sorry,' she gasped.

'It's just pre-wedding nerves,' he said patting her shoulder briskly. 'It's been far too much for you, keeping on your job to the last moment, master-minding the wedding from London, and painting the house every evening. I'm going to take you away for the weekend.'

'But I can't possibly,' she had shrieked. 'I've got *hundreds* of letters to write, and Vanessa's coming over for a bridesmaid's dress fitting, and I've got to finalise things with the caterers and the florist, and finish off the painting here . . .'

'Everything can wait,' interrupted Hugh firmly. 'It's still a fortnight to the wedding. You're stopping work at the end of the week, so you'll have a clear seven days after that to sort everything out. I'll get Eddie from the office to come and finish off the painting here. I'm going to ring the Hillingdons and see if we can spend the weekend on their boat.'

Oh not the Hillingdons, Kate was about to scream. They were a very role-reversed couple. Jonty Hillingdon ran the house, wrote cookery books, and did cookery programmes on television; Muriel, his wife, was a very successful architect who had gentlemen friends and travelled abroad a lot. They both drank too much, and gave wild parties where famous people got off with other famous people. Kate doubted whether Hugh would have liked them quite so much if they hadn't been *so* successful. They were the last people on earth with whom she felt she could relax.

But Hugh had already dialled the number. She could hear his request to stay the weekend greeted by shrieks of joy down the other end of the telephone.

'Muriel is absolutely delighted,' he said, as he put down the receiver. 'There's another couple going down to the boat tomorrow morning, but it sleeps six, so there's loads of room for us. Jonty will do all the cooking, so it'll be a nice rest.'

'I can't rest when there's so much to do,' said Kate, knowing she was being ungracious as she sulkily mopped up the paint on the floor with a cloth soaked in turpentine.

'I was actually thinking of myself,' Hugh had said evenly, pouring himself another drink. 'I've had a lot of pressure at work over the last few weeks, and you haven't been very bearable in the evenings recently, my darling. I'd quite like a break from all these scenes.'

Contrition had swept over her. 'Oh God, I'm sorry,' she muttered, scrambling to her feet. 'I'm being so selfish.'

She threw the rag on the draining board, and put her arms round him, leaning against the broad, solid back, feeling the dark blue cashmere of his jersey soft against her face. 'I've become so self-obsessed,' she moaned, 'I'll be fine after the wedding, I promise.'

Hugh had turned round and pulled her into his arms. 'I know you will,' he said, his hands feeling for her breasts. 'But you really mustn't lose any more weight, darling, or there won't be anything of you. Come on,' he whispered, his breath quickening, 'they put the spare room bed in this morning, why don't we go upstairs and Christen it?'

Before she could stop herself, Kate had stiffened. 'I've got a bit of a headache,' she said truthfully, then could have bitten her tongue off at the appalling lameness of the excuse.

Hugh had shrugged his shoulders and let her go. 'You've been having far too many headaches lately,' he snapped, 'you ought to get your eyes tested.'

And now they were driving down to the Hillingdons' floating sin palace for a weekend of relaxation. As they turned off the motorway Hugh stopped for petrol. Collecting the bill, he put it neatly folded into his wallet, beside a rather awful photograph of Kate taken at their engagement party. Hugh got bills for everything. Even when he took her out to dinner, she was passed off as one of his clients.

'What did you get for Muriel and Jonty?' he said, as he started the car up again.

'Taramasolata, smoked oysters, pâté, a melon, some asparagus, strawberries, and yes, three bottles of champagne,' said Kate, peering into the carrier bag on the back seat.

'It wasn't necessary to go that far,' said Hugh frowning, 'I've already bought them half a dozen bottles of Sancerre, and some very good claret.'

'I wanted to, they've been so kind to me,' said Kate.

Jonty and Muriel *had* been very friendly towards her, probably to compensate for the fact that they resented her annexing their most eligible spare man ("He's the only straight bachelor we know, darling," Muriel had said when they first met), and because Kate hadn't turned out to be quite the mettlesome sport they had hoped she might be. All these presents were an attempt to hide the fact that she didn't much like Jonty and Muriel either. She must try to get on with Hugh's friends, they were going to be her future.

It was too dark to write letters now, the sun had set leaving a pinky apricot glow on the horizon ahead, and the rest of the sky a drained sapphire blue. One very bright star, followed by a little star, had just appeared on the left. They were driving along country lanes now, the headlamps lighting up signposts buried deep in cow-parsley. Summer had just taken over from the spring, wild roses were closing along the hedgerow. The hawthorn blossom, although turned rusty brown, was still giving off its disturbingly sweet, soapy smell. The country always unsettled Kate, it was as though by cooping herself up in her tiny London flat she had cut herself off from all primitive instincts of the outside world.

'Half-past nine,' said Hugh, glancing at the car clock. 'We've made very good time. I could certainly use a drink.'

Kate got out her mirror, and tucked the loose strands of hair into her chignon. Hugh liked her hair up—he had a thing, he said, about the napes of women's necks—but recently she had lost so much weight, that the style only emphasised the pinched, drawn pallor of her face. She wished she'd had time to wash her hair, but she'd worked late at the office that evening, trying to get everything straight before she left at the end of the week. She dreaded giving up work and leaving all her friends there.

Kate's boss had taken her out to lunch that day in a last ditch attempt to persuade her to stay on. 'You're far too intelligent,' he had told her over the second bottle, 'to spend the rest of your life making casseroles and polishing the silver spoon in Hugh's mouth. Time to brood, Kate, is the great enemy of the married state. I can keep your job open for a month, but no longer.'

But Kate had shaken her head and refused his offer. She was so tired, all she wanted to do after she was married, between cooking dinners for Hugh's smart friends, was to sleep for six months. She was still dressed in the foxglove pink suit and black high-heeled shoes that she had worn to work, and intended to change into old clothes the moment she got on the boat.

'Here we are,' said Hugh, swinging off down a side road: a dark tunnel heavily overgrown with trees. Goosegrass and thistles scratched the paint of the car. Through the open window Kate could hear a duck quacking and the muted piping of sleepy birds. She breathed in the rank feline smell of wet nettles and damp undergrowth. Ahead gleamed the river, and there flanked by willows, her brass work gleaming in the headlights, was moored the Hillingdons' boat. She was painted dark blue, a flag with a skull and cross-bones was mounted on her bows. Red curtains glowed behind the saloon windows. Her name—the subject of much ribaldry—was painted along her bows in gold letters: *M.V. Virgin Queen*.

Muriel came rushing out of the galley. 'Darlings, you've made it!' she shouted. 'Jonty's just putting on the spuds so you've got time for several huge drinks.'

Teetering across the gangplank in her high heels, Kate stumbled into Muriel's arms, and the two women were forced to embrace each other more fondly than either of them would have wished. As Kate extracted herself from the large scented bosom and the jangling braceletted arms, she realised that Muriel was far more tarted up than she would normally have been for Hugh. Her streaked blonde hair was newly washed, and she was wearing a white, heavily-frilled shirt, hanging outside a pair of tight, black velvet trousers, which cleverly disguised a thickening waistline. The all-too-knowing Cambridge blue eyes had been carefully made up, and suntan, aided by a thick layer of tawny brown make-up, hid the network of red veins on her cheeks. She had reached an age when she tended to look better under artificial light, but she was still an extremely glamorous woman. Kate wondered who the other couple were for her to have gone to so much trouble.

In the galley, Kate found Jonty whisking about in a plastic joke apron of a naked woman's body with stripper's tassels hanging from the nipples. Above it, his whisky-soaked, tea-planter's face with its carefully brushed-forward greying hair, looked ridiculously incongruous. He was dropping mint into the boiling new potatoes.

'Isn't it the most erotic smell of the summer?' he said. 'Hello, Kate dear, you look as though you need a stiff one.'

'That could have been better put,' said Muriel roaring with laughter. She always saw *double entendres* in the most innocent of remarks. She reminded Kate of a hyena, outwardly cackling with mirth, but inwardly watchful and predatory.

'I've brought you both some goodies,' said Kate, hastily handing Jonty the carrier bag.

'Oh how lovely,' said Muriel, grabbing it and looking inside. 'But you shouldn't have, darling, you ought to be saving every penny for getting married. We must get the Bollinger on ice instantly for tomorrow's lunch, and isn't that a lovely suit you're wearing, I love pink. Why don't I look like that at the office, Jonty darling?'

'You don't get up early enough,' said Jonty.

'I've got better things to do in the morning,' said Muriel, winking at Kate.

'The best thing you can do now is to get Hugh and Kate some ice, and stop gassing,' said Jonty, handing Kate a large gin and tonic. 'If you all stay in here any

190

longer playing bumpsey daisy, you won't get any dinner.'

'I must go and change,' said Kate, as Muriel dropped an ice ball and a piece of lime into her glass.

'Go next door and introduce yourself first,' said Muriel.

Leaving Hugh to give Jonty a blow by blow account of the longevity and quality of the bottles of wine he had brought down, Kate took a slug of her drink and went next door. The saloon with its shiny wood pannelling, polished tables, and old-fashioned lamps, had been so subtly and seductively lit by Muriel, that it was a few seconds before Kate could make out the beautiful girl stretched out on one of the red leather banquettes. Her golden hair hung down her back like laburnum, and her long limbs, in the skimpy orange dress, were so smoothly and uniformly brown that they looked as though they had been dipped in a vat of milk chocolate.

'Hi,' she said, with a dazzling toothpaste-commercial smile. 'I'm Georgina Arlington.'

Why the hell didn't I spend the last twenty-nine years of my life in a beauty parlour, thought Kate.

'Hello,' she said shyly.

The beautiful girl looked her over slowly, and suddenly seemed terribly pleased about something. 'I believe you know Tod already,' she said.

The man who'd been sitting in the shadows in the corner rose to his feet. 'Hello, Katie,' he said drily.

For a second, Kate gazed into the lean brown face with its clear, all-too familiar, grey eyes. Then the smile was wiped off her face like a power cut. Her glass crashed to the floor. She clutched onto the edge of the door. She thought she was going to faint.

'Tod,' she gasped, 'is it really you?'

'Really me,' he said evenly. 'It looks as though you need a refill. Jonty! Can we have another quadruple gin and tonic.'

A couple of seconds later when Hugh entered the saloon, he found Kate on her knees, frantically rubbing gin and tonic into the rush matting with a paper handkerchief.

'Dar-ling,' he said irritably, 'I do wish you'd stop dropping things. Paint yesterday, drink today.'

'Hope it isn't you tomorrow,' said Georgina with a giggle.

Hugh looked up, took in her beauty at a glance, promptly whipped off his spectacles, and removed his pipe from his mouth.

'Good evening to you,' he said in that warm, enthusiastic voice he reserved for rich clients and important members of the legal profession. 'I'm Hugh Lancaster.' He shook hands with both Tod and Georgina.

'Did someone say Kate wanted another drink?' said Muriel popping her head round the door.

'I'm desperately sorry, Muriel, I dropped the first one,' muttered Kate, still mopping frantically to hide her confusion.

'Doesn't matter a scrap, sweetie. Jonty and I always have plastic glasses on the boat, so we can chuck them at each other with impunity. Good thing it wasn't a Bloody Mary or you'd have wrecked that beautiful suit. Are you feeling all right?' she went on as Kate scrambled to her feet. 'You look as white as a sheet.'

'I think she's just seen a guest,' said Tod, and picking up the bottle of white wine on the table, he filled up his and Georgina's glasses with a hand, Kate noticed wryly, that was perfectly steady.

'Here you are, Kate,' said Jonty, coming in and handing her a brimming glass. 'One G and T.'

'Thanks,' mumbled Kate, grabbing it. 'I'm just going to change into something more comfortable.' She fled into the next door cabin.

Muriel followed, carrying her small suitcase. 'Lucky Hugh, if this is all the luggage you've brought,' she said. 'I can't go down to the shops without a pantechnicon, I drive Jonty crackers.'

She straightened the tartan rug on the upper bunk, and replaced a wild rose that had fallen out of the vase by the window.

'How pretty the flowers are, how kind of you,' said Kate, finding every word an effort.

'But they fade so quickly, like us, darling,' said Muriel, admiring her glowing face in an ancient, speckled mirror. 'Doesn't that girl, Georgie, make one feel a hundred, and isn't *he* absolute bliss. I met him at the Royal Academy press preview last year, and have been trying to persuade him to come down here for a weekend ever since. I'd hoped we might be able to cultivate him as our new spare man—now we've lost dear Hugh to you—but he seems suddenly to have become very involved with Georgie. Sorry not to give you and Hugh the double bunk next door,' she said, once more letting out her cackle of hyena laughter, 'but as Tod and Georgie got down here this morning, it was a question of first come, first serviced so to speak. Poor Jonty and I have to shack up in the saloon after everyone's gone to bed, so we never get much kip on these trips.

'Darling,' she went on, suddenly concerned, 'you really do look washed out, are you sure you're all right? Mind you, engagements are an absolute swine. Jonty and I got so uptight, we never stopped rowing the month before our wedding, but we've managed to notch up seventeen years together fairly amicably, so don't worry too much. Change quickly and come and join the party.'

The moment Muriel had gone Kate collapsed onto the bottom bunk, covering her sweating face with her hands, trying to control the frantic thumping of her heart. Gradually, the shock of seeing Tod again gave way to horror that, after all these years, he should catch her looking so awful: with lanky, week-old hair scraped back, make-up worn off after a day's work, and dark circles beneath her eyes.

Her hands were shaking so much she could hardly undo the buttons of her suit. She hadn't even brought anything pretty to change into, just a pair of baggy old cords that had never fitted her properly, and a couple of shirts in colours that didn't particularly suit her. In her frenzy to get everything straight, all her good clothes were neatly washed and ironed at home, waiting to be transferred to the fitted cupboards of the new house.

She took down her hair, but it kinked unbecomingly where it had been drawn back into the chignon, so she put it up again. Lipstick and blusher only seemed to offset her corpse-like pallor, while eyeliner only emphasised eyes that were small and red-rimmed from too many sleepless nights.

'Oh God,' she said with a sob, 'I can't face him yet.'

She heard howls of mirth coming from the saloon and jumped in a frenzy of paranoia. Scrabbling round in her bag, she found a bottle of tranquillisers, swallowed one with a great slug of gin, and collapsed back onto the bunk.

It was nine years since she and Tod had first met and fallen in love. She'd been in her second year reading Law at Bristol University, and when she'd first taken Tod to stay with her parents in Bath they had been horrified. Tod not only had long hair and a beard, never wore a tie, and was no respecter of middle class values, but he had also chucked in a very good job in advertising to try and make the grade as a painter, and never having any money seemed always to be bumming off Kate. Kate hadn't minded the bumming at all, her parents gave her a generous allowance, and what was hers was Tod's as well. She knew he was the most generous person in the world when he was in funds, and she was convinced that one day he'd be a great painter. She didn't even mind that sometimes when he was painting he'd lose all sense of time, and turn up three hours late for a date, with only a few roses pinched from the Principal's precious garden as a peace offering.

What did finish her, however, once when she'd gone home alone for the weekend and returned a day early because she was missing him so desperately, was to have his studio door opened by a wanton-looking redhead wrapped in a green towel, and to find the redhead's clothes strewn all over the bed and the floor.

Kate had run sobbing from the flat. Tod had caught up with her in the park, wearing only a pair of jeans, his bare feet turning blue with cold on the frozen grass, and she remembered thinking how thin and underfed he looked without his shirt. Ashen-faced and trembling, they had faced each other.

'Stop it, Katie, stop crying,' he had pleaded with her. 'She doesn't mean a thing, I picked her up at a party last night, it's you that I love.'

'You can't love me,' she had screamed back, 'if the moment my back's turned, you go to bed with that . . .' She couldn't even get the words out.

'Look,' said Tod, grabbing her arms to prevent her bolting, 'I respect the fact that you don't want to sleep with anyone until you marry. I've never abused that, have I, *have I*,' he added, his fingers biting into her flesh so sharply that she winced. 'But I'm a very physical man, and I've got physical needs. I can't live like a monk. I love you, I'd do anything in the world to keep you, I'd marry you tomorrow, but we can't just live off your parents' allowance. Please try and understand.'

But she'd pulled away from him, racing through the starched leaves, out of the park. She had gone back home to Bath and, with the all-too-eager connivance of her parents, had refused ever to see him again, to speak to him on the telephone, or to answer any of his letters. Her parents, in fact, were so overjoyed that she'd finished with Tod, they didn't even mind when she completely ploughed her finals—they'd never thought a career was important for a girl—and had packed her off to South Africa for a year to recover.

For that year, she had moved through life like a sleep walker. Not a day passed without her dreaming about Tod, and longing for him. But she'd convinced herself, again heavily encouraged by her parents, that any kind of relationship with him would only bring unhappiness, because he was incapable of being faithful. Yet any man who pursued her—and there were plenty—seemed like waxworks when compared with Tod's blazing vitality.

Finally she gave up the struggle and came back to England, aware that she could no longer live without him, only to find he'd gone to live in America. Her parents made very sure that they never handed on his address out there, which he'd left behind for her.

Very carefully, she had put her heart in the deep freeze and concentrated on her career. She didn't have the will to work for her degree again, but she took a job, as a secretary to a firm of solicitors, where, with her legal knowledge and obvious intelligence, she soon made herself indispensable.

'The wonderful thing about Kate,' her boss was fond of saying smugly to the other partners, whose secretaries always took two-hour lunches and rushed off to the ladies loo clutching their floral sponge bags on the dot of five-fifteen, 'is that she never minds working late.'

Such was Kate's industry, that as the years passed her boss grew more and more successful, and was frequently able to employ Hugh Lancaster to defend his more well-heeled clients. A good-looking barrister, accustomed to success with women, Hugh had first been impressed by Kate's fragile, Snow Queen beauty, and then piqued by her complete indifference. He had laid seige: bombarding her with flowers, presents, and requests for dates, until she'd finally agreed to go out with him. After a few months, he had proposed, and she'd accepted, and he'd finally taken her to bed, and she had managed to conceal from him the fact that she had felt nothing.

Love will come, she told herself. I like and respect Hugh, my parents absolutely dote on him. I must just be patient. So she had thrown herself into plans for the wedding, filling the days and most of the nights with frenzied activity. But as the day approached, she was appalled to find herself thinking obsessively about Tod, wracked by erotic dreams of him by night and, by day, remembering the turmoil he had once reduced

196

her to, merely by kissing her. Now to crown it she was stuck on the boat with him for the whole weekend. She felt blind panic as though she were in a lift, trapped between floors in the middle of a bomb scare.

A knock on the door made her jump so hard, she banged her head on the bunk above. It was Hugh.

'Come on, darling, we're all ravenous. Jonty has raised the Chicken Supreme to such a point of perfection, he'll sulk if you keep him waiting any longer.'

'So sorry, I was dreaming,' said Kate.

'Only got fifteen days to go,' said Hugh smugly, 'and you won't need to dream anymore, you'll have the reality.'

'I'll be out in a sec,' said Kate.

As she stood up, she felt dizzy again. Without realising it, she'd finished her drink. She knew perfectly well one shouldn't mix gin and tranquillisers.

They were all sitting down at the table when she went into the saloon.

'Go on Jonty's right, next to Tod,' said Muriel, 'and have some wine, you're light years behind the rest of us.'

Kate slid onto the bench, watching Jonty carve the chicken, the sharp knife sliding through the breast.

'Hungry?' he asked her, putting two slices on her plate.

'N-not wildly,' she stammered. 'My boss treated me to lunch, so I stuffed myself midday.'

'Give her more than that,' said Muriel, as Jonty spooned mushrooms and a thick cream sauce over the chicken slices, 'the poor sweet needs feeding up. At least you won't rupture yourself carrying her over the threshold, Hugh darling.'

Sitting beside Tod, Kate was aware of his hands, with their long sunburnt fingers, spreading butter on a piece of brown bread. She still couldn't bring herself to look at him. Instead she glanced across the table at Georgie, who was certainly gorgeous. Her slanting, thickly-lashed eyes were the speckled yellow-green of a

197

William pear, and as she leant forward for the salt, the candlelight flickered on her warm, brown breasts and lovely, unlined throat. She was also gazing at Kate in fascination as if she was a priceless, centuries-old relic, unearthed on some archaeological dig. Could this faded, insipid creature really have been a girlfriend of Tod's? she seemed to be saying.

'We're all dying to hear how you and Tod know each other,' she asked. 'It must have been pretty traumatic for you to freak out like that. Did he interfere with you at Kindergarten or something? His story is you knew each other at Bristol.'

'We did,' said Kate, desperately trying to keep her voice steady. 'We went out for a bit.'

'Then she went off to South Africa,' said Tod lightly. 'And left me with a broken heart.'

'Must have been the only person who ever did,' said Muriel, shooting him a hot look.

'Was this the chap who made you fail your finals?' asked Hugh.

Kate blushed furiously. 'How did you know about that?'

'Your mother told me,' said Hugh. 'No potatoes, thanks Jonty.'

'He usually has that effect on women,' said Muriel. 'Girls committing suicide, or bolting into convents. I can never keep track of your sex life, Tod.'

'Makes two of us,' said Tod, helping himself to courgettes.

'Well, I don't intend to go into a convent, darling,' said Georgie, with a slight edge to her voice, 'I haven't got the right sort of cheekbones for a nun. This is absolutely marvellous chicken, Jonty.'

'Good,' said Jonty, filling up everyone's glasses. 'You're all being guinea pigs this weekend, I'm trying out all the recipes I'm doing for my next television series.'

'Can you cook?' said Georgie, sliding her speckled green eyes towards Hugh.

'Only basics,' said Hugh, 'I like to leave you girls to do kitchen things.'

'You're a male chauvinist guinea pig then,' said Georgie, giving him the full benefit of a smouldering glance, and deepening her cleavage by ramming her left arm against her left breast.

Hugh, for some reason, seemed to find this remark extremely funny. 'Don't tell me you're one of these feminists,' he said, smoothing his already smooth hair.

'Not at all,' replied Georgie, 'I just wish I could find a husband like Jonty, who realises the way to a woman's heart is through her stomach.'

'I've always thought it was a bit lower down,' said Muriel with a hyena cackle. 'Jonty's not very romantic, Georgie,' she went on, 'he's much more likely to quote Marika Hanbury Tennyson at one than Lord Alfred.'

'Lord who?' said Georgie, 'I don't like Lords. I had one once, and he kept wanting me to whip him. Now come on, Jonty, tell me how you make this. Then I can impress Tod's mother when she comes to London.'

'Well,' said Jonty, his blood-shot eyes sparkling, 'first you cook the salt pork and the bouquet garni in water for one hour . . .'

Hugh started talking to Muriel about mutual acquaintances who were coming to the wedding. 'Three Law Lords have definitely accepted,' he said, 'which is very gratifying.'

Tod turned to Kate. 'When are you getting married?'

'Tomorrow fortnight.'

'What time?'

'Three o'clock.'

'Hope you don't have an empty church—everyone'll be listening to the Oaks on their car radios.'

'Not my family,' said Kate. 'They're not very keen on racing.'

'Ah yes, I remember,' said Tod with a faint smile, 'Redwood Rover.'

Kate went crimson. Nine years ago Tod had been so convinced Redwood Rover was going to win the Cambridgeshire, he had persuaded Kate to pawn her pearls and lend him fifty pounds. Unfortunately, Redwood Rover had bucked his jockey off onto the rails just before the race. A few days later Kate's mother, nosing about in Kate's room, no doubt looking for incriminating evidence of her relationship with Tod, had discovered the pawn ticket in her diary, whereupon all hell had broken loose.

There was a long, agonising pause.

'Did you enjoy America?' Kate asked him. Oh, why did her voice sound as though she'd had injections for fillings on both sides of her face?

'Yeah, I did, it helped me commercially, too. Once I got established there, they started taking an interest in me over here.'

She still couldn't meet his eyes, but staring fixedly at the blond hairs on his arms, she had to fight an irresistible desire to touch them. Instead she said, 'What are you working on at the moment?'

'Well, I've just finished a mural in the new cathedral at Westmarton, and I'm getting together some pictures for an exhibition in Cork Street in September, then taking it over to Paris, and probably to New York in the spring.'

He spoke in his usual lazy, slightly husky drawl, but there was a steel tip to his voice. I've made it, he seemed to be saying, even though you and your family kicked me in the teeth.

'And Tod's going to do a bus too,' said Georgie, interrupting poor Jonty in mid-flow about how finely one must chop the fresh tarragon. 'Did you hear that, Muriel?' she went on, shouting down the table, interrupting Hugh in mid-flow about the vintage of the wine they were drinking, 'Tod's been commissioned by the Gas Board to paint a bus for their late summer advertising campaign.'

Muriel smiled warmly into Tod's eyes. 'But that's wonderful, darling, what are you going to do?'

'Purring cats and rosy-cheeked brats warming themselves in front of roaring gas fires, I suppose,' said Tod, 'I can't imagine I'll be allowed to be very *outré*.'

'But lots of lovely lolly,' said Muriel.

Tod was drawn into conversation with her and Hugh now, and Jonty, undaunted, was back on course with the Chicken Supreme:

'You heat a small pan, put in the oil, and add the diced vegetables . . .'

For a minute, Kate was free to study Tod. Since they had last met he had shaved off his beard and moustache, so one could now appreciate the lean, suntanned planes of his face and the curves of the well shaped mouth. The straight, light-brown hair was shorter too, just curling over the collar of his grey denim shirt, which matched the stormy grey of those disturbingly direct eyes. He had also filled out—obviously no longer the starving artist. He looked, in fact, as though he'd lived every day and most nights since he'd split up from Kate, to the full. He was no longer a beautiful, sensitive, romantic boy—the disciple whom Jesus loved—but a weathered, confident, overwhelmingly attractive man. As if aware of her scrutiny, he turned towards her. Immediately Kate dropped her eyes.

'How's the fishwife of Bath?' he asked. 'Frightfully excited about becoming the mother-in-law of an imminent Q.C. I should think.'

'Who's that?' said Hugh, putting his knife and fork together.

'I was just asking after your future mother-in-law,' said Tod.

'Oh, Elizabeth's a super person, isn't she,' said Hugh enthusiastically. 'And a very good bridge player too. I'm awfully fond of Henry as well, we get in a round of golf whenever possible. I couldn't be more fortunate in my in-laws,' he said, gallantly raising his glass to Kate.

'They must have changed,' said Tod flatly.

As he leaned over to fill up Georgie's glass, his arm brushed Kate, who jumped away as though she'd touched a live wire.

'You on the other hand haven't changed at all,' he said under his breath so only she could hear. 'Still the same eternally shrinking violet.'

Kate bit her lip.

'Anyone want a second helping?' said Jonty.

'Kate hasn't touched her first,' said Muriel accusingly.

Kate looked down at her plate with its congealing cream, shiny black mushrooms, and drying slices of chicken breast. She felt the sweat rising on her forehead and knew she'd be sick if she tried to eat anymore. 'I'm terribly sorry, Jonty, it was so delicious, I can't think why I'm not hungry.'

'I'll have it,' said Tod, forking up the two pieces of chicken, 'you've excelled yourself as usual, Jonty.'

Georgie cut a slice off one of the new potatoes she'd reluctantly shoved to the side of her plate. 'I can't think why you don't get fat, Tod, you never take any exercise.'

'He does,' said Muriel, looking at Kate.

'Sex doesn't count,' said Georgie, with a predatory smirk, 'I wish you'd come out jogging with me.'

'Jogging,' said Tod, 'is a totally barbaric pastime. If I'm out of doors, I like to look at things, not charge around giving heart attacks to all the local livestock.'

'I jog every morning,' said Hugh, as though that settled the matter.

'I can see you do,' said Georgie, admiringly. 'You look in really great shape. I'll come out with you tomorrow, if I wake up in time.'

'Splendid,' said Hugh, pulling in his stomach, 'I wish Kate would join us.'

'Give the poor girl a chance,' said Muriel, 'she looks shattered.'

'Perhaps you'll feel more like it, darling, once you've packed in your job,' said Hugh.

'Are you giving up work?' said Georgie enviously.

'Of course not,' said Hugh, briskly answering for Kate. 'She's going to have a full time job at home looking after me. I'm not keen on career wives, I'm sure it's the reason so many marriages break up.'

'What about Jonty and I, both slaving away?' said Muriel, indignantly.

'You two,' said Hugh, raising his glass to Muriel, 'are a delightful exception, but no-one could deny, Muriel my dear, that you have an exceptionally well-trained husband.'

'Roll out the reversal,' said Jonty gathering up the plates. 'Who'd like some strawberries? I've marinated them in *Framboise*.'

'Me, please,' said Georgie, 'I can't resist them, such an aphrodisiac. Do you remember the dramatic effect they had on me in Paris, Tod?'

Kate suddenly thought she was going to faint again. She got to her feet, unsteadily clinging onto the table.

'I promise I'll rush round and cook, and wash up tomorrow, Jonty,' she said, 'but do you mind terribly if I go to bed?'

'Course not,' said Muriel. 'Are you feeling poorly?'

'Bit tired,' Kate muttered.

'Mind you sleep in in the morning,' said Jonty.

'I'll come and tuck you up in a minute,' said Hugh playfully, 'and no reading in bed.'

'We have to go through your cabin to get to bed,' said Georgie, 'so don't get panicky and think Tod's groping for you if he suddenly comes lurching through at two o'clock in the morning.'

Only for the second time that evening Kate looked sraight into Tod's eyes.

'Don't worry,' he said, 'I'm far too ethical to try and gazump a house that's already been sold.'

He hates me, he absolutely hates me, was all Kate could think as she undressed. She was so distraught she took a couple of sleeping pills. She knew it was dangerous on top of drink and tranquillisers, but all she wanted now was oblivion. Then in total despair she fell on her knees, burying her face in the plaid rug which smelt of suntan oil, sobbing, 'Please, please help me God, I don't know what to do.'

When Hugh came to say goodnight ten minutes later, he found her fast asleep on the floor. She didn't even stir when he lifted her up and tucked her into bed.

Kate closed her eyes again and buried her face in the pillow, excluding the squawk of ducks from the river outside, and the sunlight seeping through the drawn curtains. Her head felt like a rugger ball after a Twickenham international. All she wanted to do was to go back to sleep for a month—and then, blissful thought, she'd miss the wedding. Stop it, she told herself furiously, how could she let poor Hugh down and her parents, and what about all the relations who were coming from all over the country in anticipation of two hundred bottles of Moet et Chandon and a family get-together, and the dressmaker who'd laboured so long and lovingly over her wedding dress, and worst of all her mother who trailed the length and breadth of Bond Street and Knightsbridge to find a pair of coral shoes to match exactly her David Schilling hat.

It was too late to stop the carnival. In order not to be "an old maid" as her mother so charmingly put it, and miss the boat, Kate had burned all her boats. At this moment, Tod was probably lying fast asleep in Georgie's arms after a night of heavy passion. I hope she gets pins and needles, thought Kate, groaning and pulling the pillow over her head. Through a daze of misery and longing, she could hear the clatter of washing up and the whoosh of the shower. Gingerly she peered into the bunk above, and was shocked at the relief she felt that it was empty. Hugh must have gone out jogging.

She pulled back the curtain, and winced as the sunlight charged in. Outside she could see a tangle of emerald green weeds and a mane of yellow king-cups tossing above and below the dark level of the water. It was already very hot. She winced even more at her reflection in the mirror: deathly pale, eyelids puffy and

204

red from enforced sleep, awful lank hair with a faint powdering of scurf on the middle parting. She must wash it at once.

In the galley she found Hugh, red faced and sleeked down from the shower after jogging, and exuding all the self-satisfaction of someone just returned from Early Service. He paused from reading the *Times* law reports to give her a perfunctory kiss on the cheek. Jonty was scraping new potatoes, and Muriel, looking splendidly mahogany, if slightly wrinkled round the stomach in a white bikini, was trimming the muddy ends off the asparagus. They all expressed such hearty pleasure that Kate had had such a long and wonderful night's sleep, that she started feeling guilty that they hadn't enjoyed a similar benefit.

'Let me do something,' she said.

'You are not going to lift a finger, darling,' said Muriel. 'We're all worried about you, I'm determined to send you back to London feeling really rested. Here's some coffee,' she handed one big olive green cup to Kate, and another to Hugh, who put down the *Times* with satisfaction.

'They've written three-quarters of a column on the case I defended yesterday,' he told Kate.

'Did they quote you?'

'Several times, which is gratifying.'

'How lovely, let me look.'

He handed her the paper. 'There: Burnham-Watts v The Inland Revenue.'

It was a very boring case, in which Hugh seemed to have routed the income tax people single-handed.

'I must stop at the next lock,' he said putting saccharine into his coffee, 'and see if I can get a *Telegraph*. They're bound to have reported it in more detail. When are we moving on, Jonty?'

'As soon as Tod's finished his picture. He got up at six to catch the light, says he'll be through by lunch-time.'

'Is he any good?' said Hugh.

'Oh very, I think,' said Muriel. 'In fact, if you've got a

spare grand, it would be well worth buying one of his paintings now. They're bound to rocket in value over the next few years.'

'We bought four a year ago,' said Jonty, running water over the scraped potatoes. 'We reckon we're sitting on a gold mine.'

'That's worth knowing,' said Hugh. 'My rich uncle wanted to buy us a painting as a wedding present. If it's going to be a good investment, we must steer him in Tod's direction.'

Burnham-Watts v The Inland Revenue swum before Kate's eyes. Stop discussing Tod like an issue of Unit Trusts, she thought furiously. But all she said as she handed the paper back to Hugh was, 'That's terrific, well done. You must be thrilled. Can I possibly wash my hair, Muriel?'

'Well, you could have done,' said Jonty, irritably turning the sink tap which only yielded a couple of drips, 'but that glamour pants girlfriend of Tod's seems to have used all the water. What the hell am I going to cook lunch with?'

'We can take on more water at the next lock and have the asparagus tonight,' said Muriel soothingly. 'And honestly, Kate darling, don't worry about your hair, it looks fine. Dark people are so lucky, dirty hair never shows on them.'

'Why don't you change into your bikini and get some sun?' said Hugh.

Kate felt she would like to have taken Georgie's laburnum yellow locks, like Porphyrio's lover, and wound them round her throat and strangled her.

As there was no water to wash with, Kate had to make do with cleansing cream and scraping a flannel over her body. She had to go on shore, too, to go to the loo, and stung her bottom on some nettles. When she finally got into her bikini, she found the tiny deck at the back of the boat was a mass of naked flesh. In fact, it was mostly Georgie, topless and virtually bottomless except for two tiny triangles of leopard skin. She had plugged her hairdryer on an extra lead into a power point in the saloon, and was drying her gleaming mane. Her magnificent, heavily-oiled breasts quivered with each sweep of the brush. My boobs were once as good as that, though Kate enviously. Hugh, in blue bathing trunks, binoculars round his neck for bird watching, lay a couple of feet away from Georgie doing the *Times* crossword and smoking his pipe. His solid English figure, slightly pear-shaped but kept in trim by exercise and rigorous self-control, was already turning red.

But not all the jogging in the world could ever have achieved the taut angular grace of Tod's body, with its broad brown shoulders, narrowing to lean hips, above long, long legs. He was wearing only a pair of faded blue jeans, sawn off above the knee and covered with paint. With a canvas perched on the bench seat and propped against the side of the boat, he was painting the hayfield on the opposite bank, catching the light, as the long grass turned in the warm breeze like an animal's fur. Only a dark line of beech trees on the brow of the hill divided the hay from a white hot sky above.

'It's beautiful,' breathed Kate.

Tod turned, nodded without smiling, and went back to work.

'You *do* look better. That sleep must have done you all the good in the world,' shouted Georgie above the whirr of the hairdryer.

Kate settled down between Hugh and the other side of the boat, as far away from Tod as possible, horribly aware of how unfavourably she must compare with Georgie. She hadn't seen the sun all summer. Her unpainted toe nails were slightly yellow, and she'd missed part of her leg while shaving it late on Thursday night, so black hairs sprouted above her left ankle like a little copse in the snow. At least my shoulders are so white, she thought gloomily, that any falling scurf won't show up. She settled down to her letters.

'*Dearest Vanessa*,' she wrote to one of her bridesmaids, *'so sorry you don't think the hyacinth blue suits you as well as it does Cressida.'*

Georgie was now reaching round to dry the hair at the back of the head which always stays wet longest. Her breasts rose dramatically. Hugh, Kate noticed with a wry, inward smile, was not making much progress with the *Times* crossword, he had only done two clues. Soon Muriel joined them, squashing them even more than ever. She, too, was writing a letter.

'Where's Jonty?' asked Georgie.

'Oh, getting Robert Carriered away in the galley,' said Muriel, then lowering her voice asked, 'How does one say "I'm missing you desperately" in Italian, Hugh?'

'Ti amo stupidissimo,' rattled off Hugh.

'How wonderful,' sighed Georgie, turning off her hairdryer, 'I wish I could speak languages like you.'

'I'm sure if you wear a slightly pinkier lipstick, the blue will look marvellous,' wrote Kate. God, what rubbish, she thought.

'Look, there's a blue tit,' said Hugh.

'Makes a nice change from brown,' muttered Kate under her breath.

'Where, where?' squeaked Georgie.

'Just above the meadow sweet,' said Hugh, handing Georgie his binoculars, which were still round his neck.

'I can't see,' wailed Georgie.

'To the right,' said Hugh. As she moved the binoculars, she pulled him towards her, until his shoulder was brushed against her left breast.

'Oh there it is, the little darling!' she screamed, jumping up and down with excitement. 'Isn't it sweet.'

'You're going red, Hugh,' said Muriel pointedly.

'Let me oil you,' said Georgie.

'I'm fine,' said Hugh, lying down very hurriedly.

Looking up, Kate noticed his bathing trunks were standing up like a steeple. Involuntarily, she glanced at Tod, and saw he was staring in the same direction. Then he looked up, and caught her eye and laughed. For a second she felt her face flooded with crimson, then she buried herself in her letter. What appalled her most of all was that she wasn't more upset at Hugh lusting after Georgie.

Georgie kept plaguing her with questions about the wedding. 'Are you wearing white?' she asked.

'Yes,' Kate said.

'Symbol of virginity,' said Tod, adding indigo shadows to the dark green line of the beeches. 'I would have thought you were rather old at twenty-nine, Katie, to flaunt such lack of experience.'

Kate bit her lip. That was below the belt.

'You don't look twenty-nine,' said Georgie with more kindness than conviction, applying extra oil to her shoulders.

'Where are you going for your honeymoon?' asked Muriel.

'Greece,' said Kate.

'Why are they called honeymoons?' asked Georgie.

'Because they're usually extremely sticky,' said Tod.

'Ours won't be,' said Hugh heartily, joining in the general laughter.

'Anyone for drinks?' said Jonty, appearing red-faced in the doorway, with a drying-up cloth over his shoulder.

'I'd like some of that Bollinger,' said Muriel, automatically laying her arm over her letter.

'Me too,' said Georgie.

'That would suit us nicely too,' said Hugh, sounding like an American Express ad. He seemed to have regained his composure and his flat bathing trunks.

'What about you, Tod?' asked Jonty.

Tod, who was gazing abstractedly from the landscape to his painting, didn't answer.

'To-odd,' said Georgie, 'I've never known you refuse a drink.'

'Oh sorry, whisky and lots of water please, Jonty.'

'There *is* no water,' said Jonty petulantly. 'It's all been used up. You'll have to have soda, Tod, and you'll all have to make do with kipper pâté, quiche and salad for lunch.'

'That'll be lovely,' said Georgie, quite oblivious of the malevolent look Jonty was shooting in her direction.

'Who are you writing to?' he asked Muriel, who was putting her letter into an envelope.

'The G.P.O. They sent us a final reminder,' said Muriel blandly. She got to her feet. 'I'll come and help you with drinks.'

'I'm sure she wasn't writing to the G.P.O.,' Georgie hissed to Hugh, the moment Muriel and Jonty were out of earshot. 'She wouldn't be missing them terribly.'

'She would if they'd cut her telephone off,' said Tod.

Georgie laughed. 'Perhaps she's having an affair with some gorgeous Italian count. How romantic. Do you know,' she added to Hugh, 'she told me she's taped Jonty's snoring, and she's going to play it back to him next time they have a row.'

'Suffering from seventeen-year itch, if you ask me,' said Tod, rummaging around for a tube of Cobalt. 'I wonder if Jonty has extra-Muriel affaires.'

'Shouldn't imagine so,' said Hugh knocking his pipe out briskly on the side of the boat, and obviously disapproving of the tenor of the conversation.

'It's so depressing, when you think of all the married couples who are two-timing each other,' sighed Georgie.

'Oh I don't know,' said Tod, unscrewing the tube of Cobalt, 'I've always thought that complete dishonesty between couples was the most important thing in marriage. Don't you agree, Katie?'

Kate looked up. Her heart sank. She saw nothing but comtempt and hostility in his face.

The day steadily deteriorated. Lunch was a nightmare. Everyone drank too much. Kate sat opposite Tod, and every so often caught him looking at her incredulously, as though wondering what he'd ever ·seen in her. Hugh, to Muriel's delight, was plainly very taken with Georgie. He kept crinkling up his eyes, and didn't even put on his spectacles to eat the kipper pâté, which was

210

most unusual as he was absolutely pathological about fishbones.

While Jonty was telling Kate in detail how to perfect Sole Véronique, Kate overheard Hugh say in a low voice to Georgie, 'I couldn't possibly marry a glamour puss like you, I'd find you far too distracting. I'd never get to work in the morning.'

In between such leaden pleasantries, he was also extremely pompous about politics. Tod didn't bother to disagree with him, but Kate was aware of the two men disliking each other more and more.

After lunch, Tod put the finishing touches to his painting, Jonty and Hugh fiddled with the engine, and Georgie and Kate stacked up the washing-up in the kitchen, ready for more water at the next lock.

'It seems extraordinary,' said Georgie scraping crusts into the muck bucket, 'that both of us should have been girlfriends of Tod. I mean, we couldn't be more different. I expect he liked your mind, he said you used to be very clever.'

'Very kind of him,' snapped Kate. She didn't want to discuss Tod.

'I don't know how you could bear to give him up,' persisted Georgie.

'It was Lent, and the habit stuck,' said Kate.

'But I never met anyone who tired of Tod, before he tired of them. What makes him so irresistible, I suppose, is you know you'll never have the edge over him, because he's so much more hooked on painting than anything else. Some days he's so loving, others he hardly knows I exist. When he was painting that mural in Westmarton Cathedral, he didn't come home one night. I went bananas, I was sure he was with another girl. Then I went down to the cathedral, and found him still up a ladder slapping on paint at two o'clock in the morning, with the verger fast asleep in a pew. I'd have been petrified of ghosts.'

'That's lovely, darling,' said Muriel, coming into the galley followed by Hugh. 'Tod wants just a bit longer, so we'll start up the boat in three-quarters of an hour. Jonty and I are going for a walk.'

'I'm going to sunbathe,' said Georgie.

'Had too much sun this morning,' said Hugh, touching his shoulders gingerly, 'I'm going to have a kip. You better have one too, darling,' he added.

'I'm not tired,' said Kate quickly.

'Don't lie,' said Muriel. 'You've gone white as a sheet again.'

Hugh's fingers closed round her wrist like irons.

'Come on, time for bed.'

'That's right,' said Muriel, getting the usual *double entendre* into her voice. 'But *mind* it is a rest, we'll hang a do-not-disturb sign on your door handle.'

The moment Hugh closed the cabin door behind them, he was on her like a great octopus; breathing heavily, obviously turned on by Georgie. Kate couldn't bear it.

'Someone might come through,' she muttered.

'Don't be silly,' said Hugh, ripping off her bikini top. 'Everyone knows exactly what we're up to.'

'Not now,' she said, close to tears.

'I'm fed up with all this resistance,' he snarled, pushing her back onto the bottom bunk. 'What you need, my angel, is a good screw.'

In the end he forced her, the veins standing out on his forehead, the sickly smile of passion blurring the shrewd, distinguished lawyer's features, with Kate as dry and unyielding inside as the shell of a Scotch egg. The whole coupling was a disaster.

Afterwards she lay beside him, unable to speak with the horror of it, tears coursing into her lank hair.

'You'd better sort yourself out by Saturday week,' he had blustered furiously. 'I've had enough of this ridiculously uptight behaviour.' Then turning the knife for the prosecution, 'Why the hell don't you take a leaf out of Georgie's book.'

He had barged out of the cabin, and next minute she heard him plunge into the river to cool off. She would have given anything to get off the boat and run away through the hayfields, but she couldn't bear to drag herself away from Tod, before she'd had a few minutes to talk to him alone. She lay there listening to the boat starting up, and people clambering over the roof to avoid waking her. Soon they reached the lock, and the dark green slimy wall darkened the cabin window. As the water gushed in, and the *Virgin Queen* rose to the level of the next lock, she saw Muriel coming back, glowing with illicit excitement from posting her letter, and Georgie running round a green meadow, picking buttercups with shrieks of joy. At last they moved on. She knew she ought to drag herself up and help with the washing-up, but she couldn't face another heart to heart with Georgie.

The *Virgin Queen* sailed towards evening through clear khaki waters, low fields and occasional clumps of alders.

Kate went on deck to finish her letters. Everyone was up the other end. Georgie, at the wheel, egged on by Hugh, kept nearly driving the boat into the bank amid shrieks of laughter. They sailed into a series of oxbow bends, which seemed to turn the landscape about the boat like a kaleidoscope. A spire advanced and retreated, the water darkened with the changing sky. Along the banks, water rats, voles and insects were coming out for the night. A dragonfly shot by in a flash of peacock blue. A company of ducks in close formation paddled past. Midges hovered above the deck. Gradually the envelopes piled up beside Kate.

She was vaguely aware of more shouts of mirth from the galley. Then a shadow fell across her page. It was Tod. He handed her a gin and tonic and went over to the other side of the boat, standing with his back to her, absorbed for a minute in the rays of the setting sun, which were gilding the silver willows on the opposite bank. Then he came back and sat down beside her, picking up the envelopes and glancing at the addresses.

'Lord that, Sir Charles and Lady this, Lord Chief Justice that,' he said. 'Are these your friends?'

'Mostly Hugh's.'

'Hugh and non-Hugh.'

Her laugh came out too shrilly.

'Bloody midges,' she said, slapping a grey insect who was feasting on her right ankle.

'Let them eat Kate,' said Tod, lighting a cigarette.

There was a pause.

'You look well,' she said. 'And how's your mother, is she still living in Somerset? I saw a photograph of your sister's wedding in *The Tatler* about two years ago, she looked awfully pretty. Is he a nice man she married, he looked super. I thought you might have come back for the wedding.' Her voice petered out miserably. There was another long silence. Her heart started to thump uncomfortably, she was having trouble breathing. 'Anyway,' she babbled on, frantically pleating the tails of her shirt, 'you seem to have got awfully famous since I last knew you. Have you got any exciting commissions coming up?'

'You asked me that last night,' said Tod curtly, 'and obviously didn't listen to the answer, and you're rattling like a burglar alarm.'

Because someone's just broken into me, Kate was tempted to say, and just stopped herself bursting into hysterical laughter. She took a gulp of her drink and choked. 'Goodness, you always made drinks too strong.'

The boat entered an avenue of weeping willows trailing their long green tresses in the water.

'They remind me of Georgie,' she said, looking at the bank. 'She's *so* beautiful, Tod.'

'I can't say the same for you,' said Tod bluntly. 'You look terrible. When did you go grey?'

'Grey! I haven't!'

'Look,' he picked up a strand of her hair.

'That's not grey, that's paint, I was painting the kitchen ceiling.' She started to laugh, and this time she couldn't stop.

Tod didn't laugh, he just stood looking down at her.

'You're in a mess, Katie.'

He leant over the side, and picked a white swan's feather out of the water. For a second, it lay in his palm, across the strongly marked heart and head lines. Then he gave it to her. 'That's for marrying Hugh.'

Kate gasped, and shrank away. The white feather, symbol of cowardice—it fluttered onto the deck.

'You're running away from life,' he said.

'I suppose you despise me for not marrying a sex maniac, like you.'

'I despise you for marrying someone you don't give a damn about because you're so terrified of being left on the shelf.'

'How d'you know I don't love him?' hissed Kate.

'You wouldn't have come down this weekend, looking like a road accident, not even bothering to wash your hair, slopping about in Oxfam rejects. You're all shrivelled up,' he went on brutally, 'like a plant that's dying from lack of water. Looking at you now, I wonder what the hell I ever saw in you.'

She drew back as though he'd hit her. 'Have you finished?' she said in a frozen voice.

'No I have not. You're selling out, Katie, to bridge parties, and committees and trivia, which won't mean a thing to you because you don't love him—and he doesn't love you either. He wouldn't be drooling over Georgie if he was getting his fun in the sack with you. But that was never your speciality, was it. I expect you're playing the same game as you did with me. What Katie did to Tod from a great height, and you didn't even provide a safety net.' He began to pace the deck.

Kate stood up, her trembling legs hardly holding her. 'I won't listen to another word.'

But Tod had seized her by the arms, and swung her round to face the bank. 'Do you know what building that is?'

Beyond a hayfield and quivering row of poplars were the russet ruins of an ancient church.

'That's Willingdon Priory,' said Tod. 'Nuns used to live there, but they were chucked out in the fourteenth century, for having men in and indulging in lewd behaviour. You can't suppress your sexual urges completely, Katie, you'll turn into a warped old bitch. And if you don't, he'll break you anyway—like a butterfly crushed in the waste disposal. Beneath all that bonhomie, he's an absolute shit. In a fortnight's time, you'll be married to him. The bride was dressed in a tissue of lies—my God!'

Kate tore herself away and fled to the cabin, throwing herself face down on the bed, shocked and moaning with horror. After a minute or two she scrambled to her feet, and looked in the mirror. Was she really as ugly as he said? The face that stared back, stricken and dry-eyed, seemed that of an old woman. She rushed to the loo. The smell of stale urine overwhelmed her, and she was violently sick, retching on and on, until it seemed her guts were being tugged inside out. A terrible headache took hold of her, her bones seemed to be slowly crushing her brain, and she clutched her temples in agony.

Someone banged on the door. 'Are you all right?' It was Hugh.

She couldn't bring herself to answer.

He rattled the door handle violently. 'Kate, say something.'

She opened the door, collapsing into his arms.

'What's the matter?' he said in concern.

'Migraine,' she said through gritted teeth.

He practically carried her into the cabin, and for the second night running put her to bed.

'Poor darling,' he said, obviously feeling guilty for forcing her to have sex earlier. 'You must have had too much sun. Shall I get you a doctor?' he went on, putting a sweating hand on her forehead.

She shook her head weakly. 'It'll go—if I keep still.'

She spent the rest of the evening dozing and being sick. Every so often Muriel or Hugh or Georgie put a conscience-stricken face round the door, and asked her if she needed anything. Occasionally there was a howl of mirth which was instantly hushed. Once Jonty started singing a rugger song, and was told to shut up. She knew they were relieved to be without her, and that she was casting a blight over their weekend, but felt too miserable, too ill, and too shattered to care.

Hours later, when it seemed that at last the pain in her head was beginning to recede, but not the pain in her heart, she heard them all coming to bed.

'Kate,' whispered Hugh. When she didn't answer, he pulled the sheet over her shoulders, kissed her on the forehead, and got into the creaking bunk above. Soon his breathing became a slight snore. She thought of Muriel with her tape-recorder, and wondered if that was all marriage was: an endless game of leaping to grasp the upper hand.

Soon the snoring was so loud, it seemed to rip the stuffy cabin apart. She got up and shakily crept through the saloon, where both Muriel and Jonty seemed to be snoring too, and out onto the deck. She felt dizzy and utterly exhausted.

The drained turquoise sky, full of stars, was already lightening on the horizon. Swathes of mist lay across the hayfields. The elders held up their white flowers, like lace mats, to the night. Kate sat down, breathing in their strange, acrid smell. Then remembering the sheer hopelessness of her situation, she put her face in her hands and wept. Suddenly she felt a hand on her shoulder, and nearly jumped out of her skin. A cigarette glowed in the half-light. It was Tod.

'I'm sorry, Katie,' he whispered. 'I shouldn't have given you that feather this afternoon. It was thoughtless and cruel, but I can't bear to see how much you've changed. You used to be so warm and tender and shining and beautiful.'

'And now I'm not,' sobbed Kate.

'No you're not,' he said gently. 'You remind me of a toy who's been overwound, and suddenly all the machinery gushes out, and it comes to a shuddering halt. You're on the verge of a complete crack-up. Now stop crying and listen to me.'

'I've listened to you quite enough,' said Kate with a gulp, but she stopped crying.

'You're keeping yourself busy,' he said, sitting down beside her and taking her hand, 'the way I kept myself busy after you dropped me.'

Kate caught her breath.

'Painting, painting, painting,' he went on, 'to fill up every minute of the day and night.'

'Did it affect you so much?' she whispered.

'You never considered that, did you,' he said, letting her hands drop. 'Some of the suffering went into those paintings, they were the best things I've ever done. Through losing you I grew up. I suppose I should be grateful. But now you're doing the same thing: working, working and working so you don't have time to stop and think what it'll be like once you're married. You're going to have to share his bed every night, not just endure the occasional shuffle you can walk away from, and listen to him clearing his throat and sucking on his revolting pipe, and pontificating on and on with his stupid views, and giving endless dinner parties for his frightful friends.'

'You're back on form,' said Kate her voice rising. 'Sweeney Tod, character assassinator. Hugh is, I might tell you, regarded as a considerable catch.'

'Hush,' said Tod softly, 'don't wake the whole boat.'

He put a hand on her shoulder, and she had to fight an overwhelming temptation to turn her head and kiss it.

'Break it off,' he said. 'Please, you must.'

She took a deep breath. Tod must feel something to go on haranguing her like this. 'You don't think that you and I—could perhaps try again—I mean we used to . . .' her voice petered out miserably.

'No, I don't,' said Tod far too quickly to give her even a flicker of hope. 'You and I are caput. For ten years, I've carried this idealised picture of you round in my head. I've even still got a torn photograph of you in my wallet. It's been stuck together so often with sellotape, there's hardly any picture left. The only

218

reason I came down this weekend was because Muriel said you and Hugh were coming. Any time up to yesterday evening, if someone had said Katie'll take you back, I'd have dropped everything. But now I realise, sadly, it's all over. Scratch the bark, and you won't find a trace of green underneath.'

She wanted to hurl herself into his arms, and tell him she could become beautiful, desirable, and happy once more, if only he would love her.

'But even if there's nothing between us,' he went on, lighting one cigarette from another, 'I still care for you. Christ, twenty-nine's nothing. Think of all the marriages that break up between people much older than you, and they find other people. You've years ahead in which to look for a man who'll really love you and look after you.'

'It would kill my parents.'

'Nothing but a direct hit from the nitrogen bomb would kill your mother. I suppose she's worried sick about being a grandchildless couple.'

'Well, that too,' admitted Kate. 'But they adore Hugh and I've given up my job and my flat.'

'Doesn't matter. I'll find you a job. I've got lots of mates in America, they'll fiddle you a work permit out there. If your parents chuck you out, you can come and stay with me until you get yourself together.'

'With you and Georgie?' she asked in a tight little voice.

'Sure—me and Georgie.'

'Will you marry her?'

'I might. She's decorative enough. I'd like some kids. But I seem to have lost the ability to feel very deeply about anyone anymore.'

Kate lost her temper. 'Practise what you preach,' she howled at him. 'You shouldn't marry someone unless you are crazy about them either—and you shouldn't be so flaming smug. How dare you dictate my life to me. I'll marry Hugh, and I'll make a go of it, and I bet I'm a bloody sight happier than you are.'

She stumbled down the steps and into her cabin, and

lay there shivering violently, as gradually fury gave way to utter despair. She would have liked to creep into bed with Hugh for some warmth and reassurance, but the fact that she knew he could give her none, only brought home the hopeless emptiness of their relationship. As dawn broke, and the river started waking up, her only thought was how to escape from the boat.

'Where are we?' Kate asked Muriel casually, as they washed up after breakfast.

Muriel looked out of the window at the acid green bank of fading cowparsley.

'About a mile from Crickfold Lock,' she said. 'We're going to moor just the other side of it, and have a drink with some friends called Peplow at midday, then we'll turn round after lunch, and head back to the cars.'

'I seem to have lost all sense of direction,' said Kate, even more casually. 'Where's the nearest town?'

'Great Molesforth,' said Muriel. 'It's about six miles from Crickfold Lock. Nice little market town, with a lovely Norman church. I've got some very agreeable clients there. If it weren't so far from the river we could have taken a drink off them. Little forks go in there, darling.'

Kate suddenly felt bitterly ashamed for being such a lousy guest. 'Thank you so much for having me to stay,' she said. 'You and Jonty have been so sweet.'

'Why don't the two of you stay on another day and enjoy the double bunk?' said Muriel. 'I tried to persuade Tod and Georgie, but he's got to get back to start work on his Gas Board bus.'

Hugh frowned when Kate said she didn't want to go to the Peplows. 'Have you given up altogether?' he snapped.

'I'm still a bit weak after yesterday.'

'I hope you don't mind if I go,' said Hugh, shoving tobacco down in the bowl of his pipe with a matchstick. 'Clarissa Peplow is Vera Talbot-Lacey's sister, and *he's* a judge.'

'And a good judge too,' said Kate. 'Of course you must go.'

220

'I do hope,' he added sucking at his pipe, 'that you'll behave in a more supportive fashion after we're married.'

Jonty wandered over to them, buttoning up a clean, pale blue shirt. 'I've just put the sea trout in the oven, Kate dear. Could you bear to take it out on the dot of half-past one. It's a new way of cooking it, which I think you'll all like. You just add chopped fennel, and very finely chopped garlic and then you . . .'

'That's enough, darling,' interrupted Muriel, coming out of the galley looking very nautical in a white sailor suit. 'If you take poor Kate through every fishbone we'll never get to the Peplows. And after last night I for one need a whole fur coat of the dog that bit me.'

At long last they went ashore. Kate, who was dying of impatience, could hear Georgie's shrieks as she nearly fell into the river. Gradually the voices and the laughter receded up the hill. She rushed down to the cabin, and started throwing things into her case. She was just getting out of her bikini, when she heard a step. Frantically tugging on her shirt, she kicked the half-packed suitcase under the bed—and only just in time. Tod stood in the doorway. Yesterday's sun had bleached and streaked his hair and darkened his skin to burnt Sienna. He looked like a Californian beach boy. They had not spoken since last night.

'Aren't you coming?' he said.

'No I'm not. I'm fed up with judges—and with flash, swollen-headed painters, too, for that matter,' she snapped. 'Why don't you run along like a bad boy and devastate Mrs. Peplow?'

For a second, they glared at each other, then he grinned and said, 'All right, I will.'

Out of the cabin window, she watched him walking up the hill, with the graceful, loping athletic stride that she had always found so attractive in the old days. 'Don't go,' she wanted to call out to him. But she realised it was pure masochism to prolong the weekend. Quickly she threw the rest of her clothes and the

221

great pile of letters into her case, and put on her pink suit. Even in her numb state of misery, she couldn't bring herself to travel by train in a split shirt and filthy trousers. She scribbled a quick note.

'Dearest Hugh, Terribly sorry for pushing off, but I need time to think things out. Forgive me for being so unutterably bloody this weekend. With love, Kate.'

She folded it over, wrote his name on top, and left it on the top bunk.

He won't understand, he'll be insane with rage, she thought, as she jumped onto the bank, ran along the tow path, and scuttled across the little wooden bridge onto the far side. Great Molesforth—six miles across the fields—and then she'd be free like Pigling Bland. She was in such a hurry to get out of eyeshot of the boat, that when she climbed over the first gate into a big field, she didn't bother to read the notice propped in the hawthorn hedge on the right side of the gate post. She tore across the cropped grass, feeling the thistles scratching her bare ankles. The sun blazed down relentlessly. Soon she was panting and sweating in her pink suit, but as she could still be seen from the river, she didn't let up. It was a pity she hadn't gone jogging with Hugh occasionally. The thought of him made her quicken her pace.

Two hundred yards from the river, she passed what she thought was a large black cow. Then she looked again, slowly taking in the cross little eyes, the matt of black curls on the forehead, the ring in the pinkish rubbery nose, the dangerously tossing head. She was reminded of Hugh. God, I can't get away from him was her last coherent thought. For a second she was frozen to the spot with terror, then turning on her heel, she ran for her life. The bull, suffering from the heat, maddened by flies and deprived of female company, let out an angry bellow and gave chase. Stumbling over the molehills, skidding on the cow pats, Kate raced towards the gate. She dropped her suitcase. One shoe fell off, then another. The bull was gaining on her, the thunder of his hoofs shook the ground. Her breath was coming in great sobs.

'Run for the river, for Christ's sake!' howled a voice from the bank.

With a moan of terror, twelve yards from the gate, she swung to the right. An eternity away, the stretch of water glinted in the sunshine. I'll never make it, she thought desperately. The bull was going so fast, he couldn't stop, and bucketed past her crashing into the hawthorn hedge. Surprisingly quickly, he extracted himself, and set off once more in maddened pursuit. She was only twenty-five yards from the river now, but he was gaining on her. She could feel his hot breath on her legs. Her throat was too dry even to scream. Ahead was a wall of nettles. For a second she faltered.

'Jump!' howled the voice in anguish.

Steeling herself, she charged through the dense, agonising dark green wall, then she felt a sharp pain on her right side, and a leaden weight crashed into the small of her back, knocking all the breath out of her body, as it catapulted her into the river. I'm going to drown and it doesn't matter, she thought, as the oily filthy water closed over her head. She hadn't any energy left to swim. Next minute, someone had grabbed her and tugged her choking to the surface. It was a few seconds before she realised it was Tod. He towed her to the other side, and none too gently hoisted her up onto the bank.

'Where did he get you?' he said, as he scrambled up beside her, his hair, face and clothes plastered with black river mud.

'This side, I think,' she said weakly, putting a hand on her ribs.

Despite her protests, he ripped off her jacket to reveal a deep graze down her right side.

'Bloody little idiot,' he swore at her, mopping at the graze with the jacket sleeve. 'Another inch, and he'd have gone for your lungs.'

'I couldn't help it. I didn't know there was a bull in the field.'

'Where were you going anyway?'

'Home—to get away from you. Oh my God,' she put her hands in her skirt pocket.

'What's the matter?'

'I must have dropped my latch keys.'

Back on the boat, realising how near to death she had been, she started to tremble violently. Tod poured her a quadruple brandy.

'Get that inside you. Then have a shower, and wash the dirt away from that cut. I'll try and find the farmer and get him to move his bull, so we can retrieve some of your belongings.'

Her knees were still knocking together as she turned on the shower. To hell with Muriel's water supply she thought, as she washed first herself and then her hair. The joy of being clean again almost distracted her from the agonising nettle stings burning her legs. When she went back to the cabin, she found her note to Hugh lying on the bottom bunk. She was sure she'd left it on the top. As she tore it into little pieces, she wondered if Tod had read it.

When he came back, he found her in the saloon wrapped in a faded red towel, her long dark hair dripping down her back like a mermaid. For a second he stood in the doorway, his face completely expressionless. The mud had dried on his shoulders and hair, and had streaked down the side of his face. He looked like a miner just up from the pits. Then he walked into the room and put her bag, suitcase and keys down on the polished table.

'Sorry, I didn't find your shoes, but the bull was getting a bit restless.'

Kate was aghast. 'Didn't you get the farmer to move him? You could have been killed.'

Tod picked up her half empty glass of brandy, and drained it. Then he laughed. 'Bully boy wasn't half as interested in me as he was in you, actually. It must have been a nice change having a male pursuing you as single-mindedly as that. Why didn't you tell him you had a headache?'

Wham, with the hand that wasn't clutching the red towel, she slapped him across the cheek.

Enraged, they glared at each other, as the marks of her fingers slowly reddened on his mud-streaked face. Fists clenched, Tod took a step towards her.

'Whoo-oo,' said Muriel's voice, slightly tight, from the gang plank. 'Hello, angels,' she said, bursting into the saloon. 'Where *did* you get to, Tod. I'm *absolutely* starving, how about you both?'

Then she stopped, slowly taking in Kate dripping in her towel, Tod caked in mud, and the suitcase.

'What's going on?' she said, lighting up with excitement at the prospect of trouble.

Kate opened her mouth and shut it again.

'Nothing,' said Tod curtly, putting his hand up to hide the finger marks. 'Kate fell in, I pulled her out, and she had first shower.'

Suddenly Kate was aware of a terrible smell of burning coming from the galley. 'Oh God,' she said, going green. 'I forgot to turn the oven off.'

Next minute Jonty burst in, magenta in the face with fury. 'It's too bad,' he exploded. 'My sea trout is burnt to a cinder, and all the water's run out again.'

'It's been a marvellous weekend,' said Hugh, as he kissed Muriel and got into his car.

'I'm desperately sorry about the sea trout,' said Kate for the thousandth time to Jonty.

Hugh wound down the window, to speak to Tod and Georgie. 'We'd love you both to come to the wedding. Shall we send you an invite?'

'Yes please,' said Georgie, turning a glowing brown face up to Tod. 'I love weddings.'

'I can't make it, I'm afraid,' said Tod. 'I've got to go to Paris as soon as I've finished painting the bus.'

'But I could go,' said Georgie, 'and join you on Sunday.'

'Of course, if you want to,' said Tod flatly.

He had gone round to Kate's side, and was standing drumming his fingers on the car roof. Then he bent down and kissed her on the cheek. 'I hope you'll be very happy,' he said softly. 'I'll give you the best divorce lawyer in town as a wedding present.'

'I hope Georgie can come,' said Hugh, moving into the fast lane on the motorway. 'The Law Lords would lap her up. Not very sorry Tod can't. Your parents were quite right, darling, he wouldn't have done for you.'

He's already done for *you*, thought Kate, and she got out her writing case.

'Still more thank-you letters,' said Hugh, getting out his pipe. 'You are a busy bee.'

'Just one more,' she said.

The sun at ten degrees was casting the tall shadows of moving cars onto the grass verge. Kate put her address and telephone number very clearly at the top of the page.

'Dearest Tod,' she wrote, *'I have decided not to marry Hugh after all. Thank you for making me realise it would have been a dreadful mistake for both of us. With all my love and God bless you, Katie.'*

Next morning at the office she typed his address on a brown envelope, so as not to upset Georgie, and posted it.

At first everyone was very understanding when she told them she couldn't marry Hugh. Hugh himself was kind but patronising. He immediately drove her down to her parents' house in Bath, explaining to them that Kate was in a highly over-emotional state and that Tod had been on the boat stirring it. Her mother and father told her to get a good night's sleep, she'd obviously been overdoing things. The doctor was called in to give her a sedative, and said she mustn't go back to the office for the last week.

Her boss understood perfectly, she had already left everything in apple pie order—he and all her friends from the office would see her at the wedding.

The next day when she showed no sign of changing her mind, the doctor was called back and spent an hour alone talking to Kate in the drawing-room. 'I'm terribly sorry, Elizabeth,' he said when he came out, 'but I don't find Kate the slightest bit deranged. She's bitterly sorry for upsetting everyone, but she's decided it would be wrong for her to marry Hugh, and that's that. Far better now—than in six months' or six years' time. Don't be too hard on her, it's taken a great deal of courage.'

It was Elizabeth Drayford who needed the sedatives after that. The scenes that followed were worse than Kate could ever have dreamed. Her father blustered and shouted, Hugh was bitter and vicious. He kept pointing out that he'd been made to look a complete idiot in front of his legal superiors, and what was to become of the new house and the speech proposing the toast of the bridesmaids, which he'd been perfecting for weeks.

Worst of all, her mother attacked her non-stop, one moment hysterical, the next vindictive. 'After all that work and planning,' she had screamed, 'you've let us all down. Throwing away the perfect husband just to become an old spinster. What I can't understand is *why*, when he's such a charmer, so brilliant, and such a good bridge player, and if you think you're going to spend the rest of your life mooning around here, you've got another think coming. Your father and I were going to turn your room into a second spare room. Lots of our married friends prefer not to sleep in the same room when they come and stay, you know.'

'Don't worry,' said Kate, trying to sound soothing, 'I'll go and live somewhere else, you don't have to bother with me anymore.'

'But why, why, WHY!'

'Hugh doesn't love me.'

'He would if you were nicer, you've been so awful to him lately.'

'And I don't love him.'

'That's the stupidest reason of all. You *like* him.'

'No I don't, I think he's a pompous prig and a bully, and he makes my flesh creep when he touches me and

227

when he sucks on his revolting pipe.' Kate gave a sob as she echoed Tod's words.

'Do you think I loved your father in that alleycat way when I first married him?'

'You never loved him,' screamed Kate. 'That's why I'm such a mess. I never saw any love or affection between the two of you when I was a child. I was far too frightened of giving myself to Tod all those years ago, because you always drilled into my head that sex was wicked and horrible. Well, now I know it's only wicked and horrible with someone you don't love—like Hugh.'

'How dare you speak to me like that,' said her mother, turning an ugly blotchy red all down her neck. 'It's all Tod's fault, he's an absolute swine. You were quite happy to marry Hugh before you went on that boat. Anyway,' she went on with savage satisfaction, 'Hugh tells me Tod's got a beautiful young girlfriend of his own, and wasn't showing a scrap of interest in you. I bet he thought you'd let your looks go.'

And on and on, round and round went the torrents of abuse, continually re-cycling like a fountain, as for the next eleven days Kate steadily packed up all the three hundred wedding presents—cushioning the fragile ones with packing straw—and took them down to the post office to return them to all the judges and important lawyers who had so graciously sent them. At least I'll be able to get a job as a packer after this, she thought wryly.

But despite all the ranting, she found it rather like being in a submarine at the bottom of the ocean when a storm is raging above sea level. She was desperately aware that she had upset everyone and had behaved appallingly, but she could think only of Tod. She knew she had nothing to hope for. He had brutally spelt out on the boat that he no longer loved her. Yet she still sustained herself on the crumbs of hope that he might think better of her because she'd had the guts to break it off with Hugh, and perhaps acknowledge the letter she had written telling him.

228

As the days passed the telephone never stopped ringing, with relations and friends wanting to know if the wedding was really off. The doorbell also went continually, with neighbours dropping in on the pretext of offering sympathy to Elizabeth Drayford, but really avid to find out the grisly details of the break-up, because Elizabeth had been so smug about her daughter's dazzling match. And at each ring of the telephone or front doorbell, Kate's heart leapt that it might be Tod, but it never was. Nor was there any word from him amongst the pile of letters of commiseration which came in twice a day, and which she so feverishly scanned.

It was Friday night. The wedding would have been tomorrow and Tod must now have left for France. Kate had staked her all on a million to one chance that he might come back, and she had lost. She now had to face the fact that her world was in smithereens. She felt only relief that Hugh had gone, but how was she to drag herself through the rest of her life. Wasn't it A.E. Housman who had written: *'He who loves more than once, has never loved at all.'*

This weekend, too, she must find a room to live in, and then a job. After she'd paid, out of her own pocket, for the cake, the bridesmaids' dresses, the breaking-off announcement in the *Times*, the postage for returning the parcels, the deposit on the marquee, and a hundred and one other extras, she had only two hundred pounds left in the bank. It was enough perhaps for a plane ticket to Ethiopia or Katamoja, where she could work for people whose sufferings were so dreadful that hers would seem trivial by comparison.

She was thankful for the first time since returning from the boat weekend to be alone in the house. Her mother and father had gone to a drinks party on the other side of town. Her mother, who'd lost two pounds in weight as a result of all the stress, went off looking very pretty in the dress and the new coral shoes she

229

had bought for Kate's wedding. This had triggered off yet another volley of abuse.

'I loathe and detest having to wear this,' was Elizabeth Drayford's parting shot. 'But after all the expense we've been put to, I shan't be able to afford anything else to wear for years.'

Left alone, Kate had a bath, washed all the packing straw dust out of her hair, and put on an old pair of pink denim trousers and a faded purple t-shirt. Then she went out into the garden. A thrush was singing, the air was full of the scent of honeysuckle and orange blossom, giant, dark blue delphiniums spiked the violet dusk. Pearly pink roses seemed to quiver in the stillness. Her father, she realised with a stab of remorse, had lovingly tended every plant to a pitch of perfection just in time for the wedding.

There was no time on the blank face of the sundial. Just like me, she thought miserably. I've reached the age of twenty-nine with nothing to show for it—except messing up other people's lives. She shivered and clutched her arms above the elbows for warmth. She must go in and do something about supper for her parents.

As she put the shepherd's pie into the oven, a key turned in the lock. Her heart sank, they were back already—her mother punchy and glittering-eyed from a surfeit of dry Martinis.

'Too humiliating,' she said, easing her feet out of the coral shoes. 'Everyone asked about the wedding. They all think you've been too awful, Kate. And Tom and Sue had their daughter and son-in-law there, with a heavenly baby in a carry cot. Sue took me upstairs to admire it. "Poor Elizabeth," she said, "I don't expect you'll ever have any little grandchildren now."'

Elizabeth Drayford got out her handkerchief and blew her nose loudly. 'Did you manage to get through to your Uncle Trubshaw and tell him the wedding was off?' she went on in a more bullying tone.

'I've been ringing all day, but haven't got an answer,' said Kate, 'so I've sent a telegram.'

'Well, I hope it gets through, I don't want Trubshaw turning up expecting a binge and having to entertain him all weekend.'

'Why don't you go and change out of that lovely dress, Elizabeth?' said Henry Drayford, who knew that if there was another scene he wouldn't get any dinner for ages.

'Everyone admired it,' said her mother resuming her martyred tone as she went upstairs, 'but all I could think of was that I should have been wearing it in happier circumstances.'

Kate sighed, nearer to breaking and despair than at any time in the last fortnight. She tipped the broad beans into a pan of boiling water.

'The garden's looking absolutely lovely, Daddy,' she said in a faltering voice, 'I've never seen it better, you must have worked so hard to make it look nice for tomorrow. I'm so sorry.'

Henry Drayford came over and patted her shoulder.

'Never mind, never mind, your mother'll get over it, everything'll seem better in a few days. Like a drink?'

She nodded, not trusting herself to speak, and watched him wander off towards the drinks tray in the drawing-room, cannoning off the kitchen door as he went.

She was just adding salt to the broad beans when she heard the roar of an engine, and a crunch on the gravel. Then she heard her mother scream.

'What's the matter?' she said, rushing into the hall in alarm.

'There's a bus coming up the drive!' screeched her mother, 'What on earth is it doing here? Henry! There's a bus outside, tell it to go away at once.'

'Think your mother's had a few too many,' muttered Henry Drayford, coming out of the drawing-room, carrying a large glass of whisky and a gin and tonic.

Kate ran to the hall window. Sure enough, a brilliant-coloured bus was coming up the drive, fantastically painted with hearts, roses, lilies, yellow irises and honeysuckle, all looped together with garlands of pale green ivy and pale pink ribbon. How beautiful was all she could think. Then she gave a gasp, and clung onto the window sill, for painted across the flowers in huge, scrawling, bright pink letters were the words: *I love Kate Drayford.*

A great lump came into her throat. She shut her eyes in disbelief, but the tears welled through them. Then she rushed to the front door, and read the words again. *I love Kate Drayford.*

Next minute the door of the driver's cabin opened, and a long, long pair of legs jumped out, with Tod at the top of them.

Kate tore across the gravel and crashed into him. 'Oh Tod, darling, darling, I thought you were in France.'

'And I thought you'd probably be out by now, on some pre-wedding stag night, whooping it up with all Hugh's relations. I didn't realise it was Friday, I got stuck in the weekend traffic.'

He put his arms round her and held her very tight. She could feel the frantic crash of his heart, and his blue shirt drenched with sweat. 'Katie darling, I know it's last ditch, but you can't marry Hugh, please don't. It'll break my heart.'

'But I'm not going to marry him,' she said half laughing, half crying, 'didn't you get my letter?'

'What letter?' he said in bewilderment.

'I posted you a letter about twelve days ago, saying I'd broken it off.'

'You didn't type the envelope?'

'Yes I did, it was a brown one. I thought Georgie might have opened it otherwise, and been upset.'

Tod gave a groan. 'Oh sweetheart. You ought to have remembered I never open bills. My God, I didn't realise. And all this time you've been waiting for me to get in touch, thinking I didn't care. I can't bear it.'

And there were tears in his eyes, as he bent his head to kiss her, holding her so tightly she thought her ribs

232

would crack. She could feel the stubble grazing her cheek, and the thick hair under her fingers, and her stomach melted like hot wax in joy, and lust and amazement. Finally, she struggled for air, and he laid his cheek against her hair, stroking her face over and over with his hand, as if to prove she was really there.

'I was such a sod to you on the boat,' he said, 'but I was so hurt. I heard you were coming down with some marvellously suitable man. I was eaten up with jealousy, all I wanted to do was to pay you back for all the unhappiness you caused me, and show you there was absolutely no possibility of your ever hurting me again.

'I even kidded myself it was all over, until that bloody bull chased you, and I realised I was still hopelessly hooked on you and I'd blown the whole thing. I would have come round earlier, but I psyched myself into thinking the only adequate peace offering was painting you a bus.'

'It's lovely,' said Kate in a choked voice. 'It's the loveliest thing I've ever seen, I can't really believe it. But what are the Gas Board going to say?'

'Well, they may kick up a bit of fuss about the caption,' said Tod softly, 'but I know it's the right one. I *do* love Kate Drayford.'

Kate pulled away and looked at him—taking in the five-day-old beard, the black rings under the bloodshot eyes, the paint-stained shirt and jeans. She suppressed a gurgle of laughter.

'Really, Tod,' she said reprovingly, 'you look terrible. You've let yourself go in the last fortnight, you used to be *so* beautiful. If you really cared for me, you'd never let me see you like this. I don't believe you've washed your hair for days.'

Just for a second there was a flicker of doubt and anxiety in his face, then he saw she was laughing. 'Bitch,' he said, pulling her into his arms. 'My God, what fools we've been to waste ten years. Uh-uh,' he muttered, looking over her shoulder towards the house, 'Regan and Cornwall are approaching.'

Kate tried to turn round, but his arms tightened like a vice around her.

'Evening, Elizabeth. Hello, Henry. Sorry to intrude upon your hour of grief.'

'How dare you roll up here,' said Elizabeth Drayford in an outraged voice. 'I'm sure you were entirely responsible for Kate breaking off her engagement.'

'I hope so,' said Tod, 'I assure you she's much better off with me. I've come to ask for your daughter's hand in marriage, Henry.'

Kate jumped violently. 'Are you sure?' she said shakily.

'Quite sure,' he said, drawing her back to him, gently stroking her hair. 'I'm not monkeying about any longer.'

'Well, it's all very irregular,' muttered Henry Drayford.

'I have to confess,' said Tod, 'that if you withhold permission, I won't take a blind bit of notice.'

'Insufferable,' choked Elizabeth ducking as a bat came dive-bombing over. 'You haven't changed at all, Tod.'

'And you're wonderfully the same too,' said Tod amiably.

Suddenly they all jumped at the sound of frantic hooting, and a very old Morris just missed the gate post, and came up the drive in a succession of jerks.

'Good God, it's Trubshaw,' said Henry Drayford.

'I thought you told me you'd sent him a telegram,' said Elizabeth shrilly. 'You can't do anything right, Kate. Now we'll have to spend the whole weekend amusing him.'

'I got a special licence today,' said Tod, taking a stunned, ecstatic Kate by the hand and leading her towards the bus. 'Tell Trubshaw if he hangs on till Monday, he can come to Katie's wedding after all.'

234

Lisa

A ripple of excitement ran through the female staff of Throgmorton and Williams the first time Paul Buchanan visited the office. He wore a blue shirt which matched the hard sapphire brilliance of his eyes, and he was so tall, so blond and so suntanned, that in the dusty gloom of the publisher's office he might have been mistaken for a Sun God, who had strayed from his path across the skies—except that a dark blue Aston Martin was parked outside the building instead of a flaming chariot.

Only one person appeared unmoved by his arrival, Lisa Aitken, Mr. Throgmorton's secretary, who came down to reception to collect him. Chatting up women was as natural to Paul Buchanan as breathing, and as he and Miss Aitken climbed three winding flights to Mr. Throgmorton's office, he had remarked with one of his famous smouldering glances, that running up these stairs all day must account for the slimness of her figure. Miss Aitken had given him a wintry smile and made no comment—not the sort of reaction Paul was used to.

Mr. Throgmorton kept him waiting a few minutes, and the delay gave Paul the opportunity to study Miss Aitken more closely, as she sat at her typewriter, her small hands moving over the keys with the speed of a concert pianist. No—she was certainly not his type, too thin, too pale, no make-up, National Health spectacles, dowdy grey dress, and pale gold hair scraped back into

235

a heavy coil at the nape of her neck. Paul preferred his women dark.

Later he was ushered into a large, untidy office and Mr. Throgmorton had peered at him over his bi-focals. Then, like a dog remembering where he has hidden a bone, he scrabbled through the papers on his desk, until he found a manuscript with a letter attached. 'Mr. Buchanan!' he beamed.

Paul nodded. Mr. Throgmorton swung around on his chair and said he would be very happy to accept Paul's novel about motor racing. Would an advance of one thousand pounds be acceptable? Paul, who received twice as much as this a month in unearned income, was surprised at the pleasure the offer gave him, and accepted it immediately.

'I think this calls for a celebration,' said Mr. Throgmorton, unlocking the corner cupboard behind him and taking out a decanter of sherry. 'I may add,' he said, polishing two glasses with a pink duster, 'that you have Miss Aitken to thank. She is an admirable secretary, you understand, but not a girl who gets very easily excited. Well, she took your manuscript home for the weekend, and came rushing in on Monday morning, in absolute ecstasies about it, and insisting that we must publish it. Thus encouraged, I read your book, Mr. Buchanan, and I agreed entirely with Miss Aitken.'

After that, Paul felt quite differently towards Lisa Aitken. He wanted to thank her there and then, but she had already left.

'Miss Aitken's home is in the West Country,' explained Mr. Throgmorton. 'She always leaves promptly on Friday to go there for the weekend.'

Paul had agreed to modify certain passages in his novel. But as his days were divided between race meetings and his father's merchant bank, where he was allegedly employed, and his evenings taken up with a string of pretty women, it was a month or so before he found time to deliver the revised manuscript. Once again he climbed the flights of stairs behind Lisa Aitken. He noticed she had charming ankles. Producing the famous smouldering glance, he said, 'I gather I have you to thank for getting my book accepted. I'm incredibly grateful.'

'I loved it,' she said simply. 'I was so busy reading it I almost went past my station. We've been thinking about a jacket. Would you like to see some of the designs?'

Her voice was soft but she had a slight stammer. Paul also noticed as they looked through the designs that her nails were bitten down to the quick and she had two darns in her tights. Paul only knew girls who tossed their tights away as soon as they laddered.

He spent some time going through the manuscript with Mr. Throgmorton and it was nearly eight o'clock before he walked out of the office into the soft spring night. Looking down the road, he saw Lisa Aitken walking towards the bus stop. Her shoulders drooped, her feet dragged. He loped after her. 'I've got my car just down the road, let me give you a lift home?'

She turned round. She looked desperately tired, her face drained of colour except for two red marks on either side of her nose where her glasses had been. 'I'm all right, thank you,' she said. 'The bus on the corner takes me all the way.' At that moment four buses sailed past in convoy. She gave a cry, ran after them, but she was too late.

Paul strolled after her grinning. 'Now you must accept my offer, you'll have to wait hours for another bus,' he said, taking her arm. She moved away as though she'd been stung, stammering that she didn't mind waiting.

Paul was used to getting his own way. 'Come on,' he said firmly, 'I *want* to give you a lift.'

'You shouldn't stay so late,' he told her as they drove down St. Martin's Lane. 'How long have you worked in publishing?'

'About two years.'

'And before that?'

'I was at drama school.'

He looked at her with interest. 'What made you give up?'

She hesitated, then said, 'I found I wasn't very good.'

He mentioned a few plays he'd enjoyed recently. She hadn't seen any of them. 'We must do something about that,' he said.

The afternoon's rain had given a new lease of life to London's gardens. The air was heavy with the scent of lilacs. It was a lovely evening, and Paul was in no hurry. Back in Knightsbridge, a beautiful girl was bathing and scenting herself for his evening's entertainment, a girl he knew would wait for him.

He took another look at Lisa, sitting beside him so quietly. The breeze had blown pale strands of hair across her face, and whipped a faint colour into her cheeks. She looked almost pretty. He was amazed to find himself saying, 'Have dinner with me tomorrow?'

'I always go away at weekends.'

'Well, Monday then?'

'I work late on Monday.'

'How about Tuesday?'

She was pleating her skirt nervously with her hand. Her stammer was more pronounced than ever as she said, 'I don't think so, thank you.' Not even an excuse this time.

'Come on,' said Paul. 'Just dinner in return for getting my book accepted. No strings attached—I just like to pay my debts.'

She looked at him consideringly for a minute with those twilight eyes, as though she were weighing up the pros and cons. Then she gave a little nod. 'It's very kind of you. I'd like to, thank you.'

The moment he'd dropped her off at one of those ugly red Edwardian houses on the outskirts of Wimbledon, Paul started cursing himself. A plain, frumpy little mouse. He'd had to pull out the stops to get her to accept—and he didn't really want to take her out at all. Oh well, he thought, bored, as he roared back to London—a theatre, a quick dinner, back to his flat, then Home James, see you sometime, darling, and on o the next one. That should put paid to Miss Aitken's airs and graces.

On Monday, however, one of Paul's favourite girl-friends came back from Bermuda and he was just about to telephone Lisa on Tuesday morning and cancel dinner, when he received a letter in his morning mail.

Dear Mr. Buchanan, it said, *It was kind of you to ask me ut tomorrow night, but I find I have a previous engagement. I am sorry. Yours sincerely, Lisa Aitken.*

Paul was enraged—being stood up was an entirely new experience which he did not like. He thought of ending her the theatre tickets with a sarcastic little note. Instead, after brooding all day, he found himself driving towards Throgmorton and Williams around even o'clock. He was in luck. There she was in the bus queue, in that same grey dress of such disfiguring austerity that she'd worn on both previous occasions. Didn't she have any more clothes?

'Television's bad tonight,' he yelled, bringing his car o a screaming halt beside her. She blushed crimson and pretended she hadn't seen him. All the people in he queue were craning their necks. Paul leaned across and opened the door. 'Come on, jump in,' he said.

Lisa continued to gaze stonily in front of her.

'Miss Aitken,' he said, lighting a cigarette, 'I'm hold-ng up the traffic.'

'There's a friend of yours waving at you,' said a fat woman to Lisa. All the cars were jamming and hooting. Trembling with rage and embarrassment, she got into he car beside him and slammed the door with a vicious olt.

'Where to, Lady?' he said and just grinned at her. 'I might as well drop you off at your previous engage-ment whoever he may be.'

Lisa glared at him for a minute and then lowered her eyes. 'Mr. Buchanan,' she blurted out, 'I—well—I ied to you. I don't have an engagement but there isn't any point in my coming out with you. I'm just not your line of country.' The colour was coming and going in her cheeks.

'Surely, I'm the best judge of that,' he said gently. 'Please, Lisa.' He let his voice linger over her name. 'Here I am stranded with two tickets for *Hamlet*, please!'

'Oh,' she said longingly, 'but I'm not dressed.'

'I don't mind, if you don't,' he said, swinging the car round.

They stopped for a drink, and she asked him if she might go and tidy herself up. He was amused when she came out five minutes later. She had merely washed her face and re-coiled her hair—no scent, no lipstick, no eye make-up. It was a novelty walking into the theatre with her. Usually he took out girls who had every man in the place cricking his neck. Lisa might have been invisible for all the notice people took of her. It made him feel curiously protective.

He enjoyed the play, although he'd seen the production before. But even more, he enjoyed seeing her enjoy it so much—at one moment moved to tears, the next laughing like a child. She was so enraptured she couldn't speak for half an hour afterwards.

During dinner, under the influence of soft lights and wine, he managed to make her unbend a little, but she was still very much on the defensive. Instead of taking her back to his flat, he drove her straight home. He was far too experienced not to realise it would be insanity to attempt anything that evening.

About thirty seconds from home, she thanked him profusely for the evening, and as he stopped the car, she reached for the door handle. 'Good night and thank you,' she said, leaping out of the car.

'Hang on, baby, I'm not going to eat you,' Paul shouted out.

But she was running up the steps, fumbling for her latch key. Paul bounded after her, putting his powerful shoulders against the door, and barring her way.

Once more she raised her troubled twilight eyes to

him—she was shivering like a poplar. 'Please let me in,' she said. 'It's been lovely, but I'm very tired.'

'What about tomorrow?' Paul found himself saying.

She shook her head. 'I have to work late.'

'You've got to eat.' He took her latch key and opened the door. 'I'll pick you up about nine o'clock.'

And so it began. For the first time in his life, Paul found he was making every inch of the running. The slightest false move sent her scuttling away. When he was a child, he had tamed a squirrel, and the elation he remembered feeling the first time it took a nut from his hand, resembled the triumph he felt the first time Lisa let her hand rest in his.

She would never talk about herself. It also puzzled him that she seemed to have so little money—Throgmorton's must pay her a decent salary, yet she had very few clothes, and he suspected she often skipped her lunch.

Weekends, too, were another puzzle. She was prepared, after much coaxing, to see him most nights during the week, but every Friday she set off for the country, and didn't return until very late on Sunday night. Every suggestion that she should stay in London, or that he should drive down and visit her, was flatly refused.

'My aunt is old, and she doesn't like company,' said Lisa and that was that. Often when she was with him, her eyes would cloud over and he'd feel she was miles away.

Gradually he shed his girlfriends, not easy, they were persistent, but beside Lisa, they seemed artificial and egotistical. He laughed when he thought about it: here was Paul Buchanan—Ace Casanova—hooked on a girl he hadn't even kissed.

Then one evening when they were driving home, she suggested he might come and have dinner at her flat. The day she chose, he realised after accepting, was his birthday. He didn't tell her. He didn't want her to spend money on him. Full of curiosity, he arrived at her house.

'Happy birthday,' she said, as she let him in.

'How on earth did you know?' he said.

She smiled from ear to ear. 'You put your date of birth on our publishing contract. You're twenty-nine today.'

He grimaced. 'Fast approaching my dotage.'

She handed him a parcel. It was a wildly expensive peacock blue shirt which he had admired while they were driving down Jermyn Street a few days before.

'Darling, you really shouldn't have,' he said, taking her hands.

'Look how much you've given me,' she said gruffly.

At first the flowers, the pink birthday cake, the prawns and garlic mayonnaise which she knew he loved, and the cold chicken distracted his attention from the poverty of the room. It was tiny, with awful beige wallpaper and a narrow iron bed.

It was only after they were well into the second bottle of wine, and Lisa was clearing the plates that he realised she had no kitchen or bathroom, and had to wash up in the basement.

She wouldn't let him carry anything downstairs. 'It's your birthday, and you should be spoilt.'

He lay on the bed smoking a cigarette and wishing he could move her lock, stock and barrel into his own flat that very night. This room gave him the creeps. Someone in the next door room was practising Mozart and kept getting stuck on the same run. The scent of newly-cut grass drifted in through the open window.

Lisa came back and refilled his glass. All through the evening, in spite of the warm weather, she had had fits of shivering, but he knew better than to remark on it. She went over to the window. He watched her for a minute, then stubbed out his cigarette and went over to her. He ran his hands slowly down her bare arms. She was trembling more than ever now, and he said softly, 'Mr. Throgmorton once told me you were a girl who never gets excited. I think he's wrong. I think you've got more excitement beneath the surface than any woman I've ever met.' He turned her round to face him. 'I think you could burn a man down.'

Electric currents seemed to be passing through her, as he bent his head to kiss her. Her arms slid round his neck, and for a moment she seemed to erupt against him. Then she shoved him violently away, and threw herself sobbing wildly on the bed.

'Darling, darling, please don't be frightened,' he said stroking her pale hair until the sobs subsided into muffled apologies. 'What are you so scared of? I won't hurt you. I—' he was about to say he loved her, but it was a sentence long training had taught him never to utter. Instead he said, 'You need a holiday. Why don't we go off for a week together.'

She wouldn't raise her eyes to him as she said, 'I'm taking a week off next week.'

'Marvellous, we can go to Paris, Rome, New York, anywhere you like.'

'No,' she said quickly, 'I have to go away with my aunt.'

'But that's absurd, she has you every weekend.'

'She's old, she needs me.'

'All right. I'll come down and spend a few days with you both.'

'No!' Her voice was sharp with fear.

'Why not, where are you staying then?'

'I don't know. We'll be moving around.'

After that, they had their first full dress row, and Paul drove off into the night in a fury. He'd rung her the next day to apologise, but they'd been off hand with one another.

'Are you sure you don't know where you're staying?'

'No.'

'All right,' he said coldly. 'I'll give you a ring when you get back.'

Paul plunged into a week of dissipation. He went to endless parties, he rang up his old girlfriends, who welcomed him back with cries of joy. He drank too much. But it all tasted like ashes—the more he tried to forget Lisa, the more her image floated before him like

243

some pale, cool, water-lily. Late on Wednesday, he was wondering how he could politely ditch the beautiful Swedish girl, who was sitting heavily on his knee, when the telephone rang.

'Paul?'

'Hello?'

'Paul, it's Lisa.'

He gave a shout of joy. 'Darling, my God how marvellous, just let me turn off the stereo.' He tipped the Swede onto the floor, took the telephone into the bedroom and shut the door. 'Oh Lisa, I've missed you.'

'And I've missed you, too.' They talked nonsense for five minutes. Then she said, 'Darling, I'm coming back to London tomorrow.'

'I'll come and fetch you.'

'No, I've got to drop my aunt off. I'll be in London soon after eight.'

'Come straight to my flat,' he said.

The following evening, from seven o'clock onwards, he paced up and down the flat, smoking far too many cigarettes and drinking too many glasses of whisky. At half-past eight, the door bell rang. He raced to open it. She stood smiling in the doorway.

'Come into the light, let me look at you,' he said, leading her into the drawing-room. 'You're brown, Lisa, you look wonderful.'

'I feel wonderful, now I'm here,' she said, and he saw the love for him streaming out of her eyes. I've hooked her, he thought in triumph, I've really hooked her at last. And he went towards her and very slowly took the pins out of her hair, so it poured pale gold over her shoulders.

'God, you beauty,' he breathed, 'I'm going to make you the most beautiful woman in the world.'

Long after midnight he drove her slowly back to Wimbledon, one arm round her shoulders, the other hand negligently on the wheel, and he knew what he'd suspected all along, that beneath the iceberg, Lisa was a volcano. When they reached her house, he stopped the car, and took her in his arms.

She looked at him, her face suddenly afraid. 'Paul, here's something I must tell you.'

'And there's something I must tell you. I love you, I love you, I love you,' and he kissed her long and lingeringly. Then he smiled at her. 'Well, what is it?'

She shook her head. 'It'll keep.'

'We'll have lunch tomorrow,' he said. 'I'll pick you up from the office at a quarter to one.'

He drove back through the silent streets. The gutters were full of petals. Like confetti, he thought, and knew that tomorrow he would ask her to marry him. He let himself into his flat, and resisted the temptation to ring her again. He caught a glimpse of himself in the mirror. Really, he must wipe that silly grin off his face, he looked like the village idiot! He wandered into the bathroom. A letter lay on the floor—absentmindedly he bent down to pick it up.

Darling Lisa. He stiffened as he read on. *It was so lovely to get your postcard. I'm so pleased you and Alexander are having such a lovely holiday. It must be such a treat for you both to get away together for a long stretch. This weekend business is too unsatisfactory. Never mind, perhaps things will work out in the end. It will be lovely to have you both this weekend. The roses are magnificent and there are still a lot of strawberries. All news then, love Aunt Maggie.*

After the first blinding flash of grief, Paul merely felt numb. He read the letter over and over again, until the truth sank in. Lisa had another man. It explained everything; her nervousness, her reluctance to come out with him in the beginning, her terror that he might suddenly burst in on her weekends or visit her while he was on holiday. She had been two-timing him, the little bitch. And slowly, as he tossed and turned the night away, the numbness became a sullen, smouldering hatred.

At twelve-forty-five, as arranged, she came out of her office. She'd left her hair loose, and as she ran towards his car, two men mending the road whistled at her. Paul ground his teeth in rage.

'Hello, darling,' she said, getting into the car and

holding her glowing face up to be kissed. Paul ignored her and drove off.

'What's the matter?' she faltered. 'What's happened?'

Paul didn't answer. He turned off the main road and parked in a deserted side street. He turned towards her and looked straight in her eyes. 'How's Alexander?' he said softly.

There was no mistaking her guilt, the colour drained from her face, leaving it grey and ugly. She opened and shut her mouth. 'How did you find out?' she whispered.

'You shouldn't drop letters in my flat.'

'Aunt Maggie's letter, oh my God. Darling, I've been meaning to tell you for ages, I tried to tell you last night.'

'But not very hard,' he snapped. 'You've lined up a nice little set-up, haven't you? Me during the week, Alexander taking care of the weekends. What's the matter, won't he marry you, or is he married to someone else already?'

She gave a gasp of horror. 'Oh no, no, no! It isn't like that. You've got it all wrong. Oh Paul, please let me explain.'

'There's nothing to explain—you're a bloody little two-timing hypocrite.' He leaned across her and opened the door. 'Go back to your precious Alexander. And don't play fast and loose with other people's lives in future. It's a game nobody wins.'

Tears were pouring down her face. 'Paul,' she said wildly, 'just give me a chance to . . .'

'Get out,' he snarled, almost pushing her out of the car. The expression on her face as he drove quickly away, reminded him of women waiting at the pithead when they brought the stretchers up.

That night he went out and got drunk, drunker than he'd ever got in his life, and he went on drinking all through Saturday, and finally passed out on Saturday night. He woke up on the floor of someone's flat on Sunday morning.

He went back to his own flat, bathed and shaved and

set off for the West Country. He moved the Aston Martin as though he had the devil on his heels. Halfway there, he nearly blacked out and realised he hadn't eaten for three days. He stopped at a café and ordered egg and chips, but found, when it arrived, that he could only manage coffee.

The shadows were lengthening as he drove into the village where Lisa's aunt lived. He bought some cigarettes at the village shop and found out where the house was. Cow parsley and white campion brushed against his car as he drove down a long, winding lane. He parked some way away and lit a cigarette to calm his nerves. His knees were like jelly, his heart was pounding his body to pieces as he banged on the door. He had expected Lisa, but instead the door was answered by a middle-aged woman with a red-veined face.

'Yes,' she said unhelpfully.

'Is Lisa in?' he asked.

She looked him up and down. 'I'll see,' she said and shut the door.

A few minutes later, Lisa came to the door. Her eyes were red, she was deathly pale. 'Paul,' she gasped, 'how did—I mean, what are you doing here?'

'I'll go away if it's awkward,' he said. 'I wanted to say I was sorry. I wouldn't let you explain. I thought we might sort something out.'

'Come in,' she said.

He followed her into the drawing-room. French windows opened on to a garden blazing with flowers.

'How did you find your way here?' she asked.

'I had your aunt's letter.'

'Was it difficult to find?' She had scraped back her hair again and was wearing an old shirt and trousers. Three months ago, he'd have thought how plain she looked, now his heart ached at how much she must have suffered.

'It's a beautiful journey,' she went on, 'particularly with the wild flowers out. This is a pretty village, isn't it? The church is very old, part of it is Anglo-Saxon.

We get a lot of visitors in the summer. Aunt Maggie thought of starting a café.' Her voice was coming in breathless little jerks, she was twisting her handkerchief round and round.

'Darling,' he interrupted her very gently, 'don't be frightened. Please tell me the truth, however painful it is. Please!'

She opened her mouth to speak, when suddenly there was a bellow from the garden. 'Mummy, Mummy!' shrieked a voice and a small boy came hurtling through the French windows waving a red toy bus, caught his foot on the carpet and fell flat on his face. He burst into noisy sobs. Lisa ran and picked him up. Paul picked up the red bus.

'Is broken,' said the child, as his sobs subsided.

The driving band had worked loose. Paul fitted it back into place. 'There you are,' he said. The child stared at him with huge dark eyes, his hair even blonder than Lisa's.

'This is Alexander,' said Lisa shyly.

'Alexander,' said Paul stupidly. 'Alexander!' Relief poured over him. He took the child from Lisa. 'So you're Alexander—what a bloody fool I've been,' and he started to laugh. The child looked doubtful for a minute and then began to crow with laughter too. After a minute Paul put him down and handed him the bus. 'Go and play in the garden a minute,' he said, 'I want to have a word with your Mummy.'

Alexander's face lengthened. 'Not going back yet?' he said to Lisa.

She shook her head. 'Not yet, darling, we've got to have tea first.'

Reassured, he trotted out through the French windows.

Paul wanted to take Lisa instantly in his arms but he knew it was the wrong moment. 'What happened to Alexander's father?' he said.

'I loved him, and he loved me a bit but not enough to marry me and be saddled at once with a small baby. My mother had just re-married herself and didn't want to

248

be bothered with my problems. Right up to the end, I was going to have Alexander adopted, they told me it would be unfair to both of us if I kept him. But once I'd had him, he was so lovely, I couldn't let them take him away,' her voice broke. 'I don't earn enough to keep him in London. Fortunately my aunts rallied round. During the week he lives with another aunt about ten miles from here.'

Paul felt a great lump in his throat, and went over and held her very tightly. 'Darling,' he said, 'I feel so ashamed, I've been so unspeakably bloody about the whole thing. Please forgive me?'

'Forgive you,' she said in bewilderment. 'Forgive *you*? It's me who should be asking for forgiveness. I couldn't bear to tell you. I've only had one boyfriend since Alexander was born, nothing serious, but when I told him about Alexander, he backed off immediately. Oh Paul, I wanted to tell you, but I couldn't bear the thought of losing you. I love you so much,' tears were streaming down her face.

His arms tightened round her. 'Do you think Alexander will mind pigging it in my flat until we find a house?' he said.

Lisa looked at him in amazement. 'You mean you want both of us,' she whispered.

He nodded smiling. 'Yes, of course I do.' Then more reflectively, 'Alexander Buchanan sounds a bit of all right, doesn't it.'

The Red Angora Dress

Little by little, I could feel Andrew was going off me. It was horrible—like trying to carry water in cupped hands: however tightly one's fingers are pressed together the water trickles away. There's nothing you can do.

We've nothing in common really—he's a sports commentator on television and I'm a scruffy bookworm. In the beginning this used to fascinate him.

'You're so utterly different from anyone I've ever met,' he would keep saying in a special husky voice. Pretty corny really, but with a man as attractive as Andrew—randy Andy his friends call him—you put up with it. He really laid siege, but being the sort of man he was, as soon as I was hooked, he promptly went off me. So seven nights a week dwindled to once a week, and then once a fortnight. In fact, I thought he'd gone for good, until he obviously had a pang of conscience and rang up and asked me to a party the following Saturday.

I must get him back, I thought. I'll buy the most beautiful dress and slim.

I don't think I'll ever be able to look a grapefruit in the face again, but by Saturday, I'd lost seven pounds. The temperature had also dropped and it was freezing so hard that I was glad I had bought something warm to wear. I had blued three weeks' salary on a ravishing red angora dress with long sleeves and a high neck. It clung like a second skin, and I was all set for the great come-back.

I timed getting ready like a military operation: face pack, eye pads, early bath, not too hot so my ankles didn't swell. My hair looked great, and my make-up for once went on like a dream. In fact, I was really pleased with myself. I was just pinching some of my mother's scent when the doorbell rang.

'She'll be down in a minute,' said my mother. She sounded like Kermit introducing the guest star of the show, but I rather spoilt the effect by tripping over the carpet at the foot of the stairs.

'You look wonderful,' said Andrew in a surprised voice.

'She ought to,' said my father, tactless as ever, 'she's been getting ready since breakfast.'

'We're giving Kit a lift,' said Andrew. Kit and I don't get on but Andrew thinks he's terribly funny—so does Kit. They threw my coat in the back, and although it was arctic outside, I was warm as toast hemmed in between the two of them with the heater turned up high.

'Who's giving the party?' I asked.

'A girl called Sylvia Oxley. Her parents are away for the weekend, so she's having it at their house. She's a model so there should be a lot of theatrical and television people there.'

My heart sank—models put the fear of God into me.

'Do you think Mark'll be there?' asked Kit, fiddling with the radio.

'Who's Mark?'

'Sylvia's brother—extraordinary chap—up at Oxford, absolutely brilliant but barking mad. He spends all night whooping it up with his chums—and all day sleeping it off. Sylvia's parents are awfully worried about him.'

'I'm not surprised,' said Andrew, 'he didn't even know who was captaining Oxford in the Varsity Match.'

I hadn't seen Andrew so cheerful for ages—I soon

discovered why. The moment we arrived at the party, a girl came gushing up and flung her arms round his neck.

'Darling, I'm so pleased you've come,' she said. 'Now the party's really begun.' I felt less sick when she flung her arms round Kit as well. Perhaps she was just affectionate. She wore silver dungarees, saved from positive indecency at the back by a sheet of silver hair falling well below her waist. She had slitty eyes and a monkey face—not beautiful but dangerous. I decided she must be Sylvia Oxley.

'Angel,' she suddenly cried to Andrew. 'What have you been up to? You're covered in fur.' Andrew may have been no longer attracted to me, but my angora dress was irresistibly drawn to him—his beautiful dark suit was matted with red fluff all down his left side. Sylvia Oxley was doing some very intimate brushing down with much giggling, while a maid took me upstairs.

I was shown into a bedroom. A very thin girl in a low-cut black dress was trying to give herself a cleavage by pulling her non-existent breasts together with sellotape. The heating was tropical, and I began to doubt the wisdom of my high-necked angora even more when I saw in the mirror how pink my face had become.

I went downstairs. One look at the party, and I knew I was outclassed. The girls were fantastic: false hair, false eyelashes, false bosoms, but the whole effect was marvellous. Someone gave me a drink, and I joined Andrew and Kit who were making two very pretty models roar with laughter. Andrew was forced to introduce me.

'How's moulting Milly?' said Kit. 'You need some Bob Martins. Don't stand near me.'

'If you work for ITV,' said one of the models, ignoring me pointedly and picking at the remains of the fluff on Andrew's suit, 'you must have known Roger Berry.'

'Old Roger? Of course—how is he these days?'

'Pretty browned off really, his wife's just left him.'

'Old Roger! The one who had a different typist every lunch-time, and always claimed his wife didn't understand him.'

'She's gone off with the dentist and the furniture.'

'I don't think Audrey's dress quite comes off,' said the second model.

'It will later on in the evening, if I know Audrey,' said Kit and bore her off to dance.

'I'll go and get some more drinks,' said Andrew and disappeared.

'What a fascinating man,' murmured the first model and drifted after him in hot pursuit.

I was left on my own, I was sweltering and my face was bursting into flames. I began to itch. Trying to break into the little groups of people, I felt like a moth thrashing at a window pane.

'Come and talk to us,' said a smooth man, stuck with a plain girl, and beat a retreat almost immediately. I was left with the girl who was obviously as bored by me as I was by her.

Our eyes swivelled frantically until rescue turned up in the form of a fat, middle-aged man who said he was Sylvia Oxley's accountant.

'Come and dance,' he said to me, his eyes gleaming behind his spectacles. 'It's ages since I trod a measure,' he added as we went into the darkened room next door. He was dead right—oh, the shame of it, in front of all those beautiful, swaying people with their fixed, velvety eyes, he started twisting. I tried to dance as though I didn't belong to him, but he kept pursuing me round the room.

'Come on, it's easy when you get the knack,' he said, jiggling up and down like a ball. I looked for Andrew—he was leaning against the wall talking to Sylvia Oxley. They were quite oblivious to everyone else in the room. He put his hand out and, smoothing her hair behind her ears, smiled down at her. God, it hurt. I couldn't bear it, I left the bouncer in mid-twist and fled out of the room.

I went through a side door and found myself in a study. Flinging open both windows, I thrust my burning face out to the frosty night. Far down at the end of the garden, the river gleamed like a silver blade. When I'd cooled off a bit, I rummaged in my bag for some foundation to tone my face down, but the top had come off and it had leaked over everything.

It was only when I started looking at the books, that I noticed a boy asleep on the sofa, a pretty little white whippet lying at his feet. With his long straight nose, thick eye-lashes, and silver-blond Henry V hair, he looked like one of those mediaeval knights that lie on tombs in churches. No-one could fail to recognise that hair—this must be Sylvia's brother Mark sleeping off his excesses. He was far too beautiful to pass up. I coughed noisily. The dog looked at me reproachfully, and the boy opened one eye.

'Who on earth opened those windows?' he said in horror.

'I'm sorry, I was hot,' I said.

'Well, at least let me shut them before we all three die of pneumonia.'

He got to his feet, yawning. Sounds of revelry drifted in from next door. 'Oh dear,' he said, lighting a cigarette with a trembling hand. 'Is Sylvia having one of her horrible parties? I must say she does have appalling friends—are they worse than usual?'

'I don't know,' I said carefully, 'I haven't been here before.'

'Sylvia's lovers would turn Mrs. Gaskell in her grave. She changes her men almost as often as she changes her drawers. The only one that's lasted is a wrestler called Charlie.'

'Is he coming this evening?' I asked hopefully.

'He thinks Sylvia is still modelling in America. That's why she's on the loose. You're not a model, are you? No, you couldn't be, you've got far too nice a bottom. I bet you look terrific without any clothes on.'

'I work in a library,' I said primly.

'Do you?' he said with interest, 'the big one in the High Street?'

I nodded.

'How marvellous. I shall come and bother you with obscure queries and make you climb up ladders so I can look at your legs. I'm starving, I'm going to get something to eat. Can I get you anything?'

I shook my head.

'Well, at least let me get you a drink—we might as well enjoy ourselves at Sylvia's expense. Don't turn into a pumpkin—I'll be back in a minute.'

He wandered out of the room, the dog at his heels. I was trying to repair my face, when I heard a familiar laugh. I crept up and peered through the crack in the door. Andrew held Sylvia in his arms. They were both giggling in that insane way people do from a surfeit of desire and champagne.

'You're so utterly different from anyone I've ever met, you are absolutely unique,' Andrew was saying, husky voice to the fore. This is where I came in, I thought.

'What about your red-faced girl friend?' giggled Sylvia, pressing herself against him.

'Oh, she's rather embarrassingly persistent. You always get those hangers-on if you work in television,' said Andrew, 'I thought I might palm her off on someone else.'

'Well, you succeeded, my accountant is obviously very taken with her. I must say I think it's very chic to match one's dress so exactly to one's face.'

With Andrew's laughter braying in my ears, I ran out of the house, down the garden with the grass crackling like glass under my feet. I couldn't stop crying. I would hurl myself in the river, and then they'd be sorry. I imagined Andrew sobbing at my funeral.

The water looked unbelievably cold—it was beginning to freeze and icicles gleamed in clusters from the bridge.

'I'll perish before I drown,' I thought, and bawled

255

even louder. The cold and crying was making my nose run. As I searched for a handkerchief, I realised I'd left my bag behind. My last relics—I could see the coroner holding them up at the inquest—a thousand bus tickets and matted elastic bands floating on a sea of peach foundation, a diary full of sop about Andrew, and my mother's favourite scent.

Then I remembered that I had also used my father's razor to shave my legs, and left all the hairs in, and there were all those books I'd borrowed from the library without signing for them, and the senior librarian's home-made birthday cake, which, despite having said it was delicious, I had left in my desk drawer because I wasn't hungry. Let's face it, impromptu suicide is out for scruffs like me.

Feeling cold and foolish, I walked back to the house and found a downstairs loo where I could wash away the streaked mascara. I looked awful, but at least my face was pale instead of crimson, and I managed to tidy my hair with a nail brush.

Someone rattled at the door. I came out and was confronted by Kit's model, and she didn't look so hot either with her lipstick messed up and her hair piece over one ear—I was enchanted to see that she was pale green. I hoped she was going to be sick.

I found Mark stretched out on the sofa with a bottle of champagne beside him, reading my diary.

'Hello,' he said, 'I'm so pleased you're back. I've been enjoying your diary. I say, Andrew really has been mucking you about, hasn't he?'

'How dare you,' I said furiously. 'It's awful to read other people's diaries.'

'But I always do,' he protested. 'Most of them are dull, but yours is sweet. You should never have got mixed up with Andrew. I knew he'd go off you as soon as you went to bed with him—that sort always does.'

'Give it to me at once,' I squealed.

'Angel, don't get uptight,' he said, 'I missed you and I was so pleased when I found your bag and knew you'd have to come back. Really, you mustn't go out with this creep anymore. And talking of creeps, Sylvia's got a five-star one in tow this evening. She has excruciating taste in men anyway. But this one's big-headed as well.

'You look knackered,' he went on, 'I was going to suggest we went to another party, but I think it would be better if we found a nice quiet club.'

'Yes please,' I said meekly, 'I'll go and get my coat.'

'I'll meet you in the hall,' he said.

He kept me waiting a few minutes. He was wearing an extraordinary raccoon coat, and his hair gleamed almost white in the moonlight.

'Sorry to keep you, duckie,' he said tucking his arm through mine. 'I just had to telephone Charlie the wrestler, Sylvia's steady boyfriend, and tell him she actually was back and he should come over. Charlie's a black belt and absolutely annihilates any competition.'

He opened the door of a white E-type, and settled me in before dropping the white dog onto my knees. 'I hope you don't mind sharing a seat with Prudence. She moults horribly, but she gets an inferiority complex if she sits in the back.'

We drove towards the town. The dog nestled against me, and in the light from the street lamps, I noticed her white coat busily gathering red fluff.

The Square Peg

Clutching her parcels, Penny charged through the front door, skilfully avoided a workman on a ladder, but cannoned straight into the Sales Manager coming out of the Board Room with an important client. Gibbering apologies, she raced upstairs, tiptoed past the Personnel Officer's room, and eased herself stealthily into her office.

Miss Piggott, the Managing Director's senior secretary, looked at her watch in disapproval. 'It's nane minutes past three,' she said in her ultra refined voice. 'Don't you think you're sailin' a bit close to the wind?'

'Oh gosh, Miss Piggott, I'm sorry,' said Penny, who was the Managing Director's junior secretary, 'but I saw this divine dress and then I found these shoes to match in a sale, and then in the same sale, I saw these garden scissors. I thought you might like them.'

Miss Piggott's disapproving face softened. 'That was very thoughtful of you, Penny. How much do Ay owe you?'

'Nothing, it's a present.' Penny kicked off her shoes, and collapsed into a chair, scattering parcels among the debris on her desk. 'I brought some éclairs, three in fact, in case *he*—' she pointed contemptuously at the door leading off their office—'gets back in time.'

'He's back,' said Miss Piggott. 'He's been ringing you since two o'clock.'

Penny went pale. 'Mr. McInnes is back already? My goodness, is he in a foul mood?'

'A've known him more accommodatin',' said Miss Piggott with a sniff.

'Oh dear,' sighed Penny, tugging a comb through her dark red curls, 'I do wish darling Mr. Fraser was still here. Everything was so much nicer then.'

Mr. Fraser had run the London office of Joshua McInnes Inc. with bumbling but good-natured incompetence; and immediately he had retired last autumn, old Joshua McInnes, who had been viewing the situation from across the Atlantic with increasing dismay, had sent his younger son, Jake, to sort out the muddle.

At first the London office hadn't known what had hit them. Young Jake McInnes went through every department with a tooth-comb, and for six months everyone had shivered in their shoes. Then gradually they began to realise things were running far more smoothly. Orders poured in and the factory had enough work in hand for three years.

People stopped flattening themselves against the wall whenever Jake McInnes walked down the passage. Everyone settled down—everyone except Penny, that is, for she was catastrophically inefficient.

Mr. Fraser had kept her as a kind of office pet. He had found her useful at remembering birthdays and knowing which of the telephonist's grandchildren was down with the measles. Occasionally he had given her letters, which he always signed without bothering to read.

'Penny's beautiful and she keeps me young,' he had insisted every time Miss Payne from Personnel had agitated for her dismissal. 'She makes a good cup of coffee, and she keeps the flowers in the conference room looking simply wonderful.'

But now Mr. Fraser had gone, and Jake McInnes had taken his place, and everyone was laying bets on how much longer Penny could possibly last.

The day Penny had decided to make her shopping expedition, Jake McInnes had not been expected back until late afternoon.

'Hello, Mr. McInnes, did you have a super time?' she asked nervously as she went into his office.

Jake McInnes looked her up and down for a minute, taking in the white silk shirt, the vestigial scarlet skirt over long brown legs. 'Sit down,' he said icily.

Jake McInnes was a powerfully built man in his late twenties, with thick, dark hair, deep-set eyes the colour of mahogany, and a very square jaw. With that nasty smile playing round his mouth, he looks more like a Sicilian bandit than an American businessman, thought Penny.

They glared at each other across the vast desk.

'It's twenty minutes after three. I thought your lunch break ran from twelve-thirty to one-thirty,' he said.

'I'm sorry,' mumbled Penny, 'but I saw this perfectly marvellous dress, and then . . .'

'I don't want any excuses,' he snapped. 'I've told Miss Payne to dock two hours pay from your salary this week.' He picked up her folder. 'You must have been busy while I was away, these letters are beautifully typed.'

'Oh good,' said Penny, beaming at him.

'It's a pity,' he continued softly, 'that they bear absolutely no relation to what I dictated.'

Penny flinched as though he'd struck her.

'Don't you do shorthand?' he asked.

'Not a lot,' admitted Penny, 'but my longhand's terribly fast, so I can get the gist of things. Mr. Fraser never complained,' she added defiantly.

'That doesn't surprise me,' said Jake McInnes.

For the next half-hour he went through each letter like an examination paper, until every shred of her self-confidence was ripped to pieces. Then he tore the letters up and dropped them into the wastepaper basket.

Scarlet in the face, Penny got to her feet.

'And another thing,' he added, 'next time you make reservations at a hotel, book single rooms. I don't like arriving in the middle of the night to find I'm expected to share a double bed with Mr. Atwater.'

Penny went off into a peal of laughter, which she quickly stifled when she saw the expression of disapproval on his face.

'And one last thing,' he added, as she went out of the door. 'Put your shoes on when you come in here.'

'Was he fraightfully angry?' asked Miss Piggott.

'He wasn't pleased,' sighed Penny.

Valerie from the typing pool had just arrived with the tea. She took a cup into Jake McInnes's office, and returned a few seconds later with starry eyes.

'Isn't he beautiful,' she said to Penny. 'The way he looks at you. Not that I stand a chance when you think of all those sophisticated women who come and pick him up from Reception. That Mrs. Ellerington last week looked just like a film star. Still, there's no harm in hoping, is there?'

'You need your head examined,' said Penny shortly.

Valerie bridled and glanced at the photograph over Penny's desk of a young man whose startlingly blond good looks were somewhat obscured by a long, moth-eaten beard.

'Oh well, since you fancy those drippy lefties with dirty fingernails, I don't suppose you would go for Mr. McInnes,' she said sarcastically.

'Francis doesn't have dirty fingernails,' snapped Penny. 'And don't you dare mention him in the same breath as Jake McInnes. Francis is so gentle and sweet and unaggressive.'

'He wasn't so unaggressive when he broke that placard over the policeman's head in Trafalgar Square during that Disarmament Rally,' observed Miss Piggott.

'That's different,' said Penny scornfully. 'Francis was just showing how deeply he feels about non-violence.'

'Funny way of showing it,' said Miss Piggott, who disapproved of Francis not so much for his politics or his appearance, as for the casual way he treated Penny.

At that moment the telephone rang. Penny swooped on it. 'Hello . . . I mean Mr. McInnes's office. Francis!

Darling! Is it really you? How lovely to hear your voice.' She made a triumphant face at Valerie and Miss Piggott.

Half an hour later, she reluctantly put down the receiver, gave an ecstatic shudder and buried her face in her hands. 'He rang,' she said simply.

'So Ay noticed,' said Miss Piggott. 'Mr. McInnes did, too. He came in twice and went out looking like a thundercloud.'

'To hell with Mr. McInnes,' said Penny. 'Oh Miss Piggott, Francis still loves me. I thought he was cooling off. There's a demo on Saturday and he wants me to join him.'

Thrilled by this evidence of Francis's continuing interest, she wandered off to the typing pool to give Valerie the third éclair as a peace offering.

During the next fortnight Penny tried very hard to be more efficient, but she dropped enough bricks to build her own office block. She booked tables at the wrong restaurants, arranged meetings for the wrong days, and spilled a cup of tea over Miss Piggott's electric typewriter. She also got more and more depressed because Francis hadn't rung her, her only comfort being that he had promised to take her to the theatre the following Thursday.

Thursday dawned. Having washed her hair that morning, Penny arrived later than usual at the office. Jake McInnes sent for her immediately. 'Penny,' he said wearily.

'Oh golly, what have I done now?'

'Remember last week I wrote two letters, one to my father saying Atkinsons' were playing hard to get, but I thought we'd clinch the deal with them by the end of the month; and the other letter to Atkinsons' playing it very, very cool?'

'Yes,' said Penny. 'You signed them both.'

'And you put them into the wrong envelopes. Now get out, just get out. And I don't want to talk to Emma McBride if she rings.'

Towards the end of the morning, Penny's telephone rang.

'Can I speak to Jake?' said a soft, smoky voice.

Oh goodness, thought Penny, which one did he say he didn't want to talk to? 'Who's that speaking,' she said cautiously.

'It's a personal call,' murmured the voice.

Penny had a brainwave. 'How's your little dog?' she asked.

'He's fine, Penny, just fine.'

It must be Mrs. Ellerington, who had a peke. Penny decided to throw herself on her mercy. 'Well, Mrs. Ellerington, Mr. McInnes said he specially didn't want to talk to someone, but I can't remember who it was; you or Emma McBride, or it might have been Mrs. Lusty. I'd ask him, but he's so mad at me this morning. You haven't fallen out with him lately, have you?'

'No, but I'm just about to.' The smoky voice had hardened. 'I think you'd better put me through.'

Two minutes later, Jake McInnes came out of his office. It was the first time he'd really lost his temper with Penny and it was the most terrifying thing that had ever happened to her.

'And take down that photograph of your boyfriend,' he shouted finally. 'This is an office not a film studio.'

'Well Ay never,' said Miss Piggott, as he slammed the door behind him. 'Ay've never known him fly off the handle like that before. Perhaps he is keen on that Mrs. Ellerington after all!'

'I think I'd better look for another job,' said Penny listlessly, unpinning Francis's photograph.

'It might be advaisable; have a look in the newspaper,' said Miss Piggott. She brandished a toothbrush. 'Well, Ay'm off to the dentist. Ay shan't be back.'

'Bye. Hope it doesn't hurt too much,' said Penny, who was already poring over the Situations Vacant column.

Nothing really took her fancy, until she suddenly read:

'*Managing Director requires highly intelligent, hardwork-*

ing secretary/personal assistant. Meticulous shorthand and typing essential. Salary £8000 upwards for the right person. Apply Box 9873.'

The salary was almost twice what she was getting at the moment, and Penny thought of all the clothes she could buy. Her two cats could have liver every day.

The letter of application took her only a few minutes. She saw her new boss as a younger version of Mr Fraser, kindly and appreciative, just waiting for someone to bring sunshine into his life. She told him all about her troubles with Jake McInnes, and gave a much embellished version of her own career. Very pleased with herself, she sealed the letter and delivered it to the newpaper office by hand during her lunch hour.

Late that afternoon, Jake McInnes faced one of the toughest battles of his career. He lounged, outwardly relaxed, at the end of the long Board Room table. On either side of him sat the Board, all distinguished Englishmen, many years his senior. He was outlining the reforms he intended to make; reforms which, he must make them see, were desirable in themselves, and not just proof that, as his father's son, he was trying to throw his weight about in the London office of the firm.

Gradually as the meeting progressed, he felt he was winning the battle, antagonism was dwindling, and he was even getting a few laughs. He had just moved on to the subject of delivery, when Charles Atwater, the Sales Director, suddenly wondered if he was seeing things. For through the thickening cigar smoke, from the direction of the door, loped a rabbit. Hastily he put on his spectacles. Yes, it was a rabbit.

'Look,' he nudged the Director of Public Relations beside him.

'Good God,' said the Director of Public Relations, clapping his hands over his eyes, and resolving to give up heavy business lunches.

Jake McInnes looked in their direction. 'Have you anything to add, Charles?'

Mr. Atwater roared with laughter and pointed to the rabbit which had reached Jake McInnes's chair.

Pandemonium broke out.

'Good God, it's a rabbit.'

'Tally ho, after it, boys.'

'Perhaps it wants a seat on the Board.'

'Is that your own hare, or is it a wig? Ho, ho, ho.'

They are like a crowd of schoolboys, thought Jake McInnes, trying hard to keep his temper.

'How did it get in here?' said Mr. Atwater.

'I think I know,' said Jake McInnes, picking up the panic-stricken animal. 'If you'll excuse me a minute, gentlemen.'

He found Penny on her knees by the filing cabinet.

She looked up, cheeks red, a large smudge on her nose. 'Oh,' she said, a happy smile breaking over her face, 'you've found him. I was terrified he might have escaped into the street.'

Words failed Jake McInnes, as Penny took the rabbit from him, crooning, 'There, there, poor little love, were you frightened then?'

'Penny,' he said, 'where did you get it from?'

Penny's eyes filled with tears. 'From the market. He was the last one. The man said he'd go in the pot if no-one bought him.'

A faint smile flickered across Jake McInnes's face. 'Well, you'd better go and buy him a hutch, hadn't you?'

'It's Thursday,' said Penny. 'I haven't got any money left.'

Jake McInnes took out his wallet and handed her twenty pounds. 'Go round to the pet shop now. And I want all those letters finished by the time I come out of the meeting,' he added.

Half an hour later, the rabbit was happily installed in a smart, blue hutch, nibbling at some lettuce, and Penny was busily typing when the telephone rang. It was Francis.

'Darling,' cried Penny, 'what a treat. I am going to see you later, aren't I?' (Silly to let anxiety creep into her voice.)

Francis's voice was sulky with embarrassment. 'I can't make it after all,' he said.

'Oh, why not? You promised,' wailed Penny.

Francis explained that he had this picket duty . . .

'Well, I'll come too,' said Penny.

'No, no,' said Francis much too quickly. 'It's only a small picket.'

Penny panicked. 'I don't believe you. You've found someone else. It's that horrible blonde,' she choked. 'Oh Francis, I can't bear it.'

'Well, you'll just have to lump it,' said Francis. 'I'll give you a ring sometime.' The receiver clicked.

Penny's world seemed to be crumbling round her. In one day, she'd virtually lost her job, and had certainly lost her boyfriend. 'No-one loves me,' she said. 'No-one wants me, and I've got a bed-sitter, two cats and now a rabbit to support. Oh Francis!'

She ripped the letter she was typing out of her machine and put in a fresh sheet.

'Darling, darling,' she typed frenziedly. *'I'm so frightfully sorry. I didn't mean to disbelieve you, I was just so disappointed—'*

A shadow fell across the page. Penny lent quickly forward to hide what she was typing.

'What the hell are you doing?' Jake McInnes's voice was like a rifle shot. Penny burst into tears. She laid her head among the papers on her desk and sobbed. Jake McInnes did nothing, he just sat on the edge of Miss Piggott's desk, drawing on his cigar, waiting for her to stop.

'I'm so sorry,' she said eventually.

'What's the matter?' he said. 'Is it the boyfriend?'

Penny nodded dolefully. 'He's not going to take me out tonight after all. I think he's found another girl, an awful blonde with a forty-inch placard.'

Jake McInnes examined his fingernails. 'Well, as we both appear to have been stood up this evening . . .'

'Oh no,' said Penny in horror. 'Not you too—not Mrs. Ellerington. Was she furious about that telephone call?'

'She wasn't "fraightfully accommodating," as our Miss Piggott would say.'

Penny began to giggle.

'And as I was saying,' he went on, 'as we've both got nothing better to do, I suggest we sort out this mess.' He pointed to the chaos which spread in a ten-foot radius round Penny's desk. 'Now which is your in-tray?'

'Well, those two tables over there,' said Penny, wondering what terrible skeletons were going to come tumbling out of the cupboard.

In the end, she rather enjoyed herself. Jake McInnes had obviously decided to be nice, and she found lots of things she thought she'd lost: her passport, several cleaning tickets and a bar of chocolate.

Two hours later, the tables, desks and surrounding filing cabinets were cleared and Penny was shoving paper into a sack.

'Miss Piggott will have a shock in the morning,' she said happily.

'Just try and keep it like this,' said Jake McInnes. 'Now I think we both deserve some dinner.'

'I've got stacks of food at home,' said Penny.

'I know, half a packet of Fish Fingers in the icebox. Stop being silly, and go and fix your face.'

Penny was appalled when she took a look at herself in the mirror. Crying had devastated her make-up and there was a large smudge on her nose. Hastily she repaired the damage.

Jake McInnes took her to a very smart restaurant.

'Your usual table, Mr. McInnes,' said the waiter, leading them to a discreet corner. Penny wondered how often Jake McInnes had sat there, lavishing wine and compliments on the lovely Clare Ellerington.

Jake ordered drinks, and with them the waiter

267

brought a dish of radishes, which Penny longed to pocket for the rabbit.

'It's so lovely being hungry for a change,' she said. 'I'm so overwhelmed by Francis that I never eat a thing when he's around. I'm afraid he has definitely gone off me. I should have realised it when he started putting second class stamps on his letters instead of first class ones.'

The waiter arrived with avocado pear for Penny and oysters for Jake. For a few minutes they ate in silence, then Penny noticed that a beautiful woman at the next table was staring at Jake. How odd, she thought, and had a good look at Jake herself, taking in the breadth of the shoulders, the strong, well-shaped hands, the thick black hair. Suddenly he glanced up and caught her staring at him.

'Well?' he demanded, just like he did in the office.

Penny blushed. 'I was just thinking that you're very attractive.'

'You shouldn't say so in such a surprised tone, it isn't very flattering.'

'Well—I mean—all the typing pool are besotted with you, but, of course, I'm immune because I'm in love with Francis. And I'm never attracted to people who bully me,' she added.

'That's blackmail,' said Jake McInnes. 'From now on, have I got to put up with your crumby typing, just so you'll like me?'

'Oh no,' said Penny, 'I've decided I like you anyway, after this evening—in fact I like you very much.'

He looked at her for a long time, his eyes moving over her face. 'That makes me feel as though I've just won the Nobel Peace Prize,' he said slowly.

Penny stared back at him, unable to tear her eyes away, the colour mounting in her cheeks. The waiter arriving with their second course brought them both back to earth.

'Goodness, it looks delicious,' said Penny picking up her fork.

'Mr. McInnes,' she said in a small voice five minutes

later, looking down at her untouched plate, 'I'm terribly sorry, but I don't think I can eat this. I can't think what's happened . . . I was so hungry, and now I'm not, and it was so expensive . . .'

'It's all right,' he said gently. 'It doesn't matter.' And as he smiled at her she noticed the tired lines round his eyes, as though he hadn't been getting enough sleep lately. Suddenly she felt shy of him, and in the car going home, she sat as far away as possible with the rabbit hutch between them.

He didn't attempt to kiss her, as he delivered her to the door. 'Go to bed early,' he said. 'It might get you in on time in the morning.'

Back to square one, thought Penny—but she didn't go to bed. She wandered round her room, chattering to the rabbit and the two cats, drinking cups of coffee, and determinedly thinking how very much better-looking Francis was than Jake McInnes. She didn't attempt to localise the vague happiness which was stealing over her.

'Hello, Miss Piggott,' Penny said dreamily next morning. 'How was the dentist?'

'Fraightful,' said Miss Piggott. 'He was drillin' away for hours. Mr. McInnes wants to see you.'

'I thought he might,' said Penny, drenching herself with Miss Dior.

'Ay should watch your step if Ay were you. He seems a bit taight-lipped,' warned Miss Piggott.

Jake McInnes's face was quite expressionless when Penny went into the room. She beamed at him. 'The rabbit's very well,' she said. 'He ate lots of—'

'Sit down,' snapped Jake McInnes. 'You'd better explain this letter.' He held two pieces of paper between finger and thumb.

'Oh goodness, have I put my foot in something else?' sighed Penny.

'I think I'll read it to you,' he said silkily.

'Dear Sir, it begins. *In answer to your advertisement for a*

secretary/personal assistant, I feel I have the ideal qualifications for the job.'

'Oh,' said Penny, interested. 'Are you getting another secretary? It will be a terrible squash with me and Miss Piggott and her.'

'It goes on,' said Jake McInnes, *'I relish hard work, and my aim in life is to find a job that I can really get my teeth into!'*

'I should hire her,' said Penny. 'She sounds jolly keen.'

'You would? Well, listen to this then. *I am meticulously accurate in every way and used to acting on my own initiative.'*

Horror crept over Penny's face. 'Oh no,' she whispered, 'it can't be.'

'Now it really begins to get interesting,' he said softly. *'My reason for leaving my present job is that the Managing Director (a wonderful man) was recently replaced by a director from the parent company in America. To be quite frank, this director is one of the most tyrannical individuals you could care to meet. He has already fired dozens of my colleagues—dear people who have given many years of service to the firm. I live in dread that I may be the next to go, as he bullies me unmercifully and makes my life a misery.'*

Penny buried her face in her hands.

He looked at her sternly. 'You could be prosecuted for writing that letter,' he said. 'It's complete libel from start to finish. A good thing I got in early, and no-one else saw it.'

'I'm sorry,' muttered Penny. 'Truly I am.'

'So you should be.' Then to her amazement he threw back his head and roared with laughter. 'Used to acting on your own initiative, meticulously accurate . . . Penny, Penny . . .' He wiped his streaming eyes.

Tears of mortification welled up in Penny's eyes. 'How was I to know it was you lurking behind a box number? And then being so sweet to me last night, when all the time you were looking for someone else to fill my job. Of all the mean, cruel . . .'

'Tyrannical things to do,' said Jake McInnes, still laughing.

'I'm going,' sobbed Penny. 'I'm walking out of your hateful firm right now.'

She leapt to her feet, but before she reached the door, he caught her by the arm. 'Easy now, before you go charging out of my life, just read this memo. It came from Public Relations this morning.'

Penny looked at it suspiciously.

'Dear Jake,' she read. *'Thanks for your letter. Just to confirm that we can fit in your leggy red-head any time you choose to release her—particularly if she's as ravishing as you say. There's a vacancy on the copy side now, and she can do the occasional shift in reception. Best wishes, Jim Stokely.'*

Penny put the memo down on his desk. 'You arranged to have me transferred,' she said slowly.

He nodded. 'So I can get some work done during the day, and some sleep at night. I thought you might do rather well in Public Relations with that fertile imagination.'

Penny was still staring at him in bewilderment. 'Ravishing and distracting,' she said quietly. 'You're not just trying to get rid of me?'

He shook his head ruefully. 'I spent most of last night thinking about you; seeing you cuddling that rabbit, I realised you were wasted as a secretary. You ought to be living in the country looking after a house and animals and babies and one very lucky man.'

'I only wrote that letter because I was mad at you,' said Penny. 'I thought that you loathed me.'

'Loathed you! I've been hooked ever since I walked into old Fraser's office for the first time. It was in the middle of the afternoon, and you were painting your nails with the radio on, and the sun was streaming through your hair.'

He was coming towards her, and the expression on his face made Penny back away from him until she was trapped against his desk. He took her into his arms.

'Oh, we can't,' she said in confusion. 'Not here.'

'Why not?' said Jake McInnes. 'I'm the boss around here.' And he kissed her very hard.

'Oh my goodness,' said Penny, very pink and glowing. 'I don't think I do want to marry Francis after all.'

'And I don't think I can afford to have you sabotaging my public relations company either; you'd be much better going into private relations with me. We'll discuss it over lunch.'

Still with his arm round her, he leant across and pressed the intercom switch. 'Miss Piggott, I'm going to lunch, and I won't be back this afternoon. You're in sole charge of the office. Hire and fire at will.'

'But, Mr. McInnes,' Miss Piggott's anguished voice echoed intercommunally over the room, 'you've got a meetin'.'

'Cancel it, I've got a meeting of my own lined up.'

He released the switch and turned his attention to Penny.

'But Mr. McInnes,' said Miss Piggott, charging into the room like a herd of buffaloes, 'Ay don't think Ay can contact the people comin' to the meetin' in taime.'

She broke off suddenly as she saw Penny in Jake McInnes's arms. 'Craikey,' she said.

THE END